A BROTHERS *MALEDETTI* ROMANCE

NICHOLE VAN

Fiorenza Publishing

Published by Fiorenza Publishing
Print Edition v1.0

ISBN: 978-0-9968936-2-6

To Austenne,

You say you love the dark.
But to me you will always be
sunshine, rainbows, unicorns and
everything that is purpliciously purrrr-fect.

To Dave,

You know you are sunshine, rainbows, unicorns
and everything that is purpliciously purrrr-fect.
And I'll never remember which one
of us said it first but . . .
just don't die.

she asked
'you are in love
what does love look like'
to which i replied
'like everything i've ever lost
come back to me.'

— *nayyirah waheed,* salt.

If anyone else were to kiss me,
all they would taste is your name.

— *Clementine von Radics*

PROLOGUE

Tuscany, Italy
1809

He was slowly devolving into madness.

Lorenzo D'Angelo accepted this.

To be quite honest, he had never expected anything else.

A tragic observation, but nonetheless true.

He was called *il Conte del Maldetto*—the Damned Earl—for good reason.

Insanity was the family curse.

Lorenzo had spent the entirety of his twenty-nine years knowing he would end his life in a fog of deranged lunacy . . . just as his father and grandfather and every first-born D'Angelo heir for the previous five hundred years.

Like taxes and the resurgence of Napoleon Bonaparte, it seemed inevitable.

Lorenzo simply hadn't anticipated it happening so *soon*. His father had managed to hold off the madness until his fortieth year.

Lorenzo doubted he would be so fortunate.

No.

The voices called to him. Constantly swirling, humming, buzzing—bees that vibrated from within, threatening to shake him apart. Even laudanum did little beyond dulling the edge of his visions.

Past. Future.

It all eddied around him in a continuous stream of noise and sight and feeling. Medieval ladies giggling behind filmy veils mingled with uniformed men yelling in German and riding thunderous iron machines.

Such was the curse of the D'Angelos. The supposed 'gift' of Sight granted by gypsies to Lorenzo's ancient forebear, Giovanni D'Angelo, during the height of the Middle Ages.

I zingari. Gypsies.

They had done this. And per Lorenzo's view, it was high time the gypsies cleaned up the mess they had made.

He rode into their camp late in the afternoon—a semi-circle of covered wagons tucked around a large campfire—all nestled in a wooded, Tuscan valley. Dirty children's faces peeked out of canvas doorways, while women and men in colorful clothing finished their daily chores.

A grizzled man in a bright embroidered vest walked to the edge of the camp, greeting Lorenzo with a raised hand.

Lorenzo left less than ten minutes later, angrily cursing them all.

It was only as his horse cleared the glen that the vision slammed into him, dancing before his eyes with cruel clarity.

A trail of his ancestors. Men, desperate like himself, making their way to this same camp. Pleading with generation after generation of gypsies to break the curse, to set the D'Angelos free.

And time and again, the answer rang, identical to the words Lorenzo himself had just heard:

"We know nothing of this gift. It is an utter mystery to us. If it came from our people, the knowledge of it has been lost to history. We can do nothing to help you. Go in peace, and may God have mercy on your soul."

Sagging in his saddle, Lorenzo ran a shuddering hand over his face as the vision faded.

What was to be done? How would the D'Angelo bloodline ever be free?

Replying to his unspoken question, another vision arose. This time looking ahead. Future, not past.

Three small, dark haired boys ran up a grassy hill toward a tall woman with dancing eyes and auburn, curling hair.

Each boy the same height, the same size.

The same age.

Brothers. Triplets.

The boys tackled the woman, laughing as they all tumbled to the ground, tickling and giggling.

Lorenzo sensed the boys' power. The D'Angelo 'gift' flitted between them, but it had morphed and fractured . . . different but balanced among the three brothers.

Lorenzo felt it then, faint but clear.

Hope.

At some future point, the gift would shatter, scattering over three instead of just one.

And that was . . . good . . . wasn't it?

The fracturing of the gift had to be the D'Angelo's salvation. Because if it had any other outcome . . .

Then, indeed, God have mercy on them all.

BRANWELL D'ANGELO

PORTLAND, OREGON
AUGUST, 2010

Do you believe in love at first sight?
    The idea that you lock eyes with a stranger across a crowded room and *bam!*

It hits you.

Connection. Belonging. Familiarity.

That sense of coming home.

Un colpo di fulmine the Italians call it—a lightning strike.

It's easy to dismiss the notion of insta-love until it happens to you.

Proof is in the pudding. Isn't that how the saying goes?

Or, in my case, a scone. A lemon-glazed, strawberries-and-cream-filled scone, to be precise.

The scone sat on a pretty porcelain plate in the refrigerated case next to the coffee bar. All innocent-like, alluring, calling.

Just to clarify—the scone was not the object of my love. Simply the catalyst.

I had been back in the USA for only thirty-six hours, and I wanted just two things—an extra-large mocha latte for my jet lag and something decadently American, preferably laden with sugar and carbs.

The Jump-N-Java around the corner from the apartment I shared with my brothers easily provided both.

Those brothers, Dante and Tennyson, had begged me to get them something, too. But Dante already owed me big-time from our trip to Scotland, and Tennyson had some new girl he was gaga over, so I figured he would be out with her before I got home.

As far as I was concerned, my brothers were on their own.

Smacking my lips, I snagged the strawberry-lemon scone out of the refrigerated case with a gloved hand and got my mocha latte with the other. The delicious bit of cream and strawberry heaven was all mine—if and when I found a place to sit down. Jump-N-Java's location in a kitchy old row house was high on charm but low on available seating.

I threaded through the crowded room and up the stairs to the second floor. I always preferred eating at a small table in the upper back room. Not many customers knew the room existed, making it a blissfully *quiet* table.

And quiet, for me, was essential. Being who I was. Given my *talents*—the unusual abilities I had inherited (along with my brothers) from our Italian father.

I ducked into the small room, intent on the table. Only to come to an abrupt stop.

The table in question was already occupied.

A woman sat on one side, bent over a notebook, a crumbled croissant and empty coffee cup at her elbow. Weak morning light filtered in through the large window behind her illuminating her profile in backlit shadows.

My immediate impression was one of circles and curves and sinuous lines. Hourglass figure in a fitted t-shirt over worn capris. Freckles and a round face. A riot of curly red hair spiraling everywhere, tendrils of flame in the sun.

But no circle of a ring on her left hand.

Not sure why I noticed that small detail, but my subconscious deemed it important.

I briefly considered backing out and trying to eat in the noisier lower room. It would be rude to just sit at the table with her. Besides, eyeballing my reflection in the window—shaggy beard, dark hair, long-sleeve plaid shirt—I was more lumberjack-huge than approachable-cuddly at the moment.

But . . .

The space was so quiet; the voices of other customers reduced to a mumbling thrum. No noise from the street below. Besides, the table wasn't *that* small.

And there was something about this woman . . .

With a deep breath, I crossed the room and settled in the chair opposite her.

She didn't seem to notice, keeping her head bent as she tapped her pen against her cheek, scrunched her forehead and idly twirled one of the curls framing her face.

They were gorgeous, those curls. Corkscrew crazy, coiled and ready to launch from her head.

I pulled a straw and fork out of my pocket with gloved fingers—items I had brought from home. I always came prepared.

Nothing *ever* touched my bare skin without careful planning.

I stuck the straw into my coffee and used the fork to dig into the lemon-strawberry deliciousness. Fruity citrusy heaven exploded in my mouth and only a trace of sound.

My own breathing. The soft hum of voices from downstairs.

Perfection. I dug out another bite.

The rumble of traffic from the street. Muffled sounds.

I was about to go for bite number three when a soft voice stopped me.

"Wait, wait. Don't move."

I froze, fork hovered over a particularly decadent piece of strawberry laden gooey-ness.

I lifted my head and encountered the most amazing eyes. Blue-green and wide-set. The smell of lemon-verbena and sunshine drifted over me. That fiery red hair tumbled around the gentle curve of her jaw. Window-light sculpted the arch of her rosebud lips.

Freckles. Freckles everywhere. Stars dotting her skin.

She was . . . stunning. Magnificent. Breathtaking in an unconventional way.

Maybe it was the jet lag, or the sugar and caffeine hitting my system in a knockout one-two punch.

But . . . it jolted me hard. That bolt of lightning.

This girl . . . woman . . .

Something about her tugged at me. A siren call of wedding bells and growing old hand-in-hand.

Then I noticed her t-shirt—*The Empurr Strikes Back* scrawled underneath *Star Wars*-themed, *anime* kittens.

Yep. That sealed the deal.

I was going to fall in love with her. So hard. So fast.

My foolish heart sat up and claimed her as its own, not interested in waiting for trivial details like her name.

"Uhm, I'm sorry." She was clearly oblivious to the moment I was having. "But I can't let you eat that." She motioned toward my scone.

Alarmed, I stared down at my plate, sitting back, instantly looking for . . . what? A hair? Insect?

Granted, part of me hummed in delight that this woman cared enough to say something.

She would be like that, my woman. Thoughtful. Noticing. We were destined to be together. Naturally, she would be concerned about my well-being.

Unfortunately, I was still trying to figure out what the problem might be. My scone looked innocently scrumptious, cream and berries sprawling out.

"Sorry, give me a second." She lifted a staying finger and then carefully slid my plate to her side of the table, pushing her notebook aside.

She moved my plate into the light. Rotated it to the right. Studied it, cocking her head. And then twisted it to the left. Nodded, curls bouncing.

Pulling out her phone, she proceeded to photograph my partially eaten scone.

Okay.

Not quite sure where I had anticipated this going. But artsy-food-photos was *not* it.

"So is this some weird passive-aggressive way of getting back at me for sitting at your table uninvited?" I asked and then winced.

Unlike my brothers, Dante and Tennyson, flirting was not my forte.

"What?" She looked up.

"The photos?" I gestured toward my scone. "Payback?"

"Oh. No." She glanced down at the scone, following my eyes. And then raised her head back to mine. "Sorry. I'm a COSH."

"COSH?"

"Collector of Spotted Hearts." She motioned toward my poor, waiting-to-be-eaten scone.

I blinked.

"I mean, not that the hearts are actually spotted like leprosy or something." She bobbed her head, a soft laugh escaping. "That would be totally gross."

"Leprosy? Spotted?" The conversation was slipping away from me.

"It's *spotted* like spotting something . . . seeing it." She had the perkiest voice. Light. Lilting.

Ah. "Like found hearts?"

She beamed at me. A pearly-white smile that was slightly lopsided. "Exactly! Unfortunately, Collector of Found Hearts—C-O-F-H— doesn't work as well as an acronym, so I just go with *spotted* instead."

She was a hand-talker, fingers flailing animatedly, gesturing with her phone.

It was endearingly cute.

"Gotcha." My poor brain was slowly catching up. "So you collect things that are naturally heart-shaped?"

I believed her when she said she collected hearts. Mine was already putty in her hands.

"I take photos of them . . . yeah," she said.

I looked at my scone. Tilted my head. I supposed if you caught the angle just right, it was somewhat heart-shaped.

"I actually started out physically collecting heart-shaped things—rocks, leaves, bits of trash." She framed another photo. "But then my grandma told my aunt who passed along to my mom that she thought I had 'hoarder' tendencies, which is totally not true. A heart collection does not a hoarder make."

She waved her free hand in my direction. Snapped another photo. "But as grandma is a huge fan of *Hoarders*—the TV show, not the people—not that she dislikes them either . . . though, I guess I've never asked."

She continued to take photos as she talked, rotating the plate, pushing it in and out of the light streaming behind.

"Anyway," she continued, "my family staged this weird kinda 'heart intervention' last year trying to get me to channel my heart obsession into something more 'socially mainstream'—my mom's words, not mine. Long story, but it basically ended with my mom looking befuddled and me the proud owner of a new smart phone, so it was a total win-win."

"Befuddled?" The word slipped out before I could filter myself. "I can't remember the last time I heard someone use the word *befuddled* in casual conversation."

She paused. Aimed those amazing blue-green eyes at me. "Really? That's a pity. It's one of many conversationally underutilized words." She gave a wry lift of her shoulders and then went back to her photography.

I grinned. I was so in love.

Smart with a hint of sass.

She was perfect.

"Maudlin," I said.

She raised her head, brows drawn down.

And then understanding bloomed, along with another crooked smile.

"Sycophant," she replied, turning back to her photos.

"Perfunctory."

"Oh! Good one." She tapped her chin with her phone. "Resplendent."

"Balderdash."

"Yes. Balderdash!"

An uncomfortable silence ensued. Or, at least, it felt uncomfortable to me. I was guessing my heart-collecting, soon-to-be-girlfriend didn't mind uncomfortable silences. Which, given my track record with women and social skills in general, was probably a good thing.

Overall, I was personally . . . befuddled.

"So . . . heart photos? Isn't that a little . . . *maudlin?*" I asked.

She chuckled. A breathy will-o-wisp of sound. "Yeah. The photos were actually a brilliant idea. I started a blog of them this year." She bent over her phone screen, angling up higher. "When photographing a heart, the trick is to find the shadows. Isn't that funny?" She shot me another lopsided smile. "It's the shadows, the dark areas, that illuminate the shape. See?"

She tilted her phone in my direction.

A heart-shaped scone filled the screen, light streaming around it, creating valleys of shadows that clearly delineated the form.

Delineate. Another good word.

"I like how the sliced strawberries are little hearts too," she said.

So they were.

She turned the phone, admiring her work.

"I'll let you have this back now." She slid the plate to my side of the table. "I know my boyfriend can get cranky if I monopolize his food too long."

I froze at the word *boyfriend*, my whole universe coming to a grinding halt.

I mentally smacked my forehead.

Of course, she would have a boyfriend.

I was an idiot.

I dug back into my scone, savoring the mix of lemon and berries. Thinking.

But . . .

I could be a patient idiot.

A boyfriend was a far cry from a fiancé or a husband. I could outwait a boyfriend. I merely had to make sure I had a way to contact her before she left.

She tapped her phone twice and then set it down on the table, leaning toward me.

"So what's your brand of crazy?" she asked.

I paused, trying (again) to find the thread in the conversation.

She folded her hands on the table and continued, "I collect hearts, refuse to get out of bed before nine in the morning and use words like *befuddled*. That's my crazy. What's yours?"

"You don't get out of bed before nine?"

"Only masochists get out of bed before nine." She shot me a *duh* look. "And only a sadist would make them. I think all morning people are just faking being happy."

"Trying to make the rest of us look bad?"

"Exactly! But enough stalling, what's your crazy?"

I chewed, thinking through the enormous list of crazy that was my life. Trying to find something that was less . . . out-there than the others.

I am one of three triplets who inherited a supernatural gift of Sight from our father.

Maybe.

If I touch something with my skin, I involuntarily hear the sound around the object at the moment of its last alteration.

Equally weird.

If I touch something and concentrate, I can shuffle through the sounds around it at each moment of alteration.

Mmmm. Even I knew any of those were TMI . . .

There's a fine line between crazy and certifiable.

She took my silence the wrong way.

"If you say you aren't crazy, I will so call you on your *balderdash*. Everyone is crazy in some way."

I chuckled. "Just mentally sorting through the plethora of options."

"*Plethora*. Nice."

I shrugged, my smile too wide, as I dug back into my scone.

"How's about starting with the long-sleeve lumberjack shirt and expensive, leather driving gloves?" she asked. "You do realize it's August, right?"

"I do." I took another bite, giving her a teasing grin, hearing our last two lines as soon as the scone and strawberries hit my tongue.

You do realize it's August, right?

I do.

After another pause, I went with, "I won't eat anything green unless it's a vegetable."

She cocked her head, processing.

A beat.

"Green M&M's? Skittles? Gummy bears?" she asked.

"Nope. Leave 'em all in the bag."

"Green frosting? Sprinkles? Mold?"

"Nope. Nada. And please, no."

"That rules out stinky French cheese too, I suppose."

"Generally. Depends on how good the cheese is." I winked at her.

"Green eggs and ham?"

"Good grief, no."

"So why no green?" she asked, genuine, sincere.

The reason why was simple—vegetables were often somewhat alive, muting their sound. I only 'heard' non-living things.

Artificially green things confused me.

Not that I could say that to her. Not yet, at least. Maybe on our second date, after she broke up with her boyfriend and I explained my inherited . . . issues.

So instead, I went with, "Non-vegetal green things are the charlatans of the food world."

"That's about the best sentence I've heard all week." She gave that giggly, wispy laugh of hers. "What about avocados? I mean, they act like a vegetable, but they're really a fruit."

"Masquerading vegetables get a pass. So do herbs."

"What about kiwi?"

"The jury is still out on kiwi. They're something of a Franken-fruit, to be honest . . . all that fuzzy hair and the tiny, crunchy seeds."

She laughed again. "Please tell me you have *no* Irish heritage. You would destroy any St. Patty's Day celebration."

"None." I smiled, shaking my head. "Though, I did have an Irish roommate once. He thought I was, and I quote, 'A wee bit mad.'"

"See, crazy." She grinned that signature uneven smile I was starting to adore. "I can respect that."

Silence hummed between us again. This time electricity-laden. I might be dense and awkwardly clueless with women, but even I could tell a spark when it happened.

She tucked a strand of hair behind her ear, nibbled her lip uncertainly.

"I'd better go." She looked down, gathered up her notebook and spun to place it in the purse hanging from the back of her chair.

It was now or never. There was no way I could let this girl go without having some way to contact her.

"So will my scone-heart be on your blog?"

"Of course. You should look it up. Wait." She lifted a staying hand. Like I was going anywhere. "I made business cards just last night."

"You have business cards for your blog?"

"Sure." She said it offhand, like that was a thing.

She dug through her purse and then extended a small, white card to me.

Join me at COSheart was on one side in loopy script. Handwritten. She *would* be the sort to hand-write her business cards.

The other side featured a lipstick kiss.

"Impressive." I set the card on the table. "I don't think just anyone has a heart-shaped kiss. You're a woman of many talents."

She smiled. Shrugged. Slung her purse over her shoulder and stood up. I couldn't help but notice she was a little on the tall side, maybe five seven. At six four myself, tall was good. She would fit perfectly in the curve of my arm.

"Thanks for letting me photograph your heart."

That was her parting shot.

Thanks for letting me photograph your heart.

Truer than she knew.

I watched her walk out of the room, admiring every second of that curvy figure. The riot of hair hanging down her back.

Oh yeah. This was merely the beginning. It would make an amazing story for our grandkids. I could see them now. Gingers. Redheads. Lots of freckles.

I met your grandmother when she photographed my heart . . .

Smiling, I picked up her business card in my gloved fingers.

Her lips really were heart-shaped. Two swooping semi-circles above. A pursed 'V' below.

I paused for only a second and then tugged off the glove of my right hand.

What sound had she made while kissing the card? Would I hear that breathy laugh again?

I hesitated.

And then gently touched the edge of the card.

Have I mentioned that I'm a genius?

Her voice. Excited.

The sound of the card being kissed.

I smiled.

Of course, you're a genius. I told you this would be huge, cara. *How could you ever doubt me?*

A man's voice.

My lungs seized.

A painfully *familiar* man's voice.

Come here. I want some of that sugar too, babe, the man continued.

Rustling. A soft sigh.

I never doubt you. Her voice. Quiet. *You're my perfect Tenn, remember?*

Gentle laughter.

His.

Tennyson.

No. *No!*

I had just fallen for my brother's girlfriend.

The card slipped from my numb fingers. Heaven shattering around me in brittle shards.

LUCY SNOW

PRATO, ITALY
JUNE, 2016

I woke to the sound of cathedral bells drifting through the open window.

Soft blue-white light lapped the room . . . the barest wisp of dawn. White plastered walls. White bedspread. White curtains fluttering romantically in the early morning breeze.

Art house film perfection.

It was all so self-righteously smug I wanted to puke.

I groaned and rolled away from the stupidly-bright window.

Sunrise and I have never been friends.

You can drag me out of bed anytime, but if you want my personality and good manners to actually *accompany* my body, you need to wait until after nine a.m.

I pulled the sheet over my head, blocking out the obnoxiously cheerful sunlight.

The bells *bong, bong, bonged* a lulling chant. I curled into the covers, letting the sound charm me back to sleep.

A *bing-bing* joined the bells. Insistent.

Ugh.

Phone. Text. The real culprit for waking me out of my haze so early. Groggily, I rolled over and snagged my phone off the nightstand.

Jeff. My brother.

He totally should know better than to bug me this early—

Wait. He *did* know better. That's why he texted.

Brothers.

> *Rise and shine, baby sister! We made it to Johannesburg, and we're about to board our flight to the nature reserve. No cell reception there, so we'll be out of touch for the next week. How's Grace?*

You do know what time it is, right?

Yep.

I sorta hate you right now.

I can live with that. :)

Again. Brothers.

Jeff and his wife, Jen—I know, Jeff and Jen, so cutesy . . . we called them JJ behind their backs—were celebrating their tenth wedding anniversary with a two-week African safari. Jeff worked as an internet security expert for an American company and was currently living in Prato, Italy, just outside Florence. I had taken all my time-off for the next year to come babysit my five-year-old niece, Grace, while her parents were away.

I loved my work as a wilderness therapist, leading others in backwoods survival experiences. Nothing like watching a client from Beverly

Hills arrive in high heels clutching her Prada bag with French-tipped nails and leave a little sun-burned, clean faced and smiling.

That said, I had been looking forward to this vacation and spending time with Grace. I was perfect for it, given that Italy was a familiar place for me . . . after everything . . .

I batted the thought away.

Not going to go there.

I had ended things with Tennyson once and for all two years ago. It was ancient history. Over. Done.

Not to be revisited.

I texted Jeff.

> *Lucky for you, Grace is darling. Her hay fever acted up yesterday, but she was doing better last night. She's insistent I have to see the new Knight-Snow exhibit at the museum outside of town ASAP. According to her, it's freaking awesome. You have to do jazz hands when you say that apparently.*

I smiled. Grace was nothing if not exuberant about life.
Another bing.

> *She does take after her aunt. She'll always choose fun.*

> Ha-ha. Take care you two and have a great trip. Just don't die.

> *Done and done.*

"You write-talking to my daddy?" Grace's sleepy voice filled the room as I set my phone down.

A mass of dark curls bobbed onto the bed, falling across Grace's face as she crawled toward me, dragging her ratty stuffed elephant with her.

"How's your nose, pumpkin?" I asked, as she snuggled into my side.

Grace sniffed. Testing.

"Okay. It's not snuffly anymore."

"Good." I tucked her against me, reveling in the warmth of her small body.

You would have had a child by now. Probably two.

The thought drifted through. Unbidden.

Truth. Had Tennyson and I become engaged. If I hadn't broken things off like I did.

If I hadn't fallen so far in love with the wrong D'Angelo.

Another head of dark curls punched through my memory. Darker beard. Hazel eyes—eyes so different from Tennyson's baby blues . . .

I swallowed.

The poet who claimed it was better to have loved and lost than to have never loved at all? That guy?

He was an idiot.

Because constantly being around the one thing you wanted more than anything else and knowing you could never have it—

How was I a better person for that?

I knew returning to Italy would do this . . . make old wounds ache and sting.

It was okay. I had healed. Grown up. Moved on.

Just as I was sure *they* had. Branwell and Tennyson.

I kissed Grace's forehead. She smelled of berry shampoo, sunscreen and sticky little girl.

The smells of childhood, I supposed.

Grace cuddled closer, yawning.

"When I wake up, could I have a s'nore for breakfast?" she asked. "Daddy calls them s'nores, but that doesn't mean you can only eat them at night."

"S'Nores?"

"Yeah. The things with graham crackers and smarshmellows and cholocate? I saw it in your suitcase all the way from 'Merica."

Ah.

Man, I so loved this kid. She was one of my tribe, in every way.

"Of course, Gracie Pie. You can have all the s'nores you want for breakfast. We'll roast the marshmallows over the flame on the stove."

What was the good of being an aunt if I couldn't spoil her rotten?

Besides, I was totally down with s'mores for breakfast. I had packed all the stuff to make them. Italy had access to *most* of the finer things in life. S'mores were a glaring omission.

Grace sighed happily and relaxed into me, her breathing smoothing out into that of deep sleep.

Poor thing.

Her breathing had been so stuffed the day before, allergies hitting her hard. She did sound better. Not entirely clear, but at least she could breathe.

I rubbed a hand over her back, dragging her curls through my fingers.

The curtains swirled again, twisting, curling. Absently, I wondered if they would make a heart-shape at some point. It was second-nature for me. Heart hunting.

If only I could find my own . . .

I must have drifted off again, because it seemed like only seconds later the doorbell buzzer jarred me awake.

Drowsily, I pushed the mass of my hair out of my eyes and sat up. The room was significantly brighter, the sun having climbed in the sky. Grace was no longer in my bed. She had probably snagged my tablet and headphones and snuck back to her room.

Bzzz. Bzzz. Bzzzzzz.

The doorbell sounded again. Insistent. Impatient.

Urgently demanding my attention.

BRANWELL

PORTLAND, OREGON
SIX YEARS EARLIER

Y ou must be Branwell." She gave a friendly wave from the curl of Tennyson's arm on the couch. "Hi. I'm Lucy."

I paused, halfway behind Dante, both of us still holding groceries.

"Hey." I gave her the standard guy chin lift. "Nice to meet you."

I kicked the apartment door shut, slamming a lid on my emotions just as forcefully.

I had spent the last three days prepping for the moment when we would meet again. Wondering how she would react. How I would respond.

She smiled, that lop-sided smile I hadn't been able to get out of my head. Red curls sprawled across my brother's chest, freckles dancing on her pale skin.

Not a flicker of recognition.

Alright, then.

I kept my face impassive and ordered my heart not to plummet. She didn't remember me, and I would pretend to not remember her. This was good . . . for the best. All I had to do now was forget my initial reaction to her, and we would all move on.

Tennyson pulled her closer, kissing her temple.

I turned away, setting the grocery bags on the kitchen table, ruthlessly arguing with my stupid, wayward heart.

Let. Her. Go.

LUCY

Bzzz. Bzzz.

The poor doorbell was getting a workout.

I kicked off the covers and quickly decided that my t-shirt (*Morning! My archnemesis. We meet again.*) and loose pajama bottoms (light pink with darker pink hearts) were presentable enough.

I stumbled down the long central hallway of the apartment to the front door and looked through the peephole, recognizing the older woman and thirty-something guy in the stairwell.

The upstairs neighbors. The one who was a cat-lady. And her son . . . who reminded me of a nerdier, more bumbling Italian version of Ross from *Friends*—tall with chunky glasses, curly dark hair and a loose sense of style.

All I had gathered from our previous conversations was Cat Lady loved her cats nearly as much as she wanted me to date Professor Ross.

Beyond that . . . I drew a blank.

Gah. I was so bad with names, especially complicated Italian ones.

I flipped the deadbolt and swung the door open with a smile.

Professor Ross was true to his stereotyping in a white shirt, sweater vest and dark slacks. He kept nervously pushing his chunky glasses back up his nose.

Cat Lady wore a relaxed mint green pantsuit and huge scarf, graying hair cut into a bob with oversize sunglasses tucked atop her head. She nervously twirled something in her hands. I ignored the ample cat hair clinging to her legs and arms. Who was I to judge?

She was kinda awesome in her Cat Lady-ness.

"Uhm, *ciao*," I said, trying to run a hand through my hair and realizing it was currently a massive poof-ball.

"*Sono Maria-Teresa Moretti dal piano di sopra, se mi ricordi. E questo é il mio figlio, Roberto Moretti.*" Cat Lady gestured to her son, introducing themselves.

That's right. Maria-Teresa and Roberto Moretti.

Meh. I kinda liked Cat Lady and Professor Ross better.

But their names were all I gleaned. My Italian was rudimentary at best.

Correction. My grasp on everyday, useful Italian was sparse. I knew an insane amount of lovey-dovey, gooey-cooey Italian. I was going to go out on a limb and guess that Cat Lady didn't want to be called *il mio piccolo cucciolo di amore* . . . my little love puppy. Although she would probably jump for joy if I used that line on Professor Ross.

Cat Lady rattled off something in Italian while walking past me and into the apartment, unconcerned that I hadn't actually invited her in, which was a huge part of her awesomeness.

Cat Lady don't care.

I should totally put that on a t-shirt for her—a tiny *anime* cat clutching an old purse surrounded by other cats. It would be perfect.

No. Make that *purr*-fect.

Where were we?

Cat Lady turned and stared at her son lingering in the stairwell, darting glances between myself and his mom. Cat Lady sighed and motioned for Professor Ross to join her inside. Which he did, pushing up his glasses again.

"We wish to thank you for your help yesterday," he said, accent thick.

"No problem. I'm just glad I was able to pull Michelangelo off the roof."

Grace and I had spent the better part of the previous afternoon helping Cat Lady rescue a scared calico cat. Cat Lady had supervised the rescue, chattering in Italian with the occasional English noun thrown in—her favorite words being *son, date, marry* and *babies.* Italian mothers, apparently, did not do subtly.

Professor Ross opened his mouth to say something, but his mother stopped him with a raised hand. Cat Lady then proceeded to rattle away in Italian while Professor Ross shot me apologetic glances.

Cat Lady's Italian was kinda hypnotic to listen to. Staccato, emphatic. She punctuated it all with hand gestures. I wasn't sure if she was super angry, uber-excited or just hopped up on one *doppio espresso* too many.

Her pantsuit wasn't really my style, but the woman could rock footwear. Ruby red, sparkly, low-heeled pumps with sexy little ankle straps. Totally 'I'm off to see the wizard' perfection.

I was kinda in love with Cat Lady.

She paused again, twirling that something in her hand, waiting for me to reply.

Right. I shrugged and offered a friendly smile, giving Professor Ross a *Help me* look.

"Uh, we have . . . for you," Professor Ross gestured toward his mother's hand.

Cat Lady extended her palm, revealing a silver medallion threaded on a pretty red ribbon.

"Thank you. *Grazie*." I gently lifted the medallion, noting the engraving on it—a giant-esque man lifting a small child on his back.

"For you," Cat Lady repeated her son's words in halting English. "It is *Santo Cristoforo*. For the . . . *come si dice* . . . *protezione.*" She used a finger pull down on one eye. "*Dal malocchio.*"

Uhmmm? "Protection?" I went with the only word I had understood.

"Yes. To defend against the evil eye." Professor Ross said. "The evil things. They happen."

Right. That was true.

Again. Something that would be awesome on a t-shirt.

I glanced down again at the medal.

It was probably the jet lag talking at this point.

But . . .

Had the upstairs cat lady just landed on my doorstep with her nerdy professor son in *Wizard of Oz* ruby slippers (hers, not his) to give me a Catholic saint medal to protect me from the evil eye?

Because *I* was the one needing help (psychiatric or otherwise) here?

I smiled. A happy, giddy thing.

Yep. I was so in love.

I adored Cat Lady even more than the nice Indian guru on the plane who had spent several hours theorizing who I had been in past lives.

(Spoiler alert: Thanks to Dante D'Angelo—the third member of Branwell and Tennyson's exclusive triplet club—I knew that I had generally been a peasant housewife. Which totally busted all my dreams of being a reincarnated Joan of Arc. But whatever. I bet I was a rockin' peasant housewife.)

"*Le cose maledette sono successe qui, nel questo palazzo.*" Cat Lady was saying.

I looked at Professor Ross.

"My mother . . . she feels bad things happened in this palazzo," he translated. "The medallion has been blessed for your protection."

They both stared at me. Expectantly.

Uhmm. Okay.

Medal. Danger. Evil eye. Got it.

"Thank you?" I held up the medal closed in my fist, giving a weak smile.

Professor Ross matched my wan smile. "Mamma won't leave until you . . ." He mimed looping the ribbon over his head.

Ah.

I put it on, the medallion settling against my chest.

Cat Lady beamed at me, patting my cheek. She rattled away in Italian and then turned, motioning for Professor Ross to follow.

I guess that was goodbye then.

I watched Cat Lady hobble out in her ruby slippers, Professor Ross a puppy at her heels. I couldn't stop smiling. It was all kinda priceless.

"Grace," I called as I shut the door. "Gracie-pie. Time to wake up, sleepyhead."

I touched the medallion with my fingers as I walked down the hallway. I would have to google this saint, whoever he was.

It was sweet of Cat Lady to think I needed protection. Really. It was. And the slightest bit creepy, which I counted as a bonus.

"Grace." I tapped on her bedroom door and then pushed it open.

I noticed several things at once, in seemingly backwards order.

The empty rumpled bed.

The curtains blowing through the open window.

Her ratty plush elephant lying on the floor next to a toppled Little Mermaid music box, tissue carton and princess crown.

The fact that Grace wasn't in her room.

"Grace?" I rotated and walked back into the hallway. "Gracie. Pumpkin? Where are you?"

I searched through the apartment. Heart beating faster with every step.

Each room. Empty. Barren.

"Gracie?!" Panicked now.

I ran back into Grace's bedroom, scanning one more time. I stared at the well-loved stuffed elephant leaning against the fallen Little Mermaid music box. The music box lid had popped open, reflecting Ariel in its mirror.

Only then did I finally see it.

A solitary ruby-red handprint.

Small and stark on the front of her white dresser.

Grace's hand. Inked in blood.

5

BRANWELL

PORTLAND, OREGON
SIX YEARS EARLIER

Hey guys, look at this," Tennyson said as he and Lucy walked hand-in-hand into our apartment kitchen. "Lucy made us into superheroes."

Stirring some *ragu alla bolognese* on the stovetop, I rotated enough to see Dante take a paper from Tennyson's hand. The smell of tomatoes, garlic and sausage hung in the room.

"It's not my brilliance, Tenn." Lucy giggled. The sound of sparkling sunshine. "You guys are the ones with superpowers."

"You told her?" Dante asked Tennyson. "About our GUTs?"

I raised my eyebrows. We didn't talk much about the supernatural genetic gifts we inherited from our Italian father—our Grossly Unusual

Talents or GUTs, as we called them. The acronym was a little cutesy, but we were boys. What else would we call a paranormal gift of Sight?

"Of course I told her." Tennyson grinned, kissing Lucy's forehead. "She's going to be around for a long time, if I have any say."

Lucy leaned into him, beaming rainbows and unicorns. Honestly. That woman's smile.

I noted her t-shirt: *Never fear. Distracto Girl will save you from—oh look, a kitty!*

Did she *have* to be so perfect?

"Classic. I've been dubbed PerceptiMan." Dante snorted, reading the paper. "'PerceptiMan, the superhero who can literally see history. He sees who people and things were in past lives and uses his Super Sight to observe scenes from yesteryear. But living villains rest easy. PerceptiMan only sees dead people.' Nice." Dante jabbed a finger. "I like the giant eye on the back of my cape."

I glanced over Dante's shoulder. Sure enough. A stick figure Dante with an eye on his red cape.

Dante elbowed me, pointing below his description. "You're Captain Cacophony—"

"It had to alliterate," Lucy said.

I shook my head as I read:

> *Captain Cacophony, the superhero of sound. He hears what occurred around an object the last time it changed form in some way. His superpower is all about rules: the object has to be large enough to be felt, the change has to be obviously noticeable, living things are soundless and liquids muted. But beware. If Captain Cacophony concentrates, he can hear sound through the ages.*

"So Dante gets an eye on his cape, but I have huge ears?" I stared at the drawing of me. "How is that fair?"

"It's not." Tennyson shrugged. "But who ever said our GUTs were fair?"

True that.

"Lord Destiny?" Dante looked at Tennyson's superhero description. "Isn't that somewhat precious?"

"Stop." Lucy put up a hand, punctuating the gesture with another infectious giggle. "Tennyson *is* precious to me."

We all groaned, Dante rolling his eyes.

I stomped on the jealously that punched through me.

Brother's girlfriend. Not yours.

Focus.

I pretended to study Tennyson's stick figure with his ornate telescope.

> *Lord Destiny, the empath who feels the future. Want to know what will happen five minutes from now? Lord Destiny will tell you. But rest easy. Lord Destiny only feels five minutes forward. Your long term future is safe from his empathetic heart.*

"I'm still not convinced I would call them superpowers." I tapped the paper. "More like debilitating handicaps."

"No, I won't hear criticism. They're superpowers. End of story." Lucy reached across Tennyson, beckoning her hand, demanding the paper back. "I love your GUTs. Every last one."

BRANWELL

Water flowed silently around my body.

I finished the lap, rotated under and kicked away, avoiding touching the pool wall with my feet.

No sound.

Well, there *was* sound. Water lapping. Arms splashing. My breathing.

But all those were expected noises.

No unknown voices intruded. No buzzing background hum.

In water, I was free.

Normal. Just a man.

I finished another lap, freestyle. Rotated. Kicked off. I touched the tiled pool wall with my bare feet this time.

A trowel scraping over cement. The rumble of men's voices.

Bare whispers of noise. Muted.

Had I been out of the water, the sounds would have been crisp and clear. Every *plink* of tile being laid, the griping of a guy over his cheating girlfriend.

Heaven knew, I had heard it all over the years.

Granted, had I been out of the water, I would have never chanced touching something without preparation. There was too much risk involved, the results too unpredictable.

My hands stung just thinking about it.

No, the water was like everything else in my carefully constructed world—a barrier. A buffer of protection. And if that protective buffer sometimes felt isolating more than insulating . . .

I deliberately suppressed that thought—the one that whispered a prison, no matter how necessary, was still a prison—

Not going to go there. Not today.

Reaching the other side of the pool, I kicked off again and rotated to my back, moving to the backstroke, determined to methodically focus on my morning workout.

I stared up at the Gothic groin vaults crisscrossing the ceiling as my arms cut through the water. Accent lighting arched up from the floor, skimming the walls and edging the room in a golden glow. Once medieval storage cellars underneath our family palazzo in Florence, Dante and I had converted the space into a saline swimming pool and adjoining soundproof room years ago.

My sanctuary. A haven from the family curse.

Granted, family lore held that the curse was actually a gift vigorously sought-after by a distant ancestor. But who could honestly think that? Why would anyone deliberately seek out something so destructive?

My father, grandfather and all other forebears back to the Middle Ages had been able to see, hear and feel everything that had happened or would happen in a place. Voices, images . . . scenes constantly playing out in a vivid tableau around them.

It would be enough to drive one mad.

Which was exactly what had happened to every previous D'Angelo heir through the ages.

Would I be spared the same fate? Would my brothers? Who knew.

The 'gift' had fractured at our birth, giving us each a different GUT. Tennyson got the future part of the gift. Dante and I, as identical twins who were once a single egg, shared the past portion.

That didn't mean our GUTs were equal in strength or had divided in a clear way that made sense. It would be like someone dumping a bin of garden tools onto the lawn and expecting them to form a sculpture. It could happen, but more likely, the tools would just make a mess.

That was how I saw our GUTs—potentially useful tools jumbled together into something confusingly less-helpful.

Our GUTs had developed in strength year-after-year as children and teens, only leveling off a bit once we hit adulthood. We were supposed to tell each other if things changed with our GUTs. Stay informed. Share.

The operative words in all that being 'supposed to.'

As if.

Tennyson didn't talk about it. It was anyone's guess what his GUT did currently.

I didn't mention my changes. As far as anyone knew, my GUT was strictly limited to sound. But it *had* been morphing over the past year or two.

Dante constantly *over*-shared but that was because a) he was Dante and b) his gift had been static for nearly a decade, so it was low-stakes to talk about it.

For Tennyson and me . . . not so much.

Dante and I used our GUTs in our work as art authenticators and appraisers. But I was more the grunt intellectual labor who tracked down actual physical proof of Dante's paranormal understanding. He saw the truth and then I proved it. My gift was all well and good, but trying to piece together random noises without any physical context of time or place was tricky at best—the cacophony of noise, the unexpected situations. Dante's gift of seeing was much more useful.

I was fine with the arrangement. I hated touching anything that I hadn't already altered myself for specific, well-grounded reasons.

Reasons I kept tightly to myself.

The last thing any of my family needed was one additional problem to worry about.

My GUT was like living with diabetes or some other chronic illness. It required planning at every point of my day, but with the right precautions, it was manageable.

I had my soundproof room just off the pool. A place where I could stitch in silence, carefully altering every item of clothing, every towel, sheet and pillowcase before it touched my skin.

And I had this pool of water.

Blissfully freeing.

I moved through three more laps and then paused in the middle. Floating on my back. Weightless. The water settled around me.

Deafening silence. So very rare and precious.

Perfection.

That's what I told myself.

Because to let any other emotion slip in would be . . .

I swallowed.

Loneliness was a vast, black miasma. So easy to fall into, nearly impossible to escape. All-consuming like its twin—Self Pity.

Two emotions that clamored desperately to be my constant companions.

Besides . . . *miasma.*

I'd have to add that to the list. She would have liked that one.

I kicked over to the side of the pool, mentally prepping myself for the onslaught of noise. I placed my hands on the prepared towel on the pool deck. The texture of the embroidery felt rough beneath my hands as I pushed out of the pool, water sluicing down my body.

Breathing. Cloth rustling.

The sounds of me stitching a pattern of Celtic runes around the edge of the towel, altering its sound at that moment. Fixing it into something known and . . . controlled. The ancient, three-pronged *algiz* pattern represented stylized horns and was meant to act as a shield.

Safety.

If I had to stitch something, protective runes seemed a logical choice. Pity their benefit was more psychologically soothing than magically actual.

I snagged another towel off a nearby chair and dried off.

Deep breaths. The faint hiss of a needle pulling through fabric.

I toweled off my hair and beard. Randomly, my own personal body hair held no sound for me, nor did it 'hear' sound if it brushed against something.

So I grew it all out long. Another protective layer between me and the world.

I slid my feet into rune-stitched slippers and wrapped the towel around my waist. I snagged my phone off the table, a hand-made leather case and etched screen protector kept noise to a minimum.

Light glinted off a series of thin, white scars on my right hand—the catalyst for my carefully managed world. Not that I had any intention of tumbling down the rabbit hole of *that* memory today.

I glanced at my phone screen.

Text from Dante. He needed help dating a fifteenth century manuscript. The owner thought it could be a *vade mecum* or enchiridion—a type of early how-to manual. Dante had to catch a plane tomorrow, so would I mind researching past manufacturing of . . .

I nodded and flipped to the next message, replying to another business matter.

It took a few minutes before I noticed.

Three missed calls. All from Tennyson.

He never called without a reason. Something had happened. Or *would* happen.

My heart sped up.

Tennyson answered on the second ring.

"What's up?" I asked.

"You been watching the news this morning?" Anxiety tinged with hopeless depression washed over me, the emotions laden with a sense of 'outsideness.'

And there it was. That change in my GUT.

I could 'hear' others' emotions.

My fledgling empath abilities were clearest with my brothers, Tennyson in particular. I didn't feel much from other people. But if someone told a bald-faced lie, I could hear it in their voice. I didn't sense things into the future and what I did feel was tentative and mild, not invasive the way Tennyson described his gift.

But it just made me wonder even more about my brother. If I had a touch of Tennyson's empath abilities, had he started to manifest hints of my clairaudience? Possibly even Dante's clairvoyance?

There was no manual for our GUTs—nothing saying that they had to be logical or rational or, heaven forbid, static.

Again, not that any of us talked about it. For being so close, we brothers were experts at erecting walls between ourselves.

"No. Something happen?" I asked.

A sigh. "You might say that."

His pain flickered through me. Longing. Heartache.

I imagined Tennyson running a hand through his short hair. A twist of his mouth. Face turned toward a window, looking out over the Tuscan countryside—the view from the family villa near Volterra—the place Tennyson lived away from people and their emotions.

This wasn't a taste of clairvoyance, per se. More like a solid understanding of my brother's location and physical tics. We were wombmates after all.

"Lucy . . . she's here in Italy—" His voice hitched, pained. "There's been an . . . incident."

My lungs stopped, every molecule in my body coming to attention.

Lucy . . . my *Lucia* . . . fear whispered through me.

Fear for her. For me. For Tennyson.

Instantly, emotional walls flared into place around my mind. Instinctual. Born of long habit.

Tennyson could never know how I felt about Lucy. It was my biggest secret. My personal hell.

I visualized bricking my love for her behind enormous castle walls. Tennyson could 'feel' Dante and me over a distance. Would he sense this too?

"She is?" I sat down, proud that my voice didn't sound as breathless as I felt. "Lucy's here? Is she okay?"

I focused on the shocked/surprised portion of my emotions—the ones that Tennyson would expect me to have, forcing down my own longing and heartache.

"Physically, she's safe, I think," Tennyson said.

I couldn't control the relief that pounded through me.

It had been too long since Tennyson and I played this familiar dance. The one where he was Lucy's boyfriend and talked about her all the time, and I turned myself into an emotional pretzel and pretended—somehow, someway—that I didn't love his girlfriend too.

"Apparently Jeff got a job with some company outside Florence—you remember her brother?"

The image of a stocky, ginger man with kind eyes floated through my memory. "We met a couple times. He's the oldest brother, right?"

"Yeah. Number two."

Lucy was number six of nine. Children, that is.

"Anyway, Jeff and his wife left on a trip, and Lucy is here watching their daughter. The little girl disappeared yesterday morning. Just vanished out of her bedroom sometime right after sunrise."

"Crap." Horror washed over me. Mostly mine, I was sure, but I still sensed that 'outside-ness' of Tennyson's emotions in the mix.

"My thoughts exactly. Normally, a child wandering off wouldn't be such news, but the only clue is a bloody handprint on her dresser. The police suspect foul play."

I closed my eyes, swallowing hard. Knowing what Tennyson was going to say next. No clairvoyance needed.

"As the last person who saw the girl and the only one in the supposedly locked apartment, Lucy's a suspect in her disappearance."

Oh, Lucy.

"She would *never* hurt that little girl." My voice emphatic.

"Exactly. You and I know that, but the rest of the world doesn't. And my Lucy is in a foreign country dealing with this awful thing on her own."

My Lucy . . . his possessive adjective wasn't lost on me.

"She wouldn't call me," he continued. "Not after how everything ended."

"No. She wouldn't. None of us are on her speed dial."

A pause. Tennyson was apprehensive about something. No . . . shame. He was ashamed.

What—?!

"I . . . I can't help her, Bran," he whispered. "I've sat here for the last two hours since I heard the news . . . trying to find the courage to just call her or reach out or *something—*"

I closed my eyes, that sense of shame deepening. Of failing those who relied on him yet one more time.

Oh, Tenn . . .

A hefty sigh. "I'm not strong enough right now," he continued. "I'm not in a good place. I can barely keep myself together . . ."

Preaching to the choir, brother.

"Lucy needs *help*, not my scarred, crippled . . . lameness," he said.

I winced, the self-loathing in Tennyson's words stinging. I could imagine him rubbing the stub just below his hip. The place where his left leg had been before Afghanistan and a roadside bomb.

"Dealing with this, Branwell . . . it's more than I can emotionally handle. A wise man knows when to fold his cards. So I did the one thing I *can* do. I called you."

Despair filtered through. Blackness. A desire for oblivion . . . anything to stop the pain.

That razor thin line that Tennyson always walked between coping and . . . not. Memories crowded in.

Tennyson curled on his bed. The sheet unnaturally flat where his left leg should have been.

"You going to get up today?" I asked from the doorway.

A shake of his head.

"Tomorrow?"

Another shake.

"You can't mourn Lucy forever."

Silence.

And then so softly, I barely heard . . .

"Watch me."

Another memory flitted . . .

Blood. So much blood. On the bathroom floor. Pooling in the bathtub around him.

"Dammit, Tenn . . . What have you done?"

I scrambled for a towel, anything to stop the bleeding from his slit wrists.

"You have to let Lucy go," I said. "This isn't worth your life."

"Can't," he whispered back. "Can't let her go. Have to cut myself free."

Viciously, I pushed the memories back.

Enough.

Tennyson was healing, moving on. He *was* better than he had been. Not whole. Not quite to the point of functional, but definitely into the coping stage.

We had all worked so hard to help him climb out of this pit. I refused to allow anything to push him back in.

"Will you?" Tennyson asked. "Will you help her? You and Dante? My gift is not that useful in this sort of situation anyway. I only feel emotions a few minutes into the future. Great for detecting a possible roadside bomb but not as useful when trying to find a missing child. Dante might be of some help, but he only sees dead people. Besides, he's still leaving tomorrow to join Claire in Boston with her mom going through cancer treatments and all. You, on the other hand . . ."

"Of course." No hesitation.

I would do anything for him, including cutting out my own heart. Which . . . been there, done that, bought the t-shirt.

And now I was going to do it all over again.

"Thanks, man. I owe you . . . big time." Tennyson's relief washed over me. "I can't let Lucy deal with this alone. She was never the bad guy here, just the one who was strong enough to walk away."

And there it was. The heart of the problem—pun intended. He wasn't over Lucy.

Join the club.

"I'll get Chiara to help," I said.

"Great idea. She has the right connections and loves this stuff."

Chiara, our younger sister—dark, petite and one hundred and ten percent Italian, our American mother's genes having passed her over. Chiara did enjoy a good mystery and had friends in the police community.

We talked for a moment longer and hung up. The entire time, I ruthlessly pushed aside thoughts of Lucy.

Bury her. Tamp her down. Lock your emotions in a bomb-proof bunker.

Tennyson could never know.

I called Chiara and chatted logistics. She promised to track down Lucy's contact info for me. (Translation—she was going to wait an hour and then send me the information she already had to make it look like she wasn't keeping tabs on Lucy.)

Next, I texted Dante. He was in an early morning meeting with that client about the how-to enchiridion but, assuming Chiara located Lucy for us, he would join me as soon as he could get away. Reminding me, yet again, that Dante's eagerness was a two-edged sword: he could be nosy and pushy, but he would also drop everything to help.

I climbed the three flights of stairs from the basement pool to my apartment where I showered and prepped for the day. And each time Lucy's blue-green eyes blasted through my defenses, I pushed her away.

Each remembered breathy laugh. Each bounce of excitement. Her endless cheery bubbly-ness.

I stuffed them all deep down.

A blessed numbness settled over me. Detached. Unfeeling.

The necessary state I habitually sought when anything Lucy-oriented reared its head.

It was only as I finished dressing that something slipped through the cracks.

I pulled open my dresser drawer, digging for a pair of socks, when my gloved hand brushed against a lacquered box. Inlaid with wood, it was one of the pretty boxes tourists buy in the markets around San Lorenzo in downtown Florence.

I hesitated only a second before raising the lid, absorbing everything that lay inside.

At the very top was a blank piece of paper, the edges ripped into a ragged heart shape.

I stared at it for a moment. Undecided. And then lifted it out, touching the paper heart to my bare forehead.

Paper tearing.

"Branwell, this is for you. A message for your ears only." Her voice. Soft. Giggly. "Happy birthday, big guy. I hope you have a day free of non-vegetal green things and full of choosing fun. Know that you'll always have a friend in me."

I allowed myself fifteen seconds of weakness. Fifteen seconds of watching her wild mass of hair spin around as she laughingly pulled me away from my schoolwork to go out with her and Tennyson. Waiting for her as she stopped to photograph *another* heart-shaped leaf, Tennyson chuckling at my elbow. Seeing her tear-streaked cheeks as she walked out of our apartment for the last time.

I tucked those memories and a thousand more back inside with her note, shutting the drawer with a firm click.

Long ago I had chosen my side, my team.

And it was firmly beside my brother. Not the woman we had both loved . . . and lost.

7

BRANWELL

"Hey, Branwell. Do you have a second?" Lucy's chipper voice breezed through the phone connection.

"Sure." I ran a hand over my face. Just the sound of her voice sent my stupid heart to thumping—an eager puppy straining at its leash, tail frenzied.

Down, boy.

"Tennyson is in the middle of taking that forestry test, so he's too far away to feel anything from me. Which is a good thing right now," she said. A murmur of voices. The sound of screeching metal. "I need someone to help me take my mind off things."

"Of course, Lucy. What's going on?"

She laughed, breathy. And then grunted. More metal scraping.

"Lucy? What's up?" My heart pounded harder.

"Some stoned idiot ran a red light and t-boned my car."

"What?! Are you okay?"

"Yeah, yeah. I think I'm okay. I can wiggle my feet, so that's good."
She laughed again. Was that a gasp of pain? "But talk to me, Branwell.
Distract me from thinking about the Jaws of Life."

As if on cue, metal squealed.

A voice drifted through. "Stay with us, ma'am."

Panic choked me.

"Lucy, are you still *in* the car?" I grabbed my own car keys and raced
out of the apartment.

"Uhm, yeah. But Clint and Joe here say they should have me out in
about fifteen minutes." Her voice slipped away. Muffled. "You guys said
fifteen minutes, right?"

"Yeah. Hang in there," a man shouted. "We're going to cut you free."

Terror washed me. I pushed back a vision of Lucy, bleeding and
battered, trapped in a mangled vehicle.

"I'm coming, Lucy." I slid into my own car and maneuvered out of
the parking lot. Hands shaking. "Keep talking to me. Are you in pain?"

"Some. My head hurts and I taste blood in my mouth, but I don't
think I broke anything."

A tense pause.

"You're way too calm." Anxiety fluttered against my sternum. "I
think you're going into shock."

"No, I tend to get like this in a crisis. My mom once accused me
of being the person who would scream 'Weeeee' in a plane crash." She
snorted. "It wasn't a compliment."

"Well, safe to say we found your superpower."

"What? Pathological cheerfulness?"

I chuckled. *That* was why I loved this girl . . . that right there.

"I would have gone with 'perpetual optimism'," I said.

"Eh, it's overrated." Another screech of metal. "I'll probably fall apart later, but for right now, I'm holding it together."

That's my girl.

"You just keep doing that, Lucy." I shook my head. "Keep doing that."

8

LUCY

PRATO, ITALY
2016

I have your passport. You will not leave the country." Inspector Silvia Paola, the lead investigator in charge of Grace's case, fixed me with her dark eyes.

"Okay," I nodded, blinking back tears yet again, my eyes scratchy and throat swollen.

We stood in the central hallway of Jeff and Jen's apartment, morning sunlight bouncing cheerfully through the windows. Officers had been in and out for the last few hours, asking me questions, dusting for fingerprints, asking me more questions, taking items as evidence, snapping photographs and then asking even more questions.

But so far, there had been no answers. Grace was just . . . gone. Vanished.

Worse, we hadn't been able to reach Jeff and Jen, as they were in a remote part of Africa without connectivity. They were blissfully enjoying their safari, unaware their child had disappeared into thin air.

"You may travel anywhere in Italy, as long as you let us know where you are," Paola continued in her heavily accented English.

Paola was an odd mix of femininity and cool reserve. Petite and attractive with expertly applied makeup and a sleek, bobbed haircut, she wore her police uniform like armor. No-nonsense to her core, Paola gave monosyllabic answers and employed a ruthlessly effective glare.

"This is my card." She handed me a business card, all in Italian, of course. "You are to call every morning and check in. We are allowing you to be free for now, but that can change if you are not cooperative. You will also immediately call if you remember anything else."

It wasn't a request.

Because there was only one prime suspect in Gracie's disappearance, and I had two thumbs pointed firmly at my own chest.

How could I be living this nightmare?

Numbly, I swallowed and took the card from her. "Thank you," I whispered and tucked the card into the pocket of my sweatpants.

Grace. My little Gracie . . . gone. So utterly, inexplicably vanished.

The first hours after realizing she was missing, I had assumed I would find her quickly. That she had slipped out somehow and would come bouncing back up the stairs with stories about chasing a pigeon across the cathedral piazza. I would scold her for giving me a good scare, hug her and then go get some gelato to celebrate her being alive.

But each hour that passed without any sign of Grace, I became more and more frantic. I had finally called the police yesterday afternoon, which quickly escalated from two officers on my doorstep to an entire investigative team headed by Paola. They had arrived again this morning in force, grilling me again and combing the apartment thoroughly.

Over twenty-four hours of no answers or signs or real clues had left me bereft. I had worked enough with wilderness survival and trauma to understand how important the first twenty-four hours were to any missing child situation. Nausea cramped my stomach when I thought about time slipping away.

Why, why, *why* had I gone back to sleep? Grace was my responsibility, and I *slept* through her abduction. I should have been awake. I should have been guarding over her, protecting her.

I had *one* job.

How could I ever forgive myself?

Paola turned as an officer stepped out of Grace's room, holding a crate in his hands and asking her something in rapid Italian. Paola responded. The officer shrugged and held out the crate allowing Paola, and by extension me, to see its contents—some clothes, a tissue carton, Grace's beloved stuffed elephant and her Little Mermaid music box.

More things to add to their investigation.

Paola waved the officer through and out the front door.

This continued for another hour, the officers and Paola talking back and forth.

I was counting the minutes until they left, until the apartment was mine alone. I had been able to keep myself more or less in Coping Mode—the one where I functioned and dealt with a crisis. But after nearly a day of interrogation and accusation, I was nearing nuclear melt-down stage.

"We are leaving," Paola finally announced, the last of her officers disappearing out the door. "We have a mid-morning press conference at the police station in ten minutes. Any *paparazzi* who remain here have been told they are not allowed in the palazzo without specific permission. I recommend you do not talk with them, as doing so could harm this investigation. Besides, the press can get . . . *aggressivo*. We will talk tomorrow. In the meantime, I suggest you do nothing." She swiveled to leave and then turned her head back to me. "I watch your American television, all those shows with the detectives and police. Do not play the hero and try to solve this case. Allow us to do our job."

I nodded. What could I do anyway?

Paola gave one of her signature *harrumphs* and followed her fellow officers out. I shut the apartment door with a loud *snick* behind them, resting my forehead against the cool wood door.

Fear and terror clawed at the back of my throat. My shoulders trembled.

What *had* happened to Grace? How could I have let it happen? I was the worst aunt in the history of auntness.

Wiping my raw cheeks, I walked into the living room to the left of the front door and crossed to one of the tall windows. Inspector Paola emerged from the building into the piazza below, pushing through the crowd of cameras and waving off reporters. She climbed into a police car which instantly sped off, lights flashing.

She was gone. I could fall apart now.

Turning, I collapsed into a chair, a sob stumbling from my lips. Curling into a ball, I wrapped my arms around my face, shoulders shaking in earnest.

My phone binged. Blearily through my tears, I glanced down at it resting on the end table beside my chair.

My mom texting again.

Five more *bings* followed in rapid succession.

My older sister. Another brother.

My family was understandably frantic, peppering me with a nearly constant spray of questions they needed answers to *righthisminute*.

Ugh. I was in the process of falling apart here. Couldn't they understand that? No one loved their family more than me. Seriously. We were like peanut butter and chocolate, always better together.

But this situation . . .

Panic edged in again, threatening to pull me down. I could barely hold on to my own worry and grief, much less shoulder theirs.

If only I had stayed awake . . .

There were so few clues. Just the bloody handprint and Grace gone.

No sign of forced entry. Nothing else disturbed or suspicious.

Jeff and Jen's apartment was on the second floor of an old seventeenth-century building. No balconies. And given the height of Italian ceilings, the apartment windows were a solid thirty-feet off the ground.

Nearly all the windows in the apartment had been open at the time, letting in the cool morning air. No screens or bars on any of them. Why would you need them? To get inside the apartment through a window, someone would have had to rappel from above or bring in a firetruck ladder.

But somehow, someone had.

I had spent hours wracking my brain, trying to remember every single detail.

Grace *had* come into my room that morning, right? I hadn't hallucinated that fact or dreamed it, had I?

I had been so tired from jet lag . . . not that it was an excuse for falling back asleep. Nothing could ever excuse me not being there for Grace.

Bing. Bing.

I swiped at my tears. Hiccupped.

Bzzzzzz.

The doorbell. I jumped at the sound.

Just . . . no!

It couldn't be Inspector Paola. She was at the press conference.

So who else?

A news reporter? No, thank you.

Cat Lady?

I groaned. Yes. That had to be it. She had been drifting around the fringes of the investigation, asking questions.

If I was ignoring my own mother, I had zero intention of speaking with her.

Bing. Bing. Bing.

Texts again. My mom. Two more sisters.

Please, just a few minutes.

I simply needed a moment to grieve, hyperventilate . . . have a panic attack or three.

I hiccupped and leaned back in the chair, staring at the ancient beamed ceiling, letting the tears fall.

Bzzz. Bzzz.

Go away, I mentally pleaded.

A polite knock. Followed by a longer *bzzzzzzz*.

And then . . . *bingbingbingbingbing*.

I reached out and silenced my phone. Not forever. Just for five minutes . . .

I gasped and rubbed my wet cheeks on the hem of my t-shirt, trying to gather my Coping Mode back together enough to . . . cope.

There was a source of help. I had contemplated it more seriously at three a.m. when the panic attacks and hysteria had become almost unbearable, the silence stifling.

I could get online, send a message. I wouldn't need to start with Tennyson or Branwell. Who knew if they were in Italy anyway?

I could just message Chiara. She had always been a good friend, despite everything, and she had connections within law enforcement. Even if she were still upset with me, she would help find a little girl.

I didn't blame her for siding with her brother when I made that final break with Tennyson. That's always the problem with a broken relationship. You lose so much more than simply a boyfriend.

Bzzzzzzz.

I had fallen out of romantic love with Tennyson long before I summoned the courage to rip myself away from his family.

I had loved them all. I still did.

Bzzz. Bzzz.

If only Branwell . . .

I stopped right there, a different sort of ache lodging in my chest.

I paused inside the doorway into the kitchen. I'd come from Tennyson and the hospital, knowing I'd find Branwell here. I couldn't leave without seeing him one last time.

He sat crumpled in a chair, elbows on the table in front of him, gloved hands in his long hair, hazel eyes intent as I walked into the room—

"So you're leaving?" His low voice rumbled through the gloom.

"Yeah." I swallowed. "We all know it's for the best."

"Do we?" He leaned back, hands still threaded in his hair. Brows drawn in disapproval.

I knew they wanted me to stay. All of them. Not for me, per se, but for how I calmed Tennyson. By leaving . . . I had failed them all. This clan that had somehow become my own.

But Tennyson wasn't the brother I loved. And I was so tired of living a lie. Why did my heart have to latch on to the one man I could never have?

"I just wanted to say goodbye," I whispered.

Silence. Our gazes tangled.

"Well." His voice carried through the hush. "Goodbye then." Words so quiet.

I nodded, throat thick and burning.

"Goodbye, Branwell."

I drank him in. One last look before turning and walking out the door . . .

I shook the memory off.

They didn't want to see me. I knew that.

For my part, seeing any of them again would be . . . catastrophic. I had worked so hard to move on.

But for Grace . . .

We *had* to find her. And the D'Angelo brothers could find clues hidden from the rest of us.

Tennyson's GUT focused on near-future emotions. Dante saw the past but only the dead-and-gone past, and I refused to even entertain the thought that Grace was dead.

Which left Branwell. His GUT could 'hear' if someone else had been in the apartment, if Grace had said something.

I forced down the niggling voice that whispered I was focusing on the brother I wanted to see. That Dante and Tennyson could be helpful too, if only to give hope or crush it altogether.

Bzzz. Bzzz. Bzzz.

Knock. Knock.

Okay, okay. Got it. Falling apart time was over.

I could do this. Be strong. Answer questions. Find Grace.

I was the eternal optimist—the one who coped in a crisis.

I stood up. Deep breath.

Swallowing, I walked to entryway, mentally preparing myself to face Cat Lady without being too snippy.

I threw the door open, upset words dying on my lips.

Oh. My.

It was as if my thoughts had summoned him.

Branwell . . . standing on my stoop, hand raised to knock one more time, eyes flared wide.

Looking every inch as potent as my memory painted him.

Had I conjured him?

Tall. Sun-eclipsing huge. A six foot four mountain of wide-shoulders and barrel chest.

A man-giant.

He was somehow bigger than I remembered. As if my mind couldn't fully recollect him all at once, but only as snippets of the whole—dark hair and beard, gloved hands, thick arms, trunk-like legs, intent eyes—

But to see *all* of him so suddenly . . .

My brain shut down. Literally. My coping ability shattering.

Because I did exactly what my heart had wanted to do for more years than I could quickly count—

I threw myself onto him.

Sobbing. Weeping.

Dumping my sorrow on his broad chest.

I wrapped my arms around him and held on. As if the entire world swamped me under, and he was the lifeline rescuing me from a sea of sorrow.

He was *here*. He had *come*.

Somehow. Someway.

I was too overwhelmed by Grace's disappearance—the endless police questions, the accusatory looks, my guilt, the horror of not knowing—to ask *how*. How he had found me. How he had gotten into the palazzo.

Surely some numb part of my brain noted his shock at my hug. The *oomph* of air swooshing from his lungs.

Branwell kept his life carefully structured, all with the express purpose of avoiding accidental physical contact. I knew this. I did.

No one touched him. Not without his clear permission and some planning.

But . . .

He was . . . *here*. When my entire world had shattered, Branwell had come to help.

I cried and cried. Ugly. Noisy. Totally undone.

Dimly, I noted him scooting us back into the apartment and closing the door, dropping something at his feet. And then tentatively, his arms came around me. Gentle. Kind.

And then . . . tighter.

He engulfed me. Surrounding. Warmth. Security.

Holding me with a fierce tenderness that caused my throat to ache for an entirely different reason.

It was just so typically Branwell to be the one to show up. He had always been like that. The quiet guy who worked selflessly behind the scenes to make things happen. The unsung hero.

And he was *holding* me. The perfect height to tuck my head under his chin. Big enough that my arms had to reach to surround him.

I brutally repressed a comparison with Tennyson's shorter, more wiry frame . . .

How could something so very wrong feel so impossibly right?

Oh Branwell . . . why couldn't it have been you?

I continued to sob, a stream of stuttering, "You c-c-came. Y-you came . . . youcameyoucame . . ." leaving my mouth.

Not my best moment.

Seeing Branwell required mental preparation and fortitude.

Or, barring that, a lack of crisis, an hour's forewarning and a shot of vodka.

I had nothing.

I hugged him tighter, afraid if I let go, I would crumble into pieces. My brain had short-circuited and the emotional part of me that insisted this man was *mine, mine, mine* ran amok.

I hiccupped and sniffled, breathing him in.

Warm, clean male with a hint of forest pine.

Yep. Still crying. Clinging to him like plastic wrap.

Pull yourself together, Lucy. This guy never has been, nor will he ever be, your man.

Let him go.

Literally and figuratively.

Snuffling, I told my arms to release him, to unwrap myself.

They stubbornly refused. Of course.

Granted, getting Branwell out of my system had proved a near Sisyphean task over the years.

Focusing, I forced my arms to relax their hold and took a small step back, pausing to rub the large wet spot on his chest. He clasped my upper arms in his hands.

Naturally, he wore his signature gloves—butter-soft brown leather, tightly fitted with rune stitched edges. The kind of expensive, high-end gloves you see in shop windows in Venice. The gloves disappeared under a long-sleeved shirt—this one off-white with blue-embroidered edges. Worn hip-hugging jeans and heavy leather boots rounded out his look.

His beard lifted as he swallowed and looked down at me. Golden hazel eyes met mine, lighter than I remembered in his face.

Oh boy.

"H-hey." I managed a weak smile. "N-nice to see you, Branwell. Uhmm, in case you missed it, I really appreciate you taking the time to . . . v-visit."

A faint smile ghosted over his lips.

"Nice to see you too, Lucy."

I almost closed my eyes at the sound of his voice. That deep rumble I remembered all too well.

How could I *still* be so gone on this man?

"Sorry I lost it," I whispered, sucking in a stuttery breath and dropping my eyes to his chest. "It's been an awful twenty-four hours."

"I saw the news. It looked like you could use some help." He tightened his hold on my upper arms, waiting until I raised my gaze to meet his. "We're going to find her, Lucy. We've got this for you."

I nodded, throat tight again.

After a day of recriminations—my own self-inflicted ones and Paola's thinly veiled accusations— I hadn't realized how much I needed someone on my side.

At what point would I cry myself out?

I stepped away from him and snagged a tissue from the entryway table, wiping my eyes and face. And then gave up being ladylike and blew my nose vigorously.

Out of the corner of my eye, I noted his gaze skimming me, cataloging differences and similarities.

He looked the same. Dark curly hair pulled back into a loose bun. Beard thick but neatly trimmed.

Seriously. The man was the walking, talking definition of lumbersexual.

Me . . . same red hair and freckles. Body a little curvier, face slightly more angular.

I glanced down and realized I was wearing a green t-shirt with the words 'Kiss Me I'm Irish' on the front over ratty, faded yoga pants. I had been so overwhelmed with everything, I hadn't even bothered to look at what I had on.

Add to that, every last inch of my fair, freckled skin was red and splotchy from crying. Hair a tangled mess and not a drop of make-up.

Basically, every man's fantasy . . . if said man were into the *psychotic hobo* look, which I was pretty sure Branwell wasn't.

Of course, he would see me like this—

Why are we women like this? I was in crisis. My sweet Gracie was missing. What did it *matter* how I looked?

Besides, gorgeously salon-perfect or filthy homeless waif . . . it didn't make a difference in the end. Branwell could be madly in love with me, and it would alter nothing.

Tennyson and Afghanistan and a thousand other hurts and sorrows stood firmly between us. Nothing would ever change that fact.

"Tennyson send you?" I asked, giving my cheeks one last swipe.

He nodded. "It seemed like my GUT could be of some use. So tell me what happened."

Ah, there was the Branwell I knew so well. Blunt. To the point. A man of few words. The guy who held his emotions and thoughts tight.

"Grace just . . . disappeared," I whispered. "No one knows what happened to her."

"Where did you last see her?"

"In my bedroom." I gestured down the hall. "She crawled into bed with me, and I-I fell back asleep." I hiccuped and looked at him, eyes surely full of despair. "How could I fall back asleep, Branwell? How could I abandon my sweet Gracie like that—"

"Stop, Lucy." Tone stern. "Stop. You did nothing wrong. Falling asleep with a little girl in your arms . . . you can't blame yourself."

"But, if I hadn't—"

"No. No more *what ifs*." Branwell shook his head. "The Lucy Snow I know would understand that self-reproach won't find Grace any faster." His hazel eyes drilled me.

My shoulders heaved at his words. It was true. I needed to pull myself back together. Focus on what I could fix and let go of the things that I couldn't.

"Okay." I straightened my shoulders and dabbed at my cheeks again. "After I fell asleep, the police think Grace went back to her own bedroom before she—" My voice broke.

"Got it. Will you show me?"

I bobbed my head and walked down the hall, Branwell at my heels.

I motioned him into Grace's bedroom. Like so much of the house, Grace's room was white with pops of color—white dresser, bed and nightstand, offset by bright matted prints and textiles. My sister-in-law clearly loved minimalist decor.

Branwell's large body dwarfed the space, towering over Grace's child-sized furniture. He turned in a slow circle, studying the room. He went uncannily still when he noticed the handprint on the dresser.

"That is—" He pointed at the bloody handprint.

"Terrifying." I finished on a whisper.

Branwell met my gaze. "We're going to find her, Lucy. Give me the rundown."

I blinked back tears again as I told him everything. Finding Grace gone, the paltry evidence, Inspector Paola and her accusing, threatening words.

Branwell nodded his head at the appropriate times, grunted occasionally. He prowled the room as I talked. Studying everything intently but touching nothing. He paused with his eyes on the bare twin bed—white washed wood frame with a bright pink and blue comforter. Well, there had *once* been a comforter on it.

"The police took anything that appeared disturbed as evidence," I said.

Branwell turned his head toward the dresser, looking pointedly at the ruby-red handprint again. Just seeing it caused my heart rate to spike.

"Looking for blood and other DNA evidence?"

"That was my assumption."

"What did they take?"

I scanned the room. "The bedding, obviously. Some clothes, Grace's stuffed elephant, a Little Mermaid music box. Things like that."

Branwell pursed his mouth, thinking. "I'll chat with Chiara and see about getting access to those items. They might prove useful."

He didn't say anything else for a moment, merely continued to study the room.

Seeing his huge body in motion about did me in. The careful way he moved, hands clasped behind his back. The quiet strength radiating from him.

How I had *missed* him.

Two years. Two long years of trying to move past this amazing man. Destroyed in less than five minutes.

BRANWELL

PORTLAND, OREGON
SIX YEARS EARLIER

B ranwell, you want to come with us?" Tennyson poked his head into my bedroom, lifting an eyebrow at the textbooks scattered across my desk. "You have to take a break from studying sometime, you know."

Tennyson pushed the door open wider, revealing Lucy tucked into the crook of his arm—lopsided smile on her face, red corkscrew curls escaping from her high ponytail. She sported a t-shirt with the word *Jenius* across the front.

My stupid, useless heart skipped a beat, speeding up.

Of course.

I swallowed and forced my eyes back to my brother's face, visualizing strong walls around my mind. My loyalties were to him, regardless of what my wayward heart thought.

"Where you going?" I asked.

"The Forestry Club is doing some caterpillar rehabilitation down by the river." Lucy sagged farther into Tennyson. "We'll be making tiny leaf-lined dens for them strung together by literal daisy chains."

A beat.

"Seriously?"

"Nah, I'm totally messing with you." Lucy laughed, that brilliant bubble of sound. "We're going to the movies. Come with us. Give yourself a break."

Tennyson grinned and kissed her forehead.

Yeah. As much fun as it sounded to sit in a dark theater next to the lovey-dovey two of them . . .

"The caterpillars might have sold me, but just a movie?" I shrugged. "Thanks, but no thanks. Got a test to cram for." I tapped my textbook.

Tennyson furrowed his forehead, obviously wanting to say something, but instead shrugged and slapped the door frame.

"Well, catch you later then." He turned to go, wrapping his fingers around Lucy's hand in the process.

"Have fun," she said. "Found this and thought of you."

She threw a small something at me with a good-natured, teasing grin. I snagged it out of the air with one gloved hand, watching as she waved and walked off with my brother, their happy voices floating down the hallway.

Deep breath.

I glanced down at the candy in my hand and chuckled.

A sour apple Jolly Rancher.

Bright green and shiny.

10

BRANWELL

PRATO, ITALY
2016

This was torture.

Honestly.

I loved my brother more than my own life, but this . . .

This was downright cruel.

Granted, if Tennyson knew how I felt, he would never have asked me to come here.

But Tennyson and Lucy . . . they were two sides of my heart. Declining to help either of them was not an option.

Which I guess just made me a sick masochist.

I prowled around Grace's bedroom—ostensibly trying to decide what to touch first—but mostly feeling like a cat wanting to crawl out of its skin. The room didn't hold much. A bed, dresser, nightstand. The police had clearly removed things already.

Lucy continued to outline everything that had happened, voice soft and breathy. Pain and loss lacing through every word.

I swallowed, the vision of her face as she opened the door vivid in my mind. Tear-streaked. Strained. Shocked. Surprised.

And, fleetingly, something else.

My heart wanted to label it *longing*, but that made no sense.

She had launched herself at me, practically collapsing onto my chest. So unexpected it bordered on surreal.

Lack of physical contact was the worst side effect, for lack of a better word, of my GUT.

No one touched me.

Ever.

Sure, living things have no sound. I could touch someone's skin with no noise whatsoever.

But other people's clothing, jewelry, accessories *did* have sound. And if you've ever tried to hug someone without touching their clothing . . .

As human beings, we're hard-wired for touch.

To say I yearned for human connection was an understatement. When my mom or Nonna held my hand or cupped my face—cautiously, carefully—it soothed and comforted.

But the sensation of Lucy's body snugged against mine. Warm. Soft. Flowing into me like molten chocolate—

I swallowed. Let out a slow breath.

Had she *ever* hugged me?

She was physically demonstrative and affectionate. Something I knew all too well. Watching her tease and cuddle and kiss Tennyson on a daily basis had been its own special level of hell.

But I couldn't recall ever hugging her. And, trust me, I *would* have remembered.

So when she threw her arms around me, I should have politely held her. Patted her back. Offered friendly comfort.

But the *shock* of the moment—

I had done the exact opposite. Gathered her close and held on for dear life—breathed in her scent . . . lemon verbena and fresh air. She fit so perfectly.

Lucy burned bright in my mind's eye. Same wild hair, same freckles. Same curvy body that had been made to hold against mine—

Stop. Just stop.

You have *to be beyond her by now.*

Tennyson's face flashed across my mind. Bright blue eyes, haunted. The lines of his mouth drawn in pain.

The image washed all the warmth out of me.

What was I *doing?*

Man, I was a selfish jerk. Lucy and Tennyson both faced hardships. My one and only job should be to help them. Nothing more.

"So that's where we are," Lucy said, finishing up her story. "I don't know what to do from here, Branwell."

I felt the frustration and worry in her voice, no empath ability needed. Besides, I only 'heard' emotions clearly with my brothers.

From the corner of my eye, I noted her curled against the door frame, not quite in or out of the room. She clutched her cell phone in her hands and then self-consciously tugged down on her green 'Kiss Me I'm Irish' shirt.

Ironic that shirt, in so many ways. She *had* always teased me with green things.

Her riotous red hair was piled loosely on top of her head into what could only be politely called a 'messy bun.' The slightest move looked like it would bring the whole mass down.

"The police haven't shared any theories with you, I take it?" I asked.

She shook her head, causing her hair to wobble precariously. "No, though they certainly have them. Most of them involve me, I'm sure." She paused. "You know I would never, ever hurt Grace, right?" Her words rang solid. True.

"Why do you think I'm here?"

A beat.

"Dante is coming, too," I continued. "His gift isn't as useful in this situation, but he wants to help where he can."

Neither of us said the obvious: Dante could instantly tell us if we were looking for a little girl or a corpse—search and rescue versus search and recovery.

Lucy's eyes filled again, tears and her shirt conspiring to turn them vividly blue-green. Azure eyes. Sunlight poured from the solitary window above Grace's bed, spilling through the room and tangling in Lucy's hair.

She looked so lost, so alone, her lip trembling as she swiped at her cheeks.

"Do you have any video of Grace?" I asked. "I want to hear her voice."

"So you'll recognize it?" She had always been quick, my Lucy.

"Precisely."

Sound was so much more than just sound for me. It was this hyper-aware sense. Most people could recall the face of someone they had met previously. I was okay with faces, but sounds? I had a razor-sharp memory for the unique tone of someone's voice. The timbre, accent, speech pattern—it all painted a distinct image for me.

Lucy pushed off of the door frame and crossed the room to sit on the edge of Grace's bare mattress. She swiped into her phone, hunting for some video.

"Here she is two days ago at the gelato shop."

Lucy angled the phone screen toward me and scooted slightly. I picked up the hint and sat down next to her, looking over her shoulder. Lucy disregarded the polite space I had left between us and leaned into my arm, showing me Grace.

A cute little girl gazed up at the camera—big brown eyes under a cloud of dark, curly hair. A display case of gelato behind her.

"You's videoing me Aunt Lucy?" Grace, high and piping.

"Yep." Lucy's familiar breathy voice, closer to the camera. "What kind of gelato did you say you wanted?"

Grace drew her brow down in confusion. "I just told you. I want cholocate."

"Cholocate?" Lucy again, mimicking Grace's mispronunciation.

"Yeah. Why you keep making me tell you over and over, Aunt Lucy? We need to tell the gelato man that I want cholocate." Grace waved a hand toward the bemused employee behind the counter.

Lucy giggled. "You're right. Let's get some cholocate, Gracie Pie."

The video blinked off.

Something wet hit my gloves.

I jerked a look to Lucy, who quickly sat back, wiping her eyes.

"Sorry," she hiccupped, sniffling. "Was that enough? I can find another one."

"No, it's good. I got it."

No way would I forget the sound of that cute kid.

My heart sank, leaden in my chest. Up to this point, I had been focusing on Lucy. The torment of seeing her again, wanting to ease her sorrow over Grace's disappearance.

But now . . . Grace had a face and a voice. A sense of urgency swamped me.

What *had* happened to her?

Lucy was the prime suspect. Caretakers always were. Obviously, I knew Lucy was innocent. So who had been involved with Grace's disappearance? Who else would have had access to the apartment?

There was only one way to find out.

I stood up and tugged off the glove of my right hand. A little like unsheathing a sword—a useful weapon that could cut you if you weren't careful.

Though it was warm in the room, the air felt cool and unsettled against my skin.

Some days, I thought of my gloves as a cocoon. Other days, they just felt like a trap. A chain. A physical symbol of everything that separated me from the rest of the world.

But in a situation like this . . .

"Did the police say anything about not touching the handprint?" I gestured toward the dresser drawer. The bloody print would be a safe place to start.

"They told me not to wash it off. Touching it is probably implied in that, but . . ."

"But this is an extenuating circumstance?"

"Exactly."

Lucy leaned forward, obviously anticipating what I might hear.

"Let me set your expectations," I said. "It's been over twenty-four hours since Grace vanished. Blood cells can live outside the body for hours, and I only hear non-living things. So the only sound attached to the blood will be what was going on around it when the blood cells finally died."

"Oh." She blinked. "So the chances of you hearing what happened when Grace touched the dresser—"

"—are extremely low," I finished the thought for her. "But I will listen to anything that might possibly be helpful."

"Got it." Lucy chewed on her cheek, clearly on edge.

Ever so gently, I placed the tip of my pinkie finger on an area where the blood was the thickest.

"*—think we're going to find a living body?*" *A man's voice. Italian. The rustling of a plastic bag.*

"*Beh. Who knows? It doesn't look good.*" *Another man, also Italian.*

"*The American woman is taking it hard.*" *A scraping noise.*

"*Yes, she is. Maybe a little too hard, if you catch my drift—*"

I bit back a curse. My sense of urgency ratcheted up.

I pushed back farther with my GUT, trying to hear more from the blood. All I got was a hum of muffled voices and static.

I stood back, breaking contact with the dresser, giving Lucy a slight shake of my head.

Now what?

Taking a deep breath, I surveyed the room. What objects would contain helpful sounds? And which ones would be safe?

I hated touching things that I hadn't altered first.

The risk . . . the danger . . .

I darted a glance down at the faint, thin scars running across the back of my hand.

Shiny objects were the most . . . fraught. The brass knobs on Grace's dresser screamed 'Touch Me and Die.'

So I started with the least shiny things in the room and, quite honestly, those most easily damaged and therefore most susceptible to change:

Fabrics.

Curtains. Bedding. Clothing.

If I heard something useful, then I would dig deeper into the past, listening to the sound around each moment of change. I could feel Lucy's eyes on me as I worked my way through the room.

Rustling. The chatter of voices in Chinese, Vietnamese, Hindi. The zip zip of sewing machines.

Normal.

The fabric of a child-size chair farthest from the door was the only difference.

"No! No! Grace Abigail Snow!" A woman's voice. Angry. "What are you doing with those scissors?"

"Nothin', Mama. I gots nothin'."

Fabric moving. Footsteps.

"I swear, Gracie, you will be the death of me."

I smiled. Grace was so busted. And bonus—now I knew her mother, Jen's, voice too.

I lifted my hand and touched the chair again, restarting the sound, just to better etch their voices into memory.

I concentrated on the fabric, moving farther into the past. But the next sound was of a sewing machine and factory, so no more there.

Finishing with the fabrics, I moved on to wood. I studied the window, looking for scrapes or any sign of alteration. Nothing appeared disturbed.

I touched the wooden window sill.

The swoosh of a paint brush. Far off voices calling in Italian.

I moved farther up the window, listening to the carved trim. Nothing helpful.

Tabletop, the feet of things, the dresser, armoire and wooden bed frame. Nothing atypical or unexpected. Sounds of workers painting or items scraping.

Frustrated, I studied the room again.

I had touched everything that looked like it had been altered in any way but had come up empty-handed.

Lucy met my gaze, questioning.

"Nothing unusual." I shook my head. "But let me listen to the rest of the apartment."

"Thank you for being here." Lucy stood up, rubbing her hands on her thighs. She looked pale—or rather, paler than normal.

"How long has it been since you've eaten?"

She raised her blue eyes to mine, unfocused as if thinking.

"You can't remember, can you?" I shook my head.

She shrugged.

I motioned for her to follow me back into the entryway, where I snagged the bag Nonna had packed. With Lucy at my heels, I walked into the *salotto* to the left of the front door—the living room, I supposed, in English.

The *salotto* appeared to have always been a drawing room of some sort. White walls with carved wainscoting. Worn flagstone floor laid in a diamond pattern. There was an antique fireplace at one end with a gilded mantel and mirror above, all dating from the Baroque era. Two huge floor-to-ceiling windows faced the large piazza outside. The dark beams on the ceiling had been painted at one point and traces of gold, green and red still clung to them.

A large slip covered couch—white, of course, like the rest of furniture—sat underneath the windows. Club chairs and a coffee table perched opposite. Several end tables and knick knacks rounded out the room.

Lucy curled up into a corner of the sofa, darting a questioning glance at the bag in my hands.

"Nonna figures food will cure everything." I set the sack next to her. "I have no idea what she put in there."

"Some tranquilizers and a fifth of good vodka?"

That was my plucky girl. "One could always hope."

She unpacked the bag—*panini*, grapes and two slices of my favorite lemon cake. No vodka. But comfort food never hurt in a crisis.

"I'm not hungry, so you eat up. I'm going to listen to the room." I surveyed the space.

What to avoid touching unless absolutely necessary? What was shiny?

The mirror over the mantel, the glass top of the coffee table, a silver vase on an end table. Those items had 'Touch Me at Your Own Risk' written all over them.

Like with Grace's bedroom, I started with the soft surfaces. I rested a hand on the couch slipcover.

The whirring of a sewing machine. The snip of scissors.

Nothing helpful. There *had* to be a clue somewhere.

"Who else had a key to the apartment?" I asked, pulling my hand back.

Lucy tentatively nibbled on a prosciutto and mozzarella *panino,* her appetite obviously lacking.

"As far as I know, only the people upstairs. A mother and her son—Cat Lady and Professor Ross." She said it so matter-of-factly, as if those really were their names.

"Cat Lady and Professor Ross?" A grin twitched my lips.

"I think their real names are Maria-Teresa and Roberto Moretti. But Cat Lady really likes cats. I mean, like really, really likes them." Lucy picked at the bread, barely eating anything. "And Professor Ross is this uncanny Italian version of Ross from *Friends.* Kinda nerdy and awkward, though I understand he is an actual professor."

Lucy paused, licking her lips as she met my gaze, looking so lost. She was the even keel one. I knew this. No matter how stressful things had gotten with Tennyson, she always held herself together. So it wasn't surprising she was coping better than most in her situation. But even ever-sunny Lucy had hit her limit.

Everything within me wanted to ease her pain. Or, at the very least, give her a reason to smile.

"You know the Italians have a specific word for 'cat lady.'"

"Really?"

"Yeah."

A pause.

She cocked her head at me, wild hair lurching to one side of her head. "You know you can't do that, right?"

"What?"

"You know. That thing. The one where you drop some tantalizing piece of information and leave it hanging. It drives people crazy."

"You mean it drives my *brothers* crazy?" I caved and grinned. "Because that's one hundred and ten percent why I do it."

She smiled too. Tentative but there. Lopsided. Achingly familiar.

My heart nearly stuttered to a stop.

"*Gattara*," I said.

It took her a second.

"Cat lady?"

I nodded and turned away, pulling myself together.

I touched the cloth arm of a club chair.

A loud thump. A man cursing in Italian about having to move stupid American furniture.

I moved on to the next chair. "Tell me about Cat Lady and Professor Ross."

She shrugged and gave up on the *panino*, reaching for the bag of grapes. Her hair teetered precariously. "There's not much to tell. They live above us. Cat Lady is obsessed with cats, fancy shoes and going to mass, precisely in that order. Professor Ross is obsessed with this palazzo and Jeff."

I blinked, sorting through what she had just said.

"Professor Ross is obsessed with—"

"My brother, Jeff, and this palazzo. Yep. It's a long story."

She offered no further explanation, merely swirled a couple grapes in her hand. I wasn't the only one who liked to tease.

I gave a *go on* hand roll.

"Professor Ross is one of the curators of the Etruscan museum south of town," she said.

"The one inside the Medici villa?"

"I think so. The museum houses Etruscan artifacts unearthed by an English nobleman, John Knight-Snow—"

"A relation?"

"Uh-huh. John Knight-Snow was my great-great whatever uncle. He died around 1820, I think." Lucy leaned forward and pinched off a tiny bite of lemon cake. "Ours is the only branch of the family left, descended through his younger brother. John Knight-Snow was the eighth Baron Knight—"

"Baron Knight?" I snorted. "Seriously?"

"Yep."

"Isn't that like naming a pet pig Bacon Pork?" It was a shameless attempt to get her to smile again.

It worked a little too well.

Lucy giggled.

Her laugh was puppies and rainbows—glitter-bomb sunshine all over my day.

I nearly closed my eyes at the pain of the sound.

How I had missed her.

"I know, right?" She continued to laugh. "My ancestors were an imaginative lot. Just think, we were knights before becoming barons."

I grinned. "Your illustrious ancestors went by the title Sir Knight?"

"Two hundred years of Sir Knights." She nodded, chortling. And then sobered. As if she could only escape the weight of Grace's disappearance for moments at a time.

She shook herself, hair wobbling again, two stray curls popping free.

"Your great-whatever uncle was an archaeologist?" I prompted, bringing her back.

She took in a deep breath. "Yes. He excavated several sites here in Tuscany. Apparently, Professor Ross is some sort of expert in all things John Knight-Snow, Baron Knight."

"Okay." Still trying to follow her. "But it seems almost impossibly random that Professor Ross—the Baron Knight Obsessed—and Jeff, descendant of Baron Knight, would end up as neighbors. Can I say that?"

"Yes, until I mention that John Knight-Snow lived in this building."

"Ah." All the puzzle pieces slid into place. "Professor Ross chose to live here because his favorite research topic did."

"Exactly. And then Jeff jumps at the chance to work in this part of Italy because he's heard all the family legends about crazy Gruncle Jack—"

"Gruncle?"

"Great-uncle . . . Gruncle. It's an easy way of referring to Jack. Anyway, Jeff looked up Gruncle Jack's lodging, found there was an apartment for rent in the building and snapped it up. Jeff and Jen moved in and became good friends with the upstairs neighbors, Professor Ross and his Cat Lady mom. Which, can I just say, it's weird for an educated, professional, thirty-something guy to still be living with his mom—"

Lucy broke off. Probably stopped by the droll expression on my face.

"You mean like I do?" I asked.

It was true. I currently lived in an apartment with my *nonna*, my father's mother. My mom and Chiara lived in the apartment above us.

Lucy winced. "I had forgotten about that. Though I gotta say, it's not weird with you guys, for some reason."

"Because it's a conscious choice? Not a necessity?"

"Something like that. Or maybe the fact that you obviously love each other and like spending time together."

That was also true. "So Jeff, being good friends with the upstairs neighbors, left a spare house key with them?"

"Exactly."

"I'd like to meet Cat Lady and Professor Ross," I said. "I need to learn their voices."

"I'll make sure you get a chance to chat with them. I don't know how much help they'll be, to be honest. From what I understand, they were gone for the night. Off on a spiritual retreat of some sort."

"They have an alibi?"

"Yeah. Cat Lady loves her religion, remember."

Bing, bing.

"Do you mind?" She lifted up the phone. "My family."

"No prob. I'll keep listening to the room."

Lucy bent over her phone, finally popping grapes into her mouth. After a few minutes, she moved on to a slice of lemon cake, breaking off mouse-size bits as she texted. My chest eased, knowing she had relaxed enough to truly eat.

As she ate, I listened my way through fabrics, curtains and other soft surfaces of the room. Finding nothing helpful out of the textiles, I moved onto the wood surfaces—windows, trim, furniture. I came up empty handed, nothing out of the ordinary.

What next?

I studied the gilt mantelpiece, noting a deep nick out of the finish on the left hand side. It was exactly the kind of damage I instinctively looked for. A clear indication of a moment of change.

Something had struck the mantel there. But when? Had an intruder made the mark? Or was it something much earlier?

The mantel was a genuine antique—as an art appraiser, I could tell the real deal from a later reproduction—and appeared to have been in the room for at least a hundred years, as it leaned with the floor and had slight overpaint at the bottom from the wall behind.

I knew the chances of the change having anything to do with Grace's disappearance were slim, but the mantel seemed safe enough. The paint was a soft, matte chalk and more worn than glossy. Not shiny. And even the smallest clue could be of help.

Tentatively, I raised my hand and touched the mark.

Sound bombarded me.

The clang of metal hitting wood, bouncing and then striking tile.

Harsh breathing.

The clatter of a door being opened.

"My lord? Is everything all right?"

"Get out!" A man's voice. British. Deep. Ragged. "Damn her to hell and back. How could she do this?"

"My lord?"

"I said, get out!"

Glass shattering.

The hiss of a fire flaring and popping.

The smell of woodsmoke and brandy.

Instantly, I jerked my hand away.

The *smell* of woodsmoke and brandy?

What—?!

I sniffed the air.

Nothing. Simply a hint of lavender air freshener.

But I could have sworn I had distinctly smelled woodsmoke and brandy.

That was . . . weird.

Was it just my imagination? Or was my GUT morphing again? Pushing into new territory and bleeding into one more sense?

My heartbeat sped up.

"Branwell? You okay?" Lucy's voice cut in. "Did you find something?"

I glanced back at her, still tucked on the couch. Phone in hand. Red hair dangerously askew. Her darling freckled face etched with wide-eyed anxiety.

I stared at her for a moment. And then glanced down at my hand. The thin white scars pronounced and strained.

"Nothing related to Grace." I turned back to the mantel. "I'm good."

I shook my head.

Grace or no, something was up here. And I was no coward.

I touched the mantel again.

The sounds came again, stronger, harder. Almost lunging to get to me.

The clang of metal hitting wood, bouncing and then striking tile.

Harsh breathing.

The clatter of a door being opened.

"My lord? Is everything all right?"

"Get out!" A man's voice. Definitely British. Upper class. "Damn her to hell and back. How could she do this?"

"My lord?"

Glass shattering.

The hiss of a fire flaring and popping.

The smell of woodsmoke and brandy. A thread of sweat.

Weeping. Guttural. Savage.

"Arrrrrggghh!!"

So much anguish. A heart breaking with grief.

"My lord? Are you hurt?" Concern. Fear.

"I told you to get out."

"Duly noted, my lord."

"How could she do this, Tims? She promised!"

"I know, sir. It's a terrible turn of events. 'Tis the talk of the village."

The clink of heavy crystal. The slosh of liquid.

In a high falsetto, "*I'll be yours,*' she said. '*You are my future.*' How could she——"

A gasping sob. Cloth moving.

"*Get out, Tims. Leave the glass be.*"

The thump of boots walking across a wood floor. The scrape of metal across stone.

"*This damn thing.*" *The slap of something solid against the palm of a hand.* "*I should have listened. I should never——*"

Silence.

The room darkened. A shadow of fire licked inside the hearth. The shape of a man appeared. Like smoke. There but not.

Tall. Thin. The suggestion of shirtsleeves, breeches and riding boots.

The scent of night jasmine. The taste of too much brandy.

The man clutched something long and oval with his palm.

"*I should have listened,*" *he muttered, lifting the object, staring at it. A mere breath of . . . something.* "*Love will draw out the shadow? What idiocy. It is love's doom. Love's curse.*"

He grabbed the object from the top with his opposite hand.

Blackness swooped in.

The man screamed and screamed and screamed—

The scene abruptly ceased, jarring me back to reality.

I staggered backwards.

One step. Two.

Heart pounding. Hands shaking.

As Dante would say—what the *hell*?!

I blinked, taking in the bright room. The missing smells of wood-smoke and night jasmine. The taste of brandy gone from my mouth.

That had been . . . surreal.

Had I really *seen* something too? Not clear images, to be sure, but the definite suggestion of forms. The smells and sense of taste had been strong. As clear as the sounds.

Not to mention the emotional anguish. The sense of loss still pounded. A woman had betrayed the man? Or been lost to him somehow?

But how had I gathered all this through a simple touch? It was so much more than just sound.

Feeling. Smell. Taste. A smidgen of sight. All my senses.

How? And why?

What was up? Why did my GUT decide *now* to make a huge change—

"Branwell?!" Lucy's terrified voice. So close. "What happened— "

I jumped, startled. Staggered back a step.

Everything happened fast.

I stumbled into Lucy, sending her sideways into the end table.

Which, in turn, knocked over the silver metal vase.

I reacted without thought. Pure instinct. I steadied Lucy with one hand and stretched for the vase with my other, reaching before it toppled to the floor.

I caught the silvery metal with my right, *bare* hand.

Cloth rustling. The clang of tools.

Blackness everywhere. The smell of roses. Musty. Long locked away.

No. No!

Not again.

"No!" I cried out, releasing my hold on the vase. But I was tangled in Lucy, the vase trapped between us, keeping my skin in contact.

Too late.

Always too late.

A thick blackness suddenly shrouded the vase. And out of that darkness, it came at me. Razor sharp. Claw-like.

I twisted, trying to protect myself.

Knife-sharp talons sank into my sleeve, tearing through the cloth. Seeking blood.

Ripping, shredding, pulling me down, down—

I yelled. Sharp.

Something pushed me, batting the vase away. It hit the wall with a metallic thud.

Crap!

Dazed, I stumbled backward, tripping over a chair and tumbling to the floor.

I rolled on to my side, clutching my right hand to my chest. Pain flared up my arm.

The sound of my scream echoed over and over, imprinted into my torn shirt.

Crap, crap, crap!

The burning sensation grew. Stinging. Fiery.

"Branwell!" Lucy's voice pushed through the din. "No! Branwell! You're bleeding!"

LUCY

Blood.

Branwell was bleeding.

My heart triple-skipped.

Don't hyperventilate. You're the calm one, remember?

But, as it turned out, I wasn't calm when it came to Branwell.

He lay curled on the floor, arms cradled against his chest, hissing in pain. His huge frame rolled into a ball, a horrifyingly-red stain spreading across his shirt.

"Branwell!" I collapsed to my knees, wrapping my arms around his hunched shoulders, forcibly ordering myself not to cry.

What happened? I startled him, true, but the vase . . . it hadn't appeared normal—

Panic and its close friend, Terror, pounded through my veins.

"Branwell, hon—" I nearly bit off my tongue, stopping the word *honey* just in time. "Let me see where you're hurt." I pulled on his hands.

He uncurled with a grunt and pushed against the flagstone floor with his heels, scooting himself into a sitting position. He raised his left hand to his mouth, tugging at his glove with his teeth. Giving me a clear glimpse of his right arm tucked protectively against his chest.

I gave a choked gasp. *Holy crap!*

His shirt sleeve was shredded in long strips. Like a lion had swiped him with its claws. Blood seeped through, stark against the white fabric.

Branwell succeeded in pulling off his glove and threw it aside with his teeth. He started unbuttoning his shirt, hand shaking, fumbling . . . nearly frantic. His chest heaved as if he had been running.

"Damn shirt," he rasped. "Noise. Hearing my scream."

Oh! Duh!

Whatever had happened had torn the fabric, forcing Branwell to listen to his own cry of pain over and over.

"No, no. Let me," I said.

I leaned forward and, instead of going for his buttons—'cause, let's face it, a bare-chested Branwell would annihilate what was left of my romantic self-preservation—I held up a hand, palm out . . . *stop*.

He froze.

I instantly grabbed the bloody edge of his torn sleeve and ripped it up to the shoulder seam, tearing the shredded lower half entirely away, altering the fabric again and changing its sound. I pealed the bloody fabric of the now detached sleeve off his arm.

Branwell sagged in relief.

"Thanks. I couldn't manage that one-handed." He scrubbed his left hand over his face.

His right arm dripped blood onto his jeans, so much blood it was hard to tell how badly he was hurt.

"Your jeans?" I asked, pointing to the blood. It was an alteration, wasn't it?

Branwell shook his head. "It's organic and still alive. No sound."

Ah. Creepy but true.

Noting my concerned face, Branwell pulled his arm closer to his chest.

"It's just some scratches. Gimme a sec." He hissed through clenched teeth.

Yeah. And the day I believed that—

Finally, my panic ebbed, like a switch flipped in my brain. My infamous ability to remain calm took over.

I reverted to *clinical work mode*, the one I adopted when a client took a tumble down a hill and ended up with a branch poking out of her thigh. (True story.) I had definitely seen some doozies in my time as a wilderness therapist.

I ran across the hall to the kitchen and grabbed a clean blue towel, a bottle of water and a first aid kit from a cupboard. (Certified Red Cross . . . I had given it to Jeff and Jen last Christmas).

As I walked back into the living room, Branwell's eyes met mine. Haunted. Worried.

I sat down beside him, and holding up a hand for silence again, I ripped the towel in two, altering its noise. I poured water onto one half of the towel and laid the other half across my lap. Prepped, I gently took Branwell's injured right arm and pulled it onto the dry towel. I dabbed at the blood with the wet half.

He grimaced but let me man-handle him, nodding in appreciation.

"Thank you," he said again, watching me work.

I blotted at the blood, cleaning one spot. The scratches welled with blood, but pulling on his skin showed that they were superficial. The kind of scrape that bled like crazy but, barring an infection, needed nothing more than some Neosporin and a large band-aid.

No stitches required, thank goodness.

I continued to clean his arm, pouring water onto the rag and blotting away the blood, assessing each wound as I went.

"You're good at this." Branwell motioned toward my hands with his chin.

I shrugged. "I do have wilderness first aid training."

"Really? I didn't realize Forestry Conservation covered that too."

Tennyson and I had met in the same major. We both loved the idea of working outdoors in nature. Me because I loved being around growing things. Tennyson because wilderness areas were short on humans and their emotion-laden brains.

"It doesn't," I replied, "but being a wilderness therapy guide requires first aid certification and survival skills. I'm no Bear Grylls, but I could probably pull off a tracheotomy."

"Seriously?" Impressed.

"No. I'm a total liar-liar-pants-on-fire. I *can* clean scrapes and apply bandages though."

He gave a rumbly chuckle.

We fell into silence. Me wiping away blood. Him watching. The scrapes started just below his elbow and ended at his wrist.

As I worked, a part of my brain hummed in disbelief.

I was touching Branwell's bare arm.

I repeat. His *bare* arm.

Before today, I honestly couldn't remember the last time I had seen any of Branwell's skin besides his face. He kept himself so tightly covered.

But right now . . .

His skin was pale from years of hiding from the sun. Not my own pasty-white color, of course. More of a gentle olive tone, the natural color of his Italian heritage. Dark hair dusted his arms and the back of his hands.

His hands . . .

Long fingered and thin. Veins blue and stark just under his skin. Sensitive hands. It seemed incongruous, such expressive hands on his lumberjack-esque body.

"You wanna tell me what happened?" I asked. "'Cause I'm thinking this isn't the first occurrence." I touched the thin white scars extending up the back of his hand and onto his lower arm. How could I not have known about these scars? It showed me how much and, yet, how little I knew Branwell.

Silence.

I could feel his eyes skimming me, resting on my face before staring at my own hands holding his.

My clinical, medic-detached mask slipped. My heart thumped erratically, speeding up.

I drew a finger up one of the white scars. Intellectually, I knew his skin was normal body temperature, but my feverish hormones registered it somewhere on a scale between *fiery* and *lava*.

Tension hummed.

Well, for me, at least.

Not sure what Branwell was feeling. His expression was closed and drawn. Probably worried over how Tennyson would react to this whole scenario.

"Did you see anything?" he finally asked.

"What do you mean? With the vase?

He nodded.

"I saw you cry out, like the vase was burning you," I said.

"But did you *see* anything?"

"Not really." I paused, remembering. "It's hard to say. My first thought was, 'Why is smoke coming out of that vase?' but it could simply have been a trick of the light—"

"You saw a darkness extending from the vase?"

"Sort of. It's hard to describe. It wasn't clear. Just a dimming of the light around your hand." A beat. "What did *you* see?"

A long pause . . . so drawn out, I wasn't sure Branwell was going to answer me. I went back to cleaning his wounds, not sure how to take his silence.

Finally, he inhaled, slow, measured. "I saw a claw-like . . . thing."

I stilled, shock jolting me. I wasn't sure why. Given his wounds, something had obviously slashed him.

"They sting." He clenched his jaw. "The scratches. They're never really deep but they *hurt*. Like . . . like—"

"Like there's a toxin in them?" I completed his sentence, continuing to dab away the blood.

"Exactly.

"How did it happen?" I asked.

"The first time?"

"Yeah."

He watched my hands gently cleaning his arm.

"I was thirteen. It was a teapot in Nonna's china cabinet that did it."

"A teapot?"

"Yeah, an antique silver teapot. A D'Angelo family heirloom dating from the late eighteenth century. My GUT had strengthened again that year, and I had learned how to concentrate and skim through past sounds of an object. The teapot had a small dent on the side and knowing it had been in the family for a quite some time, I was curious."

"Ah. You wanted to hear voices of your ancestors?"

"Something like that. Things were going downhill rapidly for my father. My parents had separated by that point, and we were visiting Italy for a few weeks. Being thirteen is hard enough without the added weight of watching your father slowly devolve into madness. Part of me wanted to prove that our family 'gift' wasn't completely awful. The dent hinted at a change. I figured if I heard something cool, I could tell Dante and Tennyson about it and give us all hope."

"So you touched it?"

"Yeah. I still remember the horror of wrapping a hand around the teapot and seeing this amorphous . . . *thing* come out of it. To my eye, it looked vague and shadowy, but its cutting claws were decidedly tangible. I'm not sure how I managed to let go of the teapot. My hand was bleeding and hurt so bad. I bandaged up my cut hand and told some story about a stray cat. My mom fussed over the scratches, but my dad just looked at me funny."

"Sensing your lie?"

"Probably. He never said anything, and I never asked him about the experience. Had I known how short my time would be with him, I would have." He paused. "I *should* have."

Sadness wound through his voice. Their father committed suicide when the triplets were only sixteen.

I dabbed away blood from the last scrape and wrapped his arm in the dry towel, applying pressure to ensure the bleeding stopped.

"This claw-attacking thing happened again, I take it?" I asked.

"Yeah. It's happened four other times. The only common

denominator between the attacks are the objects themselves. They've all been shiny."

"Shiny?"

"Glossy, bright, shiny. Like the teapot and silver vase. Though they haven't all been metal, so that's not a commonality. Glass and glossy plastic have also caused it."

"Sheesh, no wonder you're paranoid about touching things."

He snorted. "It's easier to just let my family assume I'm OCD and weird—"

"Wait. They don't know about these attacks?"

He inhaled, cheeks sucking inward.

That was all the answer I needed.

"Branwell!" My tone utterly scandalized. "Your family loves you. How could you not tell them—"

He silenced me with a *look*. Hazel eyes boring into mine, gold and green sparking in their brown depths.

"How do you think that would go over for them?" His deep voice vibrated in the room. "To let them know my GUT . . . what? Makes me a target for supernatural creatures?"

"Supernatural creatures? Like what?"

His shoulders gave an *I have no clue* lift.

"*Something* did this." He nodded toward his arm. "And it's clearly not a natural phenomenon."

True.

"Well, still." I grimaced. "Your family could help. You know how much Chiara likes researching this sort of thing—"

"Yes, and Dante and my mom could coddle me even more—"

"Branwell." A warning tone. "They worry about you."

He let out a humorless laugh. "Don't I know it."

"Then let them help you."

"To what end? Honestly, Lucy." He raked his free hand through his hair. Or, rather, tried to and ended up pulling out the elastic holding his man bun together. His hair tumbled around his face, dark threaded with sun-kissed curls.

He lifted his eyes back to me. Shook his head, hair moving.

"In the grand scheme of our lives, this"—he waved a hand over his injured arm—"is small potatoes. I can't even conceive of adding this burden to everyone's worries. Tennyson deals with so much more on a daily basis." He shot me a hesitant look, searching for my reaction to Tennyson's name.

Another pause, laden with things unspoken.

I cleared my throat.

"How is Tennyson?" I asked, partly to show that *I* had no problem talking about him.

"The same."

Yep.

The fact that Tennyson had sent Branwell to help me, instead of coming himself, more or less summed up his mental state—concerned but not to a place where he could face me.

"I'm sorry to hear it. You know I only want Tennyson's happiness."

Branwell nodded.

I should have left it there. Moved on. But, for some reason, I needed Branwell to understand.

"He would never have been happy with me, Branwell. I know you all think differently, but he never really loved me. Tennyson was more in love with what I represent."

Silence.

"And that is?" he asked.

"Happiness. Freedom. But, deep down, we are fundamentally different people. I loved him—I still do love him—like a brother. But that's not the type of love to build a lifetime on."

Particularly when I'm already in love with you.

Given all the uncomfortable places this conversation could go if Branwell decided to ask follow-up questions, I changed the topic.

"These scratches aren't too deep." I released the pressure on the towel. "I need to bandage them, but you also need to clean up."

Branwell glanced down at his clothing.

His shirt and jeans were a bloody mess. Literally.

"Why don't you shower," I continued, "and then I'll bandage up your arm. Jeff might have a shirt that will fit you, at least. I'll try to get the worst of the blood out of your jeans while you're washing up."

"I can clean the jeans myself."

"Are you sure?"

"I can do it."

Stubbornly self-sufficient. Branwell at his finest.

I led him down the hall, snagging a towel from the linen closet and ripping a strip from it to tame the sound.

Once I heard the shower come on, I darted into my own room and took a few minutes to change my own clothing, finding jeans, a clean t-shirt (*Bad Spellers Untie!*) and pulling my hair into a less precarious-ly-perched messy bun.

I then dug through Jeff's closet and found a long-sleeved gray t-shirt that would probably fit Branwell well enough. (*World's Okayest Brother* . . . could I give a Christmas present or what?)

Snagging a needle and black thread, I crashed on the living room couch and started to sew a zig zag design around the bottom hem. Branwell preferred sewing fancy protective runes which were beyond my rudimentary skills. But my novice stitches were better than ripping the shirt.

Besides, it was a soothing, keep-busy sort of task and I needed a chance to just . . . be. To process everything that had happened.

Grace and the horror of the past twenty-four hours. The exquisite pain of seeing Branwell again, all tied up in the guilt of how everything went down with Tennyson.

Tennyson and I had met in Portland in a forest ecology class. It was the standard college meeting. He sat next to me in class, commented on my t-shirt (*Pessimism . . . It's probably not that great*). I laughed and flirted. He invited me to study with him—

Let me just state the obvious here.

Tennyson is drop-dead *gorgeous*. The twins are good-looking guys. Branwell and Dante have that rugged masculinity thing down.

But Tennyson . . .

He's in an entirely different category.

Shorter and leaner than the twins—more soccer player than football lineman—with thick, dark hair and the most startling blue eyes. Caribbean blue. Glacier blue. Framed by long, thick lashes in a face of chiseled perfection.

Seriously. He's beautiful in a turn-heads-while-walking-down-the-street sorta way. Almost a walking ironic monument to masculine beauty.

How could a girl not be swept up by that?

At first, I could scarcely believe a guy as hot as Tennyson was that into me. My roommates drooled and whispered behind his back how lucky I was. My sisters ogled him.

It was intensely flattering.

As a boyfriend, Tennyson was kind and sweet. Despite his good looks, he wasn't hung up on himself. He was a decent, good guy. But the more he drew me into his world, the more I realized how fragmented he was.

His GUT is debilitating.

Tennyson senses the future emotions of those around him—intensely, completely—which makes living around people a daily challenge. Part of me still wondered how he managed to attend college for as long as he did. When we first met, his GUT was difficult but manageable. Over time, that changed. His GUT continued to strengthen and the constant emotional bombardment swamped him.

Apparently, I soothed his psyche. I'm a generally cheerful person. I don't know why that is . . . I just am.

Eternally optimistic.

That's how Tennyson described me.

His pocket-sunshine.

Tennyson *needed* me. Needed my steady emotions to keep him balanced. Needed to be around someone who didn't add to his pain.

And it's nice to be needed. Most of the time.

Then I met Branwell.

I had thought I loved Tennyson. And I did.

But it was nothing compared to the soul-shattering attraction I felt for Branwell.

Of course, I was immature and new to love, so it took me far too long to realize all this—that Tennyson's need, though super flattering to my ego, was heavy. Exhausting.

I was his savior.

That's a hard pedestal to maintain. No relationship can remain healthy when the parties involved are on such unequal footing. I couldn't have a bad day, because that might cause Tennyson to flounder, sending him into a tailspin. And Tennyson's dark days could be frighteningly dark. The responsibility was a millstone at times.

But when I was around Branwell, he had no expectations of me. I didn't have to stay happy and positive 24/7.

I could breathe.

Branwell was the eye of a hurricane. A sea of calm. A grounding string that would let my kite fly as high as it dared.

The yin to my yang.

The dark to my light.

My balance. My completion.

I don't know how else to describe it. I connected with him like no one before or since.

Not that he knew. Not that I could ever tell him.

I don't think Tennyson ever understood what was happening. Eventually, I reached the point where I would push forward my affection for Branwell, knowing Tennyson would just feel the emotion, the love and devotion.

Of course, I could only live a lie like that for so long. Remaining in a relationship with the wrong D'Angelo brother was unfair to Tennyson. It was unfair to me.

We all deserved better than that.

"What's on that ribbon around your neck?" Branwell's voice brought me back to the present.

My head snapped up from the stitches I was sewing.

He stood in the doorway toweling his hair with his left hand. The ragged claw marks a striation of angry red lines down his right arm. Beard combed neat. His jeans a little damp on the right side but otherwise clean, hanging low on his hips. Socks on his feet.

But from the waist up . . .

Oh. My. Word.

My lungs simply forgot how to breathe properly, my entire body jolting in shock.

Was the man *trying* to destroy me?

He didn't have a speck of clothing on from hips to the top of his head. Why would he? I was currently stitching his shirt.

Bare chest with a dusting of dark hair. Sharply defined musculature. A *six-pack*.

The image scorched my brain. Some things you simply know you'll never forget. How had I not known he sported a MMA fighter body underneath all those Free People clothes?

"Lucy? You okay?" He tilted his head, concerned.

Right.

I forced my eyes upward from his washboard abs.

Stop drooling.

"Are you blushing?" Another question.

Which just made my face burn brighter.

"Why Lucy, I do believe you *are* blushing," Branwell chuckled, a low, baffled sound. That laugh of his was a match to dry kindling, my cheeks fiery coals of red-hot flame.

He rubbed the back of his neck, turning his head in a move that could only be described as *bashful.*

Okay. The one thing hotter than a gorgeous, ripped guy? A gorgeous, ripped guy who was clueless as to said hotness.

I ducked my head and focused on the shirt in my lap. My zigzag was uneven and amateur-looking, but it would do the trick.

"Here, let me bandage your arm." I lifted my head to see him still smirking. The punk.

I motioned for him to sit on the couch. He crossed the room and perched on the cushion next to me, ensuring his naked chest didn't touch anything.

His *naked* chest . . .

Clinical mode, I sternly reminded myself.

Methodically and in silence, I snipped a gauze pad, applied it to a scrape, ripped off a strip of paper tape and wrapped his arm.

He grinned down at me.

I swallowed.

"The necklace was a gift from Cat Lady." I answered his earlier question, ignoring his obvious delight with my discomfort.

Stupid man.

"Ah." His tone implied that he had put something together. "Didn't you say she was on a spiritual retreat the night before Grace disappeared?"

"Yeah. She and Professor Ross came downstairs yesterday morning before I found Grace missing—"

"Wait. You just said they were gone."

"They were. Apparently, they had just returned. Cat Lady, being religious and all, was concerned about defending against the evil eye and handed me the medallion."

"May I?" he asked, gesturing toward the necklace.

"Of course."

I angled toward him, raising my chin.

Branwell paused and then leaned forward to better study the medallion without touching it. His body a wall of bare muscle mere millimeters away from mine.

My lungs seized.

I could feel his breath on my neck. Warm. Soft.

Keep it together, Lucy.

He smelled like Grace's berry shampoo.

That shouldn't have made me smile, but it did.

He would *love* Grace.

Which thought, fortunately, broke the spell he had cast on me.

Tears spiked instantly. The reality of the last two days came crashing back down.

Gracie Pie. She was gone.

What had *happened* to her?

Branwell sat back, instantly noting my distress.

"What's wrong?" His eyebrows flew upward.

"Sorry, sorrysorrysorry," I whispered, frantically reaching for a tissue to stem the flow. "J-just thinking about G-grace."

"Luce, no, *I'm* the one to be sorry. She is what's important here. This whole arm mess threw us off." He motioned toward his nearly bandaged arm. "We're going to find her."

I nodded, swallowing hard and fast, trying to stem the tears before they moved from sloppy to ugly. Crying wasn't going to find Grace.

Deep breath. Another.

"I can do this. Let me finish." I spread ointment over his last cut and reached for the bandage tape, cutting off a strip in the silence.

"It's a saint's medal," Branwell said as he watched me. "*San Cristoforo* . . . Saint Christopher."

I raised my head.

"If I remember my Catholic catechism, he's the patron saint of travelers and protection," he continued. "I noticed there's a shrine to him in the stairwell, too."

There *was* a shrine just inside the main door, opposite the mailboxes. A statue surrounded by fake flowers and candles.

"Professor Ross did say something about the medal being for protection. His mom was concerned for my safety."

Branwell grunted in agreement. I smoothed the last bit of bandage on his arm. Mummy-wrapped.

I handed him the altered t-shirt. He raised an eyebrow at *World's Okayest Brother* but didn't say anything. He stood up and pulled the shirt over his head, hiding all that glorious muscle.

"My question is *why?*" he asked. "Why is Cat Lady concerned for your safety?"

He pulled the long sleeves down over his bandaged arm. Or as far as he could. The shirt was clearly a size too small. It hugged his chest with shocking precision. The sleeves stopped an inch above his wrist bones.

I shrugged. "Because she is a busybody with a lot of time on her hands?"

"Or she thinks someone or something would be a danger to you. And possibly Grace by extension."

"Maybe. Though I'm still siding with busybody."

Branwell stooped and picked up his leather gloves from the floor, pulling one on to his right hand. He tucked the other one into his front pocket, leaving his left hand bare.

"Well, let's keep searching. I listened to the bathroom while I was in there and didn't hear anything. Let me see if I can find anything helpful in the other bedrooms."

He walked out into the hall.

I paused, momentarily overwhelmed. And then kicked my feet into action.

"You would do that?" I followed him into the central hall. "Something just attacked you, and you still want to touch things?"

He paused and turned to me. Eyes intent. Looming tall in the shadowed hallway.

"A mere flesh wound won't stop me from finding that little girl." Voice so emphatic.

How I loved this man.

The world instantly swam before my eyes.

I swiped away the tears. "T-thank you. I don't know how I—"

Bzzz. Bzzz. Bzzz.

I jumped.

Doorbell.

I turned toward the door, Branwell suddenly at my heels. I peeked through the peephole.

"Speak of the devil," I sniffled, wiping my eyes dry.

I shot Branwell an apologetic look over my shoulder. He was pulling his glove onto his left hand.

I opened the door to Cat Lady, dressed in another one of her famous pantsuits (this one baby blue with little pink flowers). She stood on the doorstep, wringing her hands. Agitated. Relief flooded her face as she spotted me, eyes lingering on the necklace around my neck.

"*Santa Maria piena di grazia,*" she muttered while crossing herself.

And this was why she was my new BFF. Anyone who greeted me by crossing themselves and muttering saint's prayers was a friend for life. Seriously. Everyone needs a friend like that.

Cat Lady went off in Italian, talking straight to me, my mind too frazzled to even attempt to keep up.

Branwell shifted behind me, his chest a wall of comforting warmth against my back.

Cat Lady paused, eyes pinning him.

She said something, sharp and concerned. I thought I caught the word *ragazzo*.

Boyfriend.

Or simply *boy*, perhaps.

But given the way Branwell froze, I was guessing the former.

I half turned to him. "Did she just ask—"

"—if I was your boyfriend?" he finished for me. "Indeed she did."

I mentally rattled through several responses. But I blame my poor tired brain for what happened next. Everything caught up with me—

Grace's disappearance.

Branwell's arrival.

Branwell's bloody injury.

The fact that Cat Lady took a too personal interest in my love life.

Before Branwell could reply, I wrapped a hand around his (uninjured) rock-solid bicep.

"Why, yes. Yes, he is." I sighed. "I'd love for you to meet my boyfriend, Branwell D'Angelo."

12

BRANWELL

Talk about living my own private hell.

This was it. One hundred and ten percent.

Lucy gazed up at me, love and adoration shining out of those gorgeous eyes of hers. Her soft body tucked firmly against mine. A possessive hand wrapped around my upper arm.

Everything I had ever wanted and knew I could never have.

It was bad enough I was wearing the t-shirt she had stitched, hearing her breathing and movement over and over.

But now to be her pretend boyfriend . . .

"Boyfriend?" Cat Lady sighed, continuing with that Italian thing where she rattled on as if we could understand. Which, unbeknownst to her, I could. "*Che peccato.* I was so hoping you and my Roberto"—Roberto? Oh right. Professor Ross.— "would hit it off. He just needs to find a nice girl and settle down and give me some grandbabies. But he's always off at that museum chasing after things that are better left alone . . ."

Cat Lady droned on. I started to tune her out because the more Cat Lady talked, the more Lucy sagged her weight into my arm, eventually resting her head on my bicep. Practically cuddling into me. I knew it was all an act, but that didn't stop my stupid heart from lurching.

Sweet, darling Lucy.

And still Cat Lady talked. Aside from being a *gattara*, she clearly laid claim to the title, *chiacchierona*. A chatterbox.

Quite the combo.

I kept looking for a way to interrupt her, but Cat Lady was an experienced *chiacchierona*, not making eye contact long enough for me to break in.

Clever, this one.

" . . . and, of course, now the police think that Roberto is a suspect," Cat Lady said, yanking my attention back to her, "even though he wasn't even here that morning—"

"Roberto is a suspect, too?" I asked in Italian. "Because he had a key to the apartment?"

Cat Lady paused, eyes wide and surprised, assessing me.

"You're Italian?" she asked.

"*Sì*. My father was from Florence."

Lucy pulled away from my arm to shoot me a raised eyebrow, blue eyes inquisitive in her freckled face. I gave a subtle *I'll explain in a minute* shake of my head. She lowered her eyebrows in response.

"Roberto is a suspect as well?" I prompted in Italian, turning my gaze back to Cat Lady.

Cat Lady licked her lips, recalibrating her course, and then jumped in with both feet. Talking away.

"Yes, he is. Which is just utterly ridiculous. My Roberto wouldn't hurt a fly. He loved little Grace to distraction . . . like his own daughter."

Cat Lady believed that. Her words rang solid. Truth sounded like that. Substantial. Dense.

Lucy relaxed back into me, head against my arm, clinging like I was the only thing holding her upright.

I fought the urge to shift my arm and wrap it around her waist, supporting her. As it was, her warmth readily seeped through the t-shirt, keeping every cell on that side of my body hyper-alert.

"It's a moot point," Cat Lady continued, "because Roberto was with me the whole time, so of course he had nothing to do with the little girl's disappearance."

My GUT buzzed at her words, hearing them as *hollow*. Not substantial. Empty.

Everything within me stilled.

Cat Lady was lying.

But what part of her statement was the lie? The part about her son being with her? Or the part where he had nothing to do with Grace's disappearance? Both?

I played stupid.

"What a relief that he was with you. It must be nice to know he has an alibi."

"Too true." She nodded emphatically. "Such a comfort to this mother's heart." She thumped her chest with a fist.

She firmly believed that.

Lucy relaxed even more into me. Poor thing.

I gave up fighting the urge to hold her. I tugged my arm out of her grasp and wrapped it around her curvy waist, pulling her tight against my side with a gloved hand. Practically forcing Lucy to rest her head on my chest.

I half-expected her to pull back in surprise, but she sagged into me willingly enough and even wrapped her arms around my waist. Obviously interested in keeping the 'boyfriend' ruse up.

She was heaven in my arms. Soft. Cuddly. I had to swallow back the urge to brush my lips on her hair and pull her even closer. It felt so natural, so right.

My heart howled in frustration, tugging at the chains that shackled it. Why did Tennyson have to stand between us?

Keep it together, man.

"So where were you and Roberto when Grace disappeared?" I asked Cat Lady, forcing my mind away from Lucy.

"We were at an important all-night worship service with my church group. Before the demons can be cast out, we have to properly purify ourselves, you know."

Right.

A half-truth there.

Wait—did Lucy just snuggle closer to me? *Madonna mia*—

Focus.

"And Roberto was with you the whole time?" I asked.

Cat Lady didn't like that question—it puckered her mouth like a sour lemon. "Well, of course. That's why he has an alibi."

Such empty words. Wind whistled through them.

Lie.

Bingo.

Relief washed through me. At *last*. A real clue.

Roberto, who had a key to this apartment, had not actually been with his mother during the time in question.

What had he been up to? Had he snatched Grace? Or was it something else?

We needed to talk with Roberto. Fast.

"So is Roberto home today?"

"He's at work and won't be home until late. After the museum closes, he's going down to the police station to answer their questions." Cat Lady smiled with pride. "He wants to help find Grace, too."

Truth.

Excellent. Something eased inside me knowing that Roberto was being cooperative. The police would get answers.

Cat Lady leaned forward, lowered her voice slightly. "Between you and me, Roberto needs to find a new museum to work at. The bad things happened."

I blinked, processing her words.

Le cose maledette. The bad things.

No. Not bad, per se. *Cursed.*

The cursed things.

An interesting distinction, though perhaps crucial.

Lucy stiffened slightly, arm tensing around me. What?

And then I noticed. I had begun to unconsciously rub my gloved thumb across her lower back.

Nice. Even my hands were betraying me.

I swallowed and ordered my wayward appendage to behave. Lucy relaxed again, her body melting into mine.

"The cursed things?" I asked Cat Lady.

She waved a careless hand, as if talking about old news

"You know, all the terribleness with that baron. Bad things happened here. You can feel it in the air." She flapped her hands around like a bird.

Okay.

So . . . either Cat Lady was utterly cuckoo. Or she knew more about this whole situation than the rest of us combined.

She flapped her hands twice more, rustling her pale blue pantsuit and cat earrings.

It honestly could go either way.

Worse, my stupid thumb was rubbing Lucy's back again, refusing my repeated requests to *stopitrightnow*. Fortunately this time, Lucy didn't seem to mind. She actually cuddled closer, playing the part of girlfriend to perfection.

"So the bad things happened in this palazzo?" I asked Cat Lady.

"*Sì.* Jack Knight-Snow should have left the cursed things in the ground where the shadows belong."

A chill chased my spine.

I had already heard similar words once today.

Was that Lucy's ancestor I had heard earlier? John Knight-Snow? The upset Englishman who put a dent in the mantel?

My thumb was now doing figure-eights on Lucy's spine. Stupid thing.

Cat Lady was still going strong. "When I heard little Grace had vanished, I instantly prayed they would find her—"

Footsteps sounded in the stairwell, running quickly upstairs.

Cat Lady turned around just as Dante's dark head came into view.

Lucy startled. I gave her waist a tiny squeeze, silently telling her to stay put. Jumping back would make the situation look even more suspect. She froze in place, keeping one arm wrapped around my waist. Smart girl.

"You made it," I said in English as Dante topped the last stair.

Trust me to state the obvious.

"Yeah, sorry it took longer than I thought with the client and that enchiridion. Then traffic was bad, of course. Prato is only ten miles as the crow flies, but it takes forever to get out of town."

Traffic was *always* bad coming and going out of Florence.

"Besides, have you *seen* the paparazzi out there?" Dante scrubbed a hand through his hair as he came to a halt in front of us. "I had to park two blocks away and bluff my way inside this building. So if you see the family in 4E, I'm terribly sorry that their grandfather did not actually leave them a villa in his will."

Dante's eyes darted back and forth between Lucy and myself, noting our blatant *We're a couple* stance.

Lucy stiffened even more. I could practically feel her soaring anxiety.

"Lucy, nice to see you again," Dante said, voice *very* measured. "I wish the circumstances were different, however."

"Me too." Her voice tense.

What was up?

Dante finally lifted his gaze to mine. I gave him my fiercest brother non-verbal-communication stare. The one that said, *Say nothing and I'll explain later.*

Dante flicked his eyes over my t-shirt, noting the bandages poking out the bottom of my right sleeve.

"Nice shirt," he said with a teasing jerk of his chin. One that promised retribution if I didn't explain myself as soon as possible. "I've always thought you were the *okayest* of us three."

For her part, Cat Lady stared at Dante.

He turned to her, pasting on his most charming D'Angelo smile. "Pleasure to meet you, *signora.*"

Cat Lady smiled and then looked at me. Raked me up and down. And then she turned back to Dante and did the same.

A wry grin tugged at Dante's mouth.

"This is . . .?" Cat Lady's voice trailed off into a question mark.

"My brother, Dante D'Angelo." I nodded, helpless to stop a smirk of my own.

You would think playing the Identical Twin game would get old after thirty some odd years, but it never really did.

Boys were eternally boys.

Lucy remained tense at my side, her eyes trained on my twin.

Dante looked like . . . Dante.

A classier version of me.

Same height. Same build. Same hazel eyes. Same dark hair. Same face shape.

But then we diverged. Dante wore his hair a lot shorter and sported carefully manscaped stubble. An expensive designer suit clung to his frame with military precision. Cool. Professional. Outwardly, he seemed the walking definition of 'international playboy.'

"You are . . . twins?" Cat Lady pointed between us. "Identical twins?"

Dante kept on grinning. "Yeah, but I'm the good looking one."

It was true, even if Dante laughed at the worn joke. Though we were technically identical, Dante somehow wore it better. More urbane and smooth.

"Yeah. But I'm the smart one." I ribbed him.

Also true.

I wasn't technically any smarter than Dante, merely the hulking recluse who preferred studying to socializing. From an early age, I had been so overwhelmed with listening to the world that I often forgot to interact with it. Besides, Dante had always done the talking for me.

Cat Lady turned back to me, mouth open, ready to continue her monologue.

"It was a pleasure to meet you." I held out my right hand, my left still holding Lucy.

Cat Lady reluctantly took it, doing that Italian limp handshake thing. Why they preferred dead fish handshakes, I would never understand.

Lucy took the opportunity to let go of me and turned back into the apartment, wrapping her hands around her upper arms. Dante followed her. Lucy stood tense in the hallway, facing me as I shut the door.

I took a step toward her. "Lucy—"

"Can we please get this over with?" She shot a terrified look at Dante. "I-I have to know if my little Grace is alive."

Oh Lucy.

I closed my eyes, silently berating myself. *That's* why she had tensed up once Dante arrived.

Stupid me, I had been so distracted holding her, I had utterly neglected the most important thing going on here.

Could I be a more inconsiderate jerk?

"Absolutely. Lead the way." Dante swept a hand, indicating the hallway. "Show me Grace's bedroom and a photo of Grace, if you can."

Lucy darted into the living room to grab her phone, swiping into her photos as she came back out and walked down the hall.

Before following her, Dante looked me up and down, blatantly cataloging my replacement t-shirt, bandaged arm and damp jeans and hair. He spared an even more pointed look for Lucy's retreating back.

"You gonna tell me what happened?" he asked in Italian. His concern and suspicion swirled around me.

Just what today needed.

"Later."

He grunted.

We both followed Lucy down the hall, stopping in the doorway to Grace's bedroom.

"So this is Grace." Lucy held up a picture on her phone—a darling little girl with dark curls, hugging her dad's hand.

Dante studied the photo. "She's a cutie."

Lucy nodded, the phone shaking in her hand. She bit her lip but was unable to stop two huge tears from brimming over.

All of me wanted to gather her against my chest again, comforting her.

Naturally, dumb Dante beat me to it.

I had to watch as he gave Lucy a solid hug and whispered, "We're going to find her."

Lucy pulled back, swiping at her cheeks.

Well . . .

If Dante could hug her, then so could I.

I opened my arms, and Lucy moved past Dante to collapse on my chest, body trembling in terror. My arms engulfed her, heedless of the sting from bandaged scrapes.

I met Dante's eyes over her head. He looked grim but determined as he surveyed the bedroom.

Lucy continued to shake, pressing her face into my chest. Tension hummed, palpable and thick.

Dante started with the bed frame, touching it and glazing his eyes in concentration.

Like me, Dante could focus and sift through past scenes, seeing them. No sound or other senses. Just sight. Unlike me, he wasn't limited to moments of change in an object. He could see anything at any time, provided the people involved were dead. Which, I suppose, was a different sort of alteration.

All of us hoped he *didn't* see Grace.

Because if he did . . .

Lucy whimpered, clutching me tightly, face buried in my t-shirt. I held her close, stroking her back.

After a few moments, Dante lifted his head and smiled at us.

"I'm not seeing Grace." His deep voice rumbled through the room, relief-filled.

Lucy tightened her arms around me, shoulders shaking.

"Lucy." I nudged her with my arm. "Did you hear Dante?"

Lucy nodded, face still pressed into my chest.

"He's not seeing Grace. She's alive," I continued.

Lucy's response was to cry harder, tension collapsing into emotional release.

Dante met my eyes above Lucy's head again, his gaze clearly stating he understood more than I wanted him to. I definitely had a long, uncomfortable conversation looming in my near future. No way Dante would let this go. Stupid, pathetic me . . . because soothing Lucy was worth the price.

I cuddled her closer, hungry for the sensation, knowing this would probably be the last time I would ever hold her. And she needed comfort right now.

Dante looked away and continued to study the room. He picked up some toys, a fuzzy pink blanket, touched her dresser and then her night-stand. Each time his eyes glazed in concentration.

"No Grace anywhere," he said.

Lucy hiccupped and pulled back from my chest, leaving a rapidly cooling wet spot on my shirt for the second time today.

I sternly told my arms to let her go . . . which they *very* reluctantly did.

Lucy looked up at me, eyes bright, freckles stark against her pale cheeks. "S-she's alive. She's still alive."

"Yeah." I nodded.

Dante scanned the room. "I'm not seeing much at all, to be honest. Whoever took Grace, assuming someone did, is alive too. Did you hear anything unusual, Bran?" He looked at me.

I shook my head and caught him up to date on what I had 'heard.' Dante twisted his mouth to the side, thinking.

"Did Grace use this blanket?" He pointed to the pink blanket, fuzzy and covered in princesses.

"She did," Lucy wiped her damp cheeks on her t-shirt.

"Do you mind if I keep it for now? I want to make sure Grace doesn't appear. Disconcerting, I know, but any information is good at this point."

Lucy swallowed and rapidly blinked back tears. "You're right." A whisper. "Anything is better than not knowing."

Dante sighed, turning to study the room again. "I wish I could have seen something that would help us find Grace—"

"Actually, would you mind doing one more thing?" Lucy sniffled and shot me a quick glance.

What was she up to?

"Sure." Dante draped the blanket over his shoulder. Somehow managing to pull off the pink princess look even in an Armani suit.

Figured.

"Would you mind reading objects in the living room, too?"

"Of course."

We all filed down the hallway and into the living room. Lucy swiped her cheeks a couple more times before snagging a tissue and drying her tears.

"Thanks again, Dante." Lucy sank into the sofa, curling her feet underneath her. "I heard you got married."

"I did." Every line of my twin's face changed, beaming love and devotion. "Two months ago."

"Let me guess. Tall. Blond. Leggy?"

Dante nodded, smiling wider. "Her name's Claire. You'd like her."

Lucy squirmed, knowing all-too-well that she would probably not meet Claire. "I'm sure I would. Congrats."

Lucy and I watched as Dante methodically worked his way through the room, concentrating on one object and then moving on to another.

Dante and Claire had been married a few months ago in a small private ceremony atop our family palazzo. I had moved out of the apartment I shared with Dante on the *piano nobile* and into a spare room in Nonna's apartment to give the newlyweds their own space.

Dante was flying out in the morning to join Claire in Boston. Her mother had been diagnosed with ovarian cancer earlier in the week, and Dante insisted on being at Claire's side, supporting her as she cared for her mother.

Part of me still couldn't believe Dante was married and probably already thinking about kids. Granted, we had turned thirty-one this year, so it wasn't like my mom and Nonna hadn't been nagging us for years to settle down and start giving them grandkids.

A brief image flashed through my head. Lucy pregnant, belly round, looking at me with all that adoration she had faked fifteen minutes ago as my pretend girlfriend—

The thought nearly brought me to my knees.

I swallowed. Hard. Sucking in a long, steadying breath.

I would sign up for that in a heartbeat. Tiny red-headed kids running around, spunky and sweet, just like Lucy.

My heart hungered for it with a ferocity that nearly made me nauseous.

Forcibly, I visualized a razor-sharp knife and cut the fantasy from my mind.

When . . . *when* would this torment end?

Jealousy flared. Not for the first time.

Dante was head-over-heels, to-the-moon-and-back in love with Claire. And she with him. Unlike Tennyson or myself, the love of Dante's life had simply landed in his lap. No insurmountable complications.

Everything was bigger, better and plain easier for Dante—life served up on a silver platter. While Tennyson and I had to deal with this half-life, both madly in love with a woman who wasn't meant for either of us.

Being the non-Dante part of our little triumvirate could be trying at the best of times.

I swallowed back my resentment, knowing I wasn't being fair.

Dante hated that things were simpler for him, that his GUT was just plain easier to deal with. So much so that his guilt spilled over into a mother hen-like protectiveness with Tennyson and me.

It wasn't his fault he and Claire had found their happily-ever-after. He most certainly wasn't responsible for this impossible Lucy love triangle.

And yet . . .

Resentment and jealousy were irrational emotions. Hard to understand and even harder to control.

Dante had moved on from the larger furniture, touching the knickknacks.

Lucy hopped up from the couch and grabbed the silver vase that had 'attacked' me, for lack of a better way of describing it.

"What about this one?" She handed it to Dante.

I shot her my best *Are you kidding me?* look behind Dante's back.

She gave me a signature *Try and stop me* shrug.

I knew from past experiences that the vase wouldn't harm Dante. After all, he had read Nonna's silver teapot before I touched it.

Dante stood still for about ten seconds, holding the vase and then shook off his trance.

"What were you expecting me to see?" he asked Lucy.

"I'm not sure. That's why I asked."

Dante frowned. "It's not a terribly old object. I saw an elderly woman arranging flowers in it. That's all."

Interesting but not unexpected.

"So now what?" Lucy sat down, wrapping her arms around her knees.

"We need to talk to Roberto," I said.

Lucy and Dante swiveled heads in my direction, my twin raising an eyebrow in question.

I gave them the low-down on Cat Lady's conversation, mentioning that Professor Ross's alibi was hardly airtight without going into *how* I knew.

"Cat Lady is also concerned about something bad that happened in the palazzo," I said. "She kept going on about how Lord Knight should have left things in the ground."

Dante made a humming noise, thinking. "Then Roberto becomes curator at the museum, solidifies his obsession with John Knight-Snow by befriending his great-whatever nephew, Jeff, and next thing you know, Jeff's daughter, Grace, disappears."

"Exactly. The connection is thin but there."

"So what was the deal with John Knight-Snow?" Dante asked, both of us turning to Lucy.

"I'm not sure, to be honest." Her eyes went unfocused as she dredged her memory. "I know there was some sort of scandal, and Gruncle Jack died young and childless, which is why the title and everything passed to my direct line. But that's not much to go on."

"I did hear something interesting with the mantel, Dante," I said. "An Englishman talking. It could possibly be Jack himself or, at least, related to Jack. Would you mind taking a look?"

"Of course. How old do you think it was?"

I paused. I couldn't say I had actually *seen* a man wearing early nineteenth century clothing. Dante didn't know that my gift had morphed, and I wasn't interested in having *that* particular confrontation right now.

My brothers and our secrets from each other.

"By his British accent, I would say probably around 1820 or so—"

"That is the right time period to be Gruncle Jack," Lucy chimed in.

Dante nodded and touched the mantel, again going into that unfocused trance of his. Usually he simply stared forward. But if something were interesting or unique, he would track it with his eyes.

This time, he did just that, keeping a hand on the mantel but swiveling to take in the entire room. He stood staring for several minutes. There would be about two hundred years of people and scenes to sort through until he hit the one I needed.

What would he see? My GUT was so debilitating and yet so limited at the same time. Sound was hard to contextualize. Sight was much more useful with things like this.

Dante frowned. Let go of the mantel and then touched it again. Restarting his vision, so to speak.

He stared for a moment. And then did it one more time—let go of the mantel and retouched it.

"What's up?" I asked, wanting him to speak so I could 'hear' his emotions.

My twin shook his head. "I've never seen anything like this." His confusion and surprise swamped me. "Let me check it one more time."

He did that let-go and retouch thing one more time, still shaking his head.

"Okay, that is officially the oddest thing I've ever seen," Dante finally said.

"What?" Lucy and I said at the same time.

Dante gazed back at the mantel and then studied the room, eyebrows furrowed in confusion. "I was scanning back through time just fine. People moving in and out of the room. Soldiers in uniform from both World Wars. Women in bustles and then hoop skirts that got progressively less poofy. All normal . . . everything appearing substantial and real, like I always see the past."

"Okay."

"But then I hit the early nineteenth century and a man. Tall. Thin." Dante shook his head again, lifted his eyes to mine. "He wasn't solid."

My eyebrows shot up. "What do you mean? Not solid?"

"He was . . . wispy. Like smoke, totally transparent. The weirdest part . . . it was *only* him. Servants, people visiting . . . they were all solid as could be. But the man was consistently diaphanous. See-through. Do you think that's who you heard?"

"Possibly." I was nearly one hundred percent sure that was my guy. It was too much of a coincidence otherwise.

But, for me, the entire scene had been gauzy, not just the man. Why was it different for Dante? Why did Dante see everything else as solid, but that one man was ghost-like?

It made no sense.

"What did you hear?" Dante asked me.

"It was frustratingly incomplete. This man was ranting about how he should have left something alone. That it was love's curse."

Lucy's eyes widened. "Do you both think it's Gruncle Jack?"

Yes. But I didn't want to tip my hand. So instead, I said, "He's a good candidate, but without an old portrait to compare with Dante's vision, it's hard to say."

"Mmmm, I'm not sure there are any portraits of Gruncle Jack, so we may never know."

Why was Gruncle Jack ghost-like to Dante? Was something changing for him? Why was my GUT morphing to encompass my other senses? Could we trust the information our family 'gift' was feeding us? And if not, what did that mean for missing little Grace—

Bzzz. Bzzz.

The doorbell.

We all looked at each other.

"Cat Lady." Lucy pushed herself off the couch with a sigh.

Dante and I followed her to the door.

A police officer stood on the other side.

"Lucy Snow?" he asked.

"Yes."

"Inspector Paola requested I visit you. There have been some changes."

Lucy tensed, her eyes going wide. "What happened?" A whisper.

The officer handed her a sheet of paper. "The *Giudice per le Indagini Preliminari* decided this apartment is a . . . a—" He waved his hand, searching for the words in English and then gave up. "—*una scena del crimine.*"

Lucy glanced at the paper written entirely in legalese Italian and shot me a panicked look.

"The Judge over the preliminary investigation has declared this apartment to be a crime scene," I said quietly.

"But why now? They've had a day to make that decision. Did something change?"

We all looked at the officer.

He lifted his shoulders. "I cannot say."

"Oh! What happened?" Lucy covered her mouth with her palm. Tears flooded her eyes. "My Gracie . . . Dante just saw . . . my Gracie is still alive—"

"Hey, it's probably simply a precaution." I took her by the shoulders.

Lucy collapsed against my chest for the fourth time today, not that I was counting or anything. "M-my Gracie has to be okay."

I met Dante's eyes, his gaze just as troubled as mine. The poor police officer stood nervously in the doorway, obviously unsure what to do.

"Everything will be alright, Lucy." I ran a comforting hand up her spine. "No one dies on our watch."

LUCY

Wow. That's really . . . high." Branwell craned his neck back with the rest of us, staring up as the roller coaster plummeted down the nearly vertical track.

People eddied around our group. Prize bells of carnival booths clamored. Popcorn, grease and cigarette smoke hung in the air.

"You gonna do it?" Dante asked his twin.

"I'm not sure."

Dante grunted, wrapping an arm around his girl *du jour*. Tiffany? Brittany? Gah, they changed so often I couldn't remember her name. Blond, tall and giggly. That was all you had to know about Dante and women, I had realized.

"Well, we're both in," Dante said, arm tightening around Blond Giggler.

Tennyson squeezed my own hand. I smiled and leaned into him. Branwell remained apart from our small group. Alone.

He was always alone. For some reason, that fact tugged at me, made my heart ache.

"C'mon, Branwell," I encouraged. "It looks awesome."

"He's afraid of heights," Tennyson deadpanned.

Branwell nodded, eagerly agreeing.

I snorted. There was something kinda awesome about a huge, lumberjack of a man being terrified of heights.

"You have to do it, Branwell," I said. "Choose fun. It's the Snow family motto."

"Choose fun?" He turned those hazel eyes to me.

"Yeah. Attitude is everything, in the end."

He studied me some more, eyes inscrutable.

I popped a hand onto my hip. "You guys have a family motto too, right?"

The three brothers bobbed their heads, eerily similar. Kinda hive-mindish.

"Just don't die," Branwell said.

I blinked. Darted glances at each of them.

"That's your family motto?"

"Yep." Tennyson shrugged. "My mom still says it all the time. 'Have fun at the soccer match. Just don't die'." He did a fair mimic of Judith's voice.

"And given the height of that roller coaster . . ." Branwell's voice trailed off, lost in the screams of said roller coaster plunging again.

Mmmm. "Have you ever considered adopting a less morbid family motto?" I asked. "Or at least raising the bar on it a bit? 'Just don't die' seems sorta bottom-barrel, expectations-wise."

"You clearly have never experienced Italian traffic." That was Dante.

"Ha-ha. I'm simply saying that a lack of death is hardly an admirable benchmark of success."

"Maybe, but we have a solid one hundred percent success rate." Branwell eyed the roller coaster. "And I'd really like to keep things that way."

"Well, I for one am going to 'choose fun'." Tennyson winked and tugged me toward the roller coaster line. Dante and Blonde Giggler followed.

"I'll sit and wait." Branwell motioned toward a nearby bench.

We were halfway to the roller coaster when his voice reached us. "Just don't die, you guys."

14

BRANWELL

FLORENCE, ITALY
2016

C *all me. I want to hear how things went.*
   Tennyson. Text.

It arrived just as Lucy and I pulled into the small courtyard behind the Renaissance-era family palazzo in the center of Florence. The sun was dipping toward the horizon, turning the world gold-glazed.

I carefully parked my restored 1974 Volkswagen Vanagon between Chiara's Mini Cooper and Dante's sleek BMW. The white and tangerine VW bus was my baby. My brothers dubbed her The Mystery Machine and if I let my hair grow too long, Chiara started calling me *Raggy* in her best Scooby-Doo voice. For my part, I had secretly named the VW bus Lucia, for obvious reasons—the auburn beauty that I *could* have.

It was a sad commentary on the general pathetic-ness of my life.

Lucy piled out of the van, grabbing her overnight bag from the back seat. Her red hair was escaping its bun again, rebellious curls bouncing down her neck and around her ears. Taunting.

"Are you sure this isn't a bother?" Lucy asked as we walked back to the arched passageway that ran under the apartment building to the street.

"Not at all. Guaranteed I'd hear about it for months if I had come home without you."

I *was* relieved Lucy was here with us. As the judge had declared Jeff and Jen's apartment a crime scene, Lucy couldn't remain there. Lucy had said she would go to a hotel, but Dante and I wouldn't hear of it.

Lucy had called Inspector Paola to clear the move, giving Paola our names and address in Florence. Paola was fine with it as long as Lucy, "called in everyday and stayed out of the way of investigators.'"

I had then listened as Lucy chatted with her family on the short drive back to Florence. Apparently, they had been asked to remain in the United States, as Inspector Paola didn't want more meddling Americans running about. Paola clearly had some strong prejudices. So after being grounded, Lucy's family now expected Lucy to do *more, more, more* to find answers and they wanted them *now, now, now.*

Needless to say, Lucy's voice was strained by the end of their conversation.

I propped open the door to the stairwell with my foot and took Lucy's heavy bag as she passed through.

"You don't have to carry my bag—" She stopped at the expression on my face.

"Do you seriously think Judith and Nonna raised me to be the kind of guy who would let an invited guest carry their own luggage? Male or female?"

She studied me for a long moment.

"Thank you," she finally said.

She went up the stairs before me, stopping at the first landing with its enormous wooden door—the apartment I had once shared with Dante.

Lucy knew the layout of our building. Basement was for swimming pool, gym and my sound proof room. Ground floor was the storefront for our family art appraisal and acquisitions business—D'Angelo Enterprises. First floor apartment was the twins. Second floor, Nonna. Third floor, my mom and Chiara.

Tennyson hadn't lived with us for several years, preferring to stay by himself in the family villa near Volterra. Far away from other people and their intrusive emotions.

"Dante and Claire live there now," I said, nodding toward the first floor apartment door. "I'm Nonna's new roomie. Let's keep climbing up to the third floor and my mom's apartment. Chiara will be excited to have you staying with them."

We climbed two more flights of stairs in silence. Lucy reached the top apartment just as my mom opened the door—tall and curvy, dark auburn hair neatly styled.

"Lucy, it's so good to see you." Mom gave her a tight hug. "I'm glad the boys convinced you to come here for the night. We're all praying for Grace—"

"Lucy!" A loud squeal sounded behind us.

Chiara pushed past me in a blur of color, practically plastering herself to Lucy.

Yeah. The women in my family had always been close with Lucy.

Chiara pulled back. "You poor, crazy thing. I've been following Grace's story on the news." My sister grabbed Lucy's arm and pulled her into the apartment. "You need to catch me up on *everything* . . ."

Lucy's eyes filled with tears, and she shot me a trembling look as she disappeared inside.

"Don't upset Lucy, Chiara," I called after them. "She's already been through enough—"

"It's called female therapy, Bran," Chiara yelled back. "Lucy needs some girl time. *Shoo.*"

Sisters.

My mom shot me an apologetic smile. I tromped back down to my apartment. Silence slammed into me, the apartment dark.

That's right. Nonna was having her ladies night with a group of friends. They rotated location each week, playing cards and drinking too much Chianti red.

Stepping into my bedroom, I pulled off my gloves with a sigh of relief, tossing them on a side table inside the door. I kicked off my boots, wriggling my toes inside their sound-proofing socks.

Like the pool in the basement, my bedroom was my safe space. My sanctuary. Nothing in this room could hurt me. Nothing would be unexpected.

My bedroom in Dante and Claire's apartment had been spectacular, designed to my exact tastes with huge windows and an inlaid marble floor.

This room was less flashy but still my own. Dark beamed ceiling with a herringbone wood floor. Enormous king-sized bed against the wall to the right. Two large windows directly opposite the door, thrown open to let in the summer air. Shelves on the left wall held my . . . collections.

A bowl of broken sticks.

Down pillows stacked in bins.

Braided wristbands.

A large armoire and dresser flanked the bed. Italians have no concept of a 'closet.' Wardrobe. Armoire. Closet. It was all the same word to them—*armadio*.

Sunlight washed my bedroom in shades of sunset. Vivid reds and golds wrapping around shapes, casting half the room in long silhouette.

When photographing a heart, the trick is to find the shadows . . .

Lucy's words from all those years ago tumbled through my mind. I understood what she meant—the stronger the light, the deeper the shadows, the sharper the form.

Before Tennyson's call this morning . . . I had expected to never see Lucy again. But now, she had blasted back into my life—brilliant, blinding sunshine. Dazzlingly luminous.

Lucia. My light.

Shadows define the soul. They delineate your edges, bring you into sharp focus.

Lucy stripped me bare, exposing all that I was in her radiant light—a heart that beat for her.

At what point could I finally let her go?

Correction. I *needed* to let her go.

I reached behind and fisted Jeff's too tight t-shirt, pulling it over my head and away from my skin. Stripping the sound of Lucy off my body. Literally.

Tossing the shirt into my laundry hamper, I surveyed the bandages wrapped around my right arm. The scratches had stopped stinging, but I could hear Lucy's breathing with each strip of tape over gauze. The sound of her hands moving, soothing me.

Yeah. Those needed to go too. Too much Lucy.

Too much of what I couldn't have and shouldn't dwell on.

I picked off the bandages, one-by-one, tossing them aside.

The scrapes had already started to heal, pulling together into angry thin lines stretching down my arm.

I snagged an ace bandage (already stitched and prepared in advance; I genuinely was OCD in some ways) and more antibiotic ointment from a cupboard and re-wrapped my arm.

All the while, I methodically forced down all thoughts of Lucy, stuffing my adoration of her inside an enormous steel container, mentally imagining her in the center of an indomitable safe.

All with the single purpose of keeping Tennyson from feeling my most guarded secret. Heaven only knew if it worked.

I was a complete jerk to have allowed my love of Lucy flow free as much as I had today. Holding her, comforting her. Letting her light flood me.

I needed to keep my emotions under absolute control. But being around her like this . . . just me and her, without Tennyson . . . I didn't know how I was going to survive it.

Stuff it away. Lock it up.

Finishing up with my arm, I snagged my phone.

Tennyson answered in the middle of the first ring.

"Talk to me." Impatient. Concerned. Full of pain.

I swallowed back the flood of emotion.

My empath abilities were always strongest with Tennyson. Perhaps amplified by his own?

For the umpteenth time, I wondered how much he felt from me. Supposedly, he couldn't feel emotions over distance, though he admitted to occasionally sensing things from Dante and me from afar. Did my affection for Lucy fall into that category?

So, Tenn, do you feel how madly in love I am with Lucy? Or have I been good at hiding that from you?

Questions I could never ask.

I pulled myself away from that cliff and focused on my brother, reinforcing the image of my feelings locked inside steel.

"It's all good. She's here at the house with us, Lucy is." I sat on the edge of my bed.

"That's good." Anguish washed me. A flood of despair. Tennyson's reaction to hearing Lucy's name? "How is she?"

Not good. He wouldn't even say her name.

"The same old Lucy. Upset and extremely worried about Grace but hanging in there. Though I'm betting you might have already felt that from her."

Silence.

C'mon, Tennyson. Let something slip. How's your GUT doing?

"I wish—" Apprehension. Frustration. More pain. "I wish it worked like that," he finally said, voice soft.

Truth.

"It's probably good my gift isn't that strong," he continued. That same anguish surged again through the phone connection, the same refusal to even say *her* name. "Otherwise, I don't know that I could ever be free . . ."

More truth. An image punched through: Tennyson sitting out on the large, flagstone *terrazza* that extended off the back of the family villa. Face turned toward the setting sun. Real or just my overactive imagination?

"Talk to me, Bran," he said. "What happened?"

I shook off the image and laid back on my bed, recounting the afternoon's events for him. Omitting the incident with the vase, of course, but pointing out the problems with Professor Ross . . . ehr, Roberto.

I ended with a promise to call him tomorrow with an update.

Dante walked into my room as I pushed *End*.

He kicked the door behind him, crossing his arms and leaning back into it. He had changed out into his signature tight t-shirt and jeans.

His eyes flicked to my bandaged arm.

I didn't need anything beyond simple common sense to tell me he was ticked off over my lack of communication.

"What happened?" he asked in Italian. *Cosa succede?*

I scrutinized him, rubbed a hand over my beard.

Dante stared back. Gaze firm. Determined.

He unlaced a hand and beckoned. *Spill it.*

Great. The anticipated showdown with my twin. The missing knock-out punch in this thoroughly craptacular day.

I stood, opened the armoire and pulled out my usual long sleeve, button-up shirt. Soft blue cotton. Contrasting cream stitched runes along the cuffs and hem.

"Today has been difficult." My Italian words hung in the air. *Dificile.* "Can we postpone this fight? Put it on the schedule for next week?"

"Branwell—"

I caught the weariness in his tone. Frustration. Concern. Guilt.

A desire to *fix* things.

Standard emotions for Dante when dealing with me.

I put on the shirt and started buttoning it.

My breathing. A needle sliding through fabric.

Dante shifted, face hanging down.

He shook his head. Back and forth. Left. Right.

"Please." He raised his eyes to mine. "I care about you. When you share what's happening to you"—a flicked hand toward my bandaged arm—"or what's going on in that head of yours, it means a lot to me. I'm not trying to control your life or even *fix* the problem—"

Trust Dante to mimic my own thoughts.

"—I just want to help, if I can."

His voice dripped sincerity. Genuine.

Help. That was always Dante's thing. *Let me help.*

Like I couldn't handle life on my own.

Poor Branwell and Tennyson—the broken brothers Dante had to put back together.

I *hated* the self-pitying tone of my own internal whining.

"Neither of us is leaving this room until you talk to me," he continued.

The worst part? Dante was just so damn nice about it.

I closed my eyes, forcing down that jealous, angry voice. Gah. I could be *such* a typical middle child sometimes.

I was a grown man.

Man up and grow up.

Wasn't that what my dad would say to us as teens?

Finishing with the shirt, I shucked off the damp jeans and snagged a new pair from the dresser, giving Dante my back as I pulled them on.

Silence sat heavy between us.

I could feel his eyes drilling me between the shoulder blades as I buttoned my pants.

Finally, Dante sighed. Deep. Rumbling.

"How long have you been in love with her?" he asked.

My lungs seized.

No need to clarify *who* he was referring to.

No.

This was *not* happening.

No way I was having this conversation with him.

I grabbed a pair of leather gloves from my drawer and turned, face impassive, intent on shouldering my way past my brother.

He kept his big body firmly against the door, staring me down.

Same height. Same face.

Sometimes I hated looking at him . . . seeing what my life could have been, if only—

"Stop." Dante whispered, eyes fierce. "You think you're the only one who *feels* things? Who senses stuff? I don't need a 'gift' to feel your anger. Your resentment. Your pain—"

"I'm not having this conversation." I tried to draw the gloves onto my fingers, ruthlessly ignoring the slight shake in my hands.

"You love Lucy. You're not denying it."

I pretended to be absorbed in forcing my hands into the gloves . . . with minimal success. My fingers stuck.

"I've already lost one brother to that woman, I have no intention of losing another—"

"Don't you dare!" My head snapped up, anger flooding me. "Don't you *dare* say a bad word about her. She is the most caring, sweet, kind, funny—"

"Whoa." Dante held up both hands, palms out. "I get it. Trust me, I do. But—"

Ding. Ding.

Bzzzz.

Dante's phone chimed from his pocket. My phone vibrated on the bed.

I gave up trying to get the gloves on, tossing them onto the duvet, staring at my phone in the process.

Text. Tennyson.

Stop fighting you two.

I pinched the bridge of my nose.

Honestly. Could my life just be simple? Was that too much to ask?

Silence again.

"Does he know?" Dante finally asked.

I shook my head. "I pray every day he doesn't."

Dante nodded.

I threaded my hands into my hair, angling my head back to look at the ceiling. Refusing to meet his condemning gaze.

"I met her in a coffee shop, before I knew she was Tennyson's girl-friend." The confession popped free. "It was a lightning strike."

Un colpo di fulmine.

"Damn. Branwell—" Dante's horror washed me.

"I have loved that woman with every ounce of my stupid heart for six *freaking* years." My laugh so bitter. "Watched her *with* Tennyson. Watched *over* her for him when he was in Afghanistan—"

"Branwell, good grief." Dante ran a hand over his face. Pity and dismay flooded my senses.

"—watched her break Tennyson's heart, not once but *twice*, and hated myself for feeling the smallest bit of relief both times she did it—"

"Branwell. Brother. I get it. I do." Dante pushed off the door and walked to me. Oozing that pity I so detested. "Tennyson, he's still in a bad place. This would easily send him over the edge. You know you can't pursue her—"

I laughed again. So sharp. So caustic. Fixed Dante with such a . . . *look*.

"Do you think I don't *know* that? That I don't wake Every. Single. Day. with that exact thought in my head? Forget about her. Stuff my emotions away. Lock them up so Tennyson will never know—"

Ding. Ding.

Bzzzzz.

Another text.

Seriously, you two. Knock it off.

Oy vey.

"Enough of this." I waved Dante away. "Tennyson doesn't need our added emotions right now. Obviously, they're strong enough to reach him."

"Agreed."

"I've been handling this thing with Lucy just fine for years. She doesn't know. Tennyson doesn't know. We'll find Grace, send them on their way and never see Lucy again. It'll be fine."

"Will it? What about you?" Dante started pacing, a hand back in his hair. "This is why you never date, isn't it? Why you haven't had a girlfriend in . . . forever?"

My silence was answer enough.

"I can move past her, Dante. Eventually. Time and distance will fix it."

Dante snorted. "Like it has for Tennyson?" Sarcasm ringed every syllable.

Thwack, thwack.

A tap sounded. We both turned as Chiara stepped into the room.

"Hey." She scanned us both up and down as she shut the door.

"Tennyson asked me to come down here and end your fight."

Of course.

"We're done," I said, moving to leave the room.

"No, we're not. We're just getting going." Dante's words stopped me.

"What's up?" Chiara curled up on the edge of my bed, tucking her feet underneath her. "I want details."

"You *always* want details." I stared at her. "But I'm done—"

"Branwell's been in love with Lucy from the beginning." Dante threw me under the bus.

Chiara's eyes flared wide, her mouth forming a perfect surprised 'O.'

"What the hell, man?" I shoved him. Hard.

He stumbled back but righted himself quickly. Being the same size had always kinda sucked. It made brotherly fighting less enjoyable.

"That's bad, Bran." Chiara shook her head, her shock a jolt of ice-cold water. "Like, soooo bad. So very, very, very bad."

"I know that!" I tore at my hair.

"You can't love her." My sister was merely getting started. "Bran . . . just *no*. You can't do that to Tennyson. The first time she broke up with him, Tenn ran off to Afghanistan to get over her. And then after his injury, Tenn needed Lucy to deal with the loss of his leg and avoid a complete mental collapse, but he lost it when she left again—"

"Don't you think I freaking know that?!" I shouted and then swallowed, forcing myself to calm down. "Don't you think I know that?" I repeated on a whisper.

"He nearly killed himself over her less than two years ago. This could be the final thing that sends him over the edge. You *cannot* pursue her. It would be a betrayal of such magnitude—"

"Don't you think I see Tennyson's face in that blood-soaked bathtub every time I even *think* about Lucy?"

"*Madonna!*" Chiara sagged on the bed, shoulders drooping, pushing her fists into her eyes. "This is so, so, so bad—"

"Look, you two," I interrupted. "I chose my loyalties years ago. I may not be able to pick the woman my heart decides to love, but I sure as hell can choose what I *do* about it. Why are you two in here pouring salt on my gaping wounds? It's bad enough that seeing Lucy again has ripped the scabs off of them. I've lived with this emotional torture for the past six years. It's old news. Let's move on."

I turned my back on them both, staring out the window, shoulders heaving.

Pity. Horror. Shock.

Their emotions swirled through the room.

Bzzzz.

Ding, ding.

We all swiveled to my phone.

Stop. Hug and make up. All of you.

Silence.

"Are you sure he doesn't know?" Dante asked into the quiet.

A beat.

"No, I'm not," I said, "but I try to block him. I block him from feeling me." I turned back to the window, staring over the terracotta rooftops of Florence blazing in sunset light. The distant hum of staccato Italian floated in.

More silence. This time stunned.

"You *block* him?" Dante.

"With your GUT?" Chiara.

I nodded.

"Does it work?" Chiara again.

I shrugged.

Dante hissed. Low. "Does Tennyson know you block him?"

I rolled my eyes. "I don't know. I've never actually asked him if he can sense my undying devotion to Lucy to double-check—"

"Stop with the sarcasm. You gonna tell me what else you can do?" Tension laced Dante's voice. He motioned toward my arm. "There is a lot more going on with you than just Lucy. Let's get it all out in the open."

Traffic horns drifted through the open windows. A slight breeze rustled.

"I'm fine." I shoved my hands back into my hair. Part of me hating that Dante and I even had the same mannerisms.

"With all due respect, my brother, you are *not* fine," Dante said. "You're in love with the woman who broke Tennyson's heart, and now you're hiding things from us. Important things. We had a pact. A vow. We *talk* to each other when things change with one of our GUTs—"

I laughed. A sharp bark of sound.

"What? What's that supposed to mean?" Dante snapped. Anger. Frustration.

"*You* talk about *your* GUT." I tightened the grip on my hair, still staring out the window into the dying sunlight. "Tennyson and me . . ."

"What about you and Tennyson?"

More silence.

"It's easy to talk about something when it isn't two steps away from destroying you," I whispered. "When it isn't this constantly shifting morass of . . . of sound and feeling and taste . . . and even sometimes sight."

Shock filled my senses. Followed quickly by hurt.

"How long?"

I understood his question.

How long have things been like this? How long have you held your silence?

My bed creaked as Dante sat down.

"Years, particularly the last two years. Your gift may have stabilized a decade ago but mine never did. I'm sure Tennyson's hasn't either. The changes just slowed down, but they didn't stop."

"Why?"

Why haven't you told me?

Betrayal. So much hurt.

Ugh.

"Did you really need another reason to cluck and fret over Tennyson and me? There's nothing anyone can do about it. I didn't feel the need to add my silly troubles into the mix—"

"Your troubles aren't silly," Chiara said.

"They are compared to Tennyson's."

That was completely true. My GUT was still changing, morphing, strengthening, but . . .

"It's manageable. My GUT. I've been saying it for years, and I mean it."

"So . . . you feel things too? Like Tennyson, projecting into the future?"

"No. It's immediate, like an empath. I 'hear' emotion in sound, fleeting impressions. It's strongest with you and Tennyson. It's not super intrusive or overwhelming. Not like Tennyson's GUT. "

"And what do you 'hear' right now?" Dante asked.

It flooded me. Strong. Pure.

"Love," I murmured. Swallowed. "So much love. Hurt and betrayal too. Guilt. But love is the strongest."

"That's why I'm sitting here forcing you to have this conversation. Yes, I feel hurt and betrayed, and my guilt has never been a secret. But you're my brother. I *love* you, Branwell. I want to see you happy."

I chewed on my cheek, still facing away. This was the problem with Dante. Even when I wanted to resent him, he was just so damn *lovable* it was impossible.

"Thanks." I sighed. "Thanks for putting up with me and my crap. I love you, too."

"I know."

A beat.

"I think you're supposed to hug it out now," Chiara said. "Big manly back slaps and stuff."

We both stared at her. She shrugged.

Dante shook his head. "You willing to talk about what happened to your arm?"

"Something happened to his arm?" Chiara asked.

Now Dante had done it. Chiara would *never* let this one go.

"Yeah. It's wrapped in this huge bandage," Dante said to her. "And he's not talking about it, which means it's more than the result of an overeager loofah experiment or beating away crazed attack rabbits."

Drat. Those *would* have been good explanations. Lucy had me so tied up in knots, I wasn't thinking as fast as I needed to today.

"Dude, what happened to your arm?" Chiara appeared at my side, tugging on my sleeve, trying to see my bandage.

I stepped back, pulling away. "It's nothing. Just some scratches."

Dante and Chiara stared me down.

My sister stepped forward, crowding me into the wall. She beckoned, mimicking Dante's actions from earlier. *Spill it.*

"You're not leaving this room until you talk." She folded her arms. "Consider this a family intervention."

My shoulders sagged.

Again. Sisters.

"Fine. But you asked for it." I pinched the bridge of my nose one more time. "I think a demon may be trying to kill me."

15

LUCY

PORTLAND, OREGON
SIX YEARS EARLIER

S o do you cheat?" I asked.

"What?" Branwell's head came up, sharp and fast, eyebrows drawing down over his hazel eyes. "Cheat?"

"Yeah." I nodded. We were seated at the kitchen table in the brothers' apartment, me waiting for Tennyson to get back from class.

"Like on a girlfriend?" Branwell's tone scandalized, eyes flaring in shock.

Wow. That escalated quickly.

"Uhhh, I was thinking more like an exam." I waved a hand toward the textbook in front of him—*Arabic Art through the Centuries* scrawled across the front. "Like in one of your art history classes or something?"

"Oh." He visibly relaxed, sitting back in his chair across the table. "Why do you ask?"

A clock ticked in the kitchen. Sounds from the busy street below filtered up. Absently, I noticed a plant on the table casting a heart-shaped shadow.

Branwell set his pen down and tugged on his beard with a gloved hand, his gaze fixing me. Some unreadable combination of annoyance and exasperation.

It was always like this with him. Something about me bothered him, though I hadn't put my finger on exactly what.

Did he not think I was good enough for his brother? He was protective of Tennyson. They all were and for good reason.

That didn't stop my curiosity, however. Branwell was this remote but fascinating mountain of a man, and I found myself drawn to discover more about him.

"So with a supernatural gift like yours," I said into the silence, "I was wondering if you like, I don't know, store all the answers to test questions on a tissue that you pull out during an exam. Pretend to blow your nose, hear the answers, you know . . . " My voice drifted off.

A long pause.

"No, Lucy, can't say I've ever seriously considered it." Branwell leaned forward on his elbows. "I'm not a cheater. Never have been. Never will be."

16

LUCY

I still can't believe you've had a demon attacking you for nearly twenty years, and you never once bothered to mention it," Chiara said for the third time in the last fifteen minutes.

I was with her. Branwell really should have told *someone* years ago.

We were seated around the dining table in Chiara and Judith's open-concept kitchen—me, Branwell, Dante, Chiara and Judith.

High-beamed ceilings soared above comfy, modern furniture in the large kitchen-dining-family room. The great room was decorated in a homey mix of chrome, wood and natural fabrics. An enormous marble island separated the living space and the kitchen. Basically, gorgeous

European style. Night had fallen outside, but the room was warmly lit and sparkled with light.

Earlier, Chiara and I had been sitting on the couch—me, sobbing over the events with Grace and trying to remain positive that we would find her, Chiara providing moral support and much needed therapy—when I heard their voices.

Branwell and Dante.

They were in the room below us, arguing in staccato Italian. Muffled enough that no words came through, just their angry tone. It had gone on for several minutes and then a text binged. Chiara had glanced at her phone, apologized and disappeared downstairs too.

They talked for at least another hour, voices low and tense through the floor.

Something had clearly gone down. Instinct said it was all related to Branwell's secrets which had finally been outed. Well, at least I *hoped* that was the case. Because if they were arguing about me or the situation with Grace . . .

I didn't think my heart could handle that.

That said, Chiara and Judith were as kind as ever, reminding me why I had loved them so much. And before dinner, Dante had gone out of his way to look at Grace's blanket again and reassure me she was alive.

I could already see how this was going to play out. I would get a delicious taste of the D'Angelo family, stir up a ton of old feelings and then clear out of their lives, taking the tattered pieces of my heart with me.

Finding Grace was worth any price, no matter how high. But this one was steep.

"I'm seriously appalled you didn't tell us," Chiara continued.

As Nonna was gone for the night, we had opted for delivery pizza. Because even in Italy that was a thing. I snagged another slice of cheese and pepperoni bliss and dragged it onto my plate.

"We don't know it's a demon for sure," Branwell said. "It could be a ghost or . . . hobgoblin. Who knows."

"Hobgoblin? Really?" Dante raised an amused eyebrow.

"Well, it's something," Chiara said around a mouthful of oily crust. Though it came out more like 'Welf, ith fomesing.'

Branwell picked up a bite of pizza with chopsticks, careful not to alter the food in any way before it hit his mouth.

He had held up a hand for silence before we started eating and soundlessly cut his pizza into small pieces. Altering their sound in that moment, ensuring that he could hear us talk just fine over dinner. Branwell's standard routine.

Judith nodded. "Whatever this thing might be, it *is* something tangible that can't be explained away or ignored."

"Understanding what it is would be the first step in stopping it or, at minimum, controlling it." Dante snatched another slice.

Chiara swallowed her food. "If we could do that, it might alleviate Bran's anxiety over touching shiny things."

Branwell snorted. "Make me less OCD?"

"Exactly."

"For the record, I'm not clinically OCD. Just cautious about hearing nasty things and preferring *not* to be clawed by supernatural entities."

We ate in silence for a moment. Man, Italian pizza was so *good*. I had forgotten exactly *how* good. Cheese and garlic and carb nirvana. It soothed my fraught emotions better than anything else.

Well . . . *almost.*

I deliberately squelched the memory of Branwell's comforting arms earlier in the day. The soothing thump of his heartbeat, the gentleness of his hands as I sobbed—not once, not twice, but *four* times on his chest.

So predictably pathetic.

I darted a glance at him. He had changed his clothes, but it didn't help. Branwell still looked like the human version of a hug. Big. Burly. Cuddly.

I was in *such* trouble.

"I haven't encountered anything like this demon in the family records." Chiara broke the silence. "It would stand out—one of our ancestors having physical attacks in their visions."

Chiara worked as a historical researcher for D'Angelo Enterprises and, understandably, had a deep fascination with her own family history. Given the nature of the D'Angelo curse, their ancestors kept copious personal records and had amassed a substantial library of esoteric texts, most of which were housed in the family villa in Volterra.

"With previous D'Angelo heirs, the visions and scenes—everything—have always been mental rather than physical," she continued. "Dante has died how many times in his? But they've never left a physical mark."

Both Dante and Branwell nodded their heads.

I tucked my wayward curls behind an ear. Tennyson had told me years ago about Dante's ability to experience past life regressions, some so powerful they pulled others in, like Branwell.

"What are your thoughts on it, Branwell?" I asked.

Branwell met my gaze, hazel eyes unreadable. He shrugged and set the chopsticks down next to his pizza pieces.

"You guys are all missing the bigger picture here." Branwell sat back in his chair, tugging on his beard. "Both Dante and Tennyson have touched and examined the same items that housed the . . . whatever this is—"

"We should give it a name, this demon-ish thing." Chiara tapped her lips.

"How's about we *don't* anthropomorphize the demon, Chiara." Branwell.

"Yeah. That's the first step toward claiming it as a pet." Dante.

"Oh, could I?" Chiara's eyes perked up.

I had missed this family so much.

"Dark Vader," I said.

Chiara bobbed her dark head. "I like it. Solid villain reference."

"Frankenblob." That was Judith.

"Voldesmart." We all looked at Chiara, eyebrows raised. She unfurled a free hand. "Because Branwell says the scrapes sting real bad. They *smart.*"

Ah.

The brothers rolled their eyes. I groaned.

"Chucky." Branwell picked up his chopsticks and tapped his plate. "So, as I was saying, the problem with Chucky—"

"What?! You don't just get to decide its name like that." Chiara gave a very Italian wave of her hand, a practiced mix of frustration and exasperation.

"Seriously, Bran. We should at least put it to a vote." Dante elbowed him. "Besides, why are you assigning the demon a gender?"

"Yeah. So sexist."

"My demon. My problem. My name." Branwell punctuated each word with a jab of his chopsticks. "You wanna name a demony-thing, go find your own."

I laughed a much-needed laugh. Branwell jerked his eyes to mine, staring like . . . I don't know what. Surprised, perhaps?

But . . . I loved this family so much. I had forgotten how fun it was to simply hang out with them and talk about crazy-loony stuff, like demon-naming rights.

The D'Angelos were my tribe.

I held Branwell's gaze, that ache in my heart growing. The place that would always be empty without him.

My chest tightened. Leaving him again—

I looked back down at my pizza.

Branwell cleared his throat. "I've obviously spent a lot of time thinking about Chucky. And I have reached the conclusion that the problem with Chucky is less his attempts to hurt me and more the fact that he exists at all."

A beat.

"I'm not sure I follow you." Chiara reached for her glass of water.

"Chucky proves that there is a larger supernatural world out there. A world we have never really encountered or interacted with on any conscious level."

Silence.

Dante pushed back his empty plate. "Good insight. We have supernatural-ish abilities. *Ergo*, it's not a huge stretch to believe other supernatural-ish things exist, too."

"Yes!" Chiara fist-pumped. "I call dibs on any and all hot vampires."

"Honestly?" Dante gave her a flat look. "I say *supernatural* and your instant Pavlovian response is 'hot vampire'?"

"Do you know women at all?" Chiara deadpanned.

"Why would you assume vampires—*if* they were real—would be more *Twilight* than *Nosferatu?*"

"Gotta side with Dante here, sis." Branwell nodded. "Given your track record with men, any vampire you meet is bound to be a pale-faced, creepy loser."

"Maybe." Chiara poked a finger at her brothers. "But dating a hot vampire . . . that's some bragging rights."

She did have a point. I held up a hand and we high-fived.

Branwell shook his head, a grin threatening. "Vampires aside, Chucky makes me question everything I've ever been told about us and our family curse."

"What do you mean?" I asked.

"Family lore states that, toward the end of the thirteenth century, Giovanni D'Angelo requested our family gift from gypsies. The gypsies in question were reluctant but took his money and granted the gift anyway."

"Yeah. That's old news," Chiara said.

"We also know from family journals that later gypsies claimed to know nothing about the power used to grant our 'gift' in the first place. That the knowledge was lost to history."

Another beat.

"So . . . ?" Dante trailed off.

Branwell tapped his fingers on the table. Shrugged. "What if everything everyone has always assumed about our GUTs is just plain . . . wrong?"

Silence.

Absolute silence.

Shock jolted my spine.

Chiara whistled. Low and impressed.

"Did not see that coming," she said. "But . . . you're right. All these years, we've run with the assumption that our family gift was a gypsy-born version of Second Sight—"

"But if it's not . . ." Dante scrubbed a hand through his hair. "Wow. That opens an enormous can of worms, doesn't it?"

"Exactly," Branwell agreed. "What we call a gift could actually be a legitimate curse or—"

"Or something else entirely." Chiara's eyes had gone wide. "Actual family written records start in the early 1600s. Everything before then is just oral tradition. We can trace back to Giovanni and even earlier through gravestones—the D'Angelos were always wealthy enough to have their own family chapels and crypts—but beyond that, I'm not sure how much hard evidence we have of their actual lives. In all truth, our family predilection could have started earlier or later than Giovanni's era. Family lore aside, there's no concrete reason to think gypsies were ever involved."

"It could be part of our DNA from the beginning, for example," Branwell said.

"Or somehow related to this demonic-Chucky thing."

"Maybe an ancestor was into the occult."

I sank back in my chair, mind reeling. Branwell shot me a concerned look. I sent back a weak *I'm good* smile.

He needed to stop with this sweet caring routine. It made my heart *want* things.

"*Now* do you understand why I was reluctant to mention Chucky. It changes the game and gives us even more stuff to worry about." Branwell tugged on his shirt sleeves, his right arm bulging from the bandage.

Chiara pursed her lips. "Yes and no. Knowledge and understanding are a huge part of knowing how to react. Forewarned is forearmed and all that. Besides, I'm betting you've already researched this, Bran."

He gave a casual half-nod. "Some. Not that I've found any answers. Every culture has different ideas about demonic creatures. Unlike other Western traditions, Italian folklore believes witches have a *demon* familiar, not the more common black cat or raven."

"A demon that does the witch's bidding? So like a pet demon?"

Branwell nodded.

Just like Branwell to have studied it all. He'd always been the smart one.

"That's certainly . . . intriguing." Dante folded his arms.

Chiara snorted. "Bran must have insulted a witch at some point."

"Ha-ha." Branwell propped his right foot over his left knee. "Theories about demons are plentiful. It's merely a question of what to trust."

"I would start with the Catholic church. Find a reliable priest," Chiara said to no one in particular. "People who are supposedly armed to fight demons and know a thing or two about exorcism."

"Way ahead of you, Chiara," Branwell said. "There are a couple of local Catholic groups who specialize in demon exorcisms and other occult practices. They all have euphemistic names like the 'Society of Seekers for Truth and Harmony' or the 'Brotherhood of Man and Progress'."

Branwell ran a gloved hand over his beard again and met my eyes across the table, giving an apologetic smile.

"I'm sorry, Lucy," he said to me. "You landed yourself in the middle of our family drama. None of this is helping us find Grace."

And there went that caring concern again. My heart thumped, a painful rhythm lodged in my throat.

I rested my elbows on the table. "There isn't much more we can do but wait on Inspector Paola's investigation and the police forensics."

"Not true." Chiara sat up. "Let me work my magic and see if I can get Branwell's bare fingers on the items the police took from Grace's room. That could provide some clues."

Chiara did have the most eclectic group of friends. Investigators and private detectives valued her research skills, so she had the right contacts.

"For our part, I say we visit the Knight-Snow museum first thing tomorrow morning." Branwell gestured to me and him. "Track down Dr. Roberto Moretti and ask him some hard questions."

"I like that idea," I nodded. "I'm also interested to learn more about Gruncle Jack. If Professor Ross is a suspect, maybe there are clues in my family's history that might shed some light on his obsession with us. And what, if any, involvement he might have had with Grace's disappearance."

"Good plan." Dante rapped the table with his knuckles.

"Yeah, but be careful," Chiara chimed in. "Just don't die."

The brothers laughed at the old joke, but all things considered, I was more than happy to lift a glass to that plan.

17

BRANWELL

PORTLAND, OREGON
SIX YEARS EARLIER

H ave you always had a pillow fetish?" Lucy slowly spun in a circle, taking in my room. Particularly the row of pillows nestled into brackets along one wall. "Or do you just consider bed pillows to be underutilized in interior decoration?"

I smiled, sitting back in my desk chair. She was in perfect Lucy form today. Forest green form-fitting blazer over a t-shirt showing stick-people running (*zombies hate fast food*), red hair wild and free tumbling down her back.

She continued to study the pillows lining the wall. Not tidy throw pillows, mind you. But fluffy king-size bed pillows in colorful cases. Bold stripes, solids, even polka dots.

"They're sound pillows," I said after a moment.

She turned, fixing me with her vivid blue-green eyes, tilted her head, rolled a hand. *Go on.*

"I had nightmares as a kid, so my mom made me a special pillowcase. It featured her singing 'Hush Little Baby' in a loop. From there, things just sorta . . . expanded." I waved a hand indicating the entire wall. "I choose a different one for sleeping depending on my mood."

"So what sounds are they?"

I pointed a finger, indicating the pillows in order. "Waves, white noise, forest sounds, rain, bacon sizzling—"

"Wait—what? Bacon?"

"Yep. Popping on the stove. Best sound ever."

Lucy laughed. Bright. Heart-stoppingly carefree.

Fortunately, the topic veered off from there before Lucy could ask me about the teacup of broken toothpicks on my dresser.

My noise sticks.

Most of which held the sound of her laughter.

LUCY

PRATO, ITALY
2016

I'm so sorry, but Dr. Moretti is not in yet," the young woman behind the reference desk said in passable English.

We had arrived at the *Museo dei Antichi Etruschi* right as it opened, hoping to catch Professor Ross. Perched atop a low hill and flanked by cypress trees, the Medici-era-villa-turned-museum made a striking impression with a columned portico and sweeping exterior staircase.

Now if Roberto Moretti would just show up. My heart sank. Could one simple thing go our way? We needed answers about Grace, and Professor Ross might have some. But we had to actually *find* the man first.

The previous evening had been a blur. After dinner, I had spent hours on the phone with my mom, my sister, another sister, then a third sister ending with two brothers . . . basically my entire family.

On a positive note, the authorities had finally reached Jeff and Jen on their African safari. Jeff called me right before I fell asleep. He and Jen were frantically making their way to Johannesburg and from there back to Italy, thought it would still take them at least a day to get home.

For my part, I awoke with a deeper sense of calm, Coping Mode Lucy more firmly in place. Dante hadn't seen Grace which meant she was out there, waiting to be found. We would find her. Period.

At breakfast, Chiara caught me up to speed, as Dante had already caught his plane to Boston. She had learned that the police were talking with a moving crew who had been in the area around the time of Grace's disappearance. Given the tightness of old stairwells, Italians often used a ladder-esque mechanical lift to move bulky furniture out windows. There had been a ladder crew just two palazzos down that morning. Maybe they had something to do with Grace's disappearance? Or had at least seen something?

After Chiara left for work, I had called Inspector Paola and reported in before leaving the D'Angelo palazzo. Paola was all business. Her parting shot being, "Please remain in the area, do not involve yourself in the investigation and allow the police to do their job."

Sooooo, about that . . . was it wrong if I simply pretended I hadn't heard that last part?

Visiting the museum where Roberto Moretti worked was hardly 'involving' myself, per my view. And if Roberto and I chatted as acquaintances . . . that was just neighborly friendliness, right?

Granted, the man in question had to actually *show* up first. Where had he been that night, if he wasn't with his mother? What did he know about Grace's disappearance?

"Do you know when Dr. Moretti will be in? We had an appointment with him." Branwell smiled through the lie. One of those heart-stopping smiles the D'Angelo brothers specialized in. Honey-warm. Oozing charm.

Wow.

Good thing he didn't do that too often. It was fairly lethal.

The young woman—Francesca, according to her name tag—brightened and returned Branwell's charm, measure for measure.

Not that I could blame her. He had trimmed up his beard this morning, wearing it tighter to his face—less lumberjack-bushy and more business-suave. Added to that, he had on a sleek designer suit and crisp, white shirt, open at the throat. No tie. He looked a lot like his twin, to be honest.

As I had never really hung out with Business Professional Branwell, this was a first for me. Unfortunately for my peace of mind, Business Professional Branwell was sexy as hell.

A fact that did not escape Francesca's notice.

"We expect Dr. Moretti to arrive at any time." Francesca smiled again, leaning toward Branwell. Total invitation.

I wanted to nickname her 'Desperate Hussy,' but hitting on Branwell D'Angelo hardly made anyone desperate. Optimistic, perhaps. But not desperate.

Francesca flicked a glance at me and then focused back on Branwell. The dismissive tilt of her head making it clear she didn't consider me competition.

Sheesh.

I didn't look *that* bad this morning. Granted, my hair and the Tuscan humidity had this dysfunctional on-again, off-again relationship. Some days they cordially agreed to disagree and, other days, my hair tried to frizz its way off my head.

Today was an off-again day.

But I had chosen to match Branwell's more polished attire, so I figured my teal, silk blouse tucked into a retro, high-waisted pencil skirt with kicky heels compensated for my frizzy hair.

Not that I would ever reach the same standard as Francesca. She had that Italian woman thing down—perfectly sculpted dark bob, flawless make-up, petite body wrapped in sleek couture.

I kinda really hated her.

Insecure jealousy wasn't my go-to MO, but Branwell brought it out.

"My colleague, Alessio, will replace me in a while. If you are still here, I will tell him that you are waiting to see Dr. Moretti," Francesca was saying, angling even more toward Branwell. "I have to step out for some business before lunch, but I will be back later . . ." Her voice drifted off into *hint, hint.*

"Thank you"—Branwell finally glanced at her name tag—"Francesca. I appreciate it. We'll look around the museum and touch bases in a bit."

Wait? Did Branwell wink at her?

The solitary espresso I had this morning would not be enough to counteract watching Branwell flirt with a gorgeous woman. That would require something much stronger, preferably spiked.

Had I *ever* seen Branwell flirt, come to think of it? He most certainly had never flirted with me, not that I ever expected him to.

Unbidden, the image of Branwell's hazel eyes gazing at me in adoration rocketed across my brain, detonating with the accuracy of a precision missile strike.

A thousand other images crowded behind. Branwell smiling while reaching for my hand. Laughing and tucking a stray curl behind my ear. Bending his enormous body closer, closer, eyes fixed on my mouth—

Stop! Just stop!

Longing swamped me. My heart raced.

You're worth this heartache, Gracie Pie, every last drop, I thought, *even though this situation has negated at least three years of therapy.*

How could I *still* be so gone on this man?

Branwell remained blissfully unaware of my stupid running-amok hormones. A small mercy that.

I gave Francesca a weak smile of my own and followed Branwell into the museum proper.

Straight ahead, a large glass plaque gave an overview of the Etruscans—an advanced, Hellenic civilization in central Italy which had flourished alongside ancient Athens and Sparta around 500 B.C. The plaque explained that, though the Etruscans were eventually assimilated by the Romans, their legacy lived on in many Tuscan cities, like Volterra which still had city walls and gates from that era.

Interesting.

Moving past the plaque, I scanned the museum. Glass cases stood against the large pillars supporting the barrel vaulted ceiling, artifacts behind the glass neatly labeled in both Italian and English. Accent lighting flooded up from the floor and down from nooks above, supplementing the natural light from several large windows. Security cameras were mounted in each corner, silently observing the space.

The museum ran the length of the old building, moving through pedimented doorways into four separate rooms. Midway through the first room, a door in the left-hand wall read *Soltanto per il Personale* which I took to mean 'Staff Only.'

All in all, the museum was impressive. Jack Knight-Snow had certainly been prolific in his excavations, as most of the items in the museum came from his archaeological digs.

"So now what?" I murmured to Branwell as we stopped in front of a glass case that held a large, rust-colored pot.

"We wait." His voice a low whisper. "Maybe Roberto will show up."

Branwell and I inspected the *ghirarium,* according to the card next to the object—a terracotta pot used to breed table-ready dormice, an Etruscan delicacy.

Sign me up.

"And if Roberto doesn't show?" I murmured. Just the thought . . . my alarm spiked. We *had* to talk to Professor Ross. I needed to find my Gracie.

"Then we move on to Plan B."

"We have a Plan B?"

Branwell angled his head, shooting me a comforting *duh* look.

Excellent. We had a Plan B.

We wandered among items with Latin names, like *fibula* (not the bones in the lower leg, turns out, but a golden brooch). There was pottery, gold jewelry, funerary urns, religious sculptures and several bronze mirrors with scenes etched into them.

I paused in front of a small, terracotta pot with a wide rim, reading the English description. Called a *sella caccatoia*, it was a training potty for Etruscan toddlers. Nice.

Still no Professor Ross.

"Care to share this Plan B?" I finally asked.

Branwell tucked a protective hand under my elbow, warm breath tickling my ear. "I would love to share my Plan B, but as it is slightly . . . irregular, I would prefer to keep your state of plausible deniability for as long as possible."

I was torn between feeling alarmed at his plan or charmed by his thoughtfulness.

"That's . . . comforting?" It came out a question.

Branwell just chuckled and tugged me along with him.

Another case held a collection of larger etched bronze boxes labeled *Praenestine cistae*—the ancient equivalent of a makeup case. One in particular depicted a scene of Narcissus (a mythological figure who was apparently Etruscan in origin) gazing at himself in adoration, with an inscription warning its owner to beware the vanity of being lost in one's reflection.

The wall to the right of the second room sported large panels of back-lit glass with images and writing in both Italian and English. A sign above it all clarified things.

John Alexander Frederick Knight-Snow, 6th Baron Knight.
1789 - 1818

Wow. He had only been twenty-nine when he died. So young to have accomplished so much.

The left most panel was taken up with an old charcoal drawing of a man in Regency era clothing.

Gruncle Jack, I assumed.

He looked every inch a nobleman with darkish hair swept to one side. Cutaway coat buttoned with tails hanging behind. Tasseled boots. Lighter breeches clinging to his legs. Top hat and gloves held in his right hand. A polished walking stick in his left. Despite the intervening years, he bore a passing resemblance to my own brothers.

"Handsome, wasn't he?" Branwell observed, coming to stand beside me, nearly brushing against my arm.

Heat radiated from him. Or maybe it was just my still over-excited hormones.

"Yeah. He was."

I had grown up knowing Gruncle Jack had excavated a treasure trove of Etruscan artifacts before dying childless. But that was about it. Gruncle Jack's museum biography filled in the details.

John Knight-Snow

Born into the English aristocracy on the eve of the French Revolution, John Knight-Snow, Lord Knight, displayed an early love of antiquities and archeology. His father, Richard Knight-Snow, had conducted some minor excavations in Florence while on his Grand Tour. Unfortunately, Richard Knight-Snow died in 1812 in London, leaving his excavations incomplete.

His son, John Knight-Snow, was determined to complete his father's excavations. With the end of the Napoleonic Wars making travel safe again, Lord Knight arrived in Florence in 1816. He rapidly discovered a series of Etruscan tombs complete with funerary objects, inscriptions and jewelry, most of which are displayed in this museum.

In the process of his excavations, Lord Knight uncovered a partial frieze carved with text invoking Hinthial. Lord Knight obsessed on the inscription. Unfortunately, then as now, the Etruscan language is not well-known. The name hinthial could refer to the departed human soul, literally meaning 'one who is underneath.' But in other contexts, Hinthial is a Goddess of Love, more akin to the Roman goddess, Venus.

Consequently, scholars differ on the exact meaning of the text Lord Knight uncovered. Some translate it to mean 'Hinthial guard our beloved buried prize,' yet others insist the translation is more accurately, 'Hinthial protect our beloved from the buried treasure.' While some scholars postulate that the treasure Hinthial guarded was more metaphorical than literal, Lord Knight was convinced the treasure actually existed. Between 1816 and 1818, he excavated multiple sites in the Prato region, tirelessly working to find more evidence of Hinthial's treasure.

At this point, the story of Lord Knight fades into legend. Sometime in late June, 1818, Lord Knight simply disappeared, never to be seen again.

Local folklore holds that Lord Knight did find Hinthial's treasure, but in the process, unleashed an evil, malevolent entity that caused Knight's demise. Other sources maintain that Lord Knight fell in love with an Italian noblewoman and was spurned, shattering his heart and driving him to suicide.

Despite these more fantastical theories, Lord Knight most likely died of malaria or cholera, both common illnesses at that time. Unsure how to proceed or how to contact next of kin, his servants likely interred his body in one of the many crypts that riddle Tuscany.

Despite his mysterious and untimely death, Lord Knight's legacy lives on in the artifacts he excavated and the ancient way of life he uncovered.

"Interesting." Branwell grunted beside me. "Your Gruncle Jack packed a lot of living into a few short years. We've already discussed it, but he *has* to be the guy Dante saw."

"The one who was all ghosty and transparent?"

"Yeah."

"Agreed. But if Gruncle Jack unleashed something ancient—"

"Like a demon? One of Chucky's friends?"

"Exactly like a demon—who knows what effect that would have?"

With demon thoughts on my mind, we took in the rest of the museum. Naturally, I was drawn to the glittery jewelry and mirrors—brooches and clasps carved into golden animal shapes, rings with crusty jewels. My mom claimed I was half magpie. Of course, Branwell was less enamored by shiny things, keeping every inch of skin far away.

The mirrors were particularly interesting, looking like modern hand-held mirrors, with a circular bronze head on one end and a thin handle on the other. The bronze was polished on one side with an engraving on the opposite. One mirror depicted two men reclining and talking. Another showed a woman sitting at a dressing table, surrounded by attendants fawning over her.

Vanity really hadn't changed much over the millennia.

We covered the entire museum, but there was still no sign of Professor Ross. Eventually, we circled back to the front desk and Francesca, forcing me to watch her give Branwell bedroom eyes as the two of them flirted it out.

Sheesh.

We took another tour of the museum, and I made a wish list from the small gift store.

Then more flirt, flirt, flirt with Francesca.

Lather, rinse, repeat.

After two hours, I was starting to memorize the little plaques next to each artifact and plotting Francesca's demise. Did she *have* to shoot seductive looks at Branwell's lips, as if imagining kissing him? Granted, that could just be me projecting.

Still no Professor Ross.

Between that and the flirting, I fought to contain my rising anxiety. Had Professor Ross run off with my Gracie? Was that why he was a no-show? If I gouged out Francesca's eyes, would anyone notice?

Branwell and I paused in front of the case of bronze mirrors again. Dimly, I noted that there was a blank space next to a card—a bronze mirror showing Eros or Tages forming Hinthial out of the earth. The Etruscan version of the birth of Venus, I supposed. But the actual mirror was gone.

Huh. That was an interesting coincidence.

Branwell studied the missing space with me and then pointed to a scribbled note in Italian to the side of the case.

"Out for cleaning," he whispered.

Mmmm, so maybe not such a coincidence. I was going stir-crazy, seeing mystery where none existed.

"So . . . Plan B," he murmured, talking softly out of the corner of his mouth, his mouth barely moving. It was a cool trick. Could he teach me how to do it? We apparently had a *ton* of spare time right now. Or maybe I was just too fixated on his lips . . .

"We need to know what Roberto has been up to. If I could get my bare fingers on stuff of his—"

"Like in his office?"

"Precisely. Touching his possessions could possibly tell us more than talking to him."

"Ahhh." Everything clicked into place. "That's why you've been flirting so hardcore with Francesca. Office access. Sneaky, Mr. D'Angelo."

Branwell gave me a funny look. And then glanced back toward the reception desk.

A short, wiry guy in a fitted suit coat and slacks had arrived. He ducked behind the desk with Francesca and stashed a rucksack into a drawer. He then proceeded to pin a name tag onto his jacket, all the while chatting and crowding into Francesca's space. Francesca was clearly his type of catnip.

"I don't think I'm going to be the one doing the flirting." Branwell gave me a tight grin.

Francesca extricated herself from the guy—her replacement, Alessio, I presumed—and cast Branwell one last longing look before beating a hasty retreat out the door.

Branwell grinned wider, shooting a pointed glance between me and Alessio.

Great.

"I'm a terrible flirt." I studied Alessio from the corner of my eye.

Wait. Was Alessio checking me out?

I turned my head farther in Alessio's direction, meeting his gaze, giving him a soft smile.

He raked me up and down and then returned the smile ten-fold.

Uhmm . . . okay.

"Looks like you're doing a fine job to me." Branwell grunted, annoyance in his tone.

Branwell and his mood swings. Honestly.

"Distract him," Branwell continued, doing that side-talk thing again. How *did* he do it? "While you're talking to him, I'm going to take a fact-finding detour." He glanced meaningfully at the door marked 'Staff Only' in Italian.

My heart sped up. "You want me to flirt with Alessio so he doesn't see you disappearing to rifle through Professor Ross' office? Aren't there security cameras everywhere here?"

I could feel the small cameras in the corners lasering in on my shoulder blades.

"There are but if you look closely, they're not wired to anything. Typical to have the cameras visible as a deterrent but not actually functional in any way. Bureaucratic Italian cost-saving measures."

I snuck a glance at the nearest one. Yep. No wires.

Mmmm.

"I'm pretty sure that breaking and entering is just as illegal in Italy as it is in the States." I pursed my lips.

"Plausible deniability. But if it makes you feel better, I won't be picking any locks—"

"Wait. You can pick a lock?"

He shrugged.

What the—?!

Branwell leaned toward me, warm breath tickling my ear. My eyes threatened to roll back into my head. Did the man *have* to smell so good? "If everything is on the up-and-up with Roberto, then he has nothing to fear—"

"Well, except for the invasion of his privacy."

"We need answers, Lucy. Grace is gone and Roberto might be our guy."

His words hit me with reverberating force.

Grace is gone . . .

I swallowed, telling the lump in my throat to settle down. Grace needed me to do this.

"I'm a *really* bad flirt, Branwell. I'm sure to mess this up," I confessed. "First of all, I'm hardly trophy girlfriend material with all my freckles and crazy hair. Then, I say awkward things and don't filter and get all flustered. I'll probably end up tripping and falling into Alessio's arms and, given how tiny he is, I'll flatten him to the floor."

Branwell chuckled softly, shaking his head. "Lucy, you clearly don't understand men, particularly guys like Alessio over there. You just defined how best to flirt with him."

"Mmmm. Excuse me if I put on my *skepticals*." I mimed pushing a pair of glasses up my nose.

Branwell snorted. "Please. You have this sweet, vulnerable vibe down pat. When you chat with anyone—guy or girl—you make them feel interesting and capable. Alessio would be thrilled to catch you if you fall. Trust me. Just be yourself and you'll do fine."

With that parting shot, Branwell walked off. Leaving me with my heart pounding and fluttery and not simply out of nerves.

Did he really think that about me? That I was sweet?

Ugh.

So pathetic.

Me. Not Branwell.

Fine. I could do this. For Grace, if nothing else.

With a smile, I turned and headed back to the reception desk.

Alessio perked up at my approach. That was encouraging, at least.

"Ciao," he said, "Francesca told me you are waiting to see Dr. Moretti. Is that correct?"

Deep breath.

I walked past him and leaned an elbow on top of the counter, angling my body toward his. Forcing Alessio to turn toward me, placing his back to the rest of the museum. He was really skinny up close, his jacket hanging off his shoulders. Dark hair long on top and flopping forward.

"Yes, I have been waiting." But I let my eyes say I had been waiting for *him*.

At least, I hoped they did.

I must have done something right, because his grin widened and Alessio stood a little taller. Though the standing taller thing could have simply been an attempt to match my own height. No one would ever accuse Alessio of being a large man.

Behind Alessio, I noted Branwell walk confidently toward the 'Staff Only' door, like he had every right to be there.

"I am so sorry," Alessio swept a hand through his hair, pushing it off his forehead. "Dr. Moretti called to say that he will not be in today. Something came up at a dig site, and he needs to visit there until tomorrow morning."

My head canted to the left, processing what Alessio had just said.

Normally, that wouldn't ring any alarm bells, but—

"He will be at the dig site throughout the night?"

Alessio shrugged. "That is what he said."

Nighttime work at an archaeological site? That seemed eccentric. Eccentric enough to set red flags frantically flapping.

My pulse crawled into the back of my throat. Did this have to do with my Gracie? Did he have her? Was he hurting her?

Branwell disappeared through the 'Staff Only' door.

"Perhaps it is a matter I could help you with?" Alessio grinned wide. Every line of his tiny body hinting at all the fine ways he would be willing to help me.

Lovely.

I could do this . . . keep Alessio distracted until Branwell returned. I had to. My sweet Gracie was depending on me.

19

BRANWELL

I pushed through the 'Staff Only' door and walked purposefully into the empty hallway. Head high and challenging.

When somewhere you shouldn't be, act like you belong and brazen your way through. That was my theory.

The 'Staff Only' door closed behind me. Fortunately, the doors stretching down the right side of the hall had plaques. I turned the handle on the door labeled *Dr. Roberto Moretti, Dirretore del Museo*. It swung open.

Honestly, these people needed to improve their security. Locking door handles would be a good start.

I stepped into Roberto's office and flipped on the light, shutting the door behind me. Unless Roberto returned, I was good for a few minutes at least.

Let Lucy work her magic.

She baffled me sometimes. How could she not understand how

attractive she was? Alessio had done an almost comical double-take the second he saw her. I was pretty confident his flirting with Francesca had been for Lucy's benefit. An immature attempt to make her jealous, prove his manliness.

Boys.

I refused to acknowledge the stab of possessiveness that rattled through me at the thought of Lucy cozying up to Alessio.

Not helping.

This was about Grace.

I surveyed the office—a windowless, white box with plastered walls and a florescent light flickering overhead. A modern Ikea desk stood straight ahead. Two chairs faced the desk, while the wall to the left housed three large shelves covered in books and artifacts. A dusty fake ficus tree drooped in the right corner.

All neat and orderly, if decidedly utilitarian.

I stepped around and settled into the desk chair.

A computer flatscreen sat to one side of the desktop, an old-fashioned enormous appointment calendar in the middle and a tidy pile of papers on the other side. Several items rested along the edge of the desk closest to the door—the basic detritus of a conservator's job. A few photographs of excavations. A pair of fine leather gloves, cracked and old. Cleaning implements and bottles of solution beside an ancient Etruscan mirror, the mirror showed a seated male figure pulling a female figure from the ground. Ah. The mirror depicting Eros and Hinthial that was listed as 'out for cleaning.'

I quickly tugged off the glove of my left hand and hovered, assessing what to touch first. I had so little time. The desk calendar in front of me seemed the best choice. Not shiny, so little risk, and the kind of thing that changed on a regular basis as new appointments were added.

I touched today's date.

"What do you want me to say if the police show up?" A woman's voice in native Italian. Low and urgent.

Shuffling of papers. The clink of metal.

"I need time." A man's voice. *"They suspect me, but there is still research to be done. So much we don't know about Knight and the events two hundred years ago—"*

"Are you close?"

"Closer than I have ever been. 'Love will draw out the shadow.' I think that's the key."

"Yes, you've said that more than once. But assuming you find answers and things go as planned . . . what makes you think you can control it?"

The scritch-scritch *of pen on paper.*

"I have researched that, too. There are ways. People who know."

"And the little girl? What about her? Will she be unharmed?"

A pause.

"I cannot say—"

The voices ended.

My heart had lodged in my throat.

I assumed the male voice to be Roberto, as I was in his office. Who was the woman? What was this 'research'? Was Grace the little girl they hoped would be unharmed?

And 'love will draw out the shadow'? Those were the exact words I had heard Gruncle Jack say in Lucy's living room. What was the connection there?

My mind reeled with questions.

Damn. This was the big drawback to my GUT. I couldn't see the situation, so I had no idea as to context. Worse, I couldn't control how much I heard around a change. Sometimes it was more, sometimes less.

And right now, I needed *more.*

Roberto's calendar looked normal, notes for meetings with various colleagues and preservation groups. But repeatedly, he had an evening appointment with FUP. Most telling, he had a meeting with FUP on the night before Grace disappeared, the night he was supposedly with his mother. FUP . . . were those the initials of a colleague—maybe even the women I had just heard? Another conservation organization? Or something else entirely?

Frowning, I touched the calendar again, skimming back past the conversation between Roberto and the unknown woman. When I concentrated, I could fast forward sound, like an old-fashioned cassette tape. Back, back I went. Conversations between colleagues. Francesca asking day-to-day questions.

No mention of Grace by name. No other discussions of this odd 'research.'

Only one other exchange stood out.

"You need to stop attending those meetings, Roberto. People are starting to ask questions. Difficult questions." A woman's voice. *Native Italian but different from the other woman I had heard. Older.*

A sigh.

"I know, but there's no other way. This research is important, and relevant, given the events surrounding Lord Knight's death—"

"Important enough to jeopardize your career?"

"My mother is invested now. She thinks I go for her, to offer her protection. That is what I've been telling everyone: I don't want her to go alone. It is a reasonable answer."

"Is it, though? Dr. Carpaccio stopped me last week, wanting to better understand what you were into and, quite honestly, questioning your judgment. You are delving into unearthly things that are best left alone, Roberto."

Shuffling. The squeak of a chair leg across the floor.

"Something evil happened, Barbara. Lord Knight's death was more than it appears. I will get answers . . . one way or another."

"But at what cost to—"

Again, the conversation ended.

Crap.

What was Roberto into?

LUCY

I LEANED FURTHER onto the counter, slanting my head toward Alessio. Told my eyes to say, *Mmmm, I'm interested,* when the rest of me was shouting, *Get out now!*

"So tell me about this dig Dr. Moretti is on? Where is it located? It's fascinating."

And please convince me it's not as creepy as it sounds.

Alessio definitely reacted to my lame attempts to engage him, angling his wiry body my way, sending a cloud of cologne wafting around us. Uhm, *wow*. Some things were best in moderation. AXE body spray was definitely one of them.

"Dr. Moretti didn't say. He just said he needed to look at another site to complete some important research. I'm so sorry I don't know more." For the record, Alessio didn't look particularly sorry. "He visits many different places and the *telefonini* . . . uh, the cell phones, they do not work there."

The cell reception thing sounded suspicious. Italy wasn't that large of a country and, in my (granted limited) experience, wireless coverage was excellent, even in rural areas. And what could be so important that it required an overnight 'research' binge?

Professor Ross was looking more and more dubious with every passing minute. My heart pounded. Was Grace caught up in this?

"Does he go on these night digs often?" I asked.

Alessio checked me out again, eyes lingering on hips, bust, lips. Another waft of cologne. Nice. "Every now and again. He should be in tomorrow afternoon, I would imagine."

The door behind me opened and Alessio instantly sprang to his full (vertically challenged) height.

"*Ciao, Alessio.*" A woman came up to the counter, dressed in a blouse and slacks that shouted *educated professional*. She continued to rattle in Italian, staccato fast.

Alessio smiled politely and said something in return.

The lady turned to me, an expectant look on her face. Alessio switched to English. "This is Dr. Barbara Bruno, one of our museum directors. She does the, what do you say, baby farewell?"

Baby farewell? What?

When in doubt, smile and nod.

Alessio motioned toward me, while speaking to Barbara. "This woman had some questions for Dr. Moretti. Will he be in tomorrow?"

"*Spero di sì.*" The woman shook her head, but her face looked concerned. "I hope so."

She rattled off in Italian and then gave us a friendly wave before walking purposefully across the museum floor, heading toward the 'Staff Only' door.

Crap!

BRANWELL

I STUDIED THE rest of the office, trying to decide what to touch next. The glossy computer monitor was too solid and undamaged to hold any usable noise. I pressed a finger on the excavation photographs.

The whirr of a machine. The scratch of a pen.

Nothing there.

The cleaning items were equally unhelpful.

Carefully, I lifted the ancient bronze mirror with my gloved hand, inspecting it. The mirror side shimmered. Rotating the mirror around, I studied the etched scene. The foreground depicted a seated male figure, probably Eros, pulling a woman, Hinthial I presumed, from the earth. In the background, two figures were embracing while another figure was dripping liquid—blood maybe?—onto a bowl. Scrying or divination of some sort? Overall, the scene seemed completely innocuous—the typical religious iconography of ancient Greco-Roman artifacts.

The mirror clearly needed a cleaning, which meant it probably didn't have any recent noise. Listening to ancient Etruscan wasn't going to help me find Grace. Besides, the thing had 'Touch Me and Die' written all over it. Chucky would love to hide in a place like that. I would only touch it if I got desperate.

Setting it back down, I snagged my phone out of my pocket and took photos of both sides of the mirror. For good measure, I took several additional photos of the room, the calendar, the other objects. I snapped a nice close-up of the old gloves resting beside the mirror on the desk.

Setting my phone down on top of the calendar, I carefully lifted one of the antique gloves with my own still-covered right hand. Aged yellow kidskin leather that had probably once been white. Supple but old. *Very* old if the hand stitching were any indication. Large gloves. A man's gloves.

There was a small tear in one of the seams.

I transferred the glove to my bare left hand.

"Damn. You're in trouble now, Alessio." Francesca. *"Moretti will have your hide for this."*

"No, no, it's fine. The rip was already there. I just maybe made it a tiny bit larger—"

Francesca and Alessio went back and forth a bit more.

Not really helpful.

I skimmed back farther.

"Careful, the thorn will dig in deeper. Hold still, my lord." A woman's voice. *Melodic. Italian but formally aristocratic. Florentine Italian from an earlier era.*

"Had I known it would only take a thorn embedded in my flesh to convince you to hold my hand, I would have stabbed myself long before." A man's voice. *Flirtatious. Warm. Italian, as well, but with a hint of English.*

Surprise blazed through me.

Bingo.

The same male voice I had heard while touching the mantel in Lucy's living room.

Jack.

"There. That got it." The woman's voice again. *Vaguely familiar somehow.*

The rustle of cloth over cloth . . . a woman walking in petticoats.

A faint scent of lavender. Dust.

"Thank you." Jack's voice. *"You are a treasure in so many ways, Signorina Sofia."*

"A treasure? Such pretty words. You talk a fine line, my lord. Rumor has it your father was much the same during his time here."

The whisper of wind through trees. A boot kicking a rock.

"My father is a legend around these parts then?" Jack.

A sense of shoulders shrugging.

"The villagers cross themselves and swear to Saint Christopher whenever his name is mentioned."

A male chuckle. "Well, we Knights are hardly an auspicious lot, I suppose. Big, British brutes."

A feminine laugh. Light and tinkling in sound. "I do not think it was your father's height that called forth such a reaction. Rumor runs rampant that he tried to find that which should remain hidden."

Silence. Boots crunching on leaves.

The smell of woodsmoke.

"And you, Lady Sofia? Do you feel we should forgo understanding our forebears because a small group of people are frightened by customs and ideas so far removed from this time?"

"Heavens. When stated that way— Did you not study the art of subtle *argumentation in school, my lord?"*

"Tis truth—"

"Perhaps yes. Perhaps no. But what do you English say? There cannot be smoke without fire? These ideas had to originate somewhere, and the peasants on our family lands have lived here since before the Romans. Only a fool would ignore their words."

More silence.

"Am I such a fool, Lady Sofia?"

Shadowy trees flitted. The smell of green things. The heat of summer sun.

A petite woman walking ahead. High-waisted dress of white muslin fluttering in the subtle breeze. Green silk parasol twirling over her head. A shadowy sense of dark eyes and curled hair. Familiar, somehow.

She stopped and turned, bobbed a look up and down. "Perhaps, my lord."

Frustration and longing.

His or hers?

"Will you plead my case to your brother? As he is the head of your family, I require his permission to begin my excavations. I want nothing further than the chance to finish what my own father began—"

A loud *snick.*

I dropped the glove with a start. Heart racing.

Damn. That had been the door to the hallway opening.

"What . . . say?" A woman's voice drifted down the hallway. Muffled. Garbled. Indistinct. "He is . . . hours . . . miss him . . ."

I tensed, snatching my own discarded glove and darted over to the closed door, assessing my options.

Was she referring to Roberto? Would she come in here?

What to do?

LUCY

CRAP!

How to stop Barbara from disappearing through the 'Staff Only' door?

What had Alessio said? Baby farewell?

She said goodbye to babies?

No—

"Maternity leave!" I practically shouted the words, causing several heads to turn my way, including Dr. Barbara Bruno.

Whew. Got her attention, at least.

"You were on maternity leave," I said again, still too loudly. "Congrats on your baby. That's so awesome. I bet he or she is a cutie."

That's right. I was yelling at a stranger across a quiet museum floor, pretending like it wasn't ridiculously awkward.

Go me.

Barbara smiled, strained but polite. "He is. It's only been a couple of hours, but I miss him so much already."

She turned to walk through the door.

"I would love to see a photo." I called, desperate. "I adore babies so much. I am number six of nine kids, so I totally get it." I motioned for her to come back, just to be safe.

After a short pause—probably pitting her maternal pride against my possible level of psychosis—Barbara let the staff entrance door close and walked back over to us.

I mentally fist-pumped. Maternal pride for the win.

"Thanks for putting up with me," I said as she stopped at the reception desk, digging into her purse for her phone. "Babies are so much fun. I want at least ten kids—"

"Ten?!" Alessio stumbled back so fast, his little body nearly ricocheted off the wall. "Why would you want ten children? That is . . . many."

So *that's* how you separate the men from the boys—talk about your future children. Natch.

"I loved growing up in a big family." I nodded at the photo Barbara held up for me. "Oh, he's adorable. Look at those squishy cheeks. I'm Lucy Snow, by the way."

I held out my hand to Barbara. Got a limp fish handshake in return.

Honestly. Hands have bones and muscles, people. Use them.

"I'm actually a niece of John Knight-Snow," I continued.

I was just babbling at this point, anything to keep their attention. Though announcing that Gruncle Jack was truly my gruncle brought down the house.

Alessio said something loud in Italian that I translated as, 'No way!' and Barbara perked up.

I could see Alessio weighing the options . . . lots of kids versus cool ancestry. Given that he leaned toward me again and smiled huge, I was guessing he sided with cool ancestry.

Sorry, Alessio. Not gonna happen.

For her part, Barbara played a fun game of twenty questions with me, mostly trying to understand how I was related to Jack. Or trying to trip me up and expose me as a fraud.

It was sorta hard to tell.

Midway through explaining how Great-Grandpa Michael Snow had decided to settle in Portland after losing his shirt in the crash of 1929, Alessio suddenly stood straighter, looking around.

"Wasn't there a large guy with you earlier?" He walked around the desk, scanning the museum and then turned back to me. "Where did he go?"

BRANWELL

THUNK.

The door out to the museum closed

I stood in the office, listening for footsteps.

None came.

Letting out my breath, I quickly walked back over behind the desk and lifted the old glove again.

It was extremely unlikely that the issue with Jack was specifically tied to Grace's disappearance. But given the conversation I had heard earlier between Roberto and the unknown women, *they* seemed to think there was a link. And that was really all that mattered in the end.

Holding the glove in my left hand, I skimmed back to find the conversation that had been interrupted—the one between Jack and a mysterious Lady Sofia.

There had been something familiar about her. The timbre of her voice, maybe. Moreover, I was curious to see their location. Could I nudge my gift, forcing it to *show* me more? Would things work that way?

As soon as the thought flitted through, sound assaulted me. But along with the noise came the smells of grass and cypress. A sense of a warm summer wind through my hair.

Vague shadows swirled, stronger this time.

Two figures walking along a worn path, fields to one side, an overgrown stone fence to the other. The man tall and looming, dressed in a tailcoat, breeches and boots. The woman petite and feminine.

She twirled her parasol. He canted his body toward her, top hat leaning, walking stick moving as he strode.

"Will you plead my case to your brother?" Jack's voice. "As he is the head of your family, I require his permission to begin my excavations. I want nothing further than to finish what my own father began. Surely you, more than anyone, can appreciate wanting to honor your family heritage."

Lady Sofia snorted. "It is precisely because of my family heritage that my brother is so reluctant."

They strolled in silence for a moment.

"I have heard the whispered rumors about your father," Jack said. "The words the villagers say—"

"Have you?" Lady Sofia whirled toward him, voice sharp. "Did you hear the one where he warned Signore Martino that her husband would fall to his death within a week's time? Signore Martino did, you know . . . fall to his death—"

"Lady Sofia—"

"No? Or are you referring to the time Papa interrupted an accused murderer's trial, telling the magistrate that he had the wrong man and pointed a finger at the accused man's wife instead? The man was acquitted and his wife hung for the crime—"

"My lady, I meant no malice with my words—"

"Did you not?" Pain flooded her words. Love. Anguish. "My papa was a good man, Lord Knight. An honorable man. He loved us all. My brother. My sisters."

"I do not question your late father's honor."

A beat.

"Then what are you questioning, my lord?"

They walked in silence, rounding a bend. A villa rose in the distance.

Lady Sofia stopped, turning to face Jack. She lifted her face toward the sun. Dark curls framing a delicate jawline. Straight nose in a heart-shaped face.

Familiar.

"You know of what I speak, Lady Sofia. You are merely being coy with the issue. The stories that surround your father—all of your family, to be honest—speak to the supernatural. Abilities thought lost to our modern world—"

Lady Sofia turned and strode away, silencing his words and forcing Jack to jog after her.

"My lady, please!"

"No! You speak of things I cannot discuss—"

"Sofia." Jack tugged at her arm, tone pleading, slowing her to a stop.

Her gaze remained firmly on the villa in the distance. Jaw clenched, blinking furiously.

"I have not granted you leave to use my given name," she hissed.

Jack's shoulders sagged. "Lady Sofia, then. I am sorry, but there is more here than merely my own father's desire to excavate ancient artifacts. Supernatural things that seem to pertain to your own family as well. Dissemble all you want, but your father's unearthly abilities are well known. The D'Angelos have lived in Tuscany since time immemorial—"

I flinched. Hard. My concentration nearly fracturing, bumping my bare hand against the calendar and my phone.

The D'Angelos—?! How?!

I scrambled to refocus on the scene before losing it.

"Your point, Lord Knight?" Sofia said, tone icy.

A sigh. Frustration. "Villagers say the visions that plagued your father also plague your brother. That the D'Angelo men are cursed and your brother, Lorenzo, will meet your father's fate too."

Lady Sofia tensed. Panic. Fear. Grief.

"The ancients were more attuned to the supernatural world than we are in our age," Jack continued. *"There are hints that the Etruscans buried something of great spiritual power on the D'Angelo family land. A treasure above all others. Have you considered that this treasure I seek could also be related to the D'Angelo curse—"*

The scene darkened, as if a raincloud passed overhead. Jack and Sofia receded.

The smell of roses. Musty. Long locked away.

A howl of anguish. Loss.

A desperate craving for light and freedom.

Whirling, it came.

Fog. Darkness.

A shape lunged at me, claws extended. Piercing.

Dragging me under—

LUCY

I SURVEYED THE room with Alessio, pretending to look for Branwell.

"Huh. I think he said something about visiting the restroom. Maybe he got lost?"

Man, was I terrible liar.

I just needed to buy Branwell a little more time. *Please let him find something.*

Alessio shrugged and turned back to Barbara and myself.

"I should get back to work," Barbara said. "It was very nice to meet a descendant of Lord Knight. I'm sure Dr. Moretti will be sad to have missed you. Between you and me, he is too obsessed with the Knight-Snow family and the mysterious events around Lord Knight, but we all have our little things, no?"

The 'Staff Only' door behind Barbara and Alessio cracked open about three inches.

"*Buona giornata.*" Barbara waved goodbye and started to turn around.

Branwell opened the door farther.

No!

"Wait!" I snatched Barbara's hand, forcing her to turn back to me. She started, looking down at my hand holding hers.

Crap! Now what?!

"Uhmm, I love your wedding ring. It's great."

Barbara and I stared down at the plain gold band on her finger.

No diamond. No nothing. Just a thin gold ring.

I barely controlled my wince.

"Thank you . . ." Barbara's tone clearly indicated she found my mental faculties lacking. She tugged on her hand. I held it firm. "It's nothing fancy like you Americans prefer."

From the corner of my eye, Branwell slipped back into the museum proper. His suit coat was off and draped over his left arm, gloves on his hands.

Hallelujah.

"That's why I love it," I said, still studying the ring. "It's so simple. I think we tend to overdo things in the States."

Barbara pulled harder, demanding her hand back, her eyes communicating her opinion of my (defective) mental state. I let go with a too-wide grin.

"Hey! There you are!" I turned my too bright smile to Branwell as he stopped beside me. "We were starting to think you got lost in the restroom."

Branwell met my fake smile with one of his own.

"Yeah," he pretend laughed and rubbed his stomach. "Sorry about that. I must have eaten something that didn't agree with me."

Branwell had never been slow.

Thank goodness.

"I really must go," Barbara said again, tucking both hands tight against her sides and moving away with alarming speed.

Branwell straightened beside me, snapping an intent look to Barbara's back. What was up?

Eager to chat with Branwell, I said goodbye to Alessio. Branwell left a card for Professor Ross so he could call us when and if he decided to show up.

Which meant we were walking out the front door just as two police officers walked in.

We stood to the side as they approached the reception desk, talking in sharp Italian. Alessio's eyes widened and he swallowed nervously.

They exchanged a series of tense sentences.

Branwell paused for another second, listening, and then opened the door for me, directing me out into the sunny, gravel parking lot.

"What was that?" I asked, softly as we walked toward Branwell's car.

"The police are looking for Roberto. He failed to show up for questioning yesterday, and they are trying to find him."

"Not good."

"Nope." He opened the passenger side door for me.

It was only as the car door closed that I *finally* noticed.

Something wet seeping up through the suit coat draped over his left forearm.

Blood.

20

BRANWELL

I walked around to the driver's side and climbed in, wincing as my arm flexed.

"You're bleeding." Lucy fixed me with a laser-gaze. "You had another run-in with Chucky." It wasn't a question.

"Yep."

"You've gotta stop with this passive-aggressive, tough-guy wounded act. I promise there are better ways to get attention."

"Funny."

"Thank you. Want me to drive?"

That was a good question. My right arm was still bandaged and my left stung fiercely with the new scrapes. I wasn't so macho that I had a problem with Lucy driving, but I knew the frenetic mess that passed for traffic in Italy wasn't what she needed right now. Given how rigidly she sat with her palms pressed against her thighs . . .

Had brave, sunny Lucy finally hit the end of her rope? She could only stay in Coping Mode for so long . . .

I reversed and backed out, ignoring the flare of pain up my arm.

Why did the scratches have to sting so badly? I had been luckier this time around, as my suit coat blunted the attack. Both my coat and my shirt were shredded, but the scratches were shallow. That didn't stop them from burning.

"Want to tell me what happened?" she asked. Tense.

"I'm not a hundred percent sure. I was listening to a scene with your Gruncle Jack. I startled and then suddenly Chucky was coming at me—"

"From out of the scene?"

"Yeah."

"What were you touching?"

"That's the weird thing. It was just an old leather glove, nothing shiny about it."

"Mmm, so Chucky is maybe changing?"

I frowned, replaying the incident. "I jumped back, breaking the contact with the glove momentarily. And then . . ."—a flash of realization—"I touched my phone. My hand was still in contact with my phone."

"Chucky came out of your phone?"

It was puzzling. I had touched my phone thousands of times, my screen protector and leather case shielding me from the phone directly. But who knew how Chucky worked in the end? "I'm not sure. He's never attacked me from there before. I'll have to test it."

She bit her lip. "I don't like that Chucky keeps hurting you."

"I'll heal."

I thought I heard her say, "That's not exactly the problem," but I wasn't sure.

She shook her head, staring out at the passing countryside. Terracotta roofs and overgrown fields.

My mind spun with everything I had heard in Roberto's office.

Sofia D'Angelo.

Gruncle Jack had seemed to have a thing for Sofia D'Angelo. She *had* to be an ancestor. That was why she looked familiar. The resemblance to my own sister, Chiara, was uncanny, despite two hundred years of history between them. I hadn't recognized the location of the villa, though it had clearly been Tuscany somewhere. Was it a former family holding?

I scrubbed my gloved hand over my face. What now? Had Jack received permission to continue his archaeological digs on the D'Angelo lands? Had he found his treasure?

"Talk to me." Lucy turned back to face me.

I shrugged and caught her up with what I had overheard. The mysterious meetings with FUP. Those disconcerting cryptic comments about 'the girl,' some research and the unknown woman Roberto had been talking with. Their reference to the phrase Jack had said, 'Love will draw out the shadow.' The concerns of his colleagues, particularly Barbara.

I had just finished summarizing my overheard conversation between Jack and Sofia D'Angelo as we pulled through the arched corridor driveway and into the courtyard of the family palazzo in downtown Florence.

"Professor Ross is in deep. That whole reference to a little girl." Lucy shivered. "It almost seems too much of a coincidence. Do you think he took Grace?" She asked as I parked the car.

I turned, angling my body toward her. My stupid arm stung.

"It's possible. If not, he very well may know who did."

"But if Roberto knows something about Grace and she's in danger, why isn't he saying something?"

"Because Roberto is complicit in her disappearance," I finished the thought for her.

"That's what I was afraid you'd say." Lucy hung her head, nodding. I didn't need any supernatural gift to understand her discouragement and worry.

But . . . what if?

Could I nudge my GUT like I had earlier with Jack and Sofia? I already felt Dante and Tennyson's emotions involuntarily. Would a little concentration extend that to others?

And if it worked, would it be an invasion of Lucy's privacy? Was it unethical if I already surmised how Lucy was feeling? Or was I trying to justify doing something that was ethically suspect in order to feel (pun intended) that much closer to Lucy?

Unfortunately (or fortunately, depending on the point of view), just *thinking* about nudging my gift was sufficient to do the task.

Lucy's emotions opened up, like stepping outside on a summer day, warmth washing through me.

Discouragement and terror for Grace, yes. But there was a thread of something else. Heartache. Sadness. Emotions that seemed separate from her worry for Grace.

Inwardly, I frowned. That was odd. But who knew what else she was dealing with. And given how new I was to this whole empath thing, I could simply be 'hearing' her wrong.

"We'll find her, Lucy. We will," I said. "Whatever it takes."

"I know." Voice a whisper.

"How are you coping?" I had to ask it.

"Me? How am *I* coping?" She lifted wide blue eyes to mine. Freckles stark against her pale skin. "I'm hanging in there. But then I'm not the one who keeps being randomly clawed by a supernatural entity."

Fair enough.

"I'm fine." I shrugged.

She snorted. "Yeah, well, so am I. Fine, that is." Sarcasm dripped. That heartache punched through me again.

I sighed. "Alright, so let's just both agree that we're not fine—"

Lucy snorted. "I'm doing a solid impression of a kitty-on-a-wire. Dangling over a crocodile infested pool, hanging on for dear life."

Pretty much summed up how I felt. Though surprising to hear it from Lucy. But, I supposed, even perpetual rays of sunshine weren't immune to thunderclouds. It was a simple law of physics.

I ruthlessly suppressed the part of me that wanted to haul her into my arms, clutch her close and whisper that everything would be okay. That I would fight and destroy anything that threatened her.

"I'll probably end up letting go," Lucy continued.

"And falling into the crocodiles?"

"Yep. And then fighting for all I'm worth."

That was my girl.

She didn't need me anyway.

21

LUCY

PORTLAND, OREGON
SIX YEARS EARLIER

Rain pounded on the windshield. Portland weather at its most stereotypical.

I leaned forward, resting my head on the steering wheel.

Deep breath. Keep it together.

It had been a hard day . . . a fight with my sister, which had devolved into a hissing exchange with another sister, a failed science test, too much caffeine and not enough sleep, summer internship applications looming—

I swallowed. I had to pull my emotions into a healthy, happy place before walking up to the D'Angelo's apartment. Tennyson needed me to be his Pocket Sunshine, and I couldn't leave the car until I had all this emotional turbulence stuffed away.

A tap on my window startled me. I lifted my head to see a familiar, hulking figure.

Branwell with an umbrella and kind smile.

My heart skipped and then raced ahead, pounding in my throat.

I rolled down my window.

"Tennyson won't be home for a while, accident on I-5," he said. "He wanted me to tell you."

"Thanks."

Rain dripped, pattering in puddles in the parking lot.

"You okay?" Branwell asked, his warm hazel eyes lit with concern.

I nodded *sure* even as a traitorous tear escaped.

"Sorry," I swiped it away.

My bottom lip trembled. "Give me a moment to find my sunshine," I whispered too soft for him to hear.

Silence.

More rain falling. The *shush* of traffic.

"If Tennyson isn't home, I should probably go back up to campus and study," I finally said, glancing at the bulging book bag on the seat next to me.

Hanging out with Branwell probably wouldn't be the best idea. I was rapidly realizing there was a difference between my emotions for him and my feelings for Tennyson.

I adored Tennyson with all my heart. I did. He was sweet and fun and gorgeous, and I felt proud to be his girlfriend.

But Branwell . . .

Branwell spoke to something deeper within me. Something more profound.

Tennyson only held my heart. Branwell, I sensed, could own my very soul—

I ruthlessly cut off that train of thought. Branwell obviously didn't see me that way. I was with Tennyson, and given the connection between the brothers, Branwell would never be an option for me. He would never betray his brother.

"You *could* go study." Branwell fixed me with his too-seeing gaze. "Or you could wait in the apartment here. I have a pizza in the oven, and there's an *I Love Lucy* marathon on *Lifetime*. C'mon up. Chillax and laugh."

He paused, as if debating what to say next, but then continued:

"Give yourself a break, Lucy. Even the sun can be tired of shining sometimes."

22

BRANWELL

FLORENCE, ITALY
2016

Predictably, my mom fussed over my injured arm.

"I raised triplet boys with psychic abilities; I reserve the right to fret over you as adults," was her wry comment.

Mom dug out an enormous first aid kit—she *had* been a veterinarian for over twenty years—and proceeded to cut bandage strips in silence. She helped me out of my torn white shirt, Chiara and Lucy looking on, leaving me perched bare-chested on a kitchen stool.

I summarized our museum visit while Mom cleaned and then bandaged my scrapes, my arm resting on a towel. Lucy sat beside me throughout it, adding comments when necessary, but generally remaining outwardly calm, eyes politely averted from my half-naked form.

Inside, however, was a different story. Lucy churned with emotion—heartache, worry, guilt, yearning. A toxic mix.

Not good . . . on so many levels. Just that slight opening up had seemingly lifted the floodgates.

My GUT honed in on her with fierce attention.

As my mom bandaged my arm, I tried to erect walls to keep Lucy's emotions out, not wanting to invade her privacy. But a feeling would slip through every now and again, tantalizing me, daring me to reach out more.

Fortunately, Chiara came unknowingly to my rescue with a multitude of questions. I swear her first words were a question and she hadn't stopped asking more since.

"So this Sofia chick looks like me?" She reached for a piece of *Glitterati* hard candy from the bowl on Mom's table—assorted citrus flavors in sparkling wrappers.

"Spitting image. You guys could have been sisters."

"Crazy." Chiara popped a pink sour candy into her mouth, nodding at Lucy to help herself. "I gotta say, it seems almost too coincidental that Gruncle Jack had a connection with us D'Angelos. Like . . . creepy coincidental. I'll research D'Angelo history and Jack's excavation sites. See what I can dig up."

"'Dig up.' Nice pun," I snorted.

"Thank you." Chiara grinned around the candy. "That's only the tip of the research iceberg. I don't know what to make of that phrase, 'Love will draw out the shadow.' It's telling both Gruncle Jack and Roberto said it. Maybe Roberto thought Grace would be a connection between him and Jack?"

"Possible," Lucy chimed in. "Though it could also be a complete red herring."

"True. Still, I think it's most important to get my people on Dr. Roberto Moretti. Is he really on some sort of overnight 'research' bender?" Chiara asked. "We need to find him. Or, barring that, at least understand what the police suspect with regards to him."

"Yeah, what do the police know that we don't?" I asked, wincing as my mom dabbed somewhat forcibly. "Maybe Barbara Bruno knows something?"

"Yes! I'll see if I can't chat with her." Chiara pulled out a tablet and started making notes.

"Don't mention me, though." Lucy shook her head. "After my performance this afternoon, Barbara has every reason to think I'm a crazy freak."

I watched Mom carefully apply antiseptic ointment to my scrapes. "I wish I had more information about the first unknown woman I heard Roberto talking to."

"The one who made cryptic comments about the 'little girl' being harmed?" Lucy asked. A blast of anxiety punched through me before I managed to push it back.

"Exactly."

Chiara scrunched up her mouth. "Mmmm, let me see if I can flirt my way into some answers from the office staff."

"Alessio will *love* you," Lucy said without a trace of sarcasm.

"Thanks, Chiara," I said. "We should also track down this FUP that Roberto has been meeting with after hours, particularly the night Grace disappeared. It could be nothing—"

"Or everything," Mom chimed in.

"Let me google it right now." Chiara tapped on her tablet, head bent. "Should be easy enough to tell if it's an organization or a person."

Lucy reached for a handful of candy. "What about your phone, Branwell? Is Chucky in it now, too?"

My walls slipped again. Heartache flooded me. Poignant. Searing. All hers.

Whoa.

Not the loss or worry or fear I had been expecting.

But heartache.

So . . . odd. Was I just misunderstanding Lucy's emotions? This part of my GUT was new to me after all. Why heartache instead of worry?

Lucy didn't meet my gaze, concentrating instead on the small pile of candy in front of her, separating them out by color. Pink, gold, aqua . . .

I swallowed and focused on Lucy's question. I jerked my chin toward my phone where it rested on the table. "I have no idea."

"May I?" Lucy dropped the candy and picked up my phone, gingerly, turning it in her hands. A new model smart phone, it undoubtedly met the definition of 'glossy.'

Lucy pursed her lips. Obviously thinking what I was thinking: Chucky liked shiny things.

"There's only one way to find out, Luce," I said, motioning toward my bare upper body.

She hesitated.

I nodded in encouragement. Knowing was worth the risk.

Lucy touched the shiny screen to the skin on my upper right arm.

The scent of dead roses instantly assaulted me.

Convulsively, I jerked my arm away, breaking the contact before anything happened. Good to know I could do that.

"Is that a yes?" Lucy asked, breathlessly.

"Yep."

Now what? Chucky was like beach sand—determined to infiltrate everything.

Lucy stared at the phone in her bare hand, brow furrowed. "Why you?"

I angled my head at her.

"I mean, no one else draws out Chucky. He only seems to want you."

Chiara chuckled, still tapping her tablet screen. "It was just a matter of time before a supernatural entity decided to take out one of my brothers. Though I'm kinda surprised, Bran. I had all my money on Dante."

She had a fair point.

Why *was* Chucky out to get me, and me alone? Dante had touched Chucky infested things many times, so I knew he was Chucky-proof. I was less sure about Tennyson, but still—

"Alright, so I did a quick google search for FUP," Chiara continued, staring at her tablet. "Assuming that Roberto was *not* into Fuzzy Underwear for Pets—"

"His mom *is* Cat Lady." I grinned.

Chiara ignored me.

"—FUP most likely refers to *Fraternità degli Uomini e il Progresso* . . . Brotherhood of Man and Progress—"

I whistled. "That sounds familiar."

"It should. They're a Tuscany-based Catholic religious group who seem to have an unhealthy obsession with the occult. They got website links here to demons, witchcraft, seances . . . the whole cliched schtik." Chiara snorted. "Why is it the more into mystical, woo-woo stuff an organization delves, the more scientific sounding the name? Brotherhood of Man and Progress? Seriously?"

"If you make something sound scientific, then it must be credible? All this talk of demons is giving me goosebumps." Mom shook her shoulders.

"I'll give FUP a call to see if Roberto was involved with them." Chiara stood to leave. "We might be on the wrong trail here, but I'm withholding judgment for now."

"I, for one, am holding out for Fuzzy Underwear for Pets." Mom winked.

I snorted. "I would think as a former veterinarian, you would care more about the dignity of animals."

She chuckled and patted my cheek.

The impromptu meeting broke up after that.

"Mind if I come with you, Chiara?" Lucy asked, emotions thrumming through her. "I have about a thousand texts from various family members to respond to. After that, I'm bound to need some sugar and decompress time. If I think about Gracie too much, I'll go crazy." She scooped up the pile of candy in front of her. Well, all the candies but the green ones. Those she pushed in my direction as she stood up, a wistful, teasing gleam in her eye.

"Sure." Chiara walked toward the door. "Chat with your fam and then we can talk boys."

My evil sister shot me a grin behind Lucy's back as they left the room, running her eyes salaciously over my bare chest.

Yup. Payback was going to hurt Chiara when I got around to it.

The kitchen hung with silence after the door closed behind them.

Afternoon light bounced through the room.

Mom was wrapping a final strip of gauze around my arm. The scratches were more shallow than the ones on my right arm but the bandage would keep any blood off my clothes.

"Do you want to talk about Lucy?" Mom asked, voice low. Concern wafted off her.

Of course.

Dante and Chiara had shared the news.

"Not really, Mom, no offense. There's not much to say."

Mom snagged some tape. "She doesn't know you at all if she leaves you green candy." She nodded toward the pile of sparkling green on the table near my elbow.

Funny. If Mom only knew . . .

Mom finished with my arm and sat back. Curly auburn hair shot with gray framing her face. Blue eyes, so like Tennyson's, studying me.

"Be careful." She rubbed a calloused hand over mine.

"Aren't I always?"

"Yes. You have always been my quiet, cautious one."

"My loyalty is to my family."

"Yes, but this situation with Lucy . . . it's impossible—"

"I know, Mom. Trust me. I know."

"This isn't just about Tennyson." Her concern spiked. *Oy.* "I want your happiness too, more than anything. I hate seeing two of my boys so wrapped up in the same woman—"

"Mom, relax. I've been living with this for years." I pushed back from the table and used a towel to pick up my phone, surreptitiously snagging a piece of green candy in the process. "I won't do anything other than help find Grace."

Mom's gaze burned a hole between my shoulder blades as I walked out of the apartment.

Once in my own bedroom, I tossed the towel with my phone and the piece of green candy on the bed before changing into jeans and a black t-shirt. I pulled on a pair of leather gloves and sat on the edge of my bed.

Gingerly, I picked up my phone again. Nothing happened. Chucky obviously couldn't come through other objects at me.

But what had happened with my phone? Why was Chucky suddenly inside it when he hadn't been there this morning? Somehow, Chucky was able to move between objects. Or new Chuckies were able to manifest themselves in objects.

But why? To what end?

How did it work?

Had I done something inadvertently to allow Chucky access? Or was Chucky an opportunist, sliding into objects whenever he could?

And given that Chucky had appeared in Roberto's office, was there a connection between him and Chucky? Particularly as Roberto seemed to have some ties to the occult? Or was *I* the infectious agent somehow, and Chucky ended up in Roberto's office because of me?

Dante texted to say he had landed in Boston. I wrote right back, asking about Grace. With Lucy's consent, Dante had cut off a small piece of Grace's blanket, something pocket-sized that he could take with him.

His reply was succinct.

No sign of her. Looked just a few minutes ago.

Relief flooded me.

I moved on to checking my own email, responding to business requests, answering questions.

All the while, the green candy hovered at the edge of my vision until I couldn't ignore its emerald sparkle any more.

I lifted it up, twirling it in my gloved fingers. Green. Glittery. A reflective play of light and shadow. So typically *her*.

Holding it in hand, I pulled the wooden box out of my dresser. Lucy's heart-shaped note still sat on top, white and contrasting.

But aside from the note, the contents of the box were green—Jolly Ranchers, M&Ms, Laffy Taffy, Sour Punch, Starbursts—a garish smorgasbord of lime and green apple. Every candy she had ever teasingly tossed my way.

Gah. I was a hopeless sap.

Of course, that thought didn't stop me from dropping the green *Glitterati* into the mix.

Dragging a hand over my face, I sat on the edge of my bed, right knee bouncing, as I had a long back and forth conversation with myself about Lucy.

You should just let her be. She can hang out with Chiara.

Yeah, but Chiara isn't the best when it comes to empathy and Lucy is hurting. She needs a listening ear.

And are you going to be that ear? 'Cause, let's face it, what you really want to do is pull Lucy into your arms and kiss her senseless. And we all know that's not going to help anyone.

True that.

But I was Lucy junkie. Eagerly justifying my next fix. No way could I stay away, knowing she was so close, thinking she might be hurting.

And like any addict, I was out of my bedroom and halfway up the palazzo stairs before I admitted to myself where I was going.

I expected to find Lucy curled with Chiara in front of a computer, but instead my sister dryly informed me that Lucy had opted to go downstairs for a swim.

I bounded back down the stairs, warring with myself over the wisdom of bothering Lucy. Mostly landing on the side that I should let her be. Not that my feet listened.

Addicted. That was me.

Lucy was floating on her back in the water, staring at the ceiling. Light shimmered through the space, reflecting off the water and bouncing upward. A pair of reclining loungers and a table with chairs dotted the tile pool deck.

Lucy jerked upright at the sound of the door *snicking* shut, head above the rippling water, staring at me across the room.

Where she had found a swimsuit, I didn't know. I could see its green straps looped over her shoulders. Long red hair floating in the water, curling around her shoulders.

The Lady of Shalott or Ophelia came to mind, both doomed victims of love.

Not an auspicious observation.

Lucy remained motionless as the ripples quieted around her, just barely tall enough to touch the five-foot bottom on her tippy toes and keep her entire head above water.

I jammed my gloved hands into my pockets and walked to the pool's edge, humidity hanging in the room.

"How's the water?" I asked.

"It's good. Soothing." Lucy offered me a wan smile. But, like earlier, heartache punched me in the gut.

Definitely Lucy's emotions. No doubt.

She waited expectantly. Obviously wondering why I had sought her out.

"I texted Dante and asked him about Grace." I delivered my excuse of a message. "He still isn't seeing her, so that's good."

"That's great. Thanks."

I expected to feel a surge of relief from her but got another shot of heartache instead.

What gave? Why was nothing getting through to her?

Her hurt cut me. It made me want to fight. Be a caveman and pummel something to purge my helplessness.

"You want to talk about it?" I asked instead.

"Talk about it?"

"What's bothering you. Is it more than just Grace missing?"

She tilted her head back, staring at the up-lights that rimmed the perimeter of the room, hair a floating halo spiraling around her.

Something winked under the water around her neck.

Ah. Her Saint Christopher medallion. If Chucky *were* a demon, then a religious medal might offer some protection. Smart Lucy. Cat Lady would be proud.

Silence.

"Sometimes talking helps." My voice echoed off the stone walls.

"Yes. Sometimes." Lucy lifted her head upright, water streaming.

Again, I felt that longing. Pain.

It was . . . odd. Because it seemed like . . .

My mind scrambled to understand.

"Lucy, have I hurt you?" I cleared my throat. "Are you upset because of *me?*"

LUCY

I hovered in the water, tiptoes propping me up, staring at Branwell. Trying to convince my shocked lungs to function again.

Breathe. You need air to live, Lucy.

His words hung in the air between us. Confused. Wondering.

Have I hurt you?

"Because if I've done anything to cause you pain, I am *so* sorry," he continued, unwittingly digging the knife in deeper. "I would never intentionally hurt you. You have to know that, right?"

"Yes, I know."

He hadn't hurt me. Not directly.

It was the situation that destroyed me. Realizing that every man who passed through my life would forever be measured against the yardstick of Branwell D'Angelo. And be found wanting.

Seeing him. Being with him. Taunted at every turn by what I wanted more than life itself but could never have. And then knowing he was the kind of guy who would risk being clawed or worse by a random super-natural creature on the off chance he could help my little, lost Grace, a complete stranger—

I swallowed. That familiar longing and heartache swamping me—a practically physical pain. The missing half of me was standing right here, and I couldn't reach out and claim him.

Why did it have to be *this* man? Of all the men on Planet Earth? Lit-erally, the one person who would be utterly off limits? Figured I would fall prey to some demented god who got off on cruel ironies.

Branwell stood just inside the door at the edge of the pool, gloved hands jammed into his jeans pockets. Bandages extended from wrist to elbow on both arms, ending right below the short sleeves of his black t-shirt. His hair was pulled up, beard trimmed. All of him shadowy and hulking.

The water rippled between us, catching the light occasionally and throwing a ghostly blue tint onto his face.

Even in the dim glow, his gaze bored into mine.

"I only want your happiness." His low bass bounced off the arched ceiling, pounding through me. How could I have forgotten how much I adored the sound of his voice?

"And I want yours."

He didn't love me. Not like I loved him.

Sure, I knew he cared . . . a brotherly, general sort of caring.

My throat constricted. Tight. Raw.

He tilted his head. As if listening to something I couldn't hear.

"You're sad. But I don't think it has to do with Grace. At least, not all of it."

A statement. Not a question.

He *was* becoming more adapt at discerning emotion.

Yay. Just my luck.

I pushed off with my toes and arched up onto my back again, float-ing, blinking my eyes to keep my tears in place.

What could I say that wouldn't simply make everything worse?

"I'm fine, Branwell."

He snorted.

"Really, I am," I continued. "It's been a difficult couple of days. The combination of emotional and physical exhaustion . . . it's just catching up to me."

Understatement of the year there.

I licked the salty pool water off my lips. At least, I told myself that's what it was.

This wasn't me. I was the chipper one, pathological in my optimism. Pocket sunshine.

I watched Branwell out of my peripheral vision. He walked around the edge of the pool, coming closer to me.

He squatted onto his haunches, studying me floating perpendicular to him.

"Talk to me, Lucy. What's up?"

Of course, he wouldn't let this go.

I couldn't tell him the truth.

Well, you see, I realized years ago that I love you, not Tennyson. I mean, I love Tennyson, but it's not a love-love kinda thing—more like brotherly love.

But you . . . you I love like slow dancing in the rain. Like lazy afternoons cuddled on the couch watching reruns. Like tucking our kids into bed and raiding the freezer for chocolate fudge ice cream. A forever sorta love.

Those words needed to stay inside me.

But given his stronger empathetic skills, it was just a matter of time before he realized all this, I supposed.

"Lucy." His voice deepened, taking on a hint of Desi Arnaz when Lucille Ball pulled one of her shenanigans.

LooSee.

I gave a weak laugh and kicked upright, balanced on the pool bottom again, hair plastering to my skull. I turned my head toward him.

"I'm fine, Bran," I repeated. "Just sad and worried about Grace and feeling down. I probably should get some rest."

He tugged on his beard with a gloved hand. "Of course. I'm hardly suggesting you 'choose fun' but—"

"Well, I *am* swimming." I gave a tentative smile. Wobbly.

Branwell released his beard but stayed crouched, studying me. Most likely seeing—or rather, *feeling*—right through my bravado.

What else could I say or do?

"You know you can talk to me, no matter what."

I nodded.

We stared for a moment. I could see the moment he decided to let it go, to not press me more for answers I could never give him.

He looked away and focused on tugging off the glove of his right hand.

"So . . . swimming, eh?" He touched the water, dipping two bare fingers in. "How is the water—"

Branwell's voice stopped on a choked cry.

A large, dark mass poured out of the water. Oblong. Intent.

It swallowed Branwell whole, dragging him into the pool with it. Water churned, a roiling malestorm.

Chucky!

"Branwell!" My scream echoed off the curved ceiling. High. Panicked.

Sluggishly, I pushed through the water, slow-mo scrambling to reach him.

Fifteen feet. Thirteen.

The huge, black . . . whatever it was . . . spiraled up Branwell's body, reaching for his head. Like it wanted to get onto his shoulders and force him to stay under.

Branwell fought it, trying to push away and keep his mouth above water, flailing for the edge of the pool. He grabbed a breath of air just to be pulled under again.

"Branwell!"

Eleven feet. Ten.

The water churned, darkness swarming over Branwell's form. A liquid nightmare. My brain struggled to process what I was seeing. One minute Chucky was almost human-shaped ink and the next, he was a toxic, amorphous smudge.

Branwell rolled, struggling for freedom. He surfaced, craning around, looking for me as I struggled to reach him.

Eight. Seven.

His eyes locked with mine. Desperate and terrified. And then he looked below my chin.

"Metal," he gasped before Chucky dragged him under again.

What—?!

Five. Four. Three.

Frantic, I stretched my hand over the last two feet to grab him, still trying to process what Branwell had said.

Why had he said 'metal'? Metal what?

Then it clicked.

No! *Medal.*

My medal. A Christian relic.

Of course.

Sobbing, I snatched it off my throat.

One foot.

Branwell surfaced again, water boiling around him. He managed to get a hand on the tiled side of the pool, using the leverage to keep his head above water. Chucky continued to swarm around him, a smoky blob.

Grabbing hold of Branwell's arm, I pressed the medal into the dark mist under the water, thinking to drive it off with the religious icon.

Nothing happened.

My hand passed through Chucky unharmed.

Over and over, I pressed the medal into the mist. Hand shaking, lungs hyperventilating.

Nothing.

Chucky held on, twisting Branwell under yet again.

No!

With a powerful burst of strength, Branwell launched himself upward, knocking my hand in the process. The medal flew out of the pool, clinking against the stone wall. Branwell grabbed my hand, physical connection surging between us.

Chucky vanished. Leaving just as abruptly as he had arrived.

Branwell sagged against the edge of the pool, elbow resting on the pool deck, coughing and hacking.

His huge body wracked.

He had nearly *drowned*. I had almost witnessed his death—

Coping Mode Lucy shattered.

Sobbing, I stood on my tippy toes, leaning into him, running my hands over his body, checking for blood and wounds.

"B-Branwell, love . . . are you o-okay?" Hysterical. I was utterly hysterical. "Baby, where are you hurt?"

I was leaning against his chest by this point, trying to see and touch as much of him as possible. I pressed my hands into his shoulders and then his face, searching for gouges in his skin or the tell-tale pink tinge of blood in the water.

"B-Branwell, love, you h-have to talk to me," I bawled. "Where are you hurt?"

Still coughing, he raised his head and met my gaze. His eyes so wide. Stunned.

I was hugging him, crying, clutching the back of his head with both hands. Our faces only inches apart.

"W-what did you just say?" His voice barely a whisper of sound against my lips.

BRANWELL

The entire universe came to a screeching halt.

Molecules. Atoms. Time itself.

"What"—*cough*—"did you"—*hack*—"say?"

Surely I had heard her wrong.

The surge of terror and adoration coming from her couldn't be directed at me, right?

I coughed and coughed, wheezing, trying to get the pool water out of my throat and nose. Lucy continued to sob, ducking her head and burying her face in my neck.

Ignoring my words.

I gave my head a tiny shake through another coughing fit. Surely I was just hearing things. Lucy hadn't called me 'love.'

Or, if she had, she hadn't meant it like *that*.

But still . . .

I was fully clothed in a swimming pool with Lucy clinging to me, emotionally distraught.

Lucy. The woman who never fell apart.

Addicted-me longed to wrap her in a vice-like hug and bury my lips in hers.

Thinking-me patted her shoulder and opted for less confessional comfort.

"I'll be okay, Lucy." I hacked again. "Just need to breathe."

"B-but are you hurt?" Lucy pulled back, hiccupping. The emotion in her blue eyes threatening to swamp me under again.

"Aside from swallowing half the water in the pool and choking on the other half?" I gave one final cough, clearing my throat. "I'm fine. No scratches this time. Something about the water changed how Chucky came at me—"

"Thank g-goodness. What happened?"

I replayed the events in my head, using them as a distraction from the fact that Lucy still had her arms around my neck. My feet were planted solidly on the pool bottom, so she was probably simply using me to prop herself up, right?

As for Chucky, this attack *had* been different. Muted in the sense that Chucky hadn't broken skin but more fierce in that the entity had been larger, more fully *here*.

As I was fighting off Chucky, I had noted the glint of Lucy's Saint Christopher medal. Several things had clicked in my head—the shiny surface of the metal touching the glittering water, the fact that the medal had come from Roberto who had possible ties to the occult.

The second the medal had launched out of the pool, Chucky had vanished. Coincidence? Or causation?

I wasn't quite ready to grab the medal to test the theory a second time. But . . . if Chucky had infected the medal too, then perhaps something in the water had unleashed him? Given that water muted my gift, perhaps it had muted Chucky as well? Or, at the very least, prevented him from shredding me?

Crazier things had happened, I supposed.

Logic said I should probably get out of the pool, but given how Lucy was clinging to me, I wasn't in any big hurry.

She clutched my head again, her nose pressed to my ear. "You have to stop these attacks."

Her body hugged mine in the water. All sound muted, letting me hear just her. Her soft sniffles. Breath in and out of her lungs.

The racing adrenaline bled from my system, mutating into something more warm-blooded. If I turned my head even a fraction of an inch, my lips would meet hers.

This was the definition of insanity. She was killing me.

"So . . . what exactly did you say earlier?" I asked again. I should have let it go, pretended I hadn't heard anything. But I was hardly mature enough to do that. Not when it came to this and Lucy.

She sniffled. Silence.

I jostled her with my shoulder. *Talk to me, Lucy.*

She responded, not with words, but by rubbing her cheek against mine. Chilled but soft. So soft.

My entire brain short-circuited.

Ah Lucy.

Mia carissima Lucia.

"I-I thought I could deal with this," she finally whispered. "I mean, it has been over two years since I last saw you. You'd think I would grow up and move on. Get over you already."

My sluggish mind struggled to process her words.

Wait—?! Had she just said—

"Lucy?" My voice holding a thousand question marks. All of me impossibly still.

She snuffled. Hugged me tighter.

"I'm sorry, Branwell. I tried so hard. Really I did. But now you said you are feeling emotions more, and I love you so much that I'm sure you feel it all the time and must already know it, but you're too kind to say anything . . ."

Lucy was babbling. Her lips whispering into my ear, hands clutching my head.

It washed over me through the sound of her voice.

Wave after blissful wave.

Love. Adoration. Longing. Yearning.

All Lucy.

All directed at me.

Madonna.

Shock blazed through me with stunning force. Like a fist to the gut. Not a drop of air in my lungs.

Lucy.

Loved.

Me.

Me!!

How?

Since when?

And . . . why?!

Never. And I mean *never* had I thought Lucy cared for me like this.

I hoped. I dreamed. I longed . . . but to know—

My knees buckled and my arms tightened around her, sagging my weight into the side of the pool. Convulsively. Helpless to anything else.

I opened my mouth to speak but couldn't get my sluggish tongue to form words.

My brain had been sucker punched.

And still Lucy clung to me, arms around my shoulders, fingers in my hair. Nose pressed into that space between my ear and throat.

"I'm sorry. So sorry," she sobbed, over and over. "Sorry."

Crying.

Not for Grace. Not for anyone else.

For me.

Crying because she loved *me.*

If I turned my head even a fraction of an inch toward her . . . she would *kiss* me.

Her lips would be wet and chilled.

She would taste like sweet sunshine. Happiness. Hope.

And she would return my kiss with fervent enthusiasm. I could sense it in her body. In the possessive way she dug her fingers into my hair.

My heart hammered in my throat.

Addicted-me nearly did it. It would be *so* easy to give in.

Turn my head. Find her mouth.

Lose myself.

But at what cost?

Tennyson swimming in a bathtub of his own blood—the image punched through my fuddled brain.

Finally, I found my vocal chords.

"H-how long . . ." My voice trailed off.

She sniffed. Guilt thrummed through me.

Hers? Mine?

She pulled her head back, resting a cheek on my shoulder, nose still turned toward my throat.

"From the b-beginning," she sniffed. "The very beginning."

A beat. More surprise.

"The beginning?"

She nodded, rubbing her cheek against me.

This woman.

"You probably don't even remember," she said. "We met at a coffee shop before I knew you were Tennyson's brother. You let me photograph your scone cause it looked like a heart. You were this big, sweet, adorable guy and I suddenly felt . . . home."

"Home." I was mindlessly repeating her words at this point.

"Yeah." She sniffled again. "I thought I was just being fanciful. I really did like Tennyson and he was . . . flattering with his attentions. But you were always there—"

"I was."

"I had to grow up a bit more, I think. But I eventually realized that what I felt for Tennyson paled beside what I felt for you. And I couldn't live a lie anymore . . ."

Silence.

"Lucy—"

"Shh." She hushed me. Hiccupped. "P-please don't say anything. I know you don't care about me in that way. I know you are loyal to Tennyson."

Tennyson.

I clenched my jaw. I *was* loyal to my brother . . . no matter what.

Focus on your brother, you idiot. Not how crazy right it feels to hold his ex-girl-friend in your arms.

She gave a gasping breath. "I don't need to hear the 'Lucy, you know I think you're a great person *but*—' speech."

A pause.

"I *do* think you're a great person." My brief humorless laugh echoed in the room.

She sniffed. "My emotions are not your problem, Branwell. You've always made the boundary between us very clear. It's okay. We'll find Grace, and I'll leave and you'll never have to see me again."

My heart gave a painful thump. Her words ringing over and over.

I'll leave and you'll never have to see me again.

BRANWELL

CANNON BEACH, OREGON
FIVE YEARS EARLIER

I am so in love, my brother." Tennyson collapsed on the sand next to me. "How is it possible for one woman to make me so happy?"

Because that one woman is Lucy, I wanted to say.

I wisely kept my mouth shut and instead imagined the walls around my mind tightening, hoping for the millionth time, I was somehow blocking him from sensing my emotions.

It had to have worked because Tennyson's grin stretched wide, lighting up his eyes . . . eyes the color of the ocean on a sunny summer day.

Like today.

Haystack Rock glistened in the surf, slowly being surrounded by water as the tide came in. Gulls called to each other and a gentle breeze tugged at my jacket. Even on a summer day, the Oregon coast rarely drifted into warm territory.

Closer to the surf, Lucy crouched arranging shells in the sand, photographing them from various angles. Her hair swirled in the wind, a flame halo.

Feeling our combined gazes, she swiveled her head, holding up a hand to block out the sun, waving at us with her opposite fingers. Smile broad and endearingly lop-sided.

Tennyson laughed and leaned back on his elbows.

I glanced at my brother. Happiness spilled out of him, molten sunshine pouring over the rest of us.

Lucy had done this.

"She's so positive and bubbly, her mood always up. It's effortless to be around her."

Tennyson said this line a lot. As if justifying something to himself. He gestured toward the other people strolling down the beach. People with emotions Tennyson could feel.

In the past, being in crowds had overwhelmed him. We had all worried that Tennyson would become a hermit someday, living out in the wild on his own.

And then Lucy arrived.

"She soothes me, saves me from myself," Tennyson continued. "Lucy is my secret weapon. When I'm with her, everything else is easier."

But is that really love? True love? I wanted to ask him. *What about Lucy? Love should be focused on your partner, not just yourself.*

Tennyson threaded his fingers together behind his head and winked up at me.

"Lucy's the One," he said. "I can't imagine a life without her. I'm totally going to ask her to marry me."

26

BRANWELL

I made my apologies to Lucy and scrambled out of the pool, her eyes burning a hole in my retreating shoulders.

Somehow, *somehow* I resisted. I focused on Tennyson and managed to not lay my heart at her feet. The words stuck tight in my throat.

What good would they do anyway? Her feelings for me changed nothing in the end. Tennyson and his tenuous emotional state remained an unassailable wall between us.

I slammed into my bedroom and changed out of my wet clothes and re-bandaged my arms.

And then proceeded to pace for a solid thirty minutes, my brain a hive buzzing.

Whattodowhattodo . . .

My bedroom wasn't quite far enough away, turns out.

I could *feel* Lucy moving through the palazzo. The tired tread of her feet on the stairs. Her heavy heart. Maybe I was just being fanciful. Or maybe my GUT was granting my own wish to be tuned in to her. Who knew.

But if I stayed another moment here . . . I would say things, do things. Things I would hate myself forever for.

I pulled on gloves, grabbed a few items and hit the stairs, running to my car and escape.

Absurdly cheerful sunlight washed the windshield as I drove, the sun dipping lower to the horizon.

Lucy loved me.

Loved. *Me.*

The phrase thrummed over and over.

A mantra. A hallelujah. A death knell.

Until the moment those words escaped her mouth, I had never realized that my entire life was based on one simple assumption: Lucy Snow didn't love me.

I could be around her and hang out with her because I was only torturing myself.

I could help her and console her because I was only hurting myself.

Every ounce of my behavior hinged on the fact that she *did not* return my adoration.

But knowing she loved me too . . .

Loved me like I loved her.

Loved me like Tennyson loved her.

Tennyson and Lucy. Two halves of my heart.

The worst part?

There was no way I could avoid hurting one of them now.

I was forty minutes south of Florence before I understood where I was instinctively heading. Towering, narrow cypress trees lined the road, pointing the way.

The family villa outside Volterra—Tennyson's current residence of choice.

I pulled my emotions inward, imagining a tight wall around them.

Chiara called in the middle of my drive. I put her straight to speaker phone.

"A quick call to the local FUP chapter confirmed that Roberto and his mother are devoted members—"

"Hello to you, too."

"Don't be snarky." Chiara never missed a beat. "Apparently, the police have been questioning other FUP members about their activities based on information they got from Barbara Bruno. As for Barbara herself, she's cooperating with the police, but she doesn't know much. Just that colleagues were asking pointed questions about Roberto's involvement with the occult and FUP. Maria-Teresa—"

"Cat Lady?"

Chiara snorted. "Right. Cat Lady. Anyway, word is she's been cooperating with police, too. She might be an avid member of FUP, but she doesn't know what Roberto is researching. She insists something bad happened to John Knight-Snow in her palazzo, and she and Roberto attend the FUP meetings in order to better protect themselves from the evil."

"Should we follow-up with Cat Lady?"

"Meh. I don't think she has more information beyond what we already know, honestly. For their part, FUP is none-too-happy about being dragged into this whole mess. They insist nothing in their esoteric practices would ever threaten a child but . . ."

"Who knows how Roberto has interpreted their belief in the occult, or why he was so interested in attending FUP's meetings?"

"Yeah, unlike his mother, he doesn't strike me as being particularly spiritual."

"Agreed and based on what I heard from objects at the museum earlier today, Roberto obviously thinks something supernatural happened to Gruncle Jack. That conclusion could just be a natural outgrowth of an inherent fascination with the occult—"

"Or the opposite . . . Roberto investigating supernatural phenomena to better understand what he thinks Jack is rumored have found."

"True. It's hard to say."

"Not to mention Grace. I'm still trying to see how she factors into this."

"I've considered it." I heaved a deep sigh. "Roberto going AWOL is a huge concern. I can't believe it's just coincidence. He clearly knows something and is either an accomplice to Grace's disappearance—"

"Or perhaps another victim of our abductor?"

"Exactly. Too many questions and not enough answers."

"I'm going to keep digging for dirt on Roberto. I'll be in touch."

Chiara hung up, leaving my mind spinning.

What was Roberto up to? Was all of this tied to something Jack had found so many years ago? And, again, was Chucky showing up because I was spreading him somehow? Or did his presence have a connection to Sofia D'Angelo and the events surrounding Gruncle Jack two centuries ago?

Countryside whizzed past me for another thirty minutes before the towers of Volterra rose from a hilltop in the distance. I turned off the highway before reaching the steep climb to the town proper and headed down a worn lane. I rolled the car to a stop in front of the family estate.

The D'Angelo villa was more of a compound than a single house. Once a fortified medieval castle complete with a crenelated tower, the keep walls had been absorbed by a larger, columned Renaissance palace, each generation adding their little stamp.

That said, the old castle walls still ran around two sides of a large courtyard with a small, ancient family chapel snuggled into one corner. Enormous double-doors guarded the entrance. I slipped through a smaller gate inset into them, crossed the courtyard and through the heavy main door, walking into the villa proper.

Why was I here, in the end? Entreating Tennyson for permission? Pleading for absolution? Or simply reaffirming my connection and commitment to my brother?

A soft *woof* and the slow shuffle of padded feet greeted me as I closed the front door. I smiled as an overweight, sad-eyed hound dog ambled over, tail wagging.

"Hey, Elvis." I knelt down, scratching behind his ears. "How's my favorite rock star?"

Elvis woofed again and nudged my hand higher, insisting I get the angle just right.

Figured.

He *had* always been something of a diva.

Elvis the Hound Dog was one of the small side perks of having a brother who could see the shadows of former lives.

For a time, my mom had a white rat, Boney, who Dante swore was the reincarnation of Napoleon Bonaparte. Unfortunately, the lifespan of white rats is short, so Boney had hopefully moved on to bigger karmic things.

Elvis, on the other hand . . .

Dante said the dog's shadow featured Elvis Presley in his suave Hollywood days, not his later paunchy, polyester years.

But still. A hound dog? Could the universe have been more predictable?

Cosmic retribution? Perhaps.

Or just a comforting sign that someone, somewhere had a droll sense of humor.

In any case, Elvis adored Tennyson and howled like nothing else anytime he heard 'All Shook Up.'

I gave Elvis a final rub and walked through the house, the dog at my heels.

I found Tennyson lounging on the back terrazza, feet (well, foot) propped up, reading a book. A prosthetic leg rested against the side of his lounge chair.

Off the terrace, green fields and the occasional farmhouse stretched into the distance. Humidity hung heavy, coating the undulating hills in hazy mist. The sun sank toward the horizon, raking the world in golden light.

Tennyson raised his eyebrows as I swung into a lounge chair next to him, stretching my own legs out. He studied me with those haunted blue eyes of his.

"I didn't know you were coming." A thread of accusation wove through his words.

For Tennyson, very little in life was unexpected.

"Surprise." I laced my gloved fingers behind my head. Elvis wandered over to Tennyson, settling by his side on the pavement. "Nice sunset."

"Please." Tennyson snorted, turning his head back to the view but leaning down to scratch Elvis' head. "I don't need an ounce of clairvoyance to know this isn't a purely social call."

Touché.

I studied Tennyson from the corner of my eye. He had bulked up a bit through the shoulders. Age and eating more finally moving his body from lean to fit.

Everything was externally perfect about my brother.

Perfect face, perfect smile . . . he could ooze charm and polish when needed. Fiercely loyal and idealistic.

That was good.

His emotional state, however . . .

"What's up?" he asked.

I pushed outward with my GUT, wanting to 'hear' the emotions in his words. Past his mild annoyance at my unannounced arrival.

It was like forcing my way through a thin barrier—

Pain. Self-loathing. Futility. Despair.

His emotions surged through me. A potent cocktail.

"Talk, Bran. How's everyone?" he asked again.

Lucy . . . sharp and clear it came from him, as if he had said the word. Tennyson's concern and anguish and love for her—Lucy. *That's* what he wanted to talk about. The subtext of his questions.

What a mess.

"Lucy's fine. Left her gossiping with Chiara—"

Tennyson whipped his eyes to mine. "I didn't ask about Lucy specifically."

"Didn't you?"

Silence.

He stared me down, a combination of accusation and puzzlement.

"Look, Tenn." I scrubbed a hand over my beard. "We all need to start talking more. Not just me."

"Talk?"

"Yeah. About us. About our GUTs."

Silence.

Crickets literally chirped. Fireflies flitted in the grass.

Tennyson continued to face me, a solitary eyebrow raising higher in question.

"I feel your emotions," I finally said.

His head reared back slightly. "You do?" Surprise jolted through me.

"You didn't know that? That I'm becoming something of an empath?"

He shook his head, eyes eagle-sharp, probing.

"I can't feel you anymore." Accusation in his tone.

"You can't? Since when?"

"For years, honestly. Sometimes I get hints of things from you when you're far away—"

"You knew Dante and I were arguing yesterday—"

Tennyson snorted. "Yeah, but that was all Dante. I could tell he was concerned and angry at you. Dante's an open book. But from you, I get nothing. I haven't for . . . forever."

Relief flooded me. There was no way he knew about Lucy and me.

"It's like you block me somehow," Tennyson continued, his brows drawing down into a perfect V.

I swallowed. "I do. Block you, that is."

He stared me down. "How?" Short. Blunt.

"I'm not sure, to be honest. I just imagine walls around my mind that prevent emotions from escaping."

"That's it?"

"Yeah."

Tennyson paused. I could practically see the thoughts darting across his brain.

"I'm not sure how I feel about you sensing my emotional state," he said. "It's a like a solid taste of my own medicine, I suppose. The irony, of course, is that it's not reciprocal. You feel me, but I don't feel you." He paused. "Why do you block me?"

Mmmm, how to respond to that? "For all those reasons you just said. I don't like people in my head."

My emotions were my own. How unprecedented was it that I could shut him out? Had there always been this kind of protection component to our family gift? Could Tennyson learn to shut me out too?

"Do you sense other people over a distance?" I asked.

Tennyson shrugged. "Not usually. It's mostly Dante, to be honest. Sometimes Chiara and Mom. It used to be you, too, when we were younger but not anymore."

"Do you sense people who aren't related, like Lucy?" Did he know of Lucy's supposed feelings for me?

He shook his head. "No. I've never sensed her over long distances. I have to be in the same room."

More relief.

"How long have you been an empath?" Tennyson asked.

"Not too long. A year, maybe two." I paused and then went on. "At first, it was simply vague impressions, but it keeps getting stronger. More pronounced."

It felt like it had been strengthening in just the past few days, to be honest.

"Our GUT . . . it's like a muscle, I've decided." Tennyson sat back. "The more you flex and work it, the stronger it becomes."

A beat.

"That's how it's been for you, isn't it?"

Tennyson ignored me. Instead, he scooted to one side of his chair and patted the space next to him. Elvis perked up his sad-eyes and managed to hop up on the third try, curlicuing his bulk into my brother's side.

"My GUT saved lives in Afghanistan," Tennyson stroked Elvis' flank. "I could sense attacks before they happened, so naturally, every day I was pushing, seeking, eager to sense danger before it struck—"

The irony being that he hadn't foreseen his own terrible injury. But then, Tennyson's gift had never worked on himself.

"But all that mental exercise came at a price. Are you sure you want my honesty?" He stretched his arms in front of him, like a cat, and rubbed a hand over his face before continuing to pet Elvis. If I couldn't feel his deep despair, I would never suspect it. Had he always been this skilled at hiding?

"Yes." No hesitation.

"Who will you tell?"

"No one you don't want me too. We both know how hard it is to deal with Dante and Mom sometimes."

"They mean well . . ."

"But pity can be enabling."

"Yeah." Tennyson drew in a deep breath, his pain hitting me again. A fractured, razored thing. "It's like this. Before Afghanistan, I would just feel emotions a little into the future. Now, it's taken on a whole new component. I will often see and hear, as well as feel and it often is farther into the future. I'm more attuned to my gift, which is never a good thing."

"It's like our GUTs are merging into each other. I haven't had any visions of the future, but the other senses bleed into my 'hearing' of the past."

A pause.

"Can you control it?" Tennyson asked. "If you can block me, does that control extend to other parts of your GUT?"

I shook my head. "No. Not the involuntary part. I wish I could."

"Me too, brother. Me too."

We sat in silence for a few minutes, eyes trained over the pastoral landscape.

"Chiara mentioned something has been attacking you." Tennyson broke the quiet. "A demon?"

"You mean Chucky?"

That got me a laugh.

I caught Tennyson up to date on everything.

"So Chucky is coming out of previously 'safe' things?"

"Yeah. It's . . . awful. He has been in things belonging to Gruncle Jack, things connected to Roberto, mundane objects I use all the time. It's . . . crazy. He's like a virus, infecting everything."

Tennyson pursed his lips. "I think you're on to something there, Branwell."

"I am?"

"What if Chucky really is an infectious agent?"

"Interesting. So if he is able to infect things, how does it work? Am

I the infectious agent? Is that why he only attacks me?"

Another beat.

"Are you sure about that? That he only attacks you?"

I pulled my phone out of my pocket and held it out to him with my gloved hand. Uber-careful-like. After Chucky's dramatic day, I was loath to touch anything.

Tennyson studied the phone. He carefully lifted his bare index finger and rested it on the glossy screen.

We both stared at his finger. Nail neatly trimmed.

Nothing happened.

"Alright, so Chucky does seem to have it in for you and you alone." Tennyson shrugged. "Can't say I blame him. You are a *fine*-looking man."

A bit of heat touched my cheeks. No one ever called me handsome. I was used to being the invisible brother. The in-between child. The one who was damaged enough to not be of help like Dante, but not so damaged that I demanded TLC, like Tennyson.

"Thanks," I muttered.

Tennyson waved away my discomfort.

"So to summarize," he said, "Chucky likes shiny things and you— not necessarily in that order. Grace is missing but alive, according to Dante. Roberto is on the lam, obsessed with the occult and researching something esoteric related to Lucy's Gruncle Jack. There are hints that this something may include Grace due to Roberto's obsessive interest in her family. We also know that Gruncle Jack had some connection to the D'Angelos."

"Yeah, that's pretty much where we are. Speaking of Grace, I brought this." I pulled out a piece of Grace's princess blanket, the part that Dante hadn't taken with him to Boston. Fuzzy pink fleece with princesses.

Tennyson took the cloth from me, holding it in his fingers.

"Could you look for Grace?" I asked. "For Lucy."

"Look?"

Pain arched through me. Loss. Tennyson's.

"You said you were seeing more nowadays. Could you nudge your gift and peer into Grace's future?"

Tennyson paused, staring down.

"There's no guarantee I'll see anything. And even if I do, it's only a possibility." He balled the blanket between his hands. "Nothing is set in stone."

"I know. But I figure it doesn't hurt to try."

He shot me a hesitant look. "Anytime I open myself up to my gift, there's no telling what will happen."

"But for Lucy . . ."

"But for Lucy, I'll give it a go."

Anything for her.

He didn't need to say the words. I heard them anyway.

Tennyson wrapped the blanket around each palm and then closed his eyes, head down. Concentrating.

He sat that way for several minutes. Breath even. Shoulders tense.

Elvis wiggled closer, resting his jowly chin on Tennyson's thigh.

Silence hung, which meant I felt nothing from my brother. No sound, no emotion.

Eventually, Tennyson raised his head, mouth pulled down to one side.

"Well?"

"It's hard to say," he said, face puzzled. "I saw Grace running into Lucy's arms, both of them laughing."

"That's good—"

"Yes, but they were in a strange place. A dark hall . . . one of those wide central entryways full of pillars and dim light you find in a Renaissance palazzo."

"A future image?"

He nodded. "A possible future, at least. Not everything I see happens. The scene was contradictory. Lucy and Grace were so happy, but the place itself felt . . . ominous."

"Do you think Grace is okay?"

Tennyson met my eyes with his vivid blue ones. So haunted.

"Truthfully? I have no idea. But for Lucy's sake, let's say . . . sure." He turned his gaze out over the landscape. Pain and despair. "Anything for Lucy."

27

LUCY

PORTLAND, OREGON
FIVE YEARS EARLIER

Branwell!" I pushed open the front door and yelled into the apartment. "Could you lend me a hand?"

He looked up from the couch, textbook resting on his legs. Did the man ever *not* study? He ran his eyes over my person, specifically my right arm. Raised an eyebrow.

"Uh, Lucy. You do realize there is a garden gnome on your hand, don't you?"

I glanced down at the maniacally smiling gnome in his red hat currently surrounding my right arm up to my elbow.

"Yes. It's why I need you to lend me *your* hand."

Silence.

"I'm assuming you don't mean that literally." Branwell's lips twitched. "Care to elaborate?"

I shrugged. "Margie—you know, Margie? The sweet old lady across the street from me?—anyway, she was cleaning Phil's base"—I pointed a free finger at Phil the Gnome—"and lost her wedding ring inside. I decided to help get it out because my hand is smaller and less arthritic but, well, you can see how that turned out."

We both stared at Phil in his stylish green jacket. Phil maintained his mental-patient grin.

"I was hoping you had two free hands and some vaseline to help . . ." I mimed sliding Phil off my arm. "Margie only had denture cream."

More silence. Branwell's smile stretched wider.

"Vaseline? Don't you mean a hammer?" Branwell stood up. "I think Dante has one some—"

"No!" I covered poor Phil's sensitive ears with my left hand. "Shhh, Phil will hear you."

A long pause.

"Right. Let me find that vaseline."

Branwell's chuckle followed him out of the room.

28

LUCY

FLORENCE, ITALY
2016

The morning after spilling my biggest secret, I woke up with a conflicted heart.

On the one hand, Branwell now knew the thing he was Never Supposed to Know. He had been shocked and dismayed but, in true Branwell form, otherwise kind and understanding.

The eternal gentleman.

On the other hand, there was something truly cathartic in finally setting my darkest secret free. How many years? Six? Keeping my love tightly leashed, never letting on how much I cared. All gone and shattered now.

But, instead of being debilitatingly mortified, I felt oddly liberated. I refused to feel shame for loving a man as wonderful as Branwell. The situation was what it was.

I knew my revelation changed nothing. Tennyson would always be between us. Branwell would never betray his brother. I adored Branwell's fierce sense of loyalty. How could I be upset when it didn't work to my advantage?

So, I did what I always did when faced with situations like this . . . focused on what I could control (my own feelings and behavior) and let go of what I couldn't (Branwell and his relationship with Tennyson) and got on with my day.

There was a strong nugget of truth in Tennyson calling me his Pocket Sunshine. Always onward and upward. That was me.

Besides, all it took was a solitary thought of Grace to put everything with Branwell into perspective. Unrequited love was small potatoes when compared to a missing child. But, even there, Branwell had helped. He had taken Grace's blanket to Tennyson and asked his brother to look into Grace's future. Chiara had come upstairs with the news after Branwell returned, describing to me what Tennyson had seen.

I don't know how Tennyson saw into Grace's future. But the knowledge that Grace and I might be happily reunited filled me with such hope. And then this morning, Dante texted saying he still saw no sign of Grace.

All these reasons explained why I was feeling more upbeat. My Gracie was alive, out there and waiting to be found. I firmly believed it.

My mom called while I was prepping a few items for the day, wanting an update on the investigation. Jeff and Jen were delayed in Johannesburg due to bad weather but hoped to be back in Italy within the next eighteen hours.

Of course, two sisters and a brother texted me in quick succession after my mom hung up, all with questions I diligently answered.

No new leads.

Roberto is still a prime suspect and has disappeared.

No, I haven't remembered anything else.

Yes, I'm doing everything I can to find answers.

I then made my daily, check-in call to Inspector Paola. Her comments echoed those I had said to my family and then some.

"We have no new leads and are trying to locate Roberto." Her accented English crisp. "I was told you visited the museum staff yesterday with a bearded man, asking after Roberto. Is that true?"

Her tone clearly communicated her displeasure.

Great.

"Yes, ma'am," I replied. No way I was lying to the police.

"*Uffa.*" Paola made an exasperated noise. "That is unacceptable. You must allow us to do our job. I cannot have you, or others like this bearded man, interfering with our investigation. We have allowed you to remain out of police custody, but that can change if you continue to disturb our work. Do you understand?"

There was only one answer to that. "Of course," I said, meekly.

Naturally, as soon as I hung up with Paola, my mom and sisters went right back to texting, begging me to be more proactive in finding Grace.

Basically, I was stuck.

I had the police on one side, insisting I sit tight and let them do their job—AKA, rock. And my family on the other, demanding I *Do Something* to locate Grace—AKA, hard place.

Sheesh.

I finished getting ready and wandered into the great room, greeting Chiara with a smile. She had been busy overnight too, researching.

We were at the kitchen table, bent over her laptop looking at known dig sites associated with Jack Knight-Snow when Branwell walked into the apartment.

Sitting behind Chiara, I forgot to be circumspect in my appreciation of his fine physique, letting my eyes run over him from top to bottom. He was in perfect Branwell form—loose gray button-down shirt with embroidered edges, jeans, gloves, man bun and groomed beard. No bulges underneath his shirtsleeves, so his scrapes must have healed enough to no longer need bandages.

Branwell met my gaze, startled, clearly not expecting me to be so openly obvious. Though he did smile at my oversized, lounging t-shirt. (*Apathetics Unite! Or don't. Whatever.*)

I shot him a reassuring smile and ducked my head, my cheeks burning. I needed to behave. I couldn't do anything in front of his family that would give rise to difficult questions.

But behind their backs or when we were alone? Could we negotiate something of a truce, one where I could be a little less guarded?

"Alright. No news on Roberto," Chiara was saying. "He is a person of supreme interest for everyone right now. The museum people have clammed up, claiming they have no comment due to the on-going investigation. Which means I have no way of finding out who this mysterious woman-friend of Roberto's might be. That said, I do have a small lead. Come look at this, Bran." Chiara motioned with her fingers, oblivious to the tension between Branwell and myself.

Branwell sat down on the *other* side of his sister. As far away from me as possible, given the scenario.

A thread of hurt twinged through me, but I ruthlessly pushed it down. He had never been, nor ever would be, mine. Learning that I loved him changed nothing, in the end. If anything, it made him more wary. I got it.

"Here's a map of all the known archaeological dig sites." Chiara angled the computer screen toward him. "I managed to pull some family records of land we've owned in centuries past, but I'm still working to compile a more comprehensive list. That said, there are a couple sites that look promising, as they are close to D'Angelo lands and have been part of Roberto's excavations too."

Branwell examined the map, studiously *not* looking at me. "It's such a long shot to assume that anything related to Jack and Sofia might be a factor in Grace's disappearance."

"True. But it's the only lead that we can pursue right now." Chiara shrugged. "Gruncle Jack uncovered something that Roberto is obsessed with understanding. Roberto has implied that this *something* is supernatural in origin."

"And just the *assumption* of a connection between the object and

Gruncle Jack's bloodline could be enough for Roberto to act, particularly if he's obsessed with the occult and wacko," I said.

"True." Branwell grunted, studying the map some more. "In the end, retracing Roberto's steps and researching Jack and Sofia's connection might be the best approach. Particularly as we keep hitting roadblocks with trying to find Roberto himself."

"Read my mind, bro."

Branwell and Chiara spent a solid thirty minutes pulling each location up on Google Maps street view and discussed them.

I chewed on my bottom lip as they talked, replaying Inspector Paola's words from earlier. I was pretty sure she wouldn't take kindly to me showing up at Etruscan archaeological digs related to Roberto Moretti.

"You're being awfully quiet over there," Branwell said, leaning forward to look at me across the keys of Chiara's laptop. "You good with our ideas?"

I swallowed and nodded. "Yeah, I think you guys are spot on."

Branwell raised his eyebrows, prompting me to elaborate.

"Inspector Paola had some choice words this morning about our visit to the museum yesterday. She basically told me to stay out of her investigation—and by extension, you guys too—or she would lock me up."

"What? She can't do that." Branwell's brows drew down into a line of thunderclouds. He paused and then looked at his sister. "Wait . . . can she do that?"

"Yes and no." Chiara pursed her lips. "Italian law is similar to American law when it comes to investigating crimes. They can't lock up Lucy without probable cause. That said, if Paola gets a bee in her bonnet, she could find enough 'probable cause' to convince a magistrate."

"Do you know her? Inspector Paola?" I asked.

"Sorta. She's extremely competent but hard-nosed . . . basically, a woman in a macho man's world with a giant chip on her shoulder."

"Gotcha." Branwell sat back with a sigh. "She's essentially daring Lucy to knock that chip off."

"Yep," Chiara agreed.

"Sooooo . . ." I drew out the sound. "What do we do?"

"We be careful." Chiara tapped her fingers on the table. "As long as no one sees you guys, no one will know."

"Agreed," Branwell said.

"How though?" I still doubted. "I mean, these are important ancient sites."

"Eh, Italy is not like the States where archaeological sites are rare and, therefore, watched over. There are just too many. You honestly could dig a hole anywhere in this country and hit artifacts." Branwell motioned toward the sites highlighted on the satellite map. "All three of these places, for example, are in the middle of fields out in the countryside. There shouldn't be anybody nearby other than the occasional farmer, so they would be a good place to start. Like Chiara said, we'll just be careful."

That decided, we moved back to discussing logistics and saving GPS coordinates for the three locations. Branwell and I were going to do fieldwork. Literally.

Decisions made, we broke up our impromptu meeting.

I firmly believed in what Tennyson had seen. We were going to find Grace. She was okay and out there waiting for us.

I changed into jean shorts and a cream short-sleeved blouse that, for once, didn't say anything. I gave myself a mental pep talk as I pulled on hiking boots and grabbed my phone and purse. I had come to a decision to ask Branwell for one thing that I had always wanted. Just for today.

I met Branwell on the stairs, coming out of his apartment.

He jammed his hands into his pockets. Face impassive. Eyes wary.

"Hey you." I smiled, tentatively. "Is it going to be super uncomfortable hanging out together today?"

"It's a definite possibility." He edged back, even more cautious.

No sense dancing around the topic. I was a 'get all the awkward out into the open' kinda person. Sort of a personal mantra, actually.

I should put *that* on a t-shirt. (It would be a little long but I could acronym it: GATAOITO. Mmmm . . . or maybe not. Work in progress.)

Focus, Lucy.

I had an agenda. All I needed was Branwell's cooperation.

"Let's talk about this like adults," I said, hooking a hand through his arm, careful to make sure nothing of mine touched his bare skin. I pulled him down the stairs, talking quietly. "I know you're loyal to Tennyson, as you should be. I adore you with every last breath in my body. I do. But I also know that nothing can come of that adoration. That it's completely and utterly one-sided—"

"Lucy—" Branwell began with a sigh, obviously getting ready to launch into a spectacular speech that he had mentally prepared overnight.

I did know my man.

"Let me finish and then you can have your say, Bran."

I stopped at the bottom of the stairs and released his arm, turning to him. Hazel eyes tangled with mine. My heart lurched.

Yeah. I was going to pay big time for this later.

"Let me have today," I whispered. Pleading. "Only today and no more, I promise."

"Today for what?" His voice rumbled through me.

"To be myself and not have to guard every word out of my mouth. Obviously Grace is my priority, but I could use just a little bit of fun right now, too. Something to help keep my spirits up."

His shoulders sagged, looking utterly defeated. "Luce, of course I want to help, but—"

"I'm not asking you to join in." I quickly clarified. "Maybe just save the eye rolls for when my back is turned. Please?"

I clasped my hands to my chest, bounced on my tiptoes and batted my eyelashes.

"Pretty, pretty please?" More eyelash batting.

He looked away from me. Uncomfortable but somehow so boyishly endearing my whole heart flipped.

"Do you have any idea how cute you are?" The words slipped out of my mouth.

"What?" His head whipped back to me.

"You're cute." I grinned and took his arm again.

His brow furrowed. "I'm a giant bear of a broken man who can't even touch a doughnut without planning and mental preparation," he snorted. "Hardly anyone's definition of cute."

I bumped him with my shoulder. "Lucky for you, I have a thing for giant bear men with a penchant for doughnut planning. And for today and today only—you're mine. Agreed?"

Silence. And then finally, "Agreed. For today."

I beamed at him in reply. "Thank you. You won't regret this."

Well . . . hopefully not too much.

Branwell looked apprehensive as we walked to the car. It would be okay. I would take care of him, just as he had always taken care of me.

We settled into Dante's BMW, as the June temps had moved from merely scorchingly hot to hellishly brutal overnight, and Branwell's VW bus didn't have air conditioning.

I curled up in the passenger seat and proceeded with Operation Adore Branwell.

Gah. He was such a good sport. Seriously.

First, I connected my phone to the bluetooth and started up his playlist. (Title: Brantastic.)

"I have a playlist?" He edged us into traffic along the Arno.

"Yep. Absolutely. It's a compilation of your favorite songs."

A long pause.

"You know my favorite songs? You sure you don't have stalker tendencies?"

"Giant bear men. I have a thing, remember?"

The trip-hop groove of Portishead and Beth Gibbons' angsty alto filled the car.

"Glory Box?" Branwell gave a surprised chuckle, naming the track. "Man, I forgot how much I love this song."

Exactly. That was *entirely* the point of the playlist.

"Please tell me you have some Caro Emerald on there too?"

I laughed. "What do you think?"

His huge spreading grin about did my heart in. Honestly.

We then debated the pros and cons of European versus American music for a solid ten minutes.

"I'm just saying that Americans seem to have passed the baton of musical innovation—"

I stopped, watching as Branwell navigated a particularly hairy stretch of traffic, finally merging onto the *autostrada* heading south.

"Thanks." He shot me a glance.

I shrugged. "No prob."

Silence.

"You know me so well," he said.

Truth there. He didn't like talking when he hit bad traffic.

"So where was I?" I asked. "That's right, American musical sensibilities . . ."

We talked through music, skimmed over the current political landscape—American *and* European, because *ugh*—and were hotly debating which Bourne movie was the best when we pulled up to the first excavation site.

Glancing down the hill toward a temporary shade tent, I noted a few grad students scraping away in the sweltering heat, working on a wall of stones.

Branwell and I exchanged a look as he put the car into park. Both of us obviously thinking the same thing—Paola couldn't know I had been here. My red hair and freckles were a little too memorable.

"Stay in the car and duck down low," he said. "If they don't see you, I don't think they'll connect us. Besides, Paola didn't personally tell *me* to stay away from Grace's investigation."

I nodded and reclined my seat back. Of course, that didn't stop me from peeking as Branwell approached the wary grad students. He chatted with them, smiling, but their body language remained cautious. Clearly, we weren't the first people to come around asking questions.

Branwell tugged off his glove and gingerly touched a couple of the stones as he walked around.

After a few minutes, he waved goodbye to the group and walked back up the hill. He shook his head as he climbed into the car.

"Nothing on the surface," he said, putting the car in gear, "and it's not worth the risk to go looking further."

"Next site?"

"Yep."

I pulled out some Haribo sour gummy bears as we drove, plopping the bag down on the console between us. Branwell raised an eyebrow at them.

"Don't worry," I assured him. "I snipped each bear to change the sound and pulled out all the green ones." I rattled a separate bag of strictly green gummy bears.

"Thank you." Branwell grinned, tossing a pink bear into his mouth.

He promptly froze and then burst out laughing.

Oh! That laugh.

Deep, rumbling, entirely soul melting.

"Did I mention they're now sour *punny* bears?" I asked.

He shook his head, still grinning. Popped another bear in his mouth, cocking his head to listen to the sounds I knew only he could hear.

He laughed again.

"Oh, gosh," he gasped, leaning forward. "That's so bad. 'What was Forrest Gump's email password?'"

I knew the answer. Naturally.

"1forrest1," I giggled.

Giving another gruff laugh, Branwell stared at the bag. "Every single one?"

"Every single one, baby. Hours of sour *pun*ishment."

Chuckling, Branwell ate another one. Paused, listening. And then laughed again.

"'Atheism is a non-prophet organization.' Honestly, how did you come up with all these?" He was clearly impressed.

"Google helped." I shrugged.

We settled back into our discussion of possible Star Wars sequels.

The whole time, part of my brain squealed like a fan girl. How many years had I dreamed about doing something like this?

Prepping food for Branwell, storing notes with each careful alteration. Discussing all our favorite topics without having to dampen my enthusiasm for his answers. Allowing years of careful behavior and emotional wall building to float free.

After the horror of the situation with Grace, my heart had needed this . . . a little bit of light in the darkness. Of course, Branwell's good natured willingness to play along just made me love him more.

We drove to the next site which was thankfully empty of people. But after an hour of wandering with Branwell listening, we found nothing helpful.

"This hasn't been too bad, has it?" I waved a hand between us as we walked back to the car, both hot and melting in the humid heat.

"Hanging out?"

"Yeah." I skipped ahead of him. "I'm not being too stalkerish, creepy weird?"

He opened the passenger door, fixing me with that typical Branwell look—one part indulgence, two parts patience.

"No." He motioned me into the car. "I'm enjoying it."

I beamed at him, leaning on the open car door. "Oh good. 'Cause I've been dying to go over some composites I made." I gestured toward my purse on the car seat.

"Composites?"

"Yeah, of our kids. I merged our faces together in Photoshop, so we know what they'd look like. And then, I figured we could stick with this whole Victorian artist naming thing you guys have going—what with Tennyson, Branwell, Dante. Our son could be Whitman and our daughter, Bronte or maybe Emerson. But I was wondering how you felt about Dickens as a name too? I mean, it seems problematic, not the least because it rhymes with 'chickens'—"

"*Lucy*—"

"Have I told you what a great Ricky Riccardo impression you do? Though you need to add more of a Latin accent when you say it—*Loosee!*"

"Oh my word, Luce, I-I—"

"I'm kidding, Branwell." I patted his arm, giggling. "Totally kidding about the kids."

Well, at least about the face Photoshopping thing. Dickens, on the other hand, had actually been a legitimate question, but whatever—

Poor guy. His shoulders sagged in relief.

I tried not to be offended.

"Ha-ha, very funny." He shook his head. A little tired and defeated. Again, channeling Desi Arnaz.

He gestured with his chin.

I climbed into the car, my eyes shooting cartoon hearts at Branwell's shoulders as he rounded the hood.

How I loved this man.

We were five hours into our impromptu tour of obscure Etruscan archaeological sites when we reached the last one.

We pulled past the site and parked in a small area of packed dirt down the road, far enough away to not call attention to our intentions. Getting out of the car, I lifted a hand to shade my eyes, surveying the scenery. Classic Tuscany with rolling hills, cypress trees growing in stately lines, vineyards and olive orchards melting into the distance. All wrapped in steamy, smoke-like humidity that had my shirt instantly sticking to my stomach.

Walking back down the road, the site itself boasted a series of overgrown, low stone walls, all situated in the middle of a loosely gated, uncultivated field surrounded by forest. The ruins encroached on the trees, fighting a silent battle with each other that the forest would eventually win.

Not another person in sight.

We slid through the gate and traipsed across the wild grasses and occasional wildflower until reaching the beginning of the stone walls. The summer heat scorched my lungs with each breath—the air so muggy and heavy you could practically chew it. I deeply regretted wearing hiking shoes instead of sandals.

If I was hot, Branwell must be dying. Long sleeves, gloves and boots? In this heat?

"So . . . now what?" I asked, swiping at the sweat dripping off my chin.

"I still have a trick up my sleeve."

"Does this trick involve an air conditioner and bucket of ice?" I fanned my face.

Chuckling, Branwell bent and unlaced one booted foot, tugging it off. His sock followed, leaving Branwell with one bare foot which he rested on his sock, careful not to touch anything else.

Well, that would help somewhat with heat dispersion. Would his shirt follow next? Granted, Branwell shedding clothing would only cause *me* to overheat more quickly.

I swallowed, trying (unsuccessfully) to not stare at his foot. Long toes with neatly trimmed nails. Tendons flashing in and out as he flexed his arch.

Huh. Never would have guessed I had a foot fetish but apparently I did.

"May I?" He motioned me closer and then placed a gloved hand on my shoulder, steadying his balance.

Even through his glove and the hot summer sun, the touch of his hand branded. It was surely more mental than actual—the electrical hum of attraction and connection. But still . . .

I looked down at his bare foot again.

Not helping.

Pull yourself together, Lucy.

"So . . . ?"

"I'm going to walk," Branwell answered my unspoken question. "Dirt retains a lot of sound, as it's constantly shifting and changing. I'll hold on to you for balance in case I have to lift my foot suddenly to stop an unwanted sound—"

"Or Chucky attack?"

"Possibly, though Chucky usually gravitates toward shiny things."

"True. Let's avoid those."

"Exactly. Just don't die."

I laughed.

Carefully, Branwell began walking the perimeter of the walls, one hand resting casually on my shoulder. He would pause occasionally, listening to conversations beyond the hum of cicadas, the distant rumble of farm equipment and the occasional chirping bird.

It was soothing, being here with him. Like all my life had been out of alignment, but with Branwell at my side, everything suddenly snapped into place.

When it all broke apart again . . . crap, it was gonna hurt.

We had walked through about a third of the site when Branwell went from casually listening to full alert. He froze in place with his head tilted, face a mask of concentration. He lifted his foot and set it down again. Starting the sound over?

"Roberto," he said. "I got Roberto."

His hand moved up my shoulder to rest on the back of my neck, his leather glove smooth against my skin. I stood still, waiting.

Branwell finished listening and lifted his foot.

"Sorry, I went digging a bit farther there."

"So Roberto?" I prompted.

"Yeah. Not too much. He and that mystery woman from his office were debating if this site could have been a shrine. The woman wasn't sure. She said it was more likely a ritual site for the oracle, Tages. But Roberto insisted it had to be a shrine to Hinthial because Lord Knight's research was thorough on the topic—"

"Hinthial again."

"No coincidence that Hinthial guarded the treasure your Gruncle Jack was looking for."

I studied the scattered remnants of walls, trying to imagine this place nearly three thousand years ago.

"So this would have been a shrine? A place of worship and pilgrimage for this Hinthial?"

"Possibly." Branwell shook his head. "Most interesting, at the end of the conversation, the woman asked if this was the place where 'it' was excavated."

"It?"

"Yep."

"Wow." I chewed my lip. "Could 'it' be related to the treasure Gruncle Jack sought?"

"Or, more likely, the treasure itself?"

29

BRANWELL

Roberto and the unknown woman's voice lingered in my mind.

"Is this the place where it was excavated, do you think?" she asked.

"Hard to say. Lord Knight was cagey about exactly which site it came from."

"The tomb here is large enough, but I find the inscriptions about Tages to be intriguing. They imply that this site was dedicated to him, not Hinthial. But why would it come from a site associated with Tages?"

"Agreed—"

What *thing* were they referring to? Was it the treasure? Or something entirely else?

"Nothing we've read or researched has definitively said Gruncle Jack actually *found* Hinthial's treasure." Lucy wiped sweat off her forehead, her hair wildly curly in the Tuscan humidity.

"True, but Roberto obviously thinks he did." I shook my head.

"Didn't one of the myths say Jack *had* found the treasure but released a malevolent force that eventually killed him?"

"Yes."

"Man, I hear the phrase 'malevolent force' and immediately think of Chucky."

She shuddered. "I don't like Chucky."

I shifted my weight, still balancing on one foot. "I wish I could say all this had something to do with Grace, but until we talk to Roberto, it's all guesswork."

"True. That said, it's almost too much of a coincidence to *not* have something to do with her." Lucy studied me, concern in her eyes. "Aren't you dying from the heat? You're kinda flushed."

The Tuscan sun punished my back. I was a lobster being steamed alive. "We could both use some water."

We headed back toward my shoe, me keeping a hand on Lucy.

The trees surrounding the excavation site drooped in the sweltering warmth. It *was* hot. Though it wasn't all due to the summer sun.

Lucy's emotions threaded around me, through me, each and every time she spoke.

Happiness. Love.

Desire.

My stomach was in knots. Heart pounding, my own blood a fierce tattoo in my ears.

How many times in the past several hours had I almost caved? Hauled her against me and confessed my heart through long, drugging kisses?

She would welcome it.

That was the worst part. Or was it the best?

I hadn't quite decided yet.

Lucy *wanted* me close.

Over and over, I felt it bubble out of her.

That sharp stab of heat and longing when she looked at my bare foot. A stronger stab when I placed my hand on her shoulder.

Again and again, I brutally pushed the thoughts aside. Not gonna happen.

I knew my decision. Lucy knew my decision.

But . . . some insidious voice kept whispering . . . what if?

What if I followed her example and gave in? Just for a day? A few hours even?

Kissed her. Cherished her. Treated her like my own. Let my love for her shine as strongly as hers did for me?

Just the thought . . .

I sucked in a breath. Painful and searing over the raw lump in my throat.

We reached my sock and shoe, but before I could kneel to put them on, she pressed a hand against my chest. "Your heart is beating way too fast. You're going to hurt it if you keep this up."

Hah. That was funny.

"You sure you're okay, Branwell?" Concern and worry.

"I'll be fine. Let me put on my shoes. Would you mind getting us some water and something sugary from the car?"

I crouched and pulled my shoe and sock back on, keeping an eye on Lucy as she crossed the field and disappeared around the trees shading the car.

Sour punny bears were my new favorite thing in the world, I had decided. Hearing Lucy's breathy voice with each bear, giggling sometimes when she found a pun extra funny—for example, *It's hard to explain puns to kleptomaniacs because they always take things literally.*

My shoe on, I stood up, waiting for Lucy to come back. Seeking some relief from the sun, I moved into the shade of the surrounding trees.

Still no Lucy.

Concerned, I stepped into the field to go find her, when the low hum of a motor announced an approaching vehicle.

Instantly, I pulled back into the forest. It was probably only a tourist out for a country drive, but why tempt fate?

Five seconds later, a blue and white striped sedan slowly drove past, *Polizia* emblazoned on its side.

A police car.

The sedan dipped below the horizon, passing out of my view.

Crap.

Where was Lucy?

Crap. Crap.

I hesitated for a few minutes, unsure what to do. Had the police seen her? Were they now tracking us? Or was this just coincidence?

I waited another second and then took a couple steps into the open, intent on finding Lucy. But the police sedan came up the road again, forcing me to retreat back into the forest.

This time, the police car stopped. Two officers and a plain clothes investigator got out. They pointed at the field, commenting on something. I strained, trying to hear what they were saying, but it was all garbled. From their expansive gestures, they were obviously discussing something about the site.

My heart pounded, worried for Lucy, wondering where she had gone.

After what felt like an eternity, the police officers got back into their car and drove off. I sat in the shade of the trees, waiting to see if they would return. Where was my girl?

Silence.

Judging it safe, I took a few steps out of the trees, only to practically run into Lucy, who had been skirting down the edge of the forest toward me, water and gummy bears in one hand, a stick in the other.

Without thinking, I snatched her into a tight hug. So relieved she was all right.

"You okay?" I asked, pulling away, surveying her up and down.

"Yeah," she nodded, "though that was close. I ducked into the forest right as they pulled up."

"I wish I could have heard them."

Lucy's eyes lit up with mischief. "Well, this is your lucky day, Mr. D'Angelo. I was close enough to hear them, but of course they were speaking in rapid-fire Italian, so I couldn't understand but . . ."

Her voice drifted off as she lifted the stick, allowing me to see that all secondary branches had been broken off it.

I smiled broadly. "Have I told you today what an absolute genius you are?"

Lucy laughed, breathy and carefree.

I pulled off a glove and reached for the stick. Voices in Italian instantly assaulted me.

" . . . *think this is the place then? The site that Moretti was supposedly researching?*"

"*Barbara Bruno seemed to think so.*"

"*No one has been here in ages.*"

A grunt of agreement.

"*What about that BMW down the road? Why is it parked here?*"

"*Who knows? Tourists, probably. There's a winery through the field. The car certainly doesn't belong to Roberto Moretti. He doesn't have that kind of money.*"

Another grunt.

"*What are the possibilities of getting a canine unit out here to sniff around?*"

"*Slim to none, I would guess. The paperwork would take weeks.*"

"*Even given all the attention this case has been getting? The press is going crazy over this little girl missing.*"

"*I can talk to Paola about putting in a requisition, but—*"

The conversation abruptly ended. Frustrated, I pushed with my gift, trying to see if I could hear more of it. Nothing.

Drat.

Lucy looked at me, a question in her eyes.

"Nothing too helpful." I recapped the conversation for her.

Lucy pursed her lips, thinking, handing me a full water bottle. I drank eagerly. The humidity and heat were punishing.

Lucy suddenly canted her head to the side, looking past me.

"Is that an excavated . . . something . . . back there?" She pointed to a small low-fenced area a bit farther into the trees.

Sure enough. On closer inspection, we found a trench about five feet deep and ten feet long. The far end of the channel disappeared under a stone overhang. Sun peeked through the trees overhead, dappling the ground.

I looked at Lucy. We both shrugged.

I stepped over the small fence—meant to keep tourists from accidentally falling in—and dropped into the trench. The sides were lined with ancient stone and the occasional flagstone peeked out from underneath my feet.

"What is this place?" Lucy asked from above me.

"My educated guess? An Etruscan tomb."

"You be careful down there."

I looked back at her. She stood at the edge of the fence, rimmed in yellow sunlight. That was always how I remembered Lucy.

Golden. The color of laughter and cheer and hope.

My hungry eyes drank her in. She had pulled her hair into a loose bun, but rebellious curls escaped to frame her jaw and graze her neck. That curvy body with a waist that instinct told me would fit my hand perfectly, all atop denim shorts and long bare legs, summer tanned. Well, as much as Lucy's freckled skin could tan.

And she loved me.

This intelligent, gorgeous, fiery, spunky, sweet, amazing creature loved *me*.

"Just don't die," she repeated, shooting me a wink.

I nodded and turned away before she saw adoration shining from my eyes.

Even if I managed to survive the next couple days without doing something impossibly stupid, how was I going to move past her? I had already spent six years trying to move on and that was *without* knowing she loved me.

But now, knowing that she did. That she wanted *us* as much as I did . . .

How could I hurt *her*?

But being with her would hurt Tennyson even more.

How could I hurt *him*?

Crap. This was such a mess and no matter what decision I made, I would end up being a Grade-A jerk to one of them.

I shook my head, pushing aside thoughts of Lucy. If I loved her at all, I would find Grace.

I pulled off my right hand glove and started gently touching things.

The clink of trowels and shovels.

Two students gossiping about two other undergraduates who were now an item.

Archaeologists asking questions about artifact dating and stone work.

I worked my way down the trench. Occasionally, I would hear Roberto's voice replying to a student question. Nothing out of the ordinary.

I touched grooves along one stone. A familiar man's voice jolted through me, speaking in accented Italian.

"What have you found, lads? More stone?"

Jack. Gotcha.

He *had* been here.

I moved down the trench, searching more diligently, moving back into time.

Over and over, I heard Jack's voice. Usually in his competent Italian but occasionally in English too. All just day-to-day stuff about the excavation.

Until I hit the series of stones leading into a small underground space at the far end of the trench.

". . . sure it is quite safe down here?" Sofia's voice. Teasing. Interested.

"Of course. The sides are not too deep, as you can see." Jack.

"It's fascinating. Will you chisel something away for me?"

Male laughter. "Considering you hinted yesterday for a piece of the moon, a mere bit of rock should pose no problem."

The sound of chisel against stone. The smell of dust and earth. Musty things long forgotten.

"Grazie. I shall treasure it," Sofia said. "The entire countryside is aflutter with your findings here, my lord."

"Jack, Lady Sofia. Please. I believe it is high time you called me Jack."

A fleeting sense of a woman dressed in sprigged muslin dress with a red velvet spencer, carefully lifting her skirts out of the dust.

"Jack then." A pause. "So you were telling me about the bronze box you uncovered—"

"The praenestine cista*?"*

"Is that what it is called?"

"Yes, that was the Roman name for them."

"Your manservant stated that you believe the contents of the praenestine cista *to be cursed?"*

A brief glimpse of shoulders shrugging. "It is difficult to say with any certainty. When dealing with these ancient artifacts, they are all cursed or blessed in some way. Oftentimes, such inscriptions were simply meant to deter thieves."

"But the inscription on it?"

"There is hardly a primer for ancient Etruscan, so I am finding it difficult to decipher the inscription with any accuracy—something about a shadow and protection or stealing. But it is anyone's guess if it was meant as a warning or a blessing."

"Perhaps. But the villagers whisper of darker things. Some say the bronze box isn't a house for a relic but, instead, a cage for a phantom. Are you concerned that you will set something free that should never have been?"

A scoffing noise. "Superstitious rumors, my lady, nothing more."

"No. I will not have you dismiss such superstition, my lord—"

"Jack."

A sigh. "Jack. As a D'Angelo, I know all too well the truth of rumor."

A pause.

"How fares your brother, then?" Jack asked. Hesitant. As if stirring a hornet's nest to life.

"Lorenzo is . . . not well. The visions are . . . difficult. My mother prays for him throughout most of the day, rocking with her rosary."

Another pause.

"What does your brother see?"

"He does not say. We do not ask. In the past, he has talked of metal machines stalking the land like smoking dragons. Wars fought between iron birds that spit fire and soldiers wearing masks like grasshoppers."

"Heavens. Visions of biblical proportions."

"Indeed. My mother does not like to hear her son talk of the end of days." A beat. "We have no hope of his recovery, only of his comfort. Laudanum allows him to sleep, at least."

The sound of birdsong. The distant bong of church bells.

"In light of your brother's poor health, will you reconsider my offer? Can your uncle not act as your guardian?" Jack asked.

"I have done nothing but consider your offer since our last encounter. My uncle has indicated that he would support our union."

"And you, Lady Sofia? Would you do me the honor of being my wife?"

"Yes." Softly. Quietly. "I do believe I would, Jack."

Their voices faded away. I sucked in a long breath.

Atta boy, Jack.

At least someone had been lucky in love.

BRANWELL

FLORENCE, ITALY
2016

"Do you think Jack and Sofia married?" Lucy asked. "Nothing I've ever read indicates that Gruncle Jack married."

We were in the car, driving back to Florence, and I had just caught her up to date on everything I had heard.

"True, but if he married in Italy and died shortly thereafter, the news may not have ever made it back to England. That said, the D'Angelo family records should list who Sofia married, so we'll get an answer."

Lucy sat back, staring out the window at the tile rooftops and sunflower fields whizzing past. Her frizzy curls fluttered in the blessedly cold AC.

"Do you think you and I are related?" She gestured between us with a green gummy bear. "If my uncle married your aunt . . . what would that make us?"

"Connected through marriage around two hundred years ago. There would be no blood tie."

"Whew. That could have been awkward. I was thinking I would have to start calling you *Cuz.*" She popped the bear in her mouth, but I still caught her teasing smile.

We arrived back in Florence to an empty palazzo, everyone else out for the evening.

I let us into my mom and Chiara's apartment, the evening sun pouring light through the tall windows along one side of the great room. The air conditioning bathed us both in welcome cold air.

Lucy wandered over to the couch, massaging her scalp while dropping her purse and shedding her shoes. She sank into the couch and raised her head, noting my stare. She smiled and patted the cushion next to her, a not-so-subtle invitation.

Why did being with Lucy have to feel *so* normal? So natural?

I toed off my own shoes and sank beside her. So close that the warmth of her body washed over me.

Lucy rested her head against the back of the couch, inches from my bicep. "Why do I feel like we keep finding more questions than answers?"

"Because we do," I answered her.

"True."

Her emotions roiled through me. Worry for Grace tempered by Lucy's own native optimism. Happiness because I was near. I sensed that she wanted to curl into my side, lay her head on my shoulder. But, controlling the impulse, she merely scooted a tiny bit closer.

How was it possible for me to be even more attuned to her in just the past twenty-four hours? How was I ever going to watch her walk back out of my life?

But . . . I had no other choice.

I could do this. I could be her friend and somehow, someway force myself *not* to reciprocate.

I pulled my phone out of my pocket and texted Chiara with gloved fingers, intent on distracting myself. I caught my sister up to date about what I had heard and asked if she could find any info about Sofia's marriage to Jack.

Chiara texted back within two minutes.

> *Jack and Sofia, eh? That would be a turn of events. I'm on it.*

Thanks, sis.

> *Also, heard from the police. It's a no-go getting a finger on the stuff taken from Grace's bedroom and not just because Inspector Paola's a control freak. Turns out, the Little Mermaid music box was given to Grace by Roberto. He apparently showed an interest in her. People say he was like a doting uncle, but that all changes once the kid goes missing. Still no sign of him. The police put out a warrant for his arrest this afternoon.*

My heart sank.

Damn Roberto. What had the man done? Where was Grace?

Chiara continued texting.

> *I found out that the police have been questioning Cat Lady again, but she doesn't seem to know anything more. I also got a call from Inspector Paola herself. She made it very clear that we need to back off and let her do her job. She's shutting us down. No more American hero crap.*

She said that?

> *Her exact words.*

I clenched my jaw, swallowing back the acid taste of frustration. Lucy leaned in, pressing her cheek against my arm. I angled my phone so she could read Chiara's texts.

Lucy sat back with a huff, irritated. "Stupid Inspector Paola. A little girl is *missing*. The prime suspect has vanished. It's not rocket science to put two-and-two together here."

"If only they could locate Roberto."

"Yeah. Or better yet, let us *help* find him. He is clearly a weirdo involved in some dangerous occult stuff, and it's not a stretch to think he has dragged Grace into his woo-woo world. Not to mention Chucky."

I stared at my phone, tilting it, trying to see anything shadowy in its shiny surface.

"Chucky *is* infecting things somehow. I still am not quite sure how he ended up in the pool yesterday."

"You said you thought it was the medal?"

"Yeah, because it was shiny and had been given to you by Roberto and Cat Lady."

"Well, Paola may have shut us down in some ways, but she can't control this. Let's test the medal for Chucky."

With a determined lift of her chin, Lucy uncurled from the couch and disappeared down the hallway, returning a moment later with the Saint Christopher medal.

She held it out to me, flat and sparkly against the palm of her hand.

Tentatively, I set my phone down on the coffee table and pulled off a glove. I paused and then rested a single fingertip against the medal.

Roses. Musty things—

I snatched my hand back.

"Chucky?" Lucy asked, setting the medal down on the coffee table beside my phone.

"Yeah," I sighed, pulling my glove back on. "It's like everything I come into contact with suddenly has Chucky in it. I'm a demon-generating Typhoid Mary."

"So you think you're the infectious agent?" She sat down next to me again. "You're the only one who can *interact* with Chucky, but it doesn't necessarily follow that you're the one transferring the Chucky infection. Correlation isn't causation and all that."

I sat back, tapping my fingers against my leg. "Alright. I'll buy that."

"The infectious agent is just as likely to be Roberto, to be honest. Your family is cursed, so it's possible that other bloodlines are cursed, too. My Gruncle Jack decides to go excavating some treasure that the ancient Etruscans felt compelled to hide. He mysteriously disappears."

"And then two hundred years later, Roberto develops a similar obsession and, *bam*, Gruncle Jack's niece disappears. Then Roberto himself disappears."

"Exactly."

"So where is Chucky in all of this?"

Lucy shrugged. "Roberto gave me the medal. Well, Cat Lady, technically but Roberto handled it too. And we're fairly confident that your phone became Chucky-infected while in Roberto's office."

"True, but again, correlation isn't causation."

She chewed on her cheek. "All we know about Chucky is that he likes to inhabit shiny things, correct?"

"Correct."

"And there's no consensus on the size or shape or even the medium of these shiny objects?" Lucy twisted her lips, thinking.

"Again, correct. He first attacked me at the age of thirteen out of a silver teapot."

"A family heirloom you said?"

"Yeah."

Lucy paused, eyes wide as if something just occurred to her. "Any chance that heirloom could have been in the family around 1820?"

A thrill chased my spine. I stared into Lucy's intense blue eyes. Mischievous curls bounced around her face.

"You are incredibly smart, you know that?" I grinned at her. "The teapot dates from the late eighteenth century."

"So it's something Sofia D'Angelo might have used?"

"Extremely likely, particularly if someone important came calling—"

"Like a British nobleman Sofia had betrothed herself too?"

"Precisely." I shook my head, pieces of the puzzle slotting into place. "That's a little too much coincidence to be entirely chance, I think."

Lucy sat back, a smug-satisfied look on her face. "Over the years, there have been other objects with Chucky?"

"Yeah, he's been in small and large things—metal, plastic and glass. The only thing he doesn't inhabit are objects with a matte surface. In fact, the more shiny something is, the more likely it is to house Chucky. But I can't see an obvious connection to Gruncle Jack or Sofia D'Angelo with other past Chucky-infested objects."

Lucy stared at my phone on the table and then surveyed the room.

"Without knowing how Chucky infects things, it's hard to trace the connection. Are you up for a little experimentation?" she asked. "Let's see if we can't deduce how Chucky contaminates things."

"I'm game."

"I'll start by removing this from the equation." Lucy picked up the medal and dropped it inside her purse. "From there, we know your phone became infected somehow, most likely while you were in Roberto's office."

She snagged a towel from the kitchen and wrapped up my phone without touching it.

"Just as a control, will you touch the towel?" She angled the little bundle toward me. "We're confident it doesn't work on fabrics and things that aren't shiny—"

"Because I've been holding my phone all day with my gloves without any problem?"

"Exactly."

I peeled off my right hand glove again and touched the towel.

The thrum of factory machines. Someone calling in Chinese.

Nothing else.

Lucy nodded in confirmation.

"Now, just to be sure again, would you mind touching the phone with your bare finger?"

She carefully unfolded my phone and stretched it out to me. I placed a single finger on its glossy surface.

Instantly, it swamped me.

The smell of musty roses and things long dead—

I snatched my hand away before the mist could engulf it.

"I take that as a 'Yes'?"

I bobbed my head.

Lucy wrapped up the phone again, placing it on the large central island in the kitchen. She then proceeded to walk through the room grabbing shiny items. An opaque glass vase. A metal cake pan. A spoon. A shiny plastic bowl.

She surveyed the items on the counter. And then frowned.

"The marble is shiny too." She swept a hand over my mom's gorgeous counter top. "Let me fix that.

Five minutes later, the entire counter was covered in bath towels, Lucy's collection of random items on top of them. Me on one side of the counter, Lucy on the opposite.

"Would you mind?" She pointed a finger, indicating I should touch everything.

I did, gently pressing a bare finger to each object.

Nothing.

Well, nothing out of the ordinary.

"Okay. Let's do it one more time, just to make sure that you're not the infectious agent. Like the first touch was priming the items somehow."

I touched everything again. And then did it a third time.

No Chucky.

"Alright," Lucy said, "I'm willing to say that you, in and of yourself, are not the infectious agent. So let's bring out the phone."

Tentatively, she unwrapped my phone.

"If Chucky acts like other infectious agents, then touch would be the method of transfer."

"I agree."

Gingerly, Lucy touched the surface of the phone to the opaque vase. She wrapped the phone again and motioned for me to touch the vase.

Carefully, I did.

Machines whirring. Voices chattering in French.

Nothing came at me.

Lucy popped a hand on her hip.

"That seemed straight forward," she said. "But apparently, it's more than touch. Let's try again, just to make sure."

We repeated the process with the vase, touching it to my phone.

Nothing.

"Weird. Let's try the spoon."

Lucy unwrapped the phone again and reached over the plastic bowl to touch the phone to the glossy serving spoon.

"Try that."

Feeling more confident, I touched the spoon for the fourth time, expecting nothing more than the clanking of large machinery.

Death. Roses. Fear. Something reaching for me—

I snatched my hand away, staggering back.

Lucy's eyes widened as she hissed in a breath. "Chucky?"

"Bingo."

Lucy frowned, studying the spoon.

"Obviously, we're missing something here," she said. "But he's still not in the vase?"

More hesitantly, I touched the vase again.

Nothing.

"Weird."

Curious, I touched the cake pan.

Nothing.

I touched the plastic bowl.

Roses. Hunger—

I darted back.

"Crap. He's in the bowl now." I wiped my finger on my jeans.

Lucy and I stared at the items. Totally puzzled.

"So . . . touch isn't necessary because until the phone got near the bowl, it wasn't infected."

"Agreed. It's something else."

"But what? A specific series of touches? Like you have to touch an infected object and then touch something shiny and then touch the object again—"

"I haven't done that here."

"Mmmm." Lucy bit her lip.

We both stared.

"So let's continue to assume there is some logic to this," I finally said. "Everything infected is glossy. That's the only common denominator—the shinier something is, the more likely Chucky is to inhabit it."

Lucy thought for a moment.

"So what are the unique properties of glossy things?" she asked.

"Things don't stick to them well."

"They bounce light."

"Yes. They're reflective." I paused. The simplicity of the answer thrumming through me. "That's it! They're reflective. Like tiny mirrors."

I touched the vase.

Still no Chucky.

"This vase is shiny, but not super shiny like the spoon. It's not quite mirror-like. But take my phone, Luce, and angle the vase until you can see the reflection of the phone in it."

"You're a bit of a genius, Bran."

Lucy snatched up my phone and rotated the vase, angling it this way and that until we both clearly saw the reflection of the glossy phone in the shiny glaze of the vase.

"Moment of truth."

I lifted my finger above the vase and then gently touched it.

Darkness. The smell of roses. A voice rising—

I yanked my hand away, grinning.

"I think we have it. Reflection might be the method of infectious transfer."

"And once something is infected, can it transfer the infection via reflection to something else?" Lucy asked.

"There's only one way to find out."

I touched the cake pan again.

No Chucky.

I motioned for Lucy to pick up the infected spoon.

She lifted it and angled it over the cake pan, again maneuvering both until we clearly saw the reflection of the spoon in the cake pan.

She set it back down, gesturing for me to touch it.

I placed a finger on the edge of the pan.

It swamped me quickly. Fast. Hard.

Death. Roses. Fear. Mist coming.

"Yay! I found it!" A little girl's voice. Distant. Echoey.

Grace!

I snatched my hand away, my heart instantly clawing its way out of my chest.

"What?" Lucy reached for my hand across the island.

Panicked, I shook my head, touching the metal pan again.

This time, there was no hesitation.

Mist and a dark claw surged out of the pan.

Grace screamed.

31

BRANWELL

Grace's scream ricocheted through my mind.

Wait . . . or was it a squeal?

"Dammit." I jerked away, staring at the back of my hand, scratched but not bloody yet.

"What's up? What happened?" Lucy came around the island, grabbing my left elbow.

"Grace," I whispered. "I heard Grace. It could only have been her voice."

"Grace?!!" Lucy shrieked, staring around the apartment and then coming back to the cake pan. "How?"

"I don't know. Her voice was wrapped up in the sensation of Chucky somehow."

I grabbed dish towels out of a drawer in the island.

"Protection. Smart." Lucy came around and helped me wrap the towels around my arm, over my shirt, until I had a solid level of protection extending from my shoulder to my fingertips, leaving only a strip of my pinkie finger exposed.

It would have to do for now. I faced the cake pan. Lucy watched on, intent.

In any other situation, I would have laughed at this scene. Two normally sane adults, one swathed mummy-like in towels, staring down a helpless cake pan like it housed a bomb.

But a little girl was lost, and this was the first definitive evidence we had of her.

"Thank you." Lucy shot me a watery smile. Fear. Hope. Worry. "Your willingness to face Chucky's claws to help Grace . . . it means a lot."

I managed a wan smile of my own, though it probably came off as more of a grimace.

How long would I be able to hang on once Chucky came at me?

Gingerly, I placed a finger on the pan.

Roses. Damp. Dust. Hunger.

Need.

Darkness rushing toward me.

"Grace!" I yelled. "Can you hear me, Grace?"

I had never tried to talk *into* something before, but if Chucky and sound could come out for me, maybe sound could go in, too.

"Gracie!" Lucy chimed in. "Gracie Pie, it's Aunt Lucy. Can you hear me?"

Chucky surged, clawing his way through the towels. Darkness engulfed my arm.

Roses. Death.

A high pitched giggle.

"It's so pretty!" Grace laughed.

Chucky's talons dug deeper, pricking me.

I jerked my hand away.

Chucky had shredded the towels but had only lightly scraped my skin in places.

What. Was. Up?!

Lucy panted, eyes glistening, staring at me.

"Well? What did you hear? Anything?" She licked her lips.

I shook my head. Baffled. "I honestly can't say, Luce. I heard Grace . . . laugh. Like she was super excited about something. She said, 'It's so pretty!' She didn't sound distressed, and she clearly didn't reply to us. It makes no sense."

Lucy's bottom lip trembled and she turned away, swiping at her cheeks.

"I'm so sorry, Luce." My shoulders sagged. "I wish I knew what was up. Let me think about it for a moment."

She waved a hand at me. "I-It's okay. It's not your fault. I just wish I knew where Grace was." Sorrow. Fear.

Lucy turned away and walked over to the windows, staring out at the setting sun. She wrapped her hands around her upper arms, as if to shield herself.

I pulled the shredded towels off my arm and grabbed my glove, pulling it on.

"Help me talk this through, Lucy. Grace didn't seem like she was in trouble. She sounded excited."

Lucy sniffed but didn't turn back to me. "You're thinking you're not hearing her real time?"

Loved my smart girl. "Exactly. I've touched the cake pan several times before and haven't heard Grace. So for many obvious reasons, least of which being that Grace has never been in this apartment, the cake pan isn't directly connected to her. The fact I'm hearing her *now* indicates that perhaps I'm picking up the echo of something."

"What do you mean?" Lucy turned to face me. An expanse of wood floor and furniture between us.

"Maybe the objects are all connected." I swept my arm wide, encompassing the Chucky-fied things on the counter. "What if each time they catch the reflection of something else, it basically creates a portal that Chucky can traverse."

"Or there could just be a lot of Chuckies."

"That is also a possibility, though each time I encounter him, it feels and smells and sounds the same."

"But . . ."

"But what if the linking also connects objects together?"

"So you could be hearing Grace's voice from another linked object?" Lucy angled her head in question. "Has that ever happened?"

"No, but we've already drawn connections between my family's silver teapot, objects in Roberto's office and Gruncle Jack's palazzo. It's not too much of a stretch from there."

Lucy gasped. "The Little Mermaid music box."

"Exactly. The item that Roberto gave Grace."

"Shiny with a mirror inside—reflective things that could have become infected with Chucky."

"Precisely. If the music box were linked too, then I could be hearing noise from it somehow, from Grace's reaction to it."

"It all comes back to Roberto. Do you think he cursed the music box? Chucky-fied it?"

"I wish I knew."

"And it makes the bloody handprint on Grace's dresser even more chilling." Lucy bit her lip again, trying to control its trembling. "I just need to know Gracie's okay, Branwell. That's all. I keep trying to hold on to Tennyson's vision, but I know he only sees possibilities of the future. Nothing is set in stone."

Ah Lucy.

She stood so resilient but so alone.

It took everything in me to not cross the room and draw her into my arms. If I did, I might not ever let her go.

"We're going to find her, Lucy. Let me text Dante and have him look for Grace again." I grabbed my phone. "That should give you some peace of mind."

"Thank you," Lucy whispered, rubbing her upper arms again.

I walked over to the couch and sat down, texting my brother with a gloved finger.

When I finished, she still stood in the same place, eyes downcast. Obviously wanting comfort but hesitant to intrude. A lump in my throat threatened to choke me. How could I ever deny Lucy anything?

"Come here." I scooted sideways on the couch and extended my arm along the back, creating a perfect Lucy-sized space for her to cuddle into.

She came willingly, sniffling, sagging her entire weight into me—head on my shoulder, knees tucked against my hips, rubbing her nose into my chest.

I wrapped both arms around her, pulling her close. Ruthlessly ordering my rebellious heart to slow down. Not that it listened.

I wanted to drag her onto my lap and kiss her until all tears had fled.

But that wasn't going to help this situation. And Lucy needed more than a libido-driven brain right now.

So I merely held her, running a hand up and down her back, murmuring comforting sounds.

The insistent buzz of my phone ringing startled us both.

Dante. Calling. Not a good sign.

I held the phone away from my ear, careful not to touch it to my skin.

"*Pronto,*" I answered in Italian, hoping Dante would catch my hint and reply in the same language.

Lucy sat up, pulling away from me, staring with those blue, blue eyes of hers. Wide and terrified.

"You're going to have to tell me what prompted your text." Dante's voice sounded agitated, even in Italian. "I looked and Grace is . . . visible."

My heart plummeted to the bottom of my feet. "What do you mean . . . visible?"

Lucy covered her hand with her mouth.

"Is she dead? Is my Gracie dead?" Panic edged into Lucy's tone. I knew she couldn't understand our Italian entirely, but her terror and grief pounded through me.

I held up a finger, asking for one minute.

"Just that," Dante said. "I can see her. Only the tiniest smidge, mind you. She's not solid—"

"Okay," I breathed. "That makes me feel slightly better."

Lucy clasped her hands and bounced in her seat. So anxious.

I shot her a weak smile to indicate that Grace might be okay.

"She's wispy. Like the faintest outline of a ghost. I've never seen anything like it."

"Except for Jack?"

"Yeah. Jack looked similar, but he was less wispy than Grace. He was more ghost-like. Grace is even more faint. Just barely visible."

A pause while I absorbed everything.

"Jack died two hundred years ago. This makes no sense. How can a little girl be just a wispy bit dead?" I pinched the bridge of my nose. "What is going on, Dante? Is your GUT morphing too, making you see things differently now? It's like the entire supernatural world decided to short circuit."

"I know, bro. I'm with you. I don't know that we can make assumptions about anything anymore. I'm sick for that little girl. How's Lucy?"

I looked at her. She was still clasping her hands under her chin, tears streaming down her face.

"*Lei non sta bene,*" I whispered, never once breaking eye contact with Lucy. *She's not doing well.* "She's hanging in there as best she can. She's fighting to stay positive."

"I'm with her. Call me later so you can fill me in. I'll keep checking on Grace to make sure she doesn't get more solid on us."

"Thanks, man."

I hung up and tossed my phone on the couch.

Lucy collapsed onto my chest, crying.

"He s-saw her, d-didn't he?" She hiccupped, huddling against me, sobbing uncontrollably.

"Shhh, Lucy. Yes, Dante saw her, but she's super wispy and faint."

Lucy cried harder and harder. "N-no! No!" she gasped. "T-Tennyson had that vision . . . Grace *has* to be okay—"

I gave up fighting my instincts. Wrapping my arms fully around her, I pulled Lucy completely onto my lap, cradling her against my chest. One arm bracketing her waist, the other stroking her hair.

And still she cried. Her heart breaking. Despair and grief crashed through me.

"Hush, *cara.*" I kissed the top of her head. "I wouldn't draw definite conclusions. Dante and I are starting to wonder if something isn't up with our GUTs. There are just too many unusual things going on here. Don't you dare lose hope."

I pulled back and used my teeth to yank my glove off my right hand, desperate to touch her, to *feel*. I threaded my palm into her hair, massaging her scalp. Anything to bring her comfort.

"H-hold me," Lucy pleaded. "Please."

I flexed my arms, pulling her a fractional inch closer. Her arms wrapped around my chest, hands fisting into my shirt at the small of my back.

"Don't believe Dante, Lucy. He isn't sure what it means." I pressed my lips to her head again. Stray red curls lapped at me, sizzling with sensation. "Everything is haywire."

Lucy clutched my body, crying, nuzzling her nose into my throat.

"Shhh, it's okay. Grace is okay. Trust what Tennyson saw," I kept whispering. Over and over. Stroking Lucy's hair, her back, hugging her tight and dropping kisses on her head.

Every sob and shake of her shoulders was a whip across my heart.

Sunset faded into twilight, color lethargically melting into the western horizon plunging the sky into blue-black night. Accent lighting popped on, bathing the room in warmth.

I held her through it all.

Eventually her sobbing quieted to mere sniffles, shoulders heaving intermittently. She stirred in my tight hold, lifting her head. Blue eyes bloodshot and despondent.

"We'll find her. I promise." My voice low in the dim room.

"Y-yes," she hiccupped, sucking in a breath. "We'll find her."

Dispirited sadness rioted through me. But right behind it . . . longing. So much longing.

A fierce yearning, racing wildfire.

We stared at each other for a small eternity. Her aqua eyes pools of sorrow, freckles stark against her pale skin, flame hair spilling everywhere. She was an abstract painting—slashes of blue and red dotted with bronze umber. She had never been more beautiful.

Her gaze dipped south, moving from my eyes to my mouth.

My breath hitched.

Gently, she pulled a hand from behind my back and, ever so softly, brushed her fingertips over my lips. Back and forth. Left to right. Feather-light. Tingling with sensation.

"Luce—" The faintest breath of air.

All I could manage, really.

Her name a warning. Or possibly a benediction.

Yearning swamped me. All mine.

Her fingers stilled on my lips. Heated. An impossible temptation.

This woman . . . how could I ever resist her?

She lifted up. Or did I bend down?

Lips suddenly replaced fingers.

Soft. So soft . . . her mouth.

Salty from her tears. Warm from my chest.

I trembled. Shaking from the sheer wonder of it.

I was kissing *her*. Kissing Lucy.

Her hand clutched my head, chest rising as she lifted her body to meet mine.

Part of me floated in wondering bliss.

The other part screamed to end this. That I needed to pull back before I crossed an unforgivable line.

But then she pressed into me, pulling me harder to her. Greedy. Hungry. Obliterating my resolve.

What a fool I had been to think I could deny her anything.

My arms flexed, intending to haul her even closer and kiss her with proper thoroughness.

That slight tensing shattered the spell.

Lucy froze. She jerked back but remained sitting on my lap.

Her hand instantly left my head, as if burned. She pressed fingertips against her lips, eyes wide and horrified.

"I'm so sorry," she gasped. "Branwell, I-I didn't mean to— I just reacted. My emotions . . . and I love you so much . . . I didn't th-think—"

She broke off, pushing farther away.

"Sorry. S-sorry."

Lucy scrambled off my lap, shoving a fist against her mouth to stifle her renewed sobs. Running from the room, not seeing my outstretched hand, silently begging her to come back.

BRANWELL

Are you seeing the heart in that?" Tennyson tilted his head sideways, watching Lucy photograph a puddle alongside the road.

I followed his lead, angling my head to the right.

"It's hard to say," I said. "Maybe the sticks floating in the water help?"

We both studied it for a moment longer. Arms crossed, shoulders leaning against our parked Jeep, waiting for Lucy.

"Well, I'm sure it will be heart-shaped once Lucy is done with it." Tennyson smiled. "Lucy never gets this stuff wrong."

Lucy took that moment to turn back to us, lopsided smile happy and carefree. My own heart stuttered.

The sun caught the lettering on her t-shirt.

Reach for the stars.

A T-Rex stood in the middle, its tiny arms stretched toward the heavens.

Yep.

That pretty much said it all.

33

LUCY

I tore out of the apartment, feet pounding up the stairs, tears tumbling. Branwell's stunned face seared into my memory. Shock. Horror.

What had I been thinking?

I *hadn't* been thinking. That was the problem.

My brain was a scrambled mush of emotions and, so, naturally with my guard so weak, I had kissed Branwell.

Idiot. I was such an imbecile.

I had to get away before his face morphed from surprise to regret. My heart couldn't take watching that amazing kiss turn into something awful and shameful in his eyes—the highlight of my life being the lowest point of his.

For about the thousandth time, I cursed whatever karmic fate had allowed me to fall so in love with *him.*

Branwell D'Angelo. The one man who could never be mine.

I reached the top of the stairs and burst out onto the enormous rooftop terrace. Heat and humidity enveloped me. Night had settled in for real but the flagstones under my feet still released stored sunlight.

Blinded by tears, I stumbled around an enormous, wisteria-covered pergola and wound my way to the far side of the terrace, collapsing against the railing, facing outward over the cityscape. The enormous dome of the Duomo, Florence's iconic cathedral, lit up the sky.

Leaning against the iron railing, I stared sightlessly across the city to the rolling hills beyond. Lights flared upward, obscuring the stars, blurring in my vision.

I hated the lights at that moment. Cheerful. Full of hope. Sending all their energy into the dark beyond, sure that something would come back to them.

What did I have?

Years of a broken relationship with a man I cared about but couldn't love as deeply as he wished. Nearly as many years desperately loving a different man who could never be mine. A niece who had vanished into thin air and might not even be alive—

"Lucy."

His voice behind me. Deep. Full of . . . some unknown emotion.

Remorse? Anger? Weariness?

I choked back another sob. My throat raw and hoarse.

"I'm s-so sorry, Branwell." I didn't turn around. Seeing his face twisted in self-loathing—or even worse, accusation—was beyond my emotional strength. "Please accept my apologies for my behavior. It won't happen again. I am a terrible friend to abuse your trust like that—"

"Lucy—"

I held up a hand, still keeping my back to him. "Please, Branwell," I pleaded. "I'll be okay. I just need a little time to pull myself together and stuff all this emotion back where it belongs—"

"*Basta.*" Branwell's hand closed over my elbow. Infinitely gentle but decidedly resolute. "Stop it. Please look at me." He applied pressure to my arm, the gesture asking but not demanding I turn around.

Swallowing, I pivoted to face him, staring at the second button on his shirt. The one right under the end of his beard. In my peripheral vision, I could see his hands. One on my elbow, the other rising to my face.

Both bare.

"Hey." His palm caressed my cheek. Soft. Pleading. "Lucy, *carissima mia*, please look at me."

What had he just called me?

My heart stuttered to a stop.

And then started again, determined to pound a hole through my chest.

Surely he hadn't meant that? Right?

Carissima mia.

My dearest one.

My tears suddenly evaporated. My face slowly raised, confusion all over it.

I wasn't sure what I expected to see in Branwell's expression.

Remorse. Concern. Closed-off determination.

Instead . . . his eyes . . .

That last thing I ever expected. All plainly written.

Stars.

Love. Adoration. Not a shadow of doubt.

The shaking started at my knees. I swallowed convulsively.

"There she is," he whispered, feathering his fingertips over my lips. "*Mia Lucia*. My own Lucy."

"Branwell—" My voice stopped on a gasp. "I don't understand. You don't have to—"

He laughed, shaking his head. As if I had said something impossibly cute but also incredibly stupid all at once.

His free hand came up to cup the other side of my head. His skin warm against my cheeks. His thumbs brushed my skin, forcing every nerve to stand at attention.

"Have to? No. There is nothing of obligation in this, Lucy."

Now he was flinging those stars at me. My knees threatened to dissolve into a puddle. I placed both my hands on his chest, steadying my quaking.

"I need you to promise me something." His eyes shone with worshipful devotion. Like I was salvation and hosanna.

I blinked. "Okay. I promise."

"You haven't even heard it yet." He grinned, teeth flashing in the dim light.

"Don't care. Anything you ask, I'll do."

That stopped him for a moment. "What did I ever do to deserve you?"

"Me?" I shook my head. "I don't understand, Branwell. I'm the one who doesn't . . ." The adoration blazing from his eyes stopped me.

He bent forward, kissing my forehead. "*Never* apologize for how you feel about me." My nose. *Kiss.* "Because I'll *never* apologize for how I feel about you." Cheek. *Kiss.* "Never." Chin. *Kiss.*

Each word was a shooting star blazing through my heart. I trembled, fisting my hands into his shirt. My lungs fighting to get enough air.

He pulled back. Met my eyes squarely with his. "I love you"—a choked gasp—"*you*, Lucy Miranda Snow. I love . . ." He gave a harsh laugh. "I love everything about you. I love the way your smile lights up a room. I love how you meet each day with a bounding optimism. I love how you love others. How you always think outside yourself—"

"Branwell, darling, you don't have to say these things—"

"Stop." He gave me a small shake. "You don't understand. I. Love. You. I have *always* loved you. You say you fell in love with me at that coffee shop, but I'm here to tell you, I fell first."

I gasped.

No. Impossible.

Wasn't it?

"I saw you before you saw me. I chose to sit at that table with you because, even in that brief moment between seeing you and meeting you, I knew. You were it. You were my heart. You took a snapshot of it, and I haven't gotten it back since."

"Branwell—" I instantly stepped closer, pulling myself up with his shirt, mouth reaching for his.

"Wait. Let me finish." He pressed his forehead against mine. "If you kiss me, I won't get another word out for a *very* long time."

I snorted. "That's sorta the point."

He laughed, short and pained. "*Cara mia.* Your love destroys me at the same time it heals. I have loved you for so many years. Watched you. Told myself over and over that you weren't for me. But after yesterday . . . knowing you feel the same way. I couldn't bear to have you think that today has been anything other than one of the *best* days of my life—"

I kissed him.

I popped on my tiptoes and covered his mouth with mine.

It was too much. I couldn't encompass everything he was saying. My brain had gone supernova.

My mind couldn't comprehend that the man I had admired and respected and adored more than any other returned the feeling. That just as long as I had been pining for him, he had been aching for me.

We were adults. We had both been in relationships before.

It should have been a controlled kiss. Finessed and refined.

But we were too starved.

Too long yearning for this and here and now.

Too long believing this moment would never, ever be a reality.

The kiss was anything but neat. Hungry. Ravenous.

His arms banded around me, both hands buried in my hair. Tilting my head to give him better access to my mouth.

He tasted like Branwell. Warm. Tender. Fierce.

With each kiss, my heart soared.

He. Loved. Me.

My Branwell. He truly was *mine*.

I tasted tears. Salty and perfect.

His? Mine?

I didn't care.

I was *kissing* him. His soft beard brushing my chin, tickling my nose.

After a long while, I pulled back. Laughing. Joy lashing me like wildfire.

I tucked my cheek against his, clutching his head with both hands.

"Please tell me you can feel my happiness," I murmured, rubbing my lips over that strip of skin on his cheek just above where his beard ended. "That you know how much I adore you."

His answer was a growled rumble and another kiss.

Thoughts pounded, trying to get in.

Insidious little buggers.

Whispering that Tennyson would *not* be okay with this.

That Branwell's love for me did not exceed his love for his brother.

That on the opposite side of the Joy of Kissing Branwell stood a Cliff of Despair—the one I would tumble down when he chose Tennyson over me.

Was my current joy worth the pain of that fall?

Foolish, foolish me.

Because . . . it was.

It absolutely was.

34

LUCY

Rain pattered through the trees, releasing the scent of pines and moss. I stood beneath my umbrella, nestled under the canopy of forest ringing the park, giving myself another five minutes—a stolen breathing space before hiking back up the hill.

Judith had invited her clan home for Sunday dinner which meant laughter and teasing and amazing pot roast with gravy. It also meant keeping my mood super positive for Tennyson and not letting an ounce of anything Branwell slip through my defenses.

Go me.

"Hey." A voice sounded through the hush.

Thinking of which.

Branwell emerged from the path behind me, rain slicking off his jacket, beard bunched inside his hood, hands in his pockets.

"Hey." I nodded back.

He stopped next to me, close but not touching. It didn't matter. The air buzzed, humming with the electricity of *him*.

Tennyson had been strongly hinting lately, dropping words like *ring* and *wedding* into casual conversation. I was rapidly approaching a crossroads.

"You good?" he asked.

"Yeah." I moved my knees and feet, keeping myself warm. "Just needed a moment."

"Understood."

Of course he did. Branwell always understood. That was a huge part of the problem, I had come to realize.

Tennyson needed me, which was nice and all. But there were *expectations* along with that need. A certain standard of emotional flatline I felt compelled to consistently meet. Not that Tennyson ever demanded it of me. It was more knowing that my steady presence was his lifeline, the living Prozac that kept him functional.

Branwell, on the other hand, offered me unconditional acceptance. No expectations.

With him I could just . . . be.

Like now.

Rain trilled on my umbrella, rustling through the trees. Soothing. Calming.

"Take your time," Branwell said, soft and patient. "I'll walk you back up the hill when you're ready."

35

LUCY

I woke the next morning to a text.

Chiara.

> *Come downstairs to the storefront when you wake up. I got something*
> *you'll want to see.*

I replied and then slumped back against my pillow, letting the events of the previous day spin through my mind. Given everything that had gone down, it was a wonder I had slept at all.

Grace weighed heavy on me. What had happened to my sweet little girl? Was this whole mess with Jack and Grace being wispy even related to her disappearance in the end? Or was it just a lingering . . . *something* coming from Gruncle Jack and his entanglement with Sofia D'Angelo? A misfire of the D'Angelo gift and completely unrelated to Grace in the end?

Who knew.

I simply wanted my Gracie back, safe and sound. I had to believe in the vision Tennyson had seen. I would go mad otherwise.

As for Branwell . . . his confession the night before still felt like a fevered dream. That if I awoke enough to focus on it, it would all melt away.

I wasn't ready to jinx myself yet.

Dragging my body out of bed, I showered and pulled on a strappy, white sundress with a thin aqua-blue cardigan and matching sandals. I was way too fair to get away with wearing sleeveless things in summer. My shoulders would fry no matter how much sunscreen I put on.

Besides, the blue color looked good with my eyes, and I wanted to look pretty today. Something more than just jeans and a t-shirt.

I replied to texts from my family. Jeff and Jen had made it to Abu Dhabi and were trying to get a flight into Florence, but no one had recently heard from them. We were all in wait-and-see mode.

From there, I made my daily check-in with Inspector Paola who reiterated, again, that I needed to stay out of her way, or else . . .

Got it.

Too quickly, I reached the point in my day where I had to face last night. Or rather the hunky, huggable guy I had kissed into the early morning hours.

Branwell . . .

I bounded down the stairs and paused in front of his apartment door.

How would he feel about me this morning? Had sleep and some space convinced him to reconsider his feelings for me? Or was he still firmly Team Lucy?

Regardless, my heart triple-skipped and danced giddily around my chest at the prospect of seeing him.

Why did life do this? Give me shocking heartache right along with unbelievable bliss?

I had lost Grace but gained Branwell.

He loved me.

I loved him.

We hadn't really discussed much beyond that last night. Quite frankly, there had been very little talking going on at all. Obviously, at some point, we were going to have a conversation about *us*.

But until then . . .

I stood in front of his door like an insecure teenager, debating which of my instincts was the most lucid and rational.

My primary impulse was to wrap myself around him like static cling, tell him how much I had missed him in the last eight hours and beg him to never let me go.

Even I knew that one had 'psycho girlfriend' written all over it.

Instinct number two said I should smile, flirt and act like we were an item.

But, were we an item? Tennyson stood between us, solid as ever. There was no getting away from that history, and I would hate to make assumptions.

So maybe I should act like we were friends until Branwell did something more than friends?

My last option was to assume nothing and keep walking down the stairs.

Hmmm. That sounded less fun.

I was debating between those last two choices when Branwell decided for me and opened the door. Broad shoulders filling the doorway, hair and beard still damp from the shower.

His eyes lit up like Christmas morning.

"Hey," I said.

Which was all I got out before he closed the distance between us, wrapped a hand around the nape of my neck and pulled me to him for a kiss.

A decidedly thorough, possessive kind of kiss. A kiss that melted my bones and ended with me plastered against his chest.

Well then.

Maybe Option One hadn't been such a crazy idea after all.

"Good morning," he murmured, pulling back to kiss my nose. "I missed you."

I laughed. Happiness bubbling through me. "I missed you too, love."

"Love," he repeated, voice almost pained.

Which resulted in another five minutes of kissing.

Branwell finally dragged himself away, both of us breathing hard. He looked down at me, eyes full of such wonder. Not a single barrier between me and his soul.

He tucked a curl behind my ear. Swallowed. "I know we're going to have to talk about *us* sometime soon. But today—just for a few hours—I don't want to think about future decisions."

"Amen." I popped up, intending to give him one last lingering peck.

Branwell had other ideas. My man could *kiss*.

After another couple minutes, it was obvious we weren't going to get anything done today if one of us didn't take charge.

"C'mon." I tugged on his hand, pulling him toward the stairs. "Chiara said she had something."

We held hands until reaching the bottom of the stairs and the door to D'Angelo Enterprises. Instinctively, we both knew that Chiara and the rest of his family should *not* witness our mutual adoration of each other.

One problem in a mountain of many when it came to anything permanent between Branwell and me.

Branwell opened the door and motioned me through.

The D'Angelo shop was typical of high-end antique stores. Marble statues stood on top of carved chests. Crystal goblets and priceless bowls were staged alongside tapestries and lace.

Chiara was chatting with an older couple about the provenance of an oil painting, it seemed. She lifted her head when we walked through the door, interrupting her conversation.

"I found something interesting in the family archives. I left it on the desk in the office for you," she said, nodding toward the back of the store before turning her attention back to her customers.

Giving his sister a 'thank you' wave, Branwell pulled me through a door and into the back office. I had never been this deep in the D'Angelo family affairs before.

In retrospect, I realized I had no preconceived notion of what Branwell and Dante's office space would be like. I guess I had just assumed it would be a utilitarian white box like most offices.

I could not have been more wrong.

Branwell pushed open a thick, wooden door and led me into an enormous, airy, light-filled space.

Running the back length of the palazzo, five huge windows flanked the wall opposite the door, level with the parking courtyard. The ceiling soared overhead with dark, aged beams. Traces of frescoes peaked out here and there on the white-washed walls.

The end of the room near the doorway held a wall of bookcases to the left and a large table-like desk strewn with papers, folders and several laptops. Farther down the room to the right, a sitting area featured heavy, masculine leather furniture angled toward a ginormous flatscreen TV.

Yeah. I could live in this room.

Branwell left the door open, Chiara's voice drifting in. But he glanced around and sneakily landed a kiss on my neck—sending goosebumps skittering down my spine—before walking over to the table.

Honestly.

After this small taste of his love, how could I ever walk away from this man?

Branwell picked up a plastic sleeve with a piece of paper inside it. I stopped next to him and slid my arm around his waist. He angled the letter for me to see too.

Yellowed with age and ragged along one edge, the paper was clearly old. Spidery script flowed across its surface. The kind of handwriting with loops and curlicues that was hardly *de rigueur* anymore, making it hard to read.

Though the fact it was written in Italian could also be a factor.

Branwell scanned it, pointing a finger at the signature—a boldly scrawled *Sofia*.

Ah.

"It's simply a letter to her uncle, telling him about some friends she visited and replying to his inquiry about her health. Polite. Normal. Nothing too telling." He flipped the plastic over in his gloved hands, studying the name written on the back. "No date either, so who knows when exactly it was written."

I looked down, a sticky note lay on the table where the plastic sleeve had been. Chiara's handwriting unmistakable.

> *Still working on the empath thing. Family records don't really breakdown the 'gift' into its component parts. It was just one mass of feeling, seeing and hearing to them. Understanding it all will take time, unfortunately.*
>
> *But this is what I have found out—Sofia D'Angelo married Antonio Perlucci in 1818. She died in childbirth in 1826 and is supposedly buried in the family chapel in Volterra (remind me to make a trip down there). I couldn't find record of any other marriage for her. No mention anywhere of a Jack Knight-Snow.*

"So hard to know what happened two hundred years ago," Branwell murmured, touching Chiara's note.

"That's why we have you. Allow me." I took the plastic from him and carefully pulled the fragile paper from the sleeve with my smaller, gloveless fingers, laying it on the table.

"Read my mind, *cara*." He grinned and hugged me, brief but greedy enough to send thrills tingling along my arms.

Releasing me, he tugged off a glove and placed a single finger on the paper, eyes going unfocused, his head angled. Listening.

He sat like that for several minutes.

I stared at him the whole time. That strip of skin visible between his ear and shirt collar. The curl threatening to escape from his man bun. The tendons flexing across the back of his hand, skin so pale from lack of sun.

Before last night, I would have looked away, watched him from the corner of my eye and pretended like my world didn't start and stop with him.

Today . . .

I boldly drank him in.

BRANWELL

I TRIED NOT to let Lucy destroy my concentration, but emotions flooded me with every sound out of her mouth.

Happiness. Joy. Love.

So much love.

It awed and humbled me. Nearly overwhelmed.

Being loved by Lucy Snow . . . somehow it exceeded every fantasy.

Guilt gnawed at the back of my mind, trying to work its way in. Reminders of Tennyson and his fragile emotional state. That finding out about me and Lucy could easily send him tumbling over the edge.

Not yet, I pleaded. *Just give me today.*

Just one day. Like Lucy had yesterday.

One day of hope. One day of pretending this could be the rest of my life.

I could block Tennyson; he would never know.

Lucy stirred next to me, snapping me back into the present.

Right. Focus.

How did Sofia D'Angelo and the family curse play into the events surrounding Jack Knight-Snow?

I shifted my finger on the parchment, sifting through the sounds. Voices trailed in and out, offering nothing relevant.

And then . . .

". . . you quite done with your letter then, dearest?" An unknown woman in aristocratic Tuscan Italian.

"Yes, Mamma. One more moment." Sofia.

A sigh. The creak of someone sitting on a bed.

"You did not finish your meal again. You must eat more—"

"I am fine."

"No, Sofia, you are not fine. You must let him go."

Silence. The scritch-scritch *of pen on paper.*

"It is time to let the dead be . . . dead," the woman continued.

"A broken heart does not heal itself in a day, Mamma."

More silence.

"It's been a year, Sofia dear." Words said so softly. "You need to live again."

"I am living."

"No, you are not. You are existing. He would not want you to be like this—"

"Enough, Mamma." A pen fell to the tabletop. "I appreciate that you dislike seeing me suffer, but I cannot move past . . . him . . . in just a month or a year or possibly even ten years. He was my heart. My very life. Without him, I cannot live. Can you not understand? I drove him to this. Encouraged him. Urged him on—"

"Sofia, he made his own choices—"

"No! His blood stains my hands as surely as if I killed him myself."

"But you did not, dearest. He made his choices, too. Any minor sins you may have committed, God has long forgiven."

"It little matters, Mamma, for I cannot forgive myself. . . ."

The scene faded out.

I searched back farther into time but heard nothing else of interest.

Sofia had to be talking about Jack, right? It seemed improbable that Sofia had buried another would-be lover, then agreed to marry Jack who promptly died, leaving Sofia to eventually marry this Antonio Perlucci fellow. No woman could be that unfortunate.

Between this letter and their conversation in the Etruscan tomb, Sofia was clearly in love with Jack. When I had listened to the dented mantel in Lucy's palazzo—was that really only three days ago?—Jack had been upset over a woman. Sofia? Had they fought, and Jack being distraught, had committed suicide? The plaque in the museum had stated that as one theory for Jack's disappearance.

This letter added to their story but was hardly the smoking gun we were searching for. Not to mention that this version of Jack and Sofia's history didn't involve Chucky, leaving our resident demon unexplained.

Love will draw the shadow out.

So . . . had Sofia and Jack had a fight and the resulting mix of love and anger attracted Chucky, causing Jack's disappearance?

"Well?" Lucy asked, leaning toward me.

I reached for her hand with my ungloved one, tucking our hands together. No sound filtering in when touching skin-to-skin. I would never tire of holding her.

We were safe for the moment, as I could still hear Chiara chatting with customers in the showroom.

I leaned back into the desk and tugged Lucy closer, looping my gloved hand around her waist. I dropped a smoldering kiss on her forehead.

Cuddling her, I caught Lucy up on what I had heard from Sofia.

"So you think Sofia and her mother were talking about Jack?"

"He seems a likely candidate."

Lucy shook her head. "We know so much about Jack and Sofia and, yet, so little."

"Agreed—" I stopped, cocking my ear toward the open door.

I had heard something.

Gently, I pulled away from Lucy and walked the few steps to the doorway, listening carefully.

A man had just walked into the shop, asking a question.

"Is this the store owned by the *Conte del Maledetto*?" the man repeated.

I recognized his voice instantly.

Finally! When we most needed a stroke of good fortune, it arrived.

We hadn't needed to find Roberto after all.

He had come to us.

BRANWELL

Y ou can't do this, Tennyson." I watched as he stuffed clothes into a huge duffel. "This is insanity. You could be killed."

"My life. My decision." Tennyson turned away, continuing to pack.

"Seriously, Tenn. A job as a military contractor and trip to Kabul are *not* going to help you get over Lucy any faster." I scrubbed my beard in frustration.

Three days.

Just three days since Lucy had rejected his proposal and ended their relationship.

I didn't know exactly how or why it went down, but I had my suspicions. I had seen Lucy suppress her own emotions over and over to keep herself steady for Tennyson. And Tennyson, in return, lapping up the comfort she offered like a drug.

That sort of relationship was many things . . . but romantic love was not one of them.

Tennyson's reaction to the break-up, however, was horrific. We had been arguing almost non-stop for the past twenty-four hours. He already had a contract in place and was catching his plane in less than two hours.

"Tenn, how is this even legally possible? You can't run off this quickly—"

He gave a haunted, bitter laugh, lifting those impossibly blue eyes to mine. "I'm a damn *psychic*, Branwell. You think I haven't seen this coming? Over and over, I could feel Lucy pulling away. Why do you think I held on to her so hard?"

He ran a ragged hand over his hair, tugging at it.

Oh Tennyson.

"Promise me you'll watch over Lucy for me while I'm gone." His tone dead serious.

Damn. Just when I thought this whole situation couldn't get any worse—

"No, Tenn. I won't promise you because you're not going anywhere."

"*Promise* me, Bran."

"No. Being upset over a breakup is normal." I lifted a placating hand. "But—reality check—you don't have to go to *Afghanistan* to get over a girl."

Tennyson snorted. "Yeah, but I think I do."

"How so?"

He placed his hands on his hips, shaking his head. "I'm tired, Bran. So very, very, tired. Tired of everyone always focusing on me. *Broken Tennyson, how can we fix him?'*—he mimicked Chiara's voice—"I'm tired of living a life narrowed down to this *pinprick* of daily coping." He pinched his fingers together.

He moved again, grabbing a stack of t-shirts and tossing them into the duffel on his bed. "It's gonna happen. Someday. Just like Dad. Just like every other first born D'Angelo. I won't be able to fight my demons anymore, and they'll probably take me out. But until then—" He paused, clenching his jaw in determination. "—until then, why not use my GUT to save lives? I'm a *psychic*. I feel emotions into the future. I can't think of a better use of my talents than as an advanced warning system for the military."

Frustration and despair ripped through me.

"You could be *killed*."

"Death happens to everyone sooner or later, Branwell." Tennyson braced his hands on his bed, his Caribbean blue eyes lasering through me. "I'm just stubborn enough to seek a method of exit that isn't my own hand."

37

LUCY

FLORENCE, ITALY
2016

Three minutes later . . . the store sign had been flipped to *Closed*, and Chiara and I were sitting side-by-side on the leather couch in the office. Branwell paced around us.

Roberto Moretti sat nervously in a chair opposite, rumpled and beaten.

Not that *we* had roughed him up. Though the thought had certainly crossed my mind. I wanted to rattle his skull and scream, *Where is my Gracie?!* until he begged for mercy and told me all his secrets.

Branwell said we couldn't do that because, "Assault is illegal," blah, blah.

Roberto looked a mess all on his own. He wore a beat-up wind breaker over ratty jeans and clutched a leather satchel against his chest, both arms wrapped around it. Hair greasy and cheeks scruffy. Forehead sweating, glasses askew. Eyes haunted and, quite frankly, desperate.

Running from the law definitely took a toll.

He had been surprised to see me with the D'Angelos.

Branwell pinched the bridge of his nose, continuing to pace back and forth. I had a tight hand on Chiara's arm. She might be tiny and petite, but she was ready to tear Roberto limb from limb to get answers.

To his credit, Roberto seemed as frantic to find Grace as we were.

"I did nothing to harm little Grace. I do not know what has happened to her," he pleaded for the fourth time in heavily accented English.

"Truth." Branwell stopped behind me. "It rings totally true."

"I still say he's lying," Chiara hissed. "I mean, seriously. How could he *not* have something to do with Grace's disappearance?" She gave a dramatically Italian wave of her hand.

Roberto cringed. "You must believe me. I love Grace like my own. I only want good for her."

Chiara and I both looked back at Branwell. "Truth." He shrugged, face baffled.

Chiara threw her hands up in disgust. "No. I don't believe it." She turned to Roberto. "Where have you been? Where were you the night Grace disappeared? If you're so innocent, why aren't you cooperating with the police?"

At the word *police*, Roberto held up his hands, panic evident. "I can explain. Give me a chance."

Chiara pursed her lips, eyes narrowed. "One more time. Tell us you had nothing to do with Grace's disappearance."

"I swear it." Roberto placed a hand over his heart, eyes sincere. "I swear on the Virgin Mary herself that I had nothing whatsoever to do with the disappearance of Grace Snow."

"Truth." Branwell sighed. "He completely believes it."

My heart sank. Were we suddenly back to square one? If Roberto hadn't taken Grace, then who had?

"Thank you, Mr. D'Angelo." Roberto sagged in relief.

"We'll believe you for now. But I'm guessing you wouldn't be here if you didn't have a hunch," Branwell continued.

"Yes, yes. I do have my suspicions. That is why I found you, the D'Angelos. I have *heard* things about your family. That you are . . . different." That last bit very cautiously stated. As if Roberto was fearful he would startle something free.

Branwell didn't react. He just rolled a gloved hand. *Go on.*

Roberto swallowed. "D-do you believe in *i demoni*?"

"Demons?" Chiara translated.

We all exchanged a loaded look.

"Sure," Branwell said.

Roberto blinked, taken aback at our blasé reaction, our bland expressions. But seriously, after the week I'd had? Simply *talking* about demons was hardly going to phase me.

Clearing his throat, Roberto continued, setting the leather satchel on the ground at his feet.

"Francesca said Lucy had visited the *museo* with a bearded giant"— Roberto waved toward Branwell—"so you know about John Knight-Snow and his excavations. Lord Knight searched for a rumored Etruscan treasure. In 1818, he discovered a *praenestine cista,* a type of decorated bronze box. Lord Knight was convinced the box contained the treasure."

That's what Gruncle Jack had said, right? I shot a glance at Branwell who nodded subtly.

"The box itself said nothing about treasure. Instead, it was covered in warnings that begged the finder to leave the box closed because a powerful shadow named Hinthial was trapped inside," Roberto said.

"Hinthial, again."

"The Etruscan goddess of love, right?" Chiara asked.

Roberto raise his shoulders in the universal Italian gesture for 'maybe.'

"Meh, it is hard to know exactly who Hinthial was to the Etruscans. The name means many things. As a female goddess, Hinthial had elements of love, but Hinthial was also considered to be the guardian of the shadow world. The problem occurs because *hinthial* can be translated as shadow *and* reflection."

My eyebrows disappeared into my hairline at the word *reflection*. Branwell shot me a grim look.

"I think it was a play on words. Hinthial the goddess and *hinthial* the noun. Because her name meant shadow and reflections, her likeness was often placed on mirrors. *Spettrale o spettro.*"

"Like the English words *spectral* and *specter*," Chiara said. "All coming from the Latin *spectrum*, meaning shadow, ghost or vision."

"The idea, for the ancients, that your reflection was a shadow of yourself." Branwell started pacing again.

"*Esatto*," Roberto said. "Exactly. A *hinthial* was a *fantasma*—"

"A phantom. A ghost." Chiara translated the word.

Roberto brightened. "Yes. Ghost or demon. In this case, one who fed on love. The inscription on the box can easily be interpreted as . . ." Roberto frowned and said something in Italian.

Chiara nodded. "'Beware the *hinthial*—the demon or ghost—inside as it can steal you,'" she translated.

Goosebumps skittered across my skin, raising to attention.

Okay. Things were starting to make sense. In the creepiest way possible.

Maybe.

"Lord Knight found the bronze box but ignored the warnings, convinced they were lies meant to discourage grave robbers. He opened the box and found an ancient Etruscan mirror inside," Roberto said. "Nothing more."

"The mirror that shows someone lifting Hinthial—or a demon-ghost thing—from the ground? Wasn't that in the museum too?" Branwell asked.

I looked at him, knowing full well he had seen the mirror on Roberto's desk, not in a display case.

Branwell gave the barest lift of his shoulders.

"*Sì.* That is exactly the mirror. Though I would argue that the demon is dragging the figure *into* the ground, not the other way around. Though, again, it is hard to know what the mirror means."

Roberto sighed and rubbed his bloodshot eyes and continued, "This is what I have been trying so desperately to understand. When he opened the *praenestine cista*, Lord Knight released something . . . unnatural."

"Not Hinthial herself?"

"No. I do not think it was the goddess herself. Rather, something the ancients begged the goddess to protect them *from*. Again, it is so confusing because the ancients would use the word *hinthial* to refer to any demon or ghost. But *Hinthial* was also the goddess of love. To them, I'm sure, it was a poetic play on words. Love can feel like a demon driving one insane, who knows? Here, let me—"

Roberto stopped, debating, looking intently at each of us. And then nodded, as if reaching a decision.

Bending over, he carefully opened his satchel and pulled out an oblong object wrapped in a velvet cloth. Carefully he unfolded it, revealing an ancient mirror. Given Branwell's hissing breath, it had to be the one from Roberto's office—the mirror that we were currently discussing.

"So . . . how did you get this out of the museum?" Branwell asked.

Roberto gave another Italian shrug. "My friend is a curator at the museum too and she . . ." He mimed shoving the mirror inside his jacket.

"That's a really nice friend," Chiara dryly observed. "A girlfriend, perhaps?"

Roberto shot her a decidedly wicked grin.

Well.

Roberto carefully spread out the velvet cloth and laid the mirror on the coffee table in front of him, engraved side up.

Fascinated, I moved around the table along with Chiara to get a better look at it. Branwell held back, staring at the mirror like it was a bomb. Was the mirror Chucky's place of origination?

"So what are we seeing here?" Chiara asked, leaning over the mirror.

Roberto perked up. "As I was saying, it is hard to know what ancient Etruscan means with any certainty, but this is the explanation that makes the most sense given the events surrounding this mirror. As you can see in the background"—Roberto pointed—"a priestess drips blood onto a scrying dish, perhaps cursing the bloodline. In this case, that could be those who disturb the demon, so Lord Knight and those related to him, like little Grace."

I nodded. So a demon—Chucky? Chucky's friends?—had cursed the

Snow bloodline. Not sure how that happened, but given everything I had experienced over the past couple days, I was willing to go along with it.

"Here, we can see two figures embracing," Roberto continued, pointing to figures opposite of the priestess. "Obviously, this is a reference to love and those in love. Rumors say that Lord Knight fell in love about the time he uncovered the mirror. So the embracing figures, perhaps, represent that as part of this situation. It is the front figure that ties the other two together. The text here says"—Roberto pointed at the etched letters at the top of the mirror—" 'The one who loves will call the shadow.' I believe Lord Knight translated it as, 'Love will draw the shadow out.' The text on the bottom here can be translated as, 'The shadow fights for freedom.' So if we look at the image in front, we see the seated bearded man being snared by the shadow coming out of the mirror. Some scholars interpret the male figure to be Tages, an Etruscan oracle."

"An oracle?" I asked, my goosebumps turning into skittering marbles tingling my skin.

Roberto waved a hand. "He is thought to be the founder of the Etruscan religion. A human man with powers of divination—the Etruscan version of the Oracle of Delphi. Basically, a person capable of physically touching the shadow."

I shot a glance at Branwell. He was staring intently at the mirror, eyes wide. I wasn't quite sure I followed it all, but it made a certain kind of sense.

"What exactly are you saying?" Chiara asked.

"I believe Lord Knight released a demon." Roberto looked at us all. "A shadow that feeds on love and is desperate for freedom. It attacked Lord Knight, taking him for its own."

"So how does Grace fit in to all of this?" I asked. "She's a little girl, not a lost lover. Why would she be involved in this at all?"

Roberto sighed. "This is where the story becomes less clear. Those of Lord Knight's blood have not interacted much with the mirror over the years. But Grace . . . she visited the museum. I showed her the mirror. The mirror had 'seen' her, so to speak. I did not think about it at the time, but I had the Little Mermaid music box at the museum too. The mirror 'saw' it—"

"Which means it could have been keyed to Chucky . . ." I closed my eyes, a lump tight in my throat.

"And if Chucky infected the music box, he easily could have snatched Grace," Branwell concluded.

"Uhm, are we seriously entertaining the idea that Chucky kidnapped Grace?" Chiara asked, eyes wide. "Cause even by my standards, that's a little out there."

I had to agree. It seemed far-fetched, but I was ready to grasp at straws.

"Who is this Chucky?" Roberto frowned in confusion.

"That's the question of the year," Chiara muttered.

Roberto opened his mouth, clearly set to launch into some professor-ish follow-up questions.

Branwell silenced him with a cutting look. "Why us?" he asked. "Why are you running from the police and lying in wait for the D'Angelos? If you are innocent, then why not talk to the police?"

"The *polizia*, they think I am guilty." Roberto sat up. "If they find me, I will be locked away. If I am in jail, I cannot research how to save Grace."

"So you *did* visit the excavation sites?" Branwell asked.

"Yes. I needed to look at the inscriptions again where Lord Knight found the mirror and *praenestine cista*. I had to make sure I hadn't missed something—"

"Did you find anything new?"

"No, unfortunately, which is why I am here. There is much talk *nelle comunità metafisiche* . . ." He rolled his hand.

"Metaphysical communities."

"Yes! *Esatto*. In the metaphysical communities, they say that the D'Angelo family is cursed. They are the *maledetti.* "

Branwell and Chiara exchanged a glance. Obviously, they had heard this rumor.

But Roberto wasn't done. He continued, "They say that a demon like the one originally trapped in Lord Knight's mirror haunts your family line, granting visions and dangerous powers but demanding a large price in return. The D'Angelo men"—a flicked glance at Branwell—"they die young and tragically. Perhaps a *hinthial* with ties to the ancient blood of Tages is present in you, too."

Every hair on my body flared to attention.

Given how still Branwell went behind me, Roberto's words had struck a nerve.

Chiara whistled, low and impressed.

"That is very . . . plausible," she murmured.

Branwell let out a low breath. "What kind of deal did my ancestor really make?"

Silence.

A clock ticked somewhere in the room. Traffic rumbled on the street outside, thumping along the enormous flagstone pavers.

"So our Chucky isn't Jack's Chucky?" I finally asked, glancing behind me at Branwell.

Chiara and Branwell exchanged an I-have-no-clue look.

"Probably not initially. That said, the D'Angelos *were* involved with Jack's excavations. Maybe some kind of connection happened then?" Chiara suggested.

"Like the D'Angelo curse primed the mirror for Chucky?" Branwell mused.

"Yeah," Chiara nodded, "or drew him out for the first time. Jack's demon being attracted to our demon? Perhaps Sofia's brother, Lorenzo D'Angelo, was around when the mirror was uncovered?"

"Good suggestion, sis. Archaeologists did do reveal parties, where they would open ancient artifacts in front of an aristocratic audience—"

"Like unwrapping mummies," I chimed in.

"Exactly."

"And if Lorenzo D'Angelo happened to be present . . ." Chiara's voice trailed off.

"Something in our cursed bloodline could have called the demon and Jack, being the one who opened the box and probably first touched the mirror, cursed his own bloodline as a result." Branwell leaned over the back of the couch.

Whew. My mind reeled.

"It would explain why Chucky is so eager for your blood, Branwell."

Roberto looked between Chiara and Branwell, obviously not having completely followed their discussion.

I pressed both hands into my eyes. "But what does this have to do with Grace?"

A beat.

"I have researched demons for the past several years." Roberto jumped into the conversation. "I know more about them than anyone. However, I cannot attract one. The demons . . . they won't visit me."

Ah. All the lights went on in my head.

"And that's a bad thing?" Chiara muttered.

"I hoped that maybe the D'Angelos would know how to draw out the demon from the mirror so I could trap it." Roberto leaned forward, eyes lit with what I could only describe as *glee.*

The man had clearly never tangled with Chucky.

Another beat.

"You think I'm some sort of Italian ghostbuster?" Branwell deadpanned.

Roberto gave an apologetic shrug. *If the shoe fits . . .*

"Wait." I held up a hand. "The mirror says 'Love will draw the shadow out—"

"Yes. Love is part of it," Roberto said. "But it is more than that. We need the right bloodline too."

"So if someone with the right bloodline loves enough . . ." Branwell's voice drifted off.

"Then the demon will come," Roberto finished the thought.

"And once you trap the demon?" Chiara asked.

"We get it to release Grace." Roberto nodded emphatically.

Alright. This was about as crazy a conversation as I'd had all year. And I had obviously already had some doozies.

But if it saved Grace . . .

"How? And when?" Branwell asked.

"Can you do it? Draw out the shadow?" Roberto asked, perhaps a little too eager.

Down, boy.

Branwell pulled up his sleeve, showing the healing scabs raking down his arm. "Chucky has a taste for my blood."

Roberto hissed and crossed himself, though he seemed more impressed than worried. "We must bring Grace back. In two days, it will be the *solstizio d'estate*—"

"Summer solstice," Branwell said.

"Yes. The longest day of the year, when the light is brightest and the shadows weakest. The time when light and love shine strongest in the shadow world. It will be the best day to prepare our trap." Roberto suddenly grinned, eyes wild and crazed at the edges.

I wasn't sure how I felt about trusting my Gracie's safety to this wackadoodle . . . but desperate times did make for strange bedfellows . . . or something like that.

Gah. I was so bad with quotes.

But Roberto could wear yak skins and howl at the moon, as long as he brought my Gracie back to me.

38

BRANWELL

FLORENCE, ITALY
2016

We talked for several more hours in the office, Roberto outlining what needed to happen. It mostly involved the Etruscan mirror, pentagrams, a water trap and some specific prayers.

Though definitely esoteric, everything he said made sense. Well, sorta. I was still fuzzy on some of the finer details, but Roberto clearly understood what needed to happen. I had no trouble believing Chucky was involved, linking between objects, perhaps sucking Grace in his web.

I just hoped that once we captured him, Chucky would cooperate and release Grace.

Roberto asked us to keep the ancient mirror. If anything happened to him—translation, if he were arrested—we could use the mirror to trap Chucky without him. Though given Roberto's exuberant enthusiasm for the process, he would find a way to be there.

We planned to meet in two days time at the last archaeological site Lucy and I had visited, the place where the mirror had been originally found. Roberto would lead us in the ritual. I would draw out Chucky, Roberto would trap him and use prayers to get the demon to release Grace.

I thanked Roberto and securely stowed the ancient mirror in the office safe.

When asked where he was staying, Roberto got cagey.

"Uh, with a . . . friend," was all he said.

"Your girlfriend?" I asked, thinking of the unknown woman I had heard in his office.

Roberto shrugged. "I cannot say she is my girlfriend, as the museum has strict rules about office relationships . . ." His voice trailed off into innuendo and a not-so-subtle wink.

"Is this the same woman who specializes in smuggling ancient mirrors out of museums?"

"My girlfriend is a person of many talents."

"Wait. Does your mother know about your girlfriend?" Lucy asked.

Roberto paled. "No, Mamma does not know and she cannot know. She will talk and talk and if the museum finds out, we could both lose our jobs. Please don't say anything."

As if. Roberto's illicit office romance was way down the list of my current concerns. But as potential blackmail ammo, it was worth remembering.

Lucy left to show Roberto out a discreet side door and then retreated upstairs. She had gotten several texts from family members she needed to respond to.

Chiara caught my arm and cornered me before I could follow Lucy.

"Branwell, I'm not stupid," she hissed in Italian. "I would have to be completely blind to miss how you and Lucy are looking at each other. The cat's out of the bag, so to speak." She held out a staying hand. "And before you rake me over the coals, let me remind you of the brother languishing down in Volterra, heartsick and heartbroken, because of this woman."

"I block Tennyson, remember? We've already had this conversation—"

"Ugh! Just because he can't feel your emotions, doesn't give you *carte blanche* to essentially betray him."

"Spending time with Lucy hardly constitutes betrayal—"

"Pah-lease! You're doing more than just 'spending time' with her."

Her words were a bullseye hit. I gritted my teeth.

"Seeing you with Lucy would *destroy* Tennyson," she continued. "He is teetering above an abyss labeled *Suicidal Depression,* and this could easily be the thing to send him catapulting over the edge. Don't do this to him. Don't do this to our family."

I turned my back on Chiara. Unable to meet the accusation in her eyes.

"I love her," I whispered, hating the whining tone of my voice. "I love her more than . . ."

"More than Tennyson's life?"

Silence.

"No." A long pause. "Never more than that."

Chiara shifted. A chair creaked.

"I'm not saying give up Lucy forever. Just give her up for now. For a year. Maybe two. Let Tennyson heal more, find a better emotional place. I know you, Branwell. If you felt in any way responsible for your brother's death . . ."

"I would never forgive myself. Don't you think I know that?" I tilted my head back, staring at the dark beamed ceiling, blinking hard. "Why do you think I resisted these feelings for so long?"

I snorted. A sad, unamused sound.

"I wanted one day, Chiara." My voice drifted through the quiet room. "A few hours of happiness with her. One day of bliss. Of pretending that this could be the rest of my life. And in the end, I couldn't even have twenty-four hours."

Chiara made a choked sigh. "I'm so sorry, Branwell. Really, I am. I love Lucy too. We all do. But sometimes we have to give up something we want for the greater good."

She was right. I hated it, but she was right.

I nodded at my sister and turned to leave the room. I wasn't sure I could resist saying something petty and mean.

Her voice caught me anyway. "Let her go, Branwell."

It was easy for her to say. It was easy for them all. They weren't being asked to sacrifice their happiness on the altar of the family.

No.

The offering was all mine.

39

LUCY

FLORENCE, ITALY
TWO YEARS EARLIER

Thanks for coming." Branwell walked up the white hospital hallway to greet me, face tired and drawn.

"Sure." I pulled my purse tighter against my body, telling my wayward heart to stop cataloging every last little detail of him. Same shirts, same jeans, same gloves. But older. More weight in his gaze. More authority. More man, less boy.

They had called me, the D'Angelo family, after nearly three years of intermittent contact. The words *roadside bomb*, *wounded* and *amputation* still rattled around my brain. I had hopped the first plane to Florence.

Branwell looked me up and down and shoved his hands into his pockets. He opened his mouth, as if to say something, and then changed his mind. Instead, he motioned for me to follow him back down the hall.

I stared from behind as we walked, drinking in every last inch of his broad shoulders and silently praying I was up to this task.

Branwell paused, turning back to me, his hazel eyes hesitant.

"Tennyson's not in a good place," he said.

"I gathered that from Judith's phone call."

He nodded.

"He *was* doing well in Kabul." Branwell shifted his weight. "Weird as it is to say, Afghanistan agreed with him. Using his gifts like that . . . helped. At least, he sounded up every time we talked . . . "

A beat.

"And now this," I prompted.

"And now this."

It hung there between us. His quiet request for my help, asking me to keep Tennyson together for them.

Like I always had.

Only . . . I wasn't that girl anymore.

"I told Judith I'd come for a visit," I said. "I'll stay as long as I can, but no strings attached. I can't . . . I can't do this again, Branwell. I won't lead him on. It's not fair to Tennyson."

Or to me . . . I silently added.

Silence.

"We appreciate you coming at all." He looked through the open door and then turned back to me. "We'll take every last minute of time you can give."

40

LUCY

FLORENCE, ITALY
2016

Chiara had obviously given Branwell an earful, their terse, staccato Italian drifting up the stairwell.

I loved Chiara but, honestly. Branwell and I had to sort this out ourselves.

Not that we had the time.

Jeff and Jen had called. They had *finally* landed in Florence. I caught them up on what I knew, not mentioning the whole thing with Roberto. I wasn't sure how my brother would react to his daughter being captured by a demon. Besides, I had let a potential suspect walk out the door.

Jeff and Jen were heading to the police station right now for an update. They wanted to see me; I wanted to see them. Which meant I needed to leave for Prato in less than an hour.

Family first, right?

After their phone call, I had decided to wait for Branwell on his own turf in Nonna's apartment. I was sitting on a chair in the dark central hallway, waiting. Sunlight streamed from every door, painting the long corridor in zebra stripes.

I liked the small pool of darkness I had claimed for myself, fitting to my mood.

Branwell entered, a taut rubber band of emotion on the verge of snapping. He stopped just inside the door, gloved hands in his hair. Knowing I was there but not looking at me.

I stared, memorizing every line of him. The way his tall body filled the space. His shoulders stretching underneath his shirt. The dark slash of his beard and hair against his skin. That sense of calm and rightness that radiated from him.

I tucked every detail away like a squirrel storing nuts. Understanding, intuitively, that I would need them for a long winter without him.

He let out a long breath.

"Jeff and Jen called," I said. "They're back and want me to meet them in an hour."

He nodded.

Nothing more.

"You wanna talk about it?" My voice hung in the gloom.

He shook his head. A single sideways jerk.

Nope.

"What is there to say?" His voice a husky whisper. "We both knew how this would end."

Truth.

My heart still plunged about a thousand feet.

Tennyson stood between us. That hadn't changed.

"He's stronger than you think." I had to say it.

I knew Tennyson . . . as well as anyone did. You didn't survive what he had without being a fighter.

"For you." Branwell stared into the living room to his right, light washing his face. "He fought for *you*. It has always been *you* for him."

My breath hitched.

"And it's always been *you* for me," I said.

Silence.

"I had hoped we could at least have a day," I continued, biting my lip. Ordering the tightness in my throat to stay put. "Just *one* day."

Branwell shoved a hand in his jeans and slumped against the closed door. He finally met my gaze.

"We're always off with the timing, aren't we?" His mouth curled into a humorless smile. "Meet each other too late, admit our feelings too late . . . just always too *damn* late."

My eyes stung. He locked his gaze with mine and extended a hand to me. Asking.

I ran to him, arms around his neck almost as fast as my lips found his. He pulled me off my feet, kissing me like a man drowning. Desperate.

The ache in my chest threatened to swallow me. So much sorrow and heartache. I clutched the back of his head tighter, willing myself not to cry.

Branwell pulled back to press his forehead against mine.

"This isn't over." Voice low and intense. "Me and you. This is *not* goodbye."

"Not goodbye," I repeated, stifling a sniffle.

"I can't say goodbye when I only barely said hello." His voice a whisper against my lips.

"Y-yeah," was my hiccuppy reply.

"The timing is simply off right now."

I nodded. "I need to focus on Grace, and you need to concentrate on Tennyson."

He kissed my nose. My cheeks. Brushed softly over my lips.

"Chiara said we should wait," he said. "Give Tennyson a year. Maybe two. Rekindle our romance when he has healed more."

I *hated* the thought of waiting.

"Why does the sacrifice always have to be yours?" Selfish of me, but

I had to ask it, to pick the scab off an old wound. "Why isn't your family worried about *your* emotional state?"

Branwell sighed, tucking my head under his chin.

"I'm stronger," he whispered. "It's that simple."

"Tennyson survived me leaving him. He could survive this too."

"But could he? You didn't see him after you left two years ago. It was . . . bad. Very bad. Close."

"Worse than trying to get himself killed in Afghanistan?"

"Much worse."

A beat.

"I didn't know that," I said.

A shrug. "Why would we tell you?"

I kissed him again, delaying, stalling. Branwell readily accepted my tactics.

It was supposed to make things better.

It didn't.

Tasting him, being held tight in his arms . . . feeling precious and understood and cared for . . .

I could already sense myself falling and falling toward the cold hard ground of reality. My heart would shatter.

"C-can you let me go? Watch me walk away without trying to work things out with Tennyson?" I finally gasped.

He shook his head, burying his nose in my hair. "No." Muffled. "I can't. I keep telling myself that I can, but really, I'm not that strong or noble." Branwell clutched me against his chest, arms engulfing me. I rested my head, listening to the steady *thump-thump* of his heart.

"You'll talk to him? To Tennyson?"

A pause.

"I have to try." Branwell brushed a kiss on the top of my head. "Maybe if I bring you up, it will be okay."

Neither one of us quite believed it. But hope was a terribly insidious thing.

"He loves you, Branwell. And once, he loved me. He would want our happiness."

"True. Though knowing something and feeling it enough to act rationally are two very different things. But for us . . ."

A long pause.

"For us, I have to try."

41

BRANWELL

TUSCANY, ITALY
2016

I dropped Lucy a block away from her brother's palazzo in Prato. Down the street, the media were already assembling in front of the building, everyone wanting to hear from little Grace's parents.

Lucy leaned across the car console and kissed me, lingering. A promise of sorts.

"I love you," she whispered against my lips. "No matter what happens, remember that. You'll always have my heart."

This woman . . .

"I love you, too." I gave her one more soft kiss before pulling back.

Lucy reached into her purse and set the bag of green sour gummy bears on the dashboard.

"Saved these for you," she said with a wink. And then she was out of the car, down the block and pushing her way through cameramen and reporters to the apartment entryway. She paused on the stoop to lift a hand goodbye.

I watched until she disappeared inside, my throat tight.

The green gummy bears taunted me on the dashboard, garishly lime in the sunlight.

My sweet Lucy.

Hesitating for only a second, I reached for the bag and opened it. Like their punny siblings, these bears also had small nicks in them.

Puzzled, I popped one in my mouth.

Lucy giggling.

"I love you beary *much."*

I grinned, chewing.

They weren't that bad, actually.

I reached for another one.

"I can bearly *stand how handsome you are."*

She hadn't, had she?

Another.

"Roawr!"

The. Whole. Bag.

Had she intended I would eat these? Or was this something she had done for her own amusement?

Didn't matter because green gummy bears had just become my new favorite food.

Driving out of Prato, I turned the car south, heading to Volterra. The scenery quickly morphed from apartment buildings to rolling countryside carpeted with olive trees and grape vines. Ancient towns perched on the top of each hill, clumps of trees clinging to the crannies below, looking like so many tonsured monks.

I didn't tell Tennyson I was coming. No sense in giving him advanced warning. The last thing I wanted him to do was gaze into the future of our conversation.

That wouldn't end well.

Instead, I mentally imagined the walls tightening around my mind, keeping Tennyson from seeing or feeling anything from me.

I was approaching Judgment Day. I spent the drive going over what I was going to say, outlining what would be the best approach to the topic. I couldn't come up with a clear path. Honestly, everything depended on Tennyson's mood and emotional state.

I pulled into the gravel parking area to the side of the villa, quietly killing the engine. The afternoon air was marginally less hot today and humidity hung in misty sheets around the hills. Birds chirped and cicadas buzzed. A tentative breeze ruffled the wisteria vines clambering up the old castle walls.

I walked through the small door in the large gates and stared across the courtyard at the entrance to the house proper. Was I really ready to have this conversation? My entire future perched on a knife's edge.

My feet turned right and took me to the chapel door before I even consciously thought it through. The small stone church hugged the castle wall on two sides, the Gothic entryway too large for the building's size.

Yes, a few moments in the chapel would be good. Center my thinking.

I pushed open the heavy wood door. The smell of mildew and musty things flowed around me, the air cool in the small space. I stepped into the dark interior, sunlight filtering through small, high windows to either side of the altar. Fumbling, I found the light switch.

Light flooded the room, illuminating ancient frescoes overhead. Christ judging in his glory. The Virgin Mary blessing the saints. Three wooden pews stood on each side of a center aisle. An ancient stone altar rested at the head of the short nave.

Small, confined, homey.

I walked the few steps to the altar and then sat on the front pew, the ancient wood creaking under my weight.

A thousand childhood memories washed in.

Tennyson laughing as we played tag, saying he had seen that we wouldn't be able to catch him.

Tennyson crying because Chiara was going to fall and break her arm and he was worried.

Tennyson finding me after our father had taken his life, wrapping me in his arms, knowing I needed comfort.

The world had not been an easy place for my brother. How could I contribute to his pain?

I was such a selfish jerk.

Rubbing gloved hands over my face, I mentally reviewed what I would say. Looking for a path forward that enabled me to keep Lucy without destroying my brother.

After several minutes, I lifted my head, noting the names etched into stones surrounding the altar, lining the walls and floor.

Ancestors. Generations of them.

Haunted men, like myself, and the women who had loved them.

Chiara said Sofia was buried here, too.

It took five minutes of hunting to find her tombstone, nestled knee-high in the left wall.

Sofia Elisabeta Chiara D'Angelo Perlucci
1794-1826

She had been just thirty-two when she died. Barely older than me.

I pulled off my glove and gingerly touched the stone, pressing my fingers into her name, the rock cold and rough under my fingertips.

Sounds, voices, smells . . . all came washing in.

I concentrated on them and pushed backward, not sure what I was looking for. It's not like I would find Jack here.

"Do you know the story?" A gravelly voice in Italian. A chisel striking stone, background noise—the sounds of a mason yard. "Lady Sofia and her English beau?"

"Aye, though I was too young at the time it happened to understand. My mum says it was a great scandal."

"That it was, boy. But all's well that ends well, I say. Pity about the English gentleman though. He took it all poorly. Nearly destroyed the church pew in the family chapel, so I'm told. Then went home and killed himself. Servant said he was there one minute and then gone the next . . ."

I pulled my hand away as the voices faded.

Huh. That had been . . . compelling.

Had they truly been referring to something that happened in *this* chapel?

I stood and surveyed the room, studying the age-darkened wooden benches. They were certainly more than old enough to date from Sofia's time.

After a few minutes of examination, I realized that the rear left pew had a significant repair on one side. I had never noticed it before, but then I had never been looking for it either.

Crouching down, I studied the fragmented wood. The right legs had been replaced.

Reaching out a hand, I carefully touched the worn wood. Again, noise flooded my senses.

Men talking. Hammers and saws working.

I sifted back in time, listening for . . . what?

Sofia? Jack?

Something familiar.

It took several minutes, but then . . .

"Leave me be, Sofia." Jack's voice. Anguished. *"You have done enough harm."*

"Jack, please. I was honest with you in this." Sofia. Pleading.

I pushed on my GUT, asking to see more. Images drifted in.

A man seated on the floor by the altar, flowers strewn over its surface. A celebration interrupted. A top hat and walking stick lay at his side. One hand threaded through his hair, the other resting on his upturned knees.

A woman paced before him. Long skirts swishing, bonnet hiding her face.

A snort of masculine laughter. Bitter. Caustic. Jack's. "Indeed, my lady. You were. Up until the point he stole you from me moments before we made sacred vows to each other—"

"Stole me?" Sofia stopped her pacing. Stared down at Jack. "Like I am a piece of chattel to be passed around at whim from man to man?"

"You know that is not what I meant," he sighed.

"I thank whatever saints may be that he interrupted our marriage ceremony. Antonio has always had my heart. I have loved him from the first time—"

"Please." Jack held up a hand. "I do not wish to hear of your devotion to another."

Sofia folded her arms. "I am sorry for how things . . . happened. How was I to know Antonio still lived? Napoleon's army was deadly, and Antonio had been reported missing nearly two years ago. As I told you, I had encouraged him to fight against the Corsican fiend and when he was lost, I was too——"

"Bah!" Pain. Frustration. "Enough, Sofia. It is done. All that remains is for you to take yourself off with him and for me to mourn what might have been."

Silence.

"I am sorry, Jack. You are a good man. I regret that my heart was never whole enough to be won."

"Sofia, my love." An unknown man's voice. "The carriage awaits."

"Your lover arrives." Jack laughed again. Mocking. "Do not keep him waiting, my dear."

Sofia turned and walked down the small aisle toward a man standing in the doorway.

"Vai con Dio," she whispered back to Jack. Go with God.

Turning, she took Antonio's hand, stepping into the light.

Jack slumped on the floor, shoulders shaking. Laughing? Crying? Both?

Suddenly, he erupted in a rage.

Leaping to his feet, he snatched up his walking stick and attacked the wooden bench before him . . .

The scene faded.

Well . . . damn.

That had been unexpected.

I stood up, Jack's anguish and despair slowly ebbing.

Suddenly, everything slotted into place. Jack arrived in Tuscany, intent on continuing his father's excavations. In the process, he met Sofia D'Angelo, fell in love and asked her to marry him. Sofia agreed because the love of her life, Antonio Perlucci, a soldier in the fight against Napoleon was presumed dead and she was heartbroken. The man, Antonio, returned and Sofia left Jack at the altar.

From that point . . . what happened? Jack disappeared, but how? I studied the ancient chapel, as if it could give me answers.

When I had first encountered Jack in Lucy's living room . . . I had felt profound loss. Had the scene in the palazzo happened after the scene here in the chapel? It would make sense.

And then what? Jack committed suicide in his grief, as the stone masons and so many others asserted?

Or was it what Roberto believed? That the presence of the D'Angelos had somehow primed Chucky to appear. Chucky, drawn to Jack's love and grief over Sofia, had snatched Jack?

Was that what was happening with me, too? Chucky coming after me more aggressively now because he could sense my anguish over Lucy? Or was it Lucy's concern for Grace that was drawing Chucky out through me?

Still so many questions. What was I to do with all this information? Too many loose threads and no clear answer.

I swallowed, pulling my glove back on, shaking my head.

Jack's despair lingered, tugging at my senses.

Razored pain. Self-loathing. A desire for nothingness.

Poor Jack.

The potent emotional cocktail hit me again, a blasting wave.

What—?!

Everything within me stilled. And then I took off at a run.

Madonna mia! No!

I wasn't feeling Jack at all.

This black despair . . . a yearning for oblivion . . .

It was all Tennyson.

42

BRANWELL

I flew out of the chapel, across the courtyard and through the old front door of the villa. Not pausing to wonder why I was suddenly feeling things like this from Tennyson. Was it the tandem nature of our GUTs that made us so in tune with each other? Who knew.

I raced up the wide, stone stairs and into the reception rooms on the *piano nobile*.

Dimly, I processed a note atop the large family dining table in the drawing room. I didn't stop to read it all. Tennyson's neat handwriting and words saying he was tired of fighting were evidence enough of his intentions.

Terror pounded through me as I raced up another set of stairs to Tennyson's room.

Empty.

Bathroom. Empty.

I could still feel his despair. The wracking pain. Hopelessness.

He had to be alive.

Please don't let me be too late. Not now. Not like this.

I raced up another flight of stairs, down a long hallway and then through a door, whirling up the spiral staircase in the tower, feet pounding, breathing hard.

The staircase ended in a ladder to a trap door—the final ascent to the top.

The trap door was open.

Elvis sat at the bottom of the ladder, whining as I rounded the corner, tail wagging.

"It's okay, boy," I whispered, giving his head a quick scratch. "I'm here now."

I met his concerned, hang-dog eyes as he continued to whimper. He nudged my pant leg as I pulled myself up the ladder.

I carefully climbed up, head popping out of the floor of the square arched loggia that was the top of the tower.

Tennyson stood dead center in the arch directly in front of me. Standing on one foot, his prosthetic leg resting on the stone floor beneath him.

Just inches between him and a solid hundred foot fall to the pavement below.

"I didn't feel you. Not even the tiniest bit." Tennyson chuckled. Humorless. Harsh. "I had to rely on old-fashioned *sound* to know you were here."

Fractured agony washed over me with each word. A serrated, vicious pain.

I grunted, climbing the rest of the way out of the trap door, standing up.

"You wanna come down out of there and talk to me." I edged my way forward, swallowing hard, hands shaking. Refusing to think about how high up we were.

Could I grab him if he jumped?

"The most ironic part?" Tennyson continued, ignoring my words. Tone casual, as if he weren't teetering on the edge of certain death. "I *want* to sense your emotions. You, of everyone else out there, I want to feel."

Tennyson suddenly flinched, swaying outward.

"Tenn!" Terrified, I lunged forward, latching a hand around his upper arm. I focused on him, stubbornly refusing to look down.

He looked at me, eyes so haunted.

"Fine," I said.

And I let it go. Blew apart the mental walls that I knew kept Tennyson out of my head. I pushed my feelings for Lucy down deep and pulled out the only emotion that mattered.

Love.

Every last ounce of love and respect and adoration I had for my brother.

My fierce loyalty to him. That I would sacrifice anything and everything for his chance at happiness.

Case in point.

Tennyson closed his eyes, breathing in and out.

No reaction.

Wait—his earlier flinch had been a reaction to my future emotions. Got it.

I kept pumping adoration and love through my mind.

"Stay with me, Tenn." I tightened my grip on his arm.

He bowed his head, looking down at my hand. And then raised his eyes to mine.

I refused to recoil at what I saw there. Such bitter despair. Pain. Suffering.

"I got you, bro," I whispered. "I'll always have your back."

Tennyson continued to stare at me, as if probing things I couldn't see.

"It's hard," he confessed. "It's not just the voices and the visions. That's only part of it."

He swallowed and his gaze went unfocused. "It's like I'm being torn apart from the inside out . . . like some vital component is missing or broken, and I don't know how to Humpty-Dumpty myself back together again."

He snorted, a black, desolate sound.

"The worst part? This"—he ran a hand up and down his body—"will never get better. There is no cure for me, Bran. No *fix*."

Was that true?

"You don't know that. There's a lot we don't understand about our GUTs, Tenn. There's always hope."

"Hope?" He scoffed, shaking his head. "I stopped believing in that a long time ago. Us D'Angelos haven't ever had the luxury of *hope*." He said it like a four-letter word, biting sharp.

"Not true." I called his bluff. "Me. You. Dante. We're different. Our situation is different. There's too much fight in you to let this win."

He winced and looked back over the sprawling countryside.

Silence.

"You love me," he said.

It wasn't a question.

"Absolutely." No hesitation. "More than my own life."

A beat.

"I love you, too," Tennyson whispered.

"Thank you."

"I want you to be happy. I really do." Words threaded with guilt.

"Glad that we got all the brother-mushy stuff out, but I'm going to be happiest if you come down here by me." I tugged on his arm. "C'mon, Tenn. The drop is a doozy, and it's making me all panicky."

"You and your issue with heights."

Tennyson leaned his head out, staring down at the ground far below. I felt a jolt of his longing, a desire for oblivion. Anything to make the agony go away.

"Please, Tenn." I squeezed his arm. "Please."

He nodded and bent his knee, allowing me to help him down, sitting with his back against the stone walls of the tower. He sagged into the flagstones, shaking with the aftermath of his decision.

Tennyson scrubbed a hand over his face, tilting his head back against the stone wall.

"Why do you put up with me, Bran? I'm such a selfish bastard."

I pulled him into my arms, holding him tight.

"You're preaching to the choir, brother. Preaching to the choir."

43

LUCY

I got the call in the late afternoon.

I had just returned to the D'Angelo palazzo, deciding to spend the night there. As their apartment was still a crime scene, Jeff and Jen were staying in a local hotel and bunking with them seemed awkward.

I cradled my phone against my ear, listening as Branwell described in short bursts what had happened, my heart dropping lower and lower. His words came at me in a disjointed mess—suicide watch, sedation, PTSD therapist, Dante flying home. A familiar routine with Tennyson, it seemed.

Sorrow and regret laced every word.

There would be no 'us.' Not now, at least.

Knowing I was the source of so much of this pain, I said nothing. I merely voiced my hope for Tennyson's recovery and hugged Chiara and Judith as they rushed out the door.

And then I waited, curled up on the couch in their great room.

The sun arched through the sky, morphing from yellow to orange to purple twilight. The jangle of my cell phone ringing startled me.

Inspector Paola's name pulsed on the screen. I hesitated before answering it, wondering why she would be calling me now that Jeff and Jen were home. But, given everything, I didn't want to land any higher on Paola's list of People I'm Irritated With.

"Hello," I said.

"Lucy Snow?"

"Yes."

"Good evening. Are you still staying with the D'Angelo family in Florence?"

"Uhmm, yes."

"A surveillance camera saw Roberto Moretti in the vicinity of the D'Angelo palazzo this morning." Inspector Paola wasted no time cutting to the chase. "Did you or any of the D'Angelo family have contact with him?"

My heart froze in my throat, constricting my breathing.

Busted! I could almost hear Paola chuckle.

Lying to the police was an *extremely* bad idea, but . . .

"Contact?" I asked, trying to buy myself more time.

"Yes. Did you see, speak to, or have any dealings with Roberto Moretti?"

Dang. That was a water-tight specific list. The woman was good.

How to answer without perjuring myself?

"I don't know where Roberto is." That was absolutely true.

Silence.

"That isn't the question I asked, Ms. Snow." Paola was not amused.

More silence.

"You do realize, Ms. Snow, that there is a warrant out for Dr. Moretti's arrest? As such, you have an obligation to notify us if you see him."

Drat. I did?

Now she told me. I chewed on my cheek, nerves skittering along my skin.

"I have repeatedly asked you to stay out of this investigation, Ms. Snow," Paola continued. "I consider it a serious mark of suspicion that you refuse to do so. Are you sure there isn't anything you would like to tell me?"

What to say?

Yeah, Roberto stopped by, we discussed ways to free Grace from a demon, he left an ancient mirror and then I waved him goodbye . . .

That answer would land me in jail or a mental hospital. Possibly both.

I settled on, "I don't have any comment, ma'am."

"I see." Paola grunted. "Thank you for your time, Ms. Snow."

She hung up with an annoyed, this-ain't-over click.

Heart pounding, I tossed my phone on the couch and wrapped my arms around myself.

Now what?

No way I was going to disturb any of the D'Angelo's with this.

I hadn't done anything wrong and besides . . . between Grace's disappearance, Tennyson's fragile emotional state and my fraught love of Branwell, my worry cup was already overflowing.

Inspector Paola was just going to have to trust us and chill. Though part of my mind buzzed, convinced that Paola was *not* the kind of person to let this go. She knew she was on to something and was going to pursue it like a dog scenting a bone.

My stomach growled, reminding me I hadn't eaten since this morning. Uncurling my legs, I walked over to the kitchen, trying to decide what wouldn't taste like sawdust. I was such a jittery mess.

A loaf of crusty bread in a bowl and a jar of Nutella settled my decision. I was in the middle of cutting a slice of bread when the door opened. I whirled around.

Branwell's enormous body filled the doorway, kicking it shut behind him.

I dropped the knife and launched myself into his arms, sobbing. He clutched me to him, arms steel bands around me.

It was like instantly coming home. Comfort surrounded me, soothing, making the horror and fear bearable.

I lifted my head and kissed him.

His kiss in return was not the gentle kiss of hello, but a far more desperate one that tasted terrifyingly of goodbye.

No. Please, no.

I had barely arrived at this place of love and belonging. I shattered at the thought of leaving it so soon.

I cried harder, clinging to him. Selfish tears for me and him. Tears of frustration at this impossible situation. Tears for all the pain and happiness and sheer *emotion* of the past several days.

Branwell held me through the storm. My sea of calm in a world gone topsy-turvy. Always the strong one.

How I loved this man.

He stroked my back and ran his fingers through my hair, letting me release my grief and sorrow. When I finally pulled back, he nabbed a kitchen towel off the island, gently wiping my face.

"Hey," he whispered.

"H-hey." I managed a stuttery facsimile of a smile.

I took the towel from him and dabbed my cheeks.

"Not much to say, is there?" I asked.

He shook his head. "We've gone through this before, so we all know the drill. My mom has Tenn on some solid sedatives. They numb his mind and make him sleep for days on end. But they also help him cope. I didn't even get a chance to talk with him about . . . things. Which, turns out, probably was for the best . . . " His voice trailed off.

I sniffed. He stared at me, heartbreaking sadness in his gaze. I didn't even need to ask. It was all written on his face.

There would be no 'us' for the time being.

"Thank you," I said.

He nodded and looked down. As if the sight of me was too painful.

I knew the feeling too well.

"I'm so sorry, Lucy." He shoved his hands into his pockets, throat swallowing convulsively.

I turned away from him and went back to the island, staring at the bread and knife. Hating what I knew he was going to say, wanting to put it off for as long as possible.

Branwell sighed and turned away from me. I heard the *shunk* of him flipping the deadbolt and then the *chink* of his phone being set on the marble countertop.

I shook my head. "Please don't say anything," I said, voice so soft. "I can't bear to hear goodbye right now."

I picked up the knife, determined to see through my blurry vision.

"That's good." Branwell moved to stand beside me. "Because I can't bear to say it."

I sliced into the bread which was a mistake given my state of mind. The knife slipped and promptly cut my palm.

Pain washed up my arm, stinging. But the physical pain was a welcome distraction. Something tangible to match my own inner turmoil.

"Careful." Branwell took the knife from me.

Hissing, I reached for a paper towel, applying pressure to stop the bleeding.

"How bad is it?" Branwell tugged at my hands, wanting to see.

I shrugged. "It's fine."

"Lucy, you're bleeding. It's not fine. Hold on. Let me grab Mom's first aid kit from the bathroom."

I watched his broad shoulders walk down the central hallway.

The wound hurt, pain radiated up from my palm. I pulled the paper towel away and leaned over the counter, angling the cut in the light to see if it was deep enough to warrant stitches.

Too distracted to notice Branwell's phone resting on the counter underneath my hands.

Too distraught to care when a single drop of blood dripped from my hand, splashing onto its glossy surface.

BRANWELL

I dug through a tall cabinet in the bathroom, finding the first aid kit behind Chiara's hairdryer. Fighting to keep my emotions together.

Things had been so close with Tennyson and now, having to face Lucy—

The depth of her devastation . . . the pain of my own.

Just one day. That tiny slice of what life *could* be . . .

Somehow I would get past the pain, let Lucy go, find solace . . . somehow . . .

With a deep breath, I walked back down the hall and into the great room.

I froze.

The room was empty.

"Lucy?"

Silence.

Quickly, I walked across the room to the kitchen island, frowning.

"Lucy? Where did you go?"

No answer.

I went to the front door, threw the deadbolt and shouted down the stairwell.

"Lucy?" Voice more urgent.

I turned back to the apartment, forcing myself to think. I had just opened the deadbolt to get out. No way Lucy had been able to open the front door and relock it in the time I had in the bathroom. Particularly without me hearing. And why would she leave without talking to me?

I turned back into the kitchen.

"Lucy?" I quickly moved through all the bedrooms, checking each one.

Nothing.

Becoming more terrified with each passing second, I darted back into the kitchen, bracing my hands on the countertop, trying to piece together what had happened—

And then I noticed it.

The solitary drop of blood on my cell phone screen.

LUCY

FALLING, FALLING, falling . . .

A nightmare. Vertigo and terror.

I didn't land; I just woke up.

Had everything else been a dream?

I opened my eyes but still couldn't see.

Cold. Black.

The smell of roses and musty things.

I was lying on ground, solid and chilly.

Tentatively, I waved a hand in front of my face, blinking, trying to see something. I only sensed the vaguest shadow.

What had happened?

Heart pounding, I carefully sat up, rotating my head to look around.

Slowly indistinct shapes began to appear out of the inky blackness.

Where was I? What was going on—

I shivered and rubbed my arms.

Suddenly, the darkness . . . *moved.*

I screamed.

BRANWELL

I STARED AT the blood for a few seconds, a thousand thoughts swirling.

Hands shaking. Heart pounding.

This was Lucy's blood. On my phone.

A shiny surface where Chucky lived.

What had her blood triggered? Where had Lucy gone?

Love will draw the shadow out.

The bloody little handprint on Grace's dresser floated to the surface of my mind. Had her blood touched something keyed in her bedroom, sucking her into Chucky's world?

Was this phantom thing inside—Chucky—really just hungry for love and took delight in snatching people of Jack's bloodline?

Or was there something more, tied to my D'Angelo heritage?

What. Was. Up?!!

Frantic, I grabbed the towel off the counter and wiped my phone clean.

I pulled the glove off my right hand and then my left, leaving both hands bare. I emptied the dish towel drawer, wrapping several around my left arm.

I stared at the phone's glossy surface.

Deep breath.

I pressed the index finger of my left hand to the phone screen, keeping my right hand ready poised above the screen.

All of me ready to grasp whatever came out.

Darkness. Roses. Death.

Chucky surged from the phone. Powerful. Seeking.

A shadowy form.

As his claws worked through the towel layers, eager for my blood, I tried to grab the wispy shape with my right hand.

Again and again, my hand passed through the mist.

Damn.

I snatched my finger off the phone, breaking the connection.

The towels on my arm were shredded, a few light scratches tingling on my arm, fresh against the older, healing scrapes.

Now what?

If I couldn't capture Chucky, maybe I could join Lucy.

I whirled, looking around the kitchen, eyes landing on the knife Lucy had used.

Two steps and I had it in my hand. I hesitated for just a second and then used the tip of the knife to prick my middle left finger. Blood welled.

Hands shaking, I held my finger over my phone.

One single drop fell. Splashing onto the glossy surface.

Nothing.

I waited. Squeezed another drop of blood.

Still nothing.

I frowned, thinking through options.

Maybe an object could only work once with the whole blood thing.

The glass vase we had used to test for Chucky was on the kitchen counter.

It was worth a try.

I walked over to it, cradling my cut finger.

Hovering my hand above the vase, I took a deep breath, body tense, adrenaline running.

I tipped my finger, allowing blood to drip onto the vase.

Nothing.

My shoulders sagged.

So . . . *my* blood didn't trigger anything. But Lucy and Grace's obviously did.

Crap. Why couldn't I find the answer to this riddle?

Would blood on my hands help me grab Chucky? He seemed to like blood.

Grimacing, I ran down the hall and emptied the linen closet. My arm mummified in layers of towels and sheets, I walked back into the kitchen.

I cut my finger a little deeper this time, smearing my blood onto both palms.

Gory but possibly effective.

This was *so* on.

Me and Chucky.

No way I was stopping until I had Lucy and Grace back. Forget the stupid summer solstice.

Tense, I prepped my right hand to grab Chucky.

I had a finger poised over the phone, ready to touch it, when it rang. Chiara's face pulsed across the screen.

I stared at my bare, blood-red hands, looked back down at the phone. Now what?

Hurriedly, I swiped my right finger across the screen as quickly as possible.

Roses. Death—

"Chiara," I answered, tapping the speaker phone icon with another fast finger.

"Is everything okay?" Concern poured through the phone connection.

Understatement of the year there.

I glanced at my swaddled arms, bare bloody hands poking out.

"Not really. Why do you ask?"

"Tennyson started acting funny about five minutes ago." She was with my mom in Volterra, watching over Tennyson. "We have him sedated, and he was sleeping fine. But then he suddenly sat up and said, 'Lucy . . . she doesn't know . . . what I saw, it will change everything.' "

My heart plummeted.

"He's still saying it, Bran," Chiara continued.

I could hear sounds murmuring behind her. Chiara must have switched to speaker phone too, because Tennyson's voice suddenly came through clearly. "Gotta tell Branwell. Lucy . . . it's changed . . . the whole paradigm . . . it's different from what he thinks."

"Do you hear that, Branwell?" Chiara came back.

"Yeah."

"He's completely out of it, by the way. Totally asleep. It's like a dream or—"

"Or another prophecy." I braced my knuckles on the pile of shredded towels, closing my fingers around my bloody palms.

"So what happened, Bran?"

"Lucy disappeared."

"What?!!"

"She's gone, Chiara. Just like Grace." I shivered, swallowing back the panic fighting its way through my chest. "She cut her hand. I walked out of the room to grab a bandaid and when I came back, no Lucy anywhere. Just a drop of her blood on my telephone."

"No! Nonono! Chucky?"

"Working on it." I sucked in a ragged breath, trying to tamp my emotions down. Losing it wasn't going to help. "He and I are about to go twenty rounds in a fight. He better not hurt her—"

Bzzz. Bzzz. Bzzz.

Doorbell. The one way down at the front of the building.

Bzzzzz.

Damn.

"Hang on, Chiara. Someone's at the *portone*. Let me call you right back."

Holding my bloody hands out, like a surgeon prepping for surgery, I walked over to the intercom and pressed the talk button with my elbow.

"*Pronto*," I said.

"Mr. D'Angelo? This is Inspector Paola from the metropolitan police force. We would like to speak with you."

45

BRANWELL

We have the surveillance tapes, Mr. D'Angelo. They clearly show Roberto Moretti leaving your storefront, and Ms. Snow waving goodbye to him. Tell me what you know about this."

Inspector Paola paced in front of me—bobbed hair, official hat and uniform, dark Italian looks. Another police officer stood stoically behind her.

We were in the back office of the family store. I had managed to quickly wash my hands and pull on gloves before letting the police into our palazzo. It didn't take a genius to understand how it would look—me answering the door with Lucy missing and my hands bloody.

Paola had been grilling me for a solid thirty minutes. Turns out the *gelateria* down the street had video footage which meant we were so busted.

"As I've been saying, Inspector, I have no idea as to the current whereabouts of Roberto Moretti." That had been my line from the start. The honest, if incomplete, truth.

"And again, Mr. D'Angelo, that is not the question I asked."

Technically, she hadn't asked a question; she had demanded. But given how Paola glared at me, I kept that observation to myself. I carefully maintained a neutral expression.

I knew she was just doing her job, and I couldn't blame her for being suspicious. But I wasn't the problem here and the sooner she and her sidekick left, the sooner I could find a way to get Lucy back.

"One more time, Mr. D'Angelo. Where is Lucy Snow?"

Wasn't *that* the question of the hour?

"As I've been saying, I don't know. She disappeared."

Absolute truth.

"When?"

"Right before you rang my buzzer."

Paola did another circuit of the room. Eyes taking in the papers on the desk, the books lining the walls.

"How did she disappear, Mr. D'Angelo?"

I shrugged. "I don't know. I left the room. When I came back, she was gone."

Paola harrumphed and stared me down some more.

"She just up and *poof*—disappeared?" Paola rotated her wrist and twirled a finger. A very *sarcastic* finger. "Sorta like little Grace Snow?"

"Yes. She just disappeared . . . *exactly* like Grace Snow."

Silence.

Paola *so* wasn't buying my explanations.

She leaned forward, dark eyes intent and way too *seeing*.

"There is blood on your shirt, Mr. D'Angelo." She motioned toward my chest. "And why are you wearing gloves on a hot summer night in the middle of June?"

Crap.

Crap. Crap.

Somehow, I managed to keep the panic off my face. I glanced down at my shirt.

Yep. Definitely blood spots along my left side.

From Paola's point of view, this looked very, very bad.

"I cut myself." I tugged off my left glove and held up my sliced middle finger. I hadn't had time to put a bandaid on it, but it had thankfully stopped bleeding.

"And the gloves?"

I shrugged. "A personal idiosyncrasy. Ask anyone. I always wear them." I pulled the glove back onto my left hand.

Paola studied me, foot tapping.

"I will ask you one more time, Mr. D'Angelo. What did Roberto Moretti want with Lucy Snow?"

I clasped my hands together in front of me. "I have no comment to that, ma'am."

She scrutinized me for a solid minute, the silence hanging heavy in the room.

Silence had never bothered me. I blankly met her stare with one of my own.

We sat like that for several minutes.

She flinched first.

"Give me one reason why I shouldn't have you arrested right now, Mr D'Angelo," she finally said.

Her words hung in the room. My adrenaline spiked.

Her request, however, was easy.

"I'm innocent." I met her eyes directly, letting my honesty shine through my words. "I have done nothing wrong. I care deeply for Lucy and little Grace and would never do anything to harm them. I want nothing more than their safe return."

Paola studied me for a moment longer, then nodded her head.

"This isn't the last of this, Mr. D'Angelo. You can expect to speak with us tomorrow. Perhaps a good night's sleep will make your memory more . . . accessible. Good night."

I rose and politely showed them the door, locking it firmly behind them.

Adrenaline humming, I walked back to the office, pulled my phone from my pocket, and collapsed into the desk chair.

My reaction to everything sank in with a vengeance.

Tennyson's suicide attempt and weird ramblings.

Lucy's sudden disappearance.

Inspector Paola's accusations.

The worry that I would end up behind bars before I could solve this problem.

My hands shook violently. Panic squeezed my lungs.

Think, man.

There had to be a solution here.

I was sure Lucy's blood on my phone had been the catalyst for something. It made too much sense. My own blood, however, didn't trigger anything.

This had to be all tied up in Jack Knight-Snow somehow. His bloodline and Chucky.

I just needed the puzzle pieces to slot into place.

Gritting my teeth, I stared down at my telephone and pulled off both my gloves. Practically daring Chucky to come and get me.

Cautiously, I touched the phone with my left index finger.

Nothing.

And then . . .

Sunlight. Love. Lemon-verbena.

Stunned, I watched as an achingly familiar shape surged out of the phone. Hand. Wrist. A bit of bare arm.

Delicate long fingers. Pale skin. Freckles.

Lucy.

Her fingers wrapped desperately around my left arm, my finger still pressed against the surface of the phone. Pulling.

"Lucy!" I yelled. "Help me! Tell me what to do?"

Silence.

I tried to grab her arm with my right hand but, again, my hand passed right through. It was surreal. To my left arm, she felt so solid, but to my right, she was just air.

Only the hand connected to the keyed phone could feel her.

I shifted my left hand, keeping my skin in contact with the phone, but rotated my wrist, so my palm was up. I wrapped my fingers around Lucy's arm.

She was solid. She was warm.

"Lucy! Love! Can you hear me?"

Silence.

She was tugging on me, like she wanted me to come in or, more likely, was trying to pull herself out.

I held on to her, trying to think through the logistics. I had to maintain contact with the phone, which meant I couldn't draw back my hand to pull her out. How could I get leverage?

After a few minutes, her hand faded back into the phone.

It was the weirdest thing. Her solidity simply . . . melted away.

Panicking for real now, I broke contact with the phone and touched it again.

Sunshine. Lemons.

Lucy's arm appeared, grasping mine.

"Bran-ell?" Her voice.

"Lucy!"

". . . help . . . stuck . . . can't get . . . mirror . . . study . . ."

Her words were garbled. Like a staticky phone connection.

Her arm faded again.

Crap.

I touched the phone again and again.

Nothing.

Crap, crap!

Mirror. Study it.

That made sense. I needed to go to the source.

I could do that.

I yanked my gloves back onto my hands and crossed the room to the office safe. A moment later, I had it open. Carefully, I removed the ancient mirror wrapped in velvet.

Placing the mirror on the large table, I carefully unwrapped it, lifting the mirror with my gloved hand.

Now what?

Roberto had a whole plan with pentagrams, chanting and a water trap right at the peak of the summer solstice . . .

I had . . . a malfunctioning family curse and a truckload of determination.

It would have to be enough.

I turned the mirror in my hand. The engraved back glinted, catching the incandescent light from overhead.

Study it, Lucy had said.

So . . . I pondered it.

The figure dripping blood into the bowl in the background left.

The couple embracing to the right.

The bearded man seated in the foreground, leaning forward, holding a mirror in his front hand, his back hand being pulled down into the ground by another figure.

Right. So how was this helpful?

Frowning, I looked at it again. Studying the scenes one more time.

It seemed more like a cautionary tale than anything to me.

You drip blood on this object, you'll get sucked in.

But we already knew that.

I examined the guy in front being forced down.

Wait.

Was that it? Or was he pulling someone *out?*

Suddenly, that explanation seemed a lot more logical. Because the guy seated in front looked *nothing* like the person in the background, dripping blood.

No, the figure dripping blood behind looked a lot like the person *rising* from the ground.

My breath hitched. A flash of inspiration. Hundreds of loose threads suddenly snapping into a cohesive whole.

What if nothing about this mirror were allegorical? What if it were not a warning but a literal handbook?

An enchiridion.

An ancient sort of *What to Do if Your Loved One Gets Stuck in another Dimension for Dummies.*

Chills chased my spine. I studied the image again.

What if I were seeing a sequence of events?

The person in the back wasn't scrying, but was the victim, dripping blood onto a reflective surface.

The man in front was not some random representation of love, but rather Tages, the oracle of the proper bloodline who could pull the person out.

The figures behind—Tages and the person who had been trapped— were embracing after being reunited.

A sense of intense *rightness* flooded me. This had to be the answer.

Okay.

I could go with that.

The key was the seated figure of Tages. How was he pulling the figure out? Were they coming from the mirror or the ground? As the mirror was in his front hand, it was hard to tell.

I squinted, studying the image.

No. The person was definitely rising from the ground, not the mirror.

Wait.

There were tiny ripples. That was *water* not solid earth.

Of course! The whole situation with Chucky had been unique in water.

The thought had barely formed before I was moving out the door, down more steps and into the pool room.

Lights flared to life, illuminating the water's surface.

Chucky had felt decidedly different in water. Larger, more solid.

Perhaps water had been the key all along.

This was worth a shot.

I snagged a stool and walked over to the water's edge.

Carefully, I mimicked the pose on the back of the mirror.

Me, sitting in the chair beside the water.

Mirror held in my left hand, reflecting into the water's surface.

Right hand extended toward the water's surface.

Nothing happened.

I stretched farther, dipping a finger in the water.

Nothing.

Sitting back, I frowned, studying the back of the mirror. And then I noticed it.

Duh.

The dude wasn't wearing gloves.

Everything here needed contact with my bare skin.

I set the mirror on my knees and pulled off my gloves, fingers shaking, tossing them on the ground behind me.

I stared down at the mirror, chest heaving.

Touching something shiny *and* ancient was terrifying.

Pandora's Box.

Hopefully not literally.

Gingerly, my left hand hovered above the mirror handle. Sucking in a fortifying breath, I grabbed it, wrapping my fingers around the cool metal.

Power surged up my arm. Charged. Eager.

A stallion pulling hard at the reins.

No sound.

That in and of itself was . . . astonishing.

I was holding something without a whisper of noise reaching me.

I savored the sensation for about half a second. Power arced through me, desperate for an outlet—tingling, burning the fingers of my opposite hand.

Angling the mirror so it reflected in the pool, I touched my fingertips to the water.

Instantly, Lucy's hand surged out, wrapping around mine.

Slightly chilled. Clinging. Desperate.

Hallelujah!

It was the oddest sight. She literally came out of the surface of the water.

I flexed and pulled, lifting her out of the pool and onto the tile floor beside me.

Coughing and shivering, dripping wet, she wobbled to her hands and knees.

"Grace"—a ragged cough—"P-please, get Grace."

I turned back to the pool and repeated the process.

Mirror, angle, water, reach.

A small hand leaped into mine. Fragile and cold.

I pulled and little Grace practically flew out of the pool.

Crying, she landed on top of Lucy, who instantly turned and gathered her niece tight against her chest. Both of them sopping wet.

Power coursed through me, arching my spine.

I dropped the mirror onto my legs, severing the contact.

My left hand tingled and stung, like hitting a baseball with a metal bat.

"Gracie, you okay?" Lucy ran her hands over Grace's body.

The tiny girl hiccupped and curled into Lucy's chest, wrapping her arms around Lucy's waist.

"Gracie, talk to me," Lucy urged, trying to see Grace's face.

"'T's okay, Aunt Lucy," she sniffed. And then she paused, looking around.

She met my gaze and angled her head in surprise.

"Who're you?" She inspected me up and down and then twisted in Lucy's lap, surveying the room again. "And where's my Gruncle Jack?"

46

LUCY

Shock blazed through Branwell at Grace's question. I could see it in the flare of his eyes. Heard it in his sharp intake of air.

"Where is he?" Grace continued to rotate her head, trying to see behind me. "We can't leave Gruncle Jack inside."

My mind reeled, barely processing the events of the past . . . however long it had been. An hour? Two?

"Branwell," I whispered, meeting his eyes.

He blinked and then jerked back to life.

"Gruncle Jack. Right." Branwell nodded. "Makes sense . . . I guess."

I pulled Gracie closer to my chest. She was *here*. She was safe and in my arms.

Now we simply had to rescue Gruncle Jack.

Flexing the fingers of his left hand, Branwell grasped the mirror with his bare palm, angling the mirror over the water. He dipped the fingers of his right hand into the pool.

I gasped.

He looked just like the engraving on the back of the mirror facing me.

Nothing happened.

And then . . .

A hand surged out of the water.

Masculine. Long, expressive fingers and a broad palm. An arm in a loose muslin shirt followed. The hand wrapped around Branwell's forearm, holding tight.

Grunting, Branwell leaned back, pulling the rest of the man's large body out of the water.

Tan breeches, boots, blue waistcoat, white shirt, auburn hair and the beginning of stubble.

Jack Knight-Snow, in the living flesh.

Wow. Just . . . *wow*.

Branwell hauled Jack onto the tile next to Grace and me, poor Jack coughing and wheezing.

Branwell jumped up and carefully set the mirror on a nearby table. He turned to help, intent on lifting Jack upright.

But Branwell's arms passed straight through Jack's torso. Branwell staggered forward and then flinched when his leg passed partially into Jack's neck.

I angled my head, finally realizing I could see the pool deck and water through Jack.

My gruncle was as transparent as any Hollywood ghost.

Alrighty then.

Out of the spelled water, Jack had no substance, though he did appear wet.

Strange.

Branwell stepped back, eyes wary.

I lifted a hand to the light. Was I transparent now too?

I looked solid.

Concern evident, Branwell stepped around Jack, looking at me.

"Are you okay?" he asked.

I nodded. "I think so."

He bent down, cupping my face with his hand. He felt solid, warm and blissfully mine. Particularly when he leaned in and kissed me.

Grace giggled in my lap and patted my shoulder, looking at Branwell.

"He's tissing you, Aunt Lucy." She reached a small hand up to Branwell's beard, stroking it. Giggled harder. "It's tickly."

I hugged Grace, kissing her soundly on her squishy cheek.

Mmmm.

I hugged and kissed her again.

She was maybe a little *too* squishy.

I held her hand up to the light, but Grace wasn't transparent. Well, not like Jack.

Thinking of which . . .

I looked around Branwell at my gruncle, slowly pushing himself to his feet.

Or, at least, he tried. But his hand went straight through the stool Branwell had been sitting on. Jack's head followed the momentum and would have cracked on the tile . . . if it had been solid enough to do so.

Rolling to his back in surprise, poor Jack sat up.

"Dash it all," he grumbled, surveying his wispy hands. "I've gone plum gauzy."

"Ooooh, you're like a ghost, Gruncle Jack." Grace laughed.

Jack shook his head. "Blast. Not sure how to fix this. 'The shadow diminishes upon return'," he quoted. "The translation makes better sense now."

Smiling, I clutched sweet Grace to me, kissing her extra-squishy cheeks over and over. Tears finally caught up with me, happiness bubbling over.

Grace was back! I wanted to dance an awkward jig around the room and laugh maniacally. I settled for squeezing Gracie so tight she squeaked.

Branwell fetched us towels—Jack's flew right through him when

Branwell tossed it his way—but I wrapped one around me and proceeded to dry Grace off, tickling her until we were both breathless with laughter.

"What happened?" Branwell asked once Grace and I were dryer and snuggled together under more towels.

I met his gaze over Grace's head. His hair was down, tumbling around his shoulders. Sleeves pushed up and Jack's scratches still starkly red on his arms. Jeans and shirt wet from pulling us free.

"Wow. It was . . ." I laughed, too breathy and stunned. "Remarkable."

TWO HOURS EARLIER . . .

MY BLOOD DRIPPED onto the phone. Just one solitary drop.

The world telescoped, and I tumbled weightless, only to wake up on my back in the pitch black. I sat up struggling to see as my eyes slowly adjusted to the dim light.

I found myself in a large hall, like the kind you see in old stately homes with marble columns and an arched barrel ceiling, dimly lit and nearly monochrome.

Out of the corner of my eye, a sudden movement darted forward.

I screamed.

A shriek that turned to a cry of joy half a second later.

Gracie was running toward me, down the length of the long hall. She launched herself onto me, pushing me to the ground.

Surely reenacting the vision Tennyson had seen.

"Aunt Lucy! You're here!" She sobbed over and over.

I clutched her small body to mine, crying with her.

My sweet Gracie was here. She was okay.

It was only when Grace calmed down that I noticed the Regency gentleman standing behind her.

Tall, auburn-brown hair, blue eyes, sharp jaw, wide cheek bones . . . Jack Knight-Snow.

We introduced ourselves.

"I am sorry and yet not that you are here," he said. "I have been so long without company. And then Miss Grace, and now you, have arrived."

Still holding Grace, I prowled the confines of the hall, Gruncle Jack at my heels. I peered cautiously around each pillar, expecting Chucky to lunge out at me at every turn.

Not that I had any idea what I would do if he did. Hit him with a blast of my eternal optimism and a pithy t-shirt saying?

"You okay, Aunt Lucy?" Gracie asked, arms around my neck.

"Just making sure you're safe, sweetie."

Jack frowned. "If you are looking for anyone else, I am afraid you are out of luck. We are the only people here."

"You sure about that?"

Jack turned to me with a solid *Are you crazy, madam?* look.

"I assure you, I have had adequate opportunity to ascertain the true depths of my solitude." Tone so very dry.

Got it.

"We are stuck here, I am afraid," Jack continued. "I have had far too much time to think about my mistakes. That blasted mirror. I should have never touched it. Let alone picked it up with blood on my hands. It primed the mirror to draw in those of my bloodline. I am positive it holds the key to our escape as well, but I am still not sure how."

A bright light about the size of a dinner plate suddenly appeared next to Jack.

Instantly, he pressed his hand into it. His own arm disappeared nearly up to his shoulder.

The whole scenario looked Twilight Zone weird.

Jack's face was a mask of concentration. "I just cannot quite get purchase on the other side," he muttered, face strained. "I try to grasp, to pull myself out . . ."

Ah.

The light disappeared and Jack staggered forward, his arm reappearing.

The light returned almost instantly.

He tried again.

The same thing happened several times, the light appearing in different places. Grace would chase around, looking for it, squealing when she saw it.

It disappeared for a while, giving me a chance to think. What if the light *was* the portal?

When the light appeared again, I was ready.

"Wait," I said, darting forward and thrusting my arm into the light like Jack had done.

If you can't beat 'em, join 'em.

I felt something solid. It *had* to be Branwell's arm. Instead of clawing at it, I rested my hand on it. A hand wrapped around my wrist. Held tight.

Nothing happened.

The light faded away and my arm fell.

Dang.

The light reappeared and I reached in again. This time, I yelled.

"Branwell."

No reply.

"Branwell, we're stuck in here. You have to get the mirror and study it and find a way to get us out."

Nothing.

The light faded.

We sat in tense silence for a while, Grace moving from my lap to Jack's. He had been perfectly solid inside the hall.

While we waited, Jack and I talked about what happened. Upset over Sofia's defection, Jack had accidentally cut his hand throwing a crystal brandy decanter against the fireplace mantel and, without thinking, touched the ancient mirror. The very scene that Branwell and Dante had seen in my living room.

Touching the mirror with his own blood had tethered Jack's bloodline to the shadow world. He was instantly sucked in. His memories of being in the large, monochrome hall were hazy. He remembered floating in a fever-like haze until a light shone in. He reached for the light, clawing at the other side, trying to pull himself out. But the light faded as abruptly as it came. Jack drifted in that odd dream-like state until the next time the light appeared, which it did several more times.

Then Grace had arrived, shaking Jack out of his lethargy for good. In talking with her, Jack pieced together what had happened.

Grace's allergies had given her a bloody nose on the morning she disappeared. She had gone to grab a tissue from the top of her dresser and had touched the Little Mermaid music box with her bloody hand. Like Branwell and me, Jack realized that the music box must have been keyed to the shadow world.

There was no Chucky, no demonic force.

Just a man stuck for nearly two hundred years in a shadow world, trying to dig his way free every time Branwell touched a keyed item.

Jack, Grace and I sat together until an enormous portal opened, and Branwell's very solid hand reached in to us.

AFTER LISTENING TO the story of my time in the shadow world, Branwell herded us upstairs to Judith's apartment where the evening had begun.

Jack constantly swiveled his head, taking in a world thoroughly different from the one he left, his face a strange mix of shock and wonder.

We all crowded into the great room of Judith and Chiara's apartment, Gracie clinging to my neck. My first instinct was to call Jeff and Jen and let them know their daughter was okay.

But Branwell shook his head, placing a hand over my phone before I could call.

"Let's think this through first," he said. "You are one of the prime suspects in Grace's disappearance. If she suddenly reappears with you, you will most likely be charged with kidnapping, and we have no way to disprove that."

That was . . . true. I hadn't thought beyond finding Grace.

And though I would do anything for Grace, going to jail unnecessarily definitely crossed a line. Not to mention how terrible orange looked with my pink skin undertones.

I set my phone down, deciding *not* to call my brother just yet.

"Let me rally the troops and see what we can come up with," Branwell said, brushing his knuckles against my neck.

I pecked his cheek and left the room to change into dry clothing, taking Grace with me. She chattered on about Gruncle Jack and how nice he was. Once I was done, I wrapped Gracie in a warm blanket and carried her back to the great room, snuggling her on the couch.

Branwell was on the phone, pacing, talking with Chiara and Judith in Volterra about Grace's return. I could hear their whoops of joy even across the room. Branwell smiled, holding his phone again in his bare hand. Without anyone in the shadow world, nothing came out of objects linked to the mirror.

Then Branwell launched into our problem, switching to speaker phone so I could be part of the conversation. How could we return Grace to her parents without casting suspicion on innocent others? After a lot of debate and input from Chiara in particular, we crafted a plan.

By this point, it was well past midnight. Gracie had fallen asleep hours ago, and Branwell had situated Jack into one of the guest bedrooms. Branwell kissed me good night and promised to be back first thing in the morning.

Gracie and I met Branwell and Chiara at the bottom of the palazzo stairwell just after sunrise. Grace was a bit of a mess, hair poking everywhere and still wearing the same pajamas she had on when she vanished. But her ragged looks were part of the plan.

We were ready. Chiara had everything in place.

Two of Chiara's trusted friends picked up Grace and drove her far south of Florence to the Abbey of San Galgano.

We had debated for hours where Grace should be 'found.' It needed to be somewhere touristy where there would be people, but not so touristy that Grace would be in danger or our helpers seen by security cameras.

San Galgano fit the bill. It was an abandoned abbey turned museum buried in the rural countryside of southern Tuscany. One person would drop Grace off close to the museum and send her walking toward it.

Two other friends would be in the museum at the time and ensure that Grace was 'found.'

After Grace left, Branwell and I waited an hour before calling Inspector Paola to tell her that I had returned. I had apparently been upset and needed to get away. Paola insisted we both come down to the police station to answer some questions.

Bless Paola. She played right into our hands.

Branwell and I were sitting with Paola when she got the call that Grace had been found.

The timing could not have been better. Not to mention the comical look on Paola's face when she realized that we were not, in fact, her prime suspects.

From there, everything exploded.

Reporters and cameras were everywhere. Jeff and Jen rushed to the station, crying. We all went to the hospital where they had taken Grace as a precaution and watched my niece be reunited with her parents.

As expected, the police were baffled by Grace's strange reappearance and had no leads. Grace herself was no help, as she just babbled excitedly about being with Gruncle Jack, an ancestor who had died two hundred years ago. The media dubbed Grace's safe return the Miracle of San Galgano.

It took several days, but everything eventually calmed down.

I returned to Prato with Jeff, Jen and Grace, but I hung out with the D'Angelos when I could. We talked endlessly about Branwell and his strange ability to open the portal using the mirror. Who knew why he had that particular gift. Without understanding the exact nature of the D'Angelo curse, it was hard to say. Chiara was absorbed in researching it. But it could be years before we had a solid answer.

We did determine that the mirror was a portal to a shadow land, a place in between life and death. The longer a person stayed in the shadow world, the more their body drifted toward death. This explained why Dante had seen Jack and then Grace. He was seeing the portion of their soul that had crossed over, so to speak. It also clarified why Jack was transparent: he was neither fully in this world or the next.

For herself, Grace was fine after a day or two—no longer squishy. Kids.

They'll bounce back from anything.

Jack, however, was not so lucky. He remained ghost-like, unable to touch things. We worried that he would need to eat or do something to survive, but he said he was fine.

When he first met Chiara, he stared and stared. And then stared some more.

"It is like seeing Sofia reborn," he whispered.

Dante assured us that Chiara was *not*, in fact, Sofia reincarnated but simply a distant relative who happened to look similar.

For her part, Chiara made some crack about Jack being a man of little substance and went about her day.

Things with Tennyson were still tense, and I saw Branwell less and less as he was wrapped up in family matters. We texted and talked on the phone, but we both knew that in a few days I would be returning to the States, and Branwell would get on with his life in Florence.

Tennyson, as he ever had been, stood between us.

I cried my heart out over it and ate too much therapeutic gelato.

It should have helped more than it did.

Branwell texted me ten days after Grace's return, two days before I was set to fly home.

Lunch tomorrow?

I stared at his words, knowing that seeing him would only make everything that much harder.

But . . . things were already awful. How much worse could seeing him make me feel?

We met at a swank cafe just off of Piazza della Repubblica in downtown Florence. My eyes instantly finding him in the crowded room.

Broad shouldered. Trimmed beard. Gloved hands. Long sleeves. Fierce eyes drinking me in like I was his *raison d'etre*.

Right back at you, my love.

Lunch was painfully lovely. Full of the lighthearted things we did say and heavy with the aching ones we didn't.

The refrain kept running through my head—*'Tis better to have loved and lost/Than never to have loved at all.*

I had *finally* looked up the author of that quote.

The irony of ironies?

Alfred, Lord Tennyson.

Tennysons everywhere tormented me with what could never be.

BRANWELL

L unch with Lucy was an exercise in masochistic torture.

Seeing Lucy, being with her, hearing her voice, knowing she wanted to be with me as much as I wanted to be with her . . . my heart shattered.

Guilt swamped me.

I couldn't fix this, no matter how hard I tried.

Tennyson was doing better. Better than I would have hoped, actually. Mom was staying with him in Volterra, helping him get back on his feet. That said, he was still too fragile to even consider broaching the topic of Lucy.

Lucy walked home with me after lunch, winding slowly through the streets of Florence. Shamelessly, I pulled her into every dark doorway for a kiss. Across the Piazza della Signoria. Down dark alleyways to Piazza Santa Croce. And then several more twisty streets to our family palazzo.

Lucy wanted to say goodbye to Chiara and check up on Gruncle Jack. He had taken up residence in our place. Nonna had always said the palazzo needed a ghost. Jack was a fine house guest, once he got through his creepy-staring-at-Chiara phase. Who knew what the long term outcome would be for him.

I waited in the kitchen while Lucy said her goodbyes and then took her hand as we walked back downstairs. I would drive her to Prato and then . . . that would be that.

My throat felt tight and scratchy. How could I let her go?

"This isn't goodbye for forever." She pulled me to a halt at the bottom of the stairs.

"Lucy, love, we've been over and over this—"

"I know, but I refuse to say I'll never see you again. What we have, Branwell . . . it feels too right."

I wrapped my arms around her, kissing her with quiet desperation. Trying to find a way forward through the jumbled emotions flying around my brain.

"I'm going to wait for you," she whispered between kisses. "I don't care how long it takes, you're worth the wait."

This woman.

"Love, you know I'll wait for you too, but Tenn . . . I don't know—"

"Shhh, you can't say that. Things might change. I love you too much—"

I silenced her with a kiss, and she responded, hands in my hair, pushing me back against the wall opposite the door. How could bear losing the one person who completed me? Despair and sadness laced every touch of our lips.

I really should have been paying better attention. Listening.
Anything.

But kissing Lucy felt so right. Like I had been born for this alone . . . to be her anchor in the storm.

Ah, my darling Lucy.

Dimly, I noted the car drive by. The slam of a car door. The crack of the *portone* opening.

I didn't register Tennyson's casual words for another second after that—

"Sheesh, you two. Get a room already."

He was a up a flight of stairs, prosthetic leg tapping, before it all sank in.

Lucy and I jumped apart, scalded.

What?!!

I blinked. Gazed down at Lucy.

Yep. Just as surprised as me.

We both looked at the stairs where Tennyson had disappeared.

Then back at each other.

Stairs.

Each other.

"Uhmm, did he just say what I think he did?" Lucy's tone decidedly matter-of-fact.

"Yeah." I replayed the scene in my head. "I'm pretty sure he did."

"I thought he was in Volterra."

"Me too."

Hand in hand, we bolted up the stairs after him. Three flights later, we found Tennyson, hunched over, raiding Mom's fridge for a Coke.

He stood up and shut the fridge as Lucy and I walked into the room, still holding hands.

"Hey." I gave him a solid *wassup* lift of my chin.

"Hey."

I reached out for Tennyson's emotions, trying to get a read on him.

Love. Determination. Amusement.

Wait . . . *amusement?*

I cocked my head in question. "You . . . wanna tell me . . ."

"What's up?"

"Yeah."

Tennyson's eyes flitted to Lucy and then down to our joined hands. Wistful. Pensive. But not anguished. Not the serrated pain I had been feeling from him lately.

Hope nudged in, a tiny tendril.

"Hey, Luce," he said with a soft smile, raising his eyes to hers.

"Tenn. It's good to see you." Lucy clutched my hand tighter. "I'm glad you're doing better."

Tennyson nodded. And then looked at me.

His jaw went up a notch. Daring me to challenge him. Over what, I wasn't sure.

"You love her?" He nudged his chin at Lucy.

What to say? I opted for the truth.

"More than life." I paused. Swallowed. "But not more than *your* life."

Tennyson bit his lip and angled his head.

"My life?" he asked, puzzlement and confusion. "What does my life have to do with you and Lucy?"

It was my turn to blink.

"Uh, because there is a history here?" I gestured between Lucy and Tennyson with my free hand.

Tennyson looked at Lucy. "Yeah, there is. But they're good memories."

Lucy nodded, answering his unspoken question. "They are, Tenn. Wonderful memories."

I frowned. "I'm . . . a little lost. You wanna explain what's going on?"

Tennyson flashed a smile, a little too wicked and knowing. "Well, I think it's pretty *obvious* what's going on here. I witnessed a solid sample of it in the stairwell—"

"*Tenn.*" Tone warning. I scowled, trying to piece this puzzle together.

Tennyson popped the top on his Coke and leaned a hip into the bar. I was utterly confused.

"So . . . I don't understand—" I stared first at Lucy. And then my brother. "You tried to *kill* yourself just two weeks ago."

"I did."

"This"—I waved a hand between him and Lucy again—"has *always* been an emotional trigger for you. Bathtub. Blood. Remember?"

A gust of air left Tennyson. He swallowed, eyes fixed on Lucy. "Yes. I remember."

"So . . . What's going on?" I glared at him. "Is this some kind of sick joke?"

Tennyson straightened, face sober. "No, Bran. I would never joke about this. But I *am* trying to be more open, like you said we should be." He fixed me with his blue, blue gaze. "As I told you, something's broken inside me. It's not just the visions and the constant feeling." He shook his head, eyes glassing as he focused inward. "It's like this shattered mess of pain and frustration and . . . and pure emotion that eats me from the inside out."

"Tenn—"

"I've let you guys think it was simply the loss of Lucy because it was easier than explaining that the problem is deeper than that. Harder to solve. Not that losing Lucy wasn't emotionally difficult." He smiled at her. Soft. Wan. Apologetic. "It's merely one component of a larger problem, one that has no solution. When I was with Lucy, it was easier to sweep my emotional fracturing under the rug. Use Lucy to prop me up."

Tennyson set his soda down, running a hand through his hair. Hissed out a low breath.

"Look . . . the whole bath tub incident woke me up," he continued. "It forced me to face the fact that this pain inside me can only be solved from *within*. I knew I had to let Lucy emotionally go, once and for all."

"But the bathtub incident was almost two years ago."

"True. But healing wounds this deep takes time. So when the situation with Grace surfaced in the news, I wanted to help but knew that I didn't have the emotional wherewithal to deal with it. Things have been . . . hard . . . lately." He swallowed. Convulsively.

"Obviously."

Tennyson nodded. "The fracturing inside me is growing. I was worried that if I spent time around Lucy, I would fall back into old patterns. Rely on her emotional optimism instead of forcing myself to be strong." He managed another wan smile. "Being an emotional parasite isn't helpful for any of us. I know that. But it didn't stop me from crawling up that villa tower."

"So you aren't upset over losing Lucy?" I asked.

"No. Not like you think. Not for over a year now. It's more the fear of having to face all this alone."

"You never have to face your trials alone. We got this for you, brother."

"I know. This whole situation with the mirror and Grace has shown me that we can't make any assumptions about our GUTs. There's a lot left for us to learn, which means there still might be a solution for me."

Hope went from a tiny stream to a pounding torrent.

So . . .

Where did that leave this situation?

"You're honestly okay with this?" I asked him, lifting Lucy's hand joined with mine.

"Yes. It's what is meant to be." He gave an apologetic lift of his shoulder. "Several months ago, I had a vision. So clear. The most lucid I have ever had . . ."

A beat.

I scarcely breathed.

"It was you and Lucy," Tennyson continued, eyes going distant. "We were all together on Cannon Beach on the Oregon coast . . . it was your wedding day."

"Oh!" Lucy gasped.

My heart stopped.

"It was . . . exquisite. You got married on the beach underneath a wooden arch, waves crashing around Haystack Rock behind. Dante bought a pastor's license off the internet so he could marry you—'cause, you know, that's Dante for you, always wanting to be in the middle of things. Branwell, you cried through your vows. Lucy alternately giggled and sobbed through hers. And then you kissed her . . ." Tennyson's voice drifted off. ". . . and it was the most sacred kiss I've ever been privileged to witness. Tender. Loving. Full of such promise and hope. Hallowed. I cried too. We all did."

Silence blanketed the room.

"This was several months ago, you say?" I asked.

"Yeah."

"And you didn't think to say anything to me?"

"I'm saying something now, aren't I?" He shot me another strained grin. "Besides, I figured if it was truly meant to be, you guys would work it out yourselves. I only see future possibilities, after all."

He winked at Lucy.

"But—"

Tennyson held out a hand, silencing me. "I know from far too many past experiences that talking about my visions can often impact their outcome. I didn't want to influence something this big. But Lucy arriving in Italy . . ."

He shrugged and took a loud sip of his soda, avoiding my gaze.

"So the vision Chiara said you were mumbling about, how it would change everything—"

"When I was sedated?"

I nodded.

"That whole night is super fuzzy, but yeah . . . it was this vision I was referring to. You two together. It *does* change everything."

Tennyson swallowed and cleared his throat, continuing, "I can't think of any two people who deserve each other more than you guys." He shifted his gaze to mine. Lucy's smile went all wobbly and teary. "And there is no man on the planet I'd rather see Lucy with than you, my brother. God bless you both."

I crushed Tennyson to me, helpless to stop the tears streaming into my beard.

"Thank you." I whispered in Italian. "I love you, brother mine. To eternity and back."

Tennyson returned my hug and we cried it out. Grown men can do that.

When we finally pulled back, he smiled at Lucy.

"I expect you to make good on my vision." Tennyson winked.

"I always said you were a perfect Tenn." Lucy laughed and wrapped her arms around Tennyson, kissing him soundly on the cheek. "Now, about that wedding. Can I get a few more details? Dress? Flowers? A girl needs to know these things."

EPILOGUE

Lucy wasted no time planning our wedding. After pining after each other for six long years, neither of us wanted a drawn out engagement. The darkness and hopelessness of our love had given way to a bright, sunshiny future. I was grateful for those hard-won shadows, as they made the blinding joy of Lucy's love more crystalline clear. But we were both anxious to move beyond and begin building a life together.

We married just three months after Grace's return—Cannon Beach on the Oregon Coast at sunset. Everything was precisely as Tennyson envisioned, all our family and friends together. To be honest, the day was actually a bit of a blur for me.

My clearest memory was that first glimpse of Lucy in her wedding dress, walking down the aisle. Most women have high expectations for that moment and, not to sabotage my own gender, I don't know how many grooms appreciate it as much as their brides expect them to.

But for me . . . it's an image I will remember vividly, even fifty years from now.

Lucy with her red hair piled on her head, a mass of elegant curls. Her dress, this diaphanous mix of tailored lace and chiffon swirling around her. Adoration and happiness flooding her expression.

My own vision blurred.

This exquisite, buoyant, confident, extraordinary woman had chosen to share her life with *me*.

Six months after our wedding, family and friends gathered again. This time on the lawn of the family villa outside Volterra on an unseasonably warm day toward the end of March. Everyone milled about, piling food onto plates and catching up.

Grace chased poor Elvis around the lawn, while Tennyson and Jeff chatted. Dante and Claire listened as Cat Lady delved into the minutiae of her latest feline acquisition. Chiara and Jen kept trying to draw out Jack, who still remained ghost-like. Roberto and his not-so-secret-any-more girlfriend (who had apparently quit her job at the museum so they could date) insisted on helping Nonna and Mom with the food.

Every single person wore a plain white t-shirt and jeans.

Except my beautiful wife.

Her white shirt hugged her rounding belly, the words *I make humans. What's your superpower?* printed across her stomach.

I smiled so wide it hurt as she approached. I would never tire of seeing Lucy pregnant with our child.

There are moments in life where you look at the distance between where you once were and where you currently stand and shake your head in disbelief.

If someone had told me a year ago I would be married to Lucy Snow and having a baby gender reveal party for our child . . . I would have laughed at the sick joke.

And yet . . . here we were.

Lucy arched an eyebrow as she drew near, popping onto her tiptoes to give me a kiss.

"I was wondering where my handsome baby-daddy went," she murmured against my mouth.

I gathered her into my arms, loving that I could hold my entire family all at once.

"You ready for this?" I asked.

She grinned, mischievously delighted. "Oh yeah!"

I laughed and grabbed her hand, pulling her toward a table stacked with sealed white cups.

A few minutes later, Chiara whistled to get everyone's attention. Lucy snugged herself against my side, one hand on her belly.

"Thank you all for coming," I began. "Lucy and I appreciate you making the effort to share this day with us. I hope you've been enjoying the food and fun—"

"Let's get on with it!" Mom called. "I want to know if I'm having a grandson or a granddaughter. I'm itching to go shopping."

Everyone laughed.

"Lucy and I don't know the gender either. So, from here, it's pretty simple. Each of you grab a cup full of colored powder." I swept a hand over the table. "And then, on the count of three, we're all going to pull off the foil top and toss the contents of our cups in the air. Blue for boy, pink for girl."

Three minutes later, we all faced each other in a circle. Nervous energy skittered down my spine. I knew what I hoped the colored powder would reveal. Lucy and I exchanged a wink.

"One, two . . . three!"

The air exploded in combination of pink *and* blue.

Everyone stared in puzzled silence.

"I think someone got the memo wrong," Tennyson said as the powder settled.

Lucy, however, squealed in excitement, jumping into my arms. I swung her around with a whoop.

At which point, my mom put it all together.

"You're having *twins*?!" she shrieked. "A boy and a girl? And you didn't tell me?!"

Lucy nodded her head, happy tears streaking through the powder on her cheeks.

Pandemonium ensued. People hugged and laughed. My mom and Nonna cried. Lucy and I had known for months that she carried fraternal twins, but we had decided to keep it a secret.

The look on my mom's face made it totally worth it.

Much later, I carried an exhausted but thoroughly happy Lucy up the stairs to our apartment in the family palazzo in Florence. Dante and Claire had given the first floor apartment to us, saying they preferred to live in her grandfather's villa just outside of town. I wasn't entirely sure that was true, but Lucy and I welcomed having a space of our own.

Lucy relaxed against my chest, arms looped around my neck.

"Happy, beautiful?" I asked, walking up the stone steps.

"Impossibly so," she murmured against my throat. "I'm so glad we're having a boy and a girl."

"It's what we both wanted, one of each."

"Exactly. I can't wait to meet them."

"Me either," I whispered. "I want to tell them everything."

"Everything?"

"Yes. I'll start with 'I met your mother when she photographed my heart.'"

AUTHOR'S NOTE

As usual, when writing a story set in the past, I have incorporated select aspects of history and then blatantly made up others. I'll attempt to sort through it all here. Though, be warned, there are (minor) spoilers.

First of all, let me express my appreciation for the entire country of Italy—Tuscany in particular. Outside of my current home state, I've lived more of my life in Tuscany than anywhere else in the world. Every time I visit, it feels like coming home.

For this book, I dug deep into Tuscany's history, going all the way back to the Etruscans who originally lived in the region and lent their name to it. All of the information I give in the book about Etruscan history and artifacts is true to the best of my understanding, though the specific mirror itself was fabricated for this story.

Additionally, the information about Hinthial and Tages is drawn from Roman accounts and archeology of the area. Hinthial was an ambiguous figure in Etruscan mythology and folklore and there remains controversy over who she was exactly to the Etruscans. Her name did have the double-meaning of Goddess of Love and ghost/phantasm, which caused me know small amount of frustration in my research. According to Etruscan mythology, Tages was the human founder of Etruscan religion and his descendants/followers acted as oracles.

To Americans, the Italian approach to archaeological excavation and conservation can appear haphazard and casual. Nothing could be farther from the truth. The Italians are hardly cavalier in their treatment of their history—there's just so much of it, they can't obsess over every little thing.

The Abbey of San Galgano, mentioned in passing at the very end of the book, is well worth a visit. The abandoned ruins are nestled deep in the Tuscan countryside. A nearby chapel actually houses the original sword in the stone—a confirmed 14th century blade embedded in a large rock.

As for Lucy and her t-shirts, most of them are actual shirts you can purchase from www.woot.com. Happy shopping.

I have created an extensive pinboard on Pinterest with images of everything I talk about in the book. So if you want a visual of anything, pop over there and explore. Just search for NicholeVan.

As with all books, this one couldn't have been written without the help and support from those around me. I know I am going to leave someone out with all these thanks. So to that person, know that I totally love you and am so deeply grateful for your help!

To Kelly Crawford . . . thanks for helping us up our family motto game. Choose Fun is a much better goal than Just Don't Die. Though in our defense, Just Don't Die really does apply to a staggering number of situations. (Paris driving, anyone?)

To my beta readers—you know who you are—thank you for your helpful ideas and support. And, again, an extra large thank you to Annette Evans and Norma Melzer for their fantastic copy editing skills and insights.

A huge thank you goes to Rebecca Spencer, Lois Brown, Jennifer Jenkins and Amy Beatty for their helpful plot suggestions, revision notes and willingness to let me cry on their shoulders.

And, as usual, this work would not have reached its fruition without the excellent editorial eye of Erin Rodabough. You have a touch of genius, my friend.

Thanks to Andrew, Austenne and Kian for your patience and adaptability. We sold our house and nearly everything we owned (including your beds) and moved into a very small space all during the writing of this book. Onward and upward to better things!

And finally, no words can express my love and appreciation for Dave. Thanks for listening to me, no matter how scattered, exasperated I am. Thank you for moving boxes and hefting heavy furniture and dealing with the frustration of this time in our lives. There is no one else I would rather have as my partner-in-crime.

READING GROUP QUESTIONS

Fair warning—these reading group questions contain spoilers.

1. In the initial brainstorming for this book, there was a lot of discussion about using the threat of Tennyson's suicide as the barrier keeping Branwell and Lucy apart. Do you feel the real possibility of a loved-one's suicide would be sufficient to prevent you from pursuing a relationship? Do you feel this conflict was realistically portrayed in the book?

2. There are flashbacks between a number of the chapters. Why do you think the author included the flashbacks? Did you like them? Why or why not?

3. Did you enjoy the secondary storyline with Jack and Sofia? Why do you think it was included in the book? Did you like how it was integrated? Did you want more or less of their story?

4. The presence of Chucky is meant to add tension and drama to the storyline. But, in the end, you find that there never was a demon. How did you feel about that revelation? Was it fun or did you feel cheated as a reader?

5. This book has something of a love triangle going between Branwell, Lucy and Tennyson. How do you feel about love triangles? Did this one work for you?

6. How do you feel about the resolution between Tennyson, Branwell and Lucy? Do you think the author handled that well or did it leave you unsatisfied? Why or why not?

7. Why is the book titled Love's Shadow? Along that same line, Branwell asserts that our shadows define our light—what does that mean to you? Do you agree or disagree?

OTHER BOOKS BY NICHOLE VAN

THE BROTHERS MALEDETTI

Gladly Beyond (Dante and Claire)
Love's Shadow (Branwell and Lucy)
Chiara and Jack (coming mid-2017)
Tennyson and Ainsley (coming late 2017)

THE HOUSE OF OAK SERIES

Intertwine
Divine
Clandestine
Refine
Outshine (coming Spring 2017, Daniel Ashton's story)
An Invisible Heiress (a novella in *Spring in Hyde Park*)

If you haven't yet read *Intertwine*, book one in the House of Oak series, turn the page for a preview.

Intertwine
HOUSE OF OAK, BOOK 1

PROLOGUE

The obsession began on June 12, 2008 around 11:23 a.m.

Though secretly Emme Wilde considered it more of a 'spiritual connection' than an actual full-blown neurosis.

Of course, her brother, Marc, her mother and a series of therapists all begged to disagree.

Thankfully her best friend, Jasmine, regularly validated the connection and considered herself to be Emme's guide through this divinely mystical union of predestined souls (her words, not Emme's). Marc asserted that Jasmine was not so much a guide as an incense-addled enabler (again, his words, not Emme's). Emme was just grateful that anyone considered the whole affair normal—even if it was only Jasmine's loose sense of 'normal.'

Jasmine always insisted Emme come with her to estate sales, and this one outside Portland, Oregon proved no exception. Though Jasmine contended *this* particular estate sale would be significant for Emme, rambling on about circles colliding in the vast cosmic ocean creating necessary links between lives—blah, blah. All typical Jasmine-speak.

Emme brushed it off, assuming that Jasmine really just wanted someone to organize the trip: plan the best route to avoid traffic, find a quirky restaurant for lunch, entertain her on the long drive from Seattle.

At the estate sale, Emme roamed through the stifling tents, touching the cool wood of old furniture, the air heavy with that mix of dust, moth balls and disuse that marks aged things. Jasmine predictably disappeared into a corner piled with antique quilts, hunting yet again for that elusive log cabin design with black centers instead of the traditional red.

But Emme drifted deeper, something pulling her farther and farther into the debris of lives past and spent. To the trace of human passing, like fingerprints left in the paint of a pioneer cupboard door. Stark and clear.

Usually Emme would have stopped to listen to the stories around her, the history grad student in her analyzing each detail. Yet that day she didn't. She just wandered, looking for something. Something specific.

If only she could remember what.

Skirting around a low settee in a back corner, Emme first saw the antique trunk. A typical mid-nineteenth century traveling chest, solid with mellow aged wood. It did not call attention to itself. But it stood apart somehow, almost as if the air were a little lighter around it.

She first opened the lid out of curiosity, expecting the trunk to be empty. Instead, she found it full. Carefully shifting old books and papers, Emme found nothing of real interest.

Until she reached the bottom right corner.

There she found a small object tucked inside a brittle cotton handkerchief. Gently unwrapping the aged fabric, she pulled out an oval locket. Untouched and expectant.

Filigree covered the front, its gilt frame still bright and untarnished, as if nearly new.

Emme turned the locket over, feeling its heft in her hand, the metal cool against her palm. It hummed with an almost electric pulse. How long had the locket lain wrapped in the trunk?

Transparent crystal partially covered the back. Under the crystal, two locks of hair were woven into an intricate pattern—one bright and fair, the other a dark chocolate brown. Gilded on top of the crystal, two initials nestled together into a stylized gold symbol.

She touched the initials, trying to make them out. One was clearly an F. But she puzzled over the other for a moment, tracing the design with her eyes. And then she saw it. Emme sucked in a sharp breath. An E. The other initial was an E.

She opened the locket, hearing the small pop of the catch.

A gasp.

Her hands tingled.

A sizzling shock started at the back of her neck and then spread.

Him.

There are moments in life that sear into the soul. Brief glimpses of some larger force. When so many threads collapse into one. Coalesce into a single truth.

Seeing *him* for the first time was one of those moments.

He gazed intently out from within the right side of the locket: blond, blue-eyed, chiseled with a mouth hinting at shared laughter. Emme's historian mind quickly dated his blue-green, high collared jacket and crisp, white shirt and neckcloth to the mid-Regency era, probably around 1812, give or take a year.

Emme continued to look at the man—well, stare actually. His golden hair finger-combed and deliciously disheveled. Broad shoulders angled slightly toward the viewer. Perhaps his face a shade too long and his nose a little too sharp for true beauty. But striking. Handsome even.

Looking expectant, as if he had been waiting for her.

Emme would forever remember the jolt of it.

Surprise and recognition.

She knew him. Had known him.

Somehow, somewhere, in some place.

He felt agonizingly familiar. That phantom part of her she had never realized was lost.

The sensation wasn't quite deja vu.

More like memory.

Like suddenly finding that vital thing you didn't realize had been misplaced. Like coming up, gasping for air, after nearly drowning and seeing the world bright and sparkling and new.

She stood mesmerized by *him* until Jasmine joined her.

"Oooh, you found him." The hushed respect in her voice was remarkable. This was Jasmine after all.

Emme nodded mutely.

"Your circles are so closely intertwined. Amazing."

Jasmine turned the locket in Emme's hand.

"What does this inscription say?" she asked.

Emme hadn't noticed the engraved words on the inside left of the locket case. But now she read them. Her sudden sharp inhalation seared, painfully clenching.

Oh. *Oh!*

The words reverberated through her soul, shattering and profound.

Emme didn't recall much more of that day—Jasmine purchasing the locket or even the little restaurant where they ate lunch. Instead, she only remembered the endless blur of passing trees on the drive home, the inscription echoing over and over:

To E
throughout all time
heart of my soul
your F

Visit www.NicholeVan.com to buy your copy of *Intertwine* today and continue the story.

ABOUT THE AUTHOR

Nichole Van is an artist who feels life is too short to only have one obsession. In former lives, she has been a contemporary dancer, pianist, art historian, choreographer, culinary artist and English professor. Though Nichole still prefers the label 'adaptable' more than 'ADD.'

Most notably, however, Nichole is an acclaimed photographer, winning over thirty international accolades for her work, including Portrait of the Year from WPPI in 2007. (Think Oscars for wedding and portrait photographers.) Her unique photography style has been featured in many magazines, including *Rangefinder* and *Professional Photographer*. She is also the creative mind behind the popular websites Flourish Emporium and {life as art} Workshops, which provide resources for photographers.

All that said, Nichole has always been a writer at heart. With an MA in English, she taught technical writing at Brigham Young University for ten years and has written more technical manuals than she can quickly count. She decided in late 2013 to start writing fiction and has loved exploring a new creative process.

Nichole currently lives in Utah with her husband and three crazy children, but that will change in January 2017 when they all move to Europe.

Though continuing in her career as a photographer, Nichole is also now writing historical romance on the side. She is known as NicholeVan all over the web: Facebook, Instagram, Pinterest, etc. Visit her author website at www.NicholeVan.com to sign up for her newsletter to be notified of new releases.

You can see her photographic work at photography.nicholeV.com and www.nicholeV.com.

If you enjoyed this book, please leave a short review on Amazon. com. Wonderful reviews are the elixir of life for authors. Even better than dark chocolate.

www.ingramcontent.com/pod-product-compliance
Lightning Source LLC
Chambersburg PA
CBHW020518260626
47156CB00006B/2046